"YOU WANT ME, DELIA!"

The word barely made it out of her constricted throat. "No."

"Yes. I can make you want me."

Ty's mouth came down on hers, forcing her lips apart in a fierce, hungry kiss.

Her protest had dissolved with the first touch of his lips on hers. She made a tiny whimpering noise in the back of her throat. She reached up and clung to both of his arms, her fingers digging into the tense, rigid muscle.

He broke the kiss, pulling away from her. "You want me, Delia-girl. But I think maybe next time I'll make *you* do the asking . . ."

A Wild Yearning

PENELOPE WILLIAMSON

AVON BOOKS ◆ NEW YORK

AVON BOOKS
A division of
The Hearst Corporation
105 Madison Avenue
New York, New York 10016

Copyright © 1990 by Penelope Williamson
Published by arrangement with the author
Library of Congress Catalog Card Number: 89-91873
ISBN: 0-380-75880-6

First Avon Books Printing: April 1990

AVON TRADEMARK REG. U.S. PAT. OFF. AND IN OTHER COUNTRIES, MARCA REGISTRADA, HECHO EN U.S.A.

Printed in the U.S.A.

RA 10 9 8 7 6 5 4 3 2 1

Chapter 1

Boston, Massachusetts Bay Colony
May 1721

"**D**elia, ye bitch, ye get yersel' back here! If I gotta be comin' after ye, girl . . ."

The door banged open, slamming hard against the wall, and a girl stumbled over the threshold. She landed on her hands and knees on the stoop with a thud, her back hunched, her breath rasping harshly in her throat.

A couple of boys were playing huzzlecaps at the dead end of the alley, and they looked up at the sound of the door crashing open. The sight of the girl, with her dark hair in tangles around her face and her eyes open wide with fear, made them scoop up their pennies and run out onto the docks.

"Delia!"

The angry, drunken bellow jolted the girl to her feet. Clinging with one hand to the rickety railing, she jumped from the stoop, swinging around . . . and skidded to a stop.

For there, weaving his way among the fishing nets spread out to dry in the sun—and directly in the path of her escape—was the stocky, barrel-chested figure of Constable Dunlop.

The constable paused and turned his back to her, staring out over the bay to watch a royal frigate as it pulled up to the Long Wharf. The girl took a cautious step forward, then froze as she saw his bulky shoulders start to turn again in her direction.

From above her came the sound of a stool falling over, followed by another bellow. "Bloody hell!" Iron pots clat-

1

tered to the floor and something thudded against the wall. ''I know ye've more hidden in here somewheres an' ye'll give it over, ye bitch, if ye know what's good for ye . . . Delia!''

As though he were a fox that had just gotten scent of a rabbit, the constable's head jerked up. Biting back a groan of despair, the girl dropped to her knees and scurried like a beetle beneath the stoop.

Only two steps tall and built of wood that had long ago begun to rot, the stoop led to a stairway which ran up from the waterfront alley to their living quarters above a dilapidated cooper's shop. Not much could fit under there but a few rats and spiders—and a skinny, seventeen-year-old girl running from a beating.

''Delia! Goddamn yer hide!''

She heard the thud of her father's feet stumbling on the stairs, followed by the squish of Constable Dunlap's shoes as he started down the slop-strewn alley. Delia pressed her face into the earth to stifle the sound of her heavy breathing; the mud was slimy against her cheek and smelled of mildew and rotting fish.

The constable's feet stopped in line with Delia's eyes. He was so close she could plainly see the splatters of mud and dung that decorated his bleached leather gaiters.

The constable hawked and sent a glob of tobacco and spittle into the dirt within inches of Delia's face. ''Hoy there, McQuaid,'' he called out. ''What's this ruckus all about, eh?''

The boards above her head groaned and sagged as her father stepped onto the stoop.

''Oh, 'tis ye, constable . . .'' Ezra McQuaid's voice had sobered a bit at the sight of an officer of the law. A man could spend twelve hours in the stocks for public drunkenness and disturbing the peace. ''Ye wouldn't happen t' have seen my Delia, would ye—a-hightailin' it outta here hell-bent for breakfast?''

The constable hawked and spat again. ''Can't say I did. But then I was looking out to bay-side. The *Moravia*'s just pulled in. It'll be a quiet night tonight, what with the press gangs out. Any man with two sound legs will be tucked up safe inside and out of sight. . . . So what's the wench done now, eh?''

"She came across sixpence I had put away for a rainy day," Ezra McQuaid said, the whine of self-pity in his voice. "Made off with it, she did, an' I mean t' give her a beltin' for it. It's a sin against God, it is, for a girl t' steal from her own da."

Oh, ye liar, Delia thought. The sixpence had been hers, and she had hidden it within a crock of lard. But he had sniffed it out with uncanny ability, the way he always could when the thirst was on him. Yet even buying cheap beer at a penny a quart, the sixpence hadn't been enough this time. It was like that with her da. Once the thirst was on him he couldn't stop until he drank himself insensible. When the beer had run out he'd come after her, demanding more money that she didn't have. Then he'd started in on her with his fist.

"You should've married the wench off long afore now," Constable Dunlop was saying, clucking his tongue in sympathy. "Let someone else take over the disciplining of her."

Ezra McQuaid's laugh rumbled like thunderclaps from deep within his big belly. "Are ye a-offerin' for her then, sir?"

"Who, me? Lord, no. She's too saucy by half."

The men shared another laugh. Then Dunlop sighed softly. "Well, I should be out about my rounds. If I run across your girl, I'll haul her back to you to face the piper, eh?"

"You do that, sir, and with my thanks. But if ye spot her working at the Frisky Lyon, best just let her be. We need the gilt, ye know, an' I can always get my licks in later."

The constable snorted a chuckle and shot another wad of spittle onto the ground. "Aye, that you can. Well, good day to you, McQuaid."

The muddy gaiters turned and disappeared. Then the boards above Delia's head creaked, and she heard the door latch clicking into place.

Quiet descended on the alley while Delia lay motionless. A breeze started up, finding its way beneath the stoop to caress her sweaty face. It brought with it the briny reek of salted cod and the knocking of the copper's mallet from the shop next door. Her da had been a copper once, before the drink had gotten hold of him.

She poked her head out from beneath the stoop, looking around slowly, like a cat let out of a basket. Then, pressing her hands into the squishy mud, she began to push herself forward.

A fist snaked down to grab her by the hair, hauling her to her feet. Delia bit back a scream as Ezra McQuaid shoved his face into hers.

His lips disappeared into his black beard, baring his teeth. "Ye thought I'd gone back inside, didn't ye, girl? But I fooled ye. Oh, aye, I fooled ye right an' proper. Where's the gilt?"

"There isn't more, Da. I swear t' ye—"

"Lying li'l slut!"

Still holding her by the hair, he shook her roughly, lifting her off her feet. He let her go, but as she started to fall, he pulled back his arm and, swinging his fist wide around, slammed it into her midriff.

Pain flooded through her, so hot and intense it robbed her of breath and brought burning vomit to her throat. The force of the blow spun her around and sent her flying face-first against the railing of the stoop. The rotted wood collapsed beneath her, wrenching the arm she had thrown out to break her fall.

He came after her. She twisted her head in panic, and for one brief moment she was frozen, mesmerized by his yellow eyes that glowed at her from beneath the shaggy fringe of his hair. She had one thought—that this time he wouldn't stop until he'd killed her.

Her hands clawed beneath her as she tried desperately to push herself to her feet so that she could run, run . . . and her fingers closed around a piece of the shattered railing. Whirling, she rose up and heaved it at his head.

Immediately she was fleeing down the alley, her bare feet slipping and sliding on the piles of refuse and slops. She heard his cry of surprise and pain, followed by a snarl of rage, and it only made her run faster. Then she was out on the wharf, her feet pounding on the wooden boards, dodging in and out among the barrels and crates, skirting a pair of pigs rooting through a heap of fish guts.

She didn't stop running until she'd passed Sear's Shipyard and the Ship Street wharf. Leaning against the rough plank boards of a rope works shed, she fought for air, her lungs heaving like bellows in her chest. Pain knifed her side where he had hit her. Gingerly, she felt her rib cage, worried something might have broken.

"Oh, Da . . ."

Tears filled her eyes, and she leaned her head back, squeezing her lids shut—but they immediately flew open again as a pair of hands landed against the wall, bracketing her face.

"Here you are, luv. I've been looking all over for you."

Delia gazed into vivid blue eyes that stared back at her from beneath a shock of curly blond hair only partially covered by a red cloth cap. "Tom . . . ye startled me."

The young man's wide mouth started to stretch into a smile, only to turn down at the corners at the last minute. "What's the matter with you then?"

Delia wiped at a stray tear that had somehow managed to escape down her cheek. "Nothin'." She drew in a shallow breath and forced a smile of her own. "An' what're ye doing out and about in the middle of a Monday afternoon? What if old Jake were t' catch ye?" Tom Mullins was bonded to Jake Steerborn, the blacksmith. If Jake found out his servant was strolling the quay when he should have been tending to the forge, Tom would be in for a flogging.

"The old bastard stepped out for a bite and a tot of rum," Tom said. "I'll not stand about in this heat and pump up a fire for someone who's not there." He flashed her a sudden grin and stroked her cheek with his knuckles. "Where've you been these last few days? I've missed you . . ."

He started to lower his lips to hers, and she turned her head aside. But he cupped her chin, pulling her head back around, and in the end she let him kiss her.

But when his hands began to fumble with the laces of her bodice and his tongue pushed through her teeth into her mouth, she suddenly remembered why she had been avoiding Tom Mullins lately and pulled away from him.

"Don't, Tom. We shouldn't. . . . Nothin' can come of it," she added after a moment. For as a bond servant he couldn't take a wife until after he'd served his indenture. "Ye've four more years yet t' work off afore we can marry an'—"

"Marry! Who said anything about marriage?" Tom's handsome features had stiffened into anger, and his hand slammed against the wall beside her face, making her jump. "Damn you, Delia, you little tease! You've given out before. Why not with me?"

Delia sucked in a sharp breath. "Who's been sayin' such things?"

"Everyone. Everyone at the Frisky Lyon."

She shoved hard against his chest, surprising him so that he took a step backward. "Well, everyone is lyin'! I'm no tart, Thomas Mullins, and if ye can think that of me then I don't care if I never set eyes on ye again!"

She pushed away from the shed wall and started down the quay, but he seized her arm, hauling her back around to face him. Thinking he was going to hit her, she steeled herself for the blow. Then she saw the anger collapse within him.

"Delia, I'm sorry . . ."

"Let go of me," she demanded through stiff lips.

He released her arm, but not before giving it a hard squeeze, hard enough to leave bruises.

"Christ, Delia, do you have any idea what it is you do to a man?" He stuffed his hands into the waistband of his homespun breeches and looked down at his bare feet. Then his head jerked back up and his face tightened. "Oh, you know. Aye, I think you know. The way you look at a man all beckoning-like with those strange gold eyes of yours. Cat's eyes. And the way you talk with that voice of yours, all rough and husky like a boy's. You know damn well how much your doing that makes a man want to—"

But Delia couldn't bear to hear any more. She whirled and ran away from him, and though he called after her she did not look back.

She'd seen the intent in his eyes. *He was all set to hit me,* she thought. Oh, he hadn't hit her this time and he might not the next, but one day his temper would get the best of him and he'd let fly with his fists . . . just like her da.

The Frisky Lyon was only one of many grog shops that dotted the waterfront, offering cheap drink to the leather aprons—the workingmen, such as the blacksmiths and coopers and stevedores who earned their livings servicing the ships that plied the bay. It was where Delia McQuaid had worked since she was fourteen.

She didn't whore though, in spite of what Tom Mullins thought, and everyone said. She waited tables, and that was a long way from whoring even to the nastiest of minds. So now, as she stood within the sagging doorway of the crowded, smoky taproom, she tried to guess which of the laughing, boisterous men has started the ugly rumors about her.

Oh, every one of them had at one time or other asked her to come up the stairs with him, but that was the way of men. She had never held it against a man for asking, as long as he kept his hands to himself and accepted no for an answer. It had been two years since she'd even had shoes for her feet, yet she could have earned the price of a pair with a single trip up the Frisky Lyon's back stairs. Pride had stopped her. Pride and a surety that if she lay just once with a man for money, she would be so deep in the gutter she would never be able to claw her way out.

Yet now some man had named her whore and everyone believed it, and the thought cut at the wick of Delia's pride, hurting worse than her bruised ribs.

"Ye're late, wench." A breath that reeked of sausages blew against Delia's ear, and she turned to look into the fleshy, pocked face of Sally Jedrup, owner of the Frisky Lyon and two other grog shops along the waterfront. Sally had a fat dimple in the middle of her chin and it puckered as she spoke. "I'll not be payin' ye good siller just so's ye can come strollin' in any sweet time ye damn well please—"

"I'm not late," Delia snapped back, although she didn't feel capable of standing up to Sally's bullying tonight. She took a wooden tray loaded with rum-filled noggins out of the woman's pudgy hands. "Where does this lot go?"

"To yon noisy clods sittin' against the wall. And mind you don't spill a drop," she called out to Delia's retreating back, "or I'll have the cost of such outta yer wages."

As Delia carried the tray to the group of topers sitting on benches in the back of the room, she noticed one of them was the blacksmith, Jake Steerborn. In spite of her disillusionment with Tom Mullins, Delia was still glad to see that, with his master otherwise occupied, the young man wouldn't be caught slacking on his chores.

Hanging on a peg above Jake's head was a gamecock trussed in a leather satchel. The bird was making a low churring sound, perhaps in pleasant anticipation of the coming fight. There was a cock platform in back of the Frisky Lyon, and all the waterfront knew a high-stakes match had been set up for later that evening between Jake's champion bird and one of Sally Jedrup's.

As Delia bent over to set the noggins on the ring-marked trestle table, the blacksmith laid his soot-stained hand on her backside. He rubbed his palm in circles on her rough petticoat made of old mattress ticking. "Will ye wager a threepence on my fighting cock tonight, Delia girl?"

Delia grabbed his thick wrist and removed the straying hand. "Ye won't find me tossin' tuppence at a lost cause," she answered tartly. In a way she was giving him fair warning for Sally Jedrup was known to coat the beaks of her birds with garlic to repulse an opponent and to shoot brandy down a cock's throat to enhance its fighting spirit.

Wrapping his arm around Delia's waist, Jake yanked her against him. "Aw, Delia, have a heart. What d' ye say we have ourselves a li'l fun afterwards?" He fished into the pocket of his leather apron. "Look here, I'll give ye a pair of silver shillings. Two silver shillings for just a few minutes of yer time—"

Delia pushed against his chest. "Let go of me, Jake."

But Jake's arm tightened, pulling her down to plant a wet, sloppy kiss on the swell of her breast where it rose from beneath the confines of her tightly laced bodice. For Delia this last assault was one too many. Reaching behind his back, she snatched up one of the noggins of rum and poured it over Jake Steerborn's head.

Jake's arm fell from around her waist. He sat in stunned silence while the burning, sticky liquid oozed in rivulets down his beefy face. Then he jumped from the bench, roaring curses.

Delia was ready for him. Swinging the wooden tray in a wide arc, she slammed it hard against the side of the blacksmith's large, shovel-shaped nose. The men around them all burst into loud laughter. Tears of pain flooded the blacksmith's eyes and he brought his hand up to his face.

"Jesus, Delia," he sputtered from behind the big palm that covered his throbbing nose. He wiggled the monstrous appendage back and forth to ensure it wasn't broken. "What did you want to go an' do a thing like that for?"

Unabashed by what she had done, Delia nevertheless started backing up, putting a healthy distance between herself and the giant blacksmith. "Ye'll learn in future to be keepin' yer filthy lips and hands to yersel', Jake Steerborn."

"I meant no harm."

"Hunh!" She turned around to find her path blocked by the broad figure of Sally Jedrup.

"What the hell do ye think yer doin', ye strumpet?" the woman leaned over to hiss in Delia's face. "D' ye want t' bring the coppers down on us for causin' a riot?"

Delia lifted the tray above her head. "Out of my way, ye filthy old bawd, or I'll brain ye as well, see if I bloody don't."

"Well, I never!" Sally exclaimed, though she did step back out of striking distance of Delia's menacing weapon. "Aye, girl, well ye can just keep on goin' then 'cause yer not workin' for me no more, ye're not. No, nor in any other grog shop on the front either, not if I have aught t' say about it." And, as Delia did keep going, out the open door of the Frisky Lyon and into the late afternoon sunlight, Sally Jedrup screamed after her, "I hope ye and yer old tosspot of a father starve, I do!"

Delia had almost reached Clark's Wharf before she realized she still held the wooden tray in her hand. She walked all the way to the end of the pier and sent the tray spinning into the bay, then started to laugh. But her throat seized up and the laughter caught in her chest.

Oh, she had made a right mess of things this day, she had. Bloodying her father's head—it would be days before she dared go home, and even then she'd better hope he was either so falling-down drunk he'd be incapable of taking his rage out on her, or too sober to want to.

And there was Tom. Like a fool she'd actually harbored dreams they might marry someday when his service was up. She'd pictured having a home of their own above a blacksmith's shop, with a row of children all sitting like building blocks around the kitchen table, her stirring something spicy and bubbling on the fire, him having a pipe and his tot and watching her with contented, sleepy eyes. Delia's throat closed as she swallowed a sob. Aye, a fool she was, taken in by Tom's handsome face and honeyed words. She didn't know which had shattered the illusion so hurtfully, his easy assumption that she could sink to whoring or the look of hate and fury in his eyes when she thought he was going to hit her.

Now this latest—losing her job at the Frisky Lyon, and all over foolish, besotted old Jake, who was only after a little fun and hadn't meant any real harm. "An' what d' ye think ye're goin' t' live on now, ye wooden-headed fool?" she berated herself aloud. "D' ye think ye can eat pride?"

Delia stood at the end of the pier as the sun began to set behind the shrouds and ratlines of the ships in the harbor. In the mouth of the estuary a fisherman sculled his dory homeward and the tide brought in strings of rockweed to wrap around the barnacle-encrusted pilings. A gull swooped down low over her head, squawking shrilly. For some reason the familiar sound brought fresh tears to her eyes. It was the loneliness of it, she supposed.

A movement at the corner of her eye caused Delia to turn back toward the row of shops jammed close together along the wharf. She watched a couple of officers from the frigate *Moravia* stroll up to the bulletin board that told which ships were in port. The few local men who had been perusing the notices of available berths quickly took themselves off. Everyone always gave the English sailors a wide berth, for the Royal Navy, with its gangs of pressmen, was not popular with the people of Boston.

Battening down a sigh, Delia retraced her steps along the pier. A brisk evening breeze had come up, stirring the piles of refuse that littered the wharf and sending a page of the *Boston News-Letter* to wrap around her legs, breaking her stride. Delia bent over to free herself from the newspaper's clutches. She was about to toss it away when a word in tall black print caught her eye.

Delia folded the newspaper into a more manageable square,

but she was not adept at reading, for she'd had little schooling. Sounding out the letters by moving her lips, she was able to make out two of the larger, darker words—*woman* and then *wife*. The rest was beyond her.

She was about to give up when a shadow fell across the newspaper. Delia looked up into the face of one of the English officers she had spotted earlier. The insignia on the epaulets of his fancy blue coat proclaimed him to be a lieutenant. He was tall and quill-thin, and his hair was pulled back into a tight queue and clubbed with eelskin. But his smile was friendly.

"Good afternoon to you, mistress," he said in an educated voice. "I was noticing you before, standing at the end of the pier, and I thought you looked a little lonely. I was wondering . . ." He smiled, and a light flush suffused his pale, hollowed cheeks.

Lonely indeed! At any other time Delia would have scoffed at the lieutenant's shopworn flirtation, but instead she decided to take advantage of his forwardness.

She gave him her most brilliant smile. "Can ye read, sir?"

The lieutenant thrust out his thin chest like a turkey cock. "Aye. Of course."

"Could ye read this for me, then? Out loud?"

Smiling, the young man took the newspaper from her. He cleared his throat, holding the paper several inches from his eyes and squinting. "Ahem," he said, and began to read:

WOMAN SOUGHT FOR WIFE. This freehold Yeoman of the Merrymeeting Settlement, Sagadahoc Territory, The Maine, finding himself in dire Circumstances upon the Death of his Wife and left with the care of two young Daughters, agrees to provide a Home for a good Woman willing in turn to assume the Responsibility of Wife to said Yeoman and Mother to his two young Daughters. Said Woman shall be of strong Mind and Body and of exemplary Christian and moral Character. Interested Parties may apply to Tyler W. Savitch, M.D., in temporary Residence at the Red Dragon Inn, King Street, Boston.

The lieutenant's voice trailed off and he stared at Delia, a pleased grin on his face. She looked back, smiling as well, but she wasn't really seeing the man. She was thinking: a farmer would have built himself a house. And there would always be plenty to eat on the table. A man left with two motherless daughters might be good to a woman who would be agreeable to caring for his children and looking after his home . . .

"The Red Dragon . . . Tyler W. Savitch, M.D.," she repeated aloud. "What does that mean—M.D.?"

"Medicinae doctor. It means the fellow went to university. Surely you aren't considering applying for the position." The young lieutenant laughed and stroked Delia's cheek. "You're too lovely to waste on some dirt-grubbing farmer in the wilderness—"

Delia plucked the newspaper from his hands. "I thank ye for yer trouble, kind sir."

"Wait!" he called out. "What about letting me buy you supper?" But Delia was already walking briskly toward King Street and the Red Dragon.

Delia stood within the large shadow cast by the town house and looked across King Street at the tightly packed row houses and shops. In the middle, standing out by virture of its grandeur—and the giant, colorfully painted signboard swinging above its doors—was the Red Dragon Inn.

No leather aprons would dare patronize the taproom of this establishment, Delia thought. No, only those of the "better sort" frequented this gentlemen's pub. She imagined how it would be inside, although she'd never before dared to set foot in any place so grand. The gentry would sip their drinks from pewter tankards while smoking on their clay pipes. They would play cards or read newspapers, but there would be no unseemly noise or behavior to disturb the genteel atmosphere.

An ostler and the porter, both done up in red and gold livery and wearing curled periwigs, stood before the entrance having a bit of a gossip. Delia had hoped to approach Tyler W. Savitch unobserved, but after waiting impatiently for several long minutes, she realized she would have to brazen her way past the stuffy inn's hallowed, and guarded, portals.

Gathering up her skirts and lifting her chin high in the air, the way she imagined a real lady would do, she approached the entrance, dodging around a broom seller, water carrier, and knife grinder as she crossed the crowded street.

"Excuse me, good sirs . . ."

The men in red and gold livery stopped talking and turned of one accord. They looked Delia over, from the mud-stained hem of her ragged, striped petticoat to the top of her head, bare of any modest kerchief or clout. The ostler was a man her father's age, short and compact with smooth skin pulled tautly over his padded features. He gave Delia another look, and his nose, pink and round like a bunny's, began to twitch.

The porter, who was taller and much younger, gave her a leering smile that revealed brown, jagged teeth. "The kitchens are round back, m'dear. Though we've no openings for a scullery maid, I fear."

Delia smiled back at him. "I've not come for work, thank ye. Do ye know where I might find a Mr. Tyler W. Savitch"—she searched her memory for the correct appellation—"M.D.? I've an appointment," she added. It wasn't a lie; well, not much of a one. After all, the advertisement had read "interested parties may apply . . ."

"Oh, so you've an appointment, do you? And I'm the King of England!" the ostler exclaimed, chuckling so hard at his own joke that his periwig tilted askew. Then the amusement abruptly left his face. "Be off with you, wench, afore I call the constables."

"Hold a moment," the porter said, pausing to open the door for a stout gentleman wearing a high-crowned beaver hat nearly as tall as he was. "There've been all sorts of females in and out to see the doctor this past week and more. Aye, and most no better than the likes of this one—begging your pardon, mistress."

The ostler cast another disparaging eye at Delia, then "tsked" and shook his head. "Strange doings, aye, strange doings . . . He's aiming to set up a bawdy house to my way of thinking."

Delia was beginning to have the same suspicion. Deciding she didn't want to see Tyler W. Savitch, M.D., after all, she started to turn away.

"Here now, mistress, the doctor's out just now," the porter called after her in a friendly way, only to spoil it by giving her a lewd wink. "But he's taken himself a suite, and you can wait for him in his sitting room."

The ostler raised questioning brows but held his silence.

For a moment longer Delia hesitated. But, she reasoned, if she didn't like the looks of the doctor, she would simply leave and that would be that. After all, nothing too horrible was likely to happen to her in such a grand place as the Red Dragon.

As Delia followed the porter inside and past the taproom, she saw that it was almost empty, except for a pair of old gentlemen wearing wigs and suits of fine black cloth, sitting before the fire and engaging in a game of backgammon. One of the old gentlemen mumbled something, and his opponent picked up an ear trumpet, shouting, "Eh, what did ye say? Speak up, Feathergrew, demme ye!" Delia bit back a laugh.

The porter did not take her up the main staircase, but instead led her through the kitchen and up a narrow flight of servants' stairs at the rear of the inn. She got a brief glimpse of a paneled carpeted hall before he pushed open a door and ushered her inside with a quick flap of his hand.

"I'm taking a risk, I am, letting you in here without permission. So mind you don't steal anything." He leaned close and smiled suggestively, bathing her face with breath that reeked of rum and stale tobacco. "I'll be downstairs, minding the entrance. Whatever the gentleman gives you after you've finished your, uh, business, I'm to get half. You understand?"

Delia understood, but she didn't answer him. She stood just inside the threshold, her eyes wide in awe, for it was the most beautiful room she had ever seen.

Carpets covered the polished parquet floor, and damask curtains framed a pair of tall, sashed windows that opened onto a tree-shaded courtyard out back. Although it had been a warm spring day, it was now starting to cool, and a fire burned invitingly in the grate. A betty lamp was already lit against the coming darkness. It bathed the furnishings—all English-made and highly polished—with a warm glow, bringing out their sheen and the grain of the wood.

Delia heard the door click shut behind her and realized with a start that she had been left alone. Smiling, humming to herself, she wandered around the beautiful room. She ran her hand over the smooth back of a wainscot chair that sat catty-cornered to the fire. She touched the things, *his* things, left out on the bureau and desk: a razor and hone, an ivory-toothed comb, a set of steel-nibbed pens with their quills kept in an elaborate brass box. Also those things which attested to his profession: a set of bone-handled lancet blades, a physician's leather bag, and a pharmacopeia in glazed apothecary pots. Incongruously, leaning in a corner against the wall by the fireplace, was a Pennsylvania rifle. Its oiled wooden stock and gray metal barrel gleamed warmly, reflecting the flames.

Delia wondered about the man who owned these things. She thought she could detect his presence in the room, a faint odor of tobacco and rich leather that seemed to hover in the air. He was a man of some wealth, she thought, for what he owned was finely crafted and of the best materials. She wondered how big his farm was, and how old his two motherless daughters were.

But what sort of man was he that he would need to advertise for a wife? Perhaps he had been left badly scarred by the pox. Or perhaps he was old. Perhaps he was simply too shy to approach a woman on romantic terms.

"Tyler W. Savitch," she whispered aloud. "What kind of man are ye?"

Although she knew she shouldn't, Delia wandered into the bedroom. There was a looking glass above the mantel, and as Delia caught sight of her own reflection she almost screamed, thinking for one brief moment that there was someone else in the room with her. This foolishness brought on a fit of nervous giggles and she covered her mouth with her hand. She looked at herself in the mirror, her eyes above her grimy hand opened wide and brimming with golden lights of amusement.

Then she noticed to her disgust that her cheeks were streaked with dried mud and her hair was matted with tiny twigs and dried leaves that she had picked up while hiding from her da beneath the stoop. What's more, her bodice, not too clean to begin with, was now stained with the rum that had splashed her when she'd doused the head of Jake Steer-born. What a sight I am, she thought, laughing aloud. No wonder the ostler had threatened to summon the constables.

She wet the hem of her petticoat with saliva and scrubbed the grime off her face as best she could, then shook out her tangled mane of black hair. She turned around, taking in the room, and her gaze fell with delight on the wide tester bed with its swelling feather mattress. The bed looked so soft she couldn't resist trying it.

Delia settled back against the down-filled pillows with a soft sigh. It was so quiet in here, back off the street and away from the rumbling carts and wagons and the shouts of the hawkers. How wonderful, she thought, her eyes drifting closed. How wonderful to be a real lady and sleep in a fine goose-feather bed like this one.

Mrs. Tyler W. Savitch, she said to herself. Mrs Tyler W. Savitch, M.D. . . .

Chapter 2

Delia rubbed her hands across smooth linen, sighing and stretching luxuriously. She snuggled her face deeper into the soft downiness of the pillow—

Her eyelids flew open, and she pushed herself upright. Lord above us, she had fallen asleep on the man's bed!

She flopped onto her back. It was dark now, and long shadows shrouded the bed where it stood in the corner against the wall. But the moon was up and full, casting harsh silvery beams through the window and mixing with the pool of soft, golden lamplight that came from the sitting room.

She uncoiled into another long stretch, curling her toes and thrusting her fisted hands above her head until she felt a twinge of pain in her sore ribs. She wondered what time it was; it seemed very late. She supposed the night watch must have wakened her by calling out the hour, and thank the good Lord for that. Imagine if the man had come back to find her lying on his bed asleep! Why, if he really were using the ploy of looking for a wife to solicit harlots for a bawdy house, he would think her a prime candidate indeed, and her cheeks flushed hot at the very idea.

Yawning, she brushed the hair from her face and rubbed her eyes. She pushed herself into a half-sitting position, resting on her elbows, and then she heard the sound of muted laughter, the rustle of clothing.

A woman's voice, soft and tremulous, said, "Oh, Ty, that feels . . . yes, there . . . oh, please."

A soft, feminine sigh was followed by a husky murmur. "There?"

"Ah, yesss . . ." And another, softer sigh.

Delia bolted up straight and stiff, looking around with wild eyes like those of a raccoon frozen by the sudden flare of a torch. By the time her sluggish brain told her legs to move, it was too late—the man and woman were already on their way into the room.

Laughing, the woman came first, pulling the man after her by the hand. But once across the threshold, she stopped and, turning, leaned against the wall. Grasping the man by the ruffle of his shirt, she pulled him to her. He nuzzled the curve of her neck with his lips and she sighed.

Delia's mouth fell open in shock. The man was not only recruiting whores, he was trying them out himself first! She thought she had better make some noise, do something, anything . . . She drew in a deep breath.

"Oh, Ty, I thought I'd go crazy tonight, watching you dance with all those simpering ingenues," the woman purred. "Tell me you thought they were all ugly and that they bored you to tears."

"They were all ugly," a deep voice drawled. "They bored me to tears."

"You didn't look my way once all night."

"I looked, Pris. I looked." He caught his breath on the last word, for the woman had opened the flap to his breeches and slipped her hand inside. She laughed deep in her throat. "Why, Tyler Savitch, I do declare. What have we here?"

For an answer he smothered her mouth with his. He pinned her to the wall with his hips while his hands moved lingeringly over her shoulders and down her arms, and her hands tugged and pushed at his confining breeches.

Delia's throat was so tight and dry she couldn't swallow. She had witnessed a lot of things at the Frisky Lyon but never anyone actually doing . . . *it*. Yet from her position on the bed she could see the man and woman plainly. They stood in half profile to her, and in the light cast by the moon Delia could tell the woman was small and fair and dressed as if she'd just come from a ball. The man wore only a shirt and breeches, and the breeches were now pushed down around his thighs. The woman's hands were pale against the darker skin of the man's buttocks as she squeezed the taut muscles almost savagely. Her bodice gaped open, exposing her breasts, and he held one of them in his cupped palm, massaging the nipple with long fingers. The woman's head fell back, and she groaned.

Delia almost groaned right along with her. A wet, hot heat flooded through her, drenching her like steam from a laundry. There was a strange feeling of tightness in her chest, as if it had been locked in a cooper's vise. Though the sound of the lovers' breathing was loud in the room, like the sough of wind through a forest, Delia didn't dare move, fearful as she now was of making even the slightest noise and giving her presence away. It was a wicked thing to be watching this, she knew. Dutifully, she squeezed her eyes shut, but they snapped open a moment later as if pried apart against her will.

The man was undulating his hips in slow, sensuous circles while he assaulted the woman's neck with his lips and tongue. She arched her back, pulling him tighter against her.

"Oh God, Ty . . . God."

His hands spanned her waist, lifting her up and bracing her against the wall. He lowered his head and sucked a nipple into his mouth.

The woman's panting breaths, loud and harsh, began to accelerate, building and building in tempo with the grinding motion of his hips. Her hands were twisted into tight fists at the small of his back, bunching up his shirt. The muscles of his buttocks clenched, unclenched. The woman moaned.

"Now, Ty, please . . . I can't stand any more. Please!"

Delia saw the man bend and lift the woman into his arms. She saw him turn toward the bed. She saw the woman grasp the man's dark hair and pull his face down to her hungry, open mouth. She saw the lovers pass out of the light into the shadows where she sat silent and watching. She saw it all and she couldn't move, couldn't move—

And then the man and woman, mouths locked together, wrapped in each other's arms, fell onto the bed . . . right on top of Delia McQuaid.

Delia screamed once—from pain as the man's broad shoulder smacked into her sore ribs. Leaping from the bed, the woman screamed and went on screaming. The man made no sound at all, but a split second later Delia felt the prick of something sharp against her neck.

"God Almighty, Priscilla, shut up! Do you want to wake all of Boston? Who in hell are you?"

It took Delia a moment to realize this last was addressed to her. When she didn't answer right away, he pressed the blade of the knife closer to her throat, nicking the skin.

"Who are you?" he said again, in a voice so cold and hard it rose the hairs on the back of Delia's neck.

"Please . . . don't kill me," she said, fear pitching her normally husky voice even lower.

The woman had gone blessedly silent, but now she let out a hysterical laugh. "Why, Ty, it's only a boy."

"I'm no boy!" Delia protested. Realizing the knife was no longer poised to slit her throat, she sat up, huffing with indignation. But when she started to get off the bed, a strong hand held her in place, pressing down on her shoulder.

"You stay right where you are. . . . Pris, fetch the lamp in here." The woman hesitated until the man said sternly, "Priscilla . . ." Then she glided from the room in a swish of skirts.

The man moved away from the bed, turning his back to pull up his breeches and button the front flap. Delia thought how she had sat crouched in silence, watching, watching that woman touching him, that intimate part of him, so boldly . . . She almost groaned aloud from the shame.

It suddenly seemed very quiet in the room, so quiet Delia could hear a clock ticking somewhere. She thought she should probably say something, perhaps introduce herself, but "How d' ye do, Dr. Savitch" didn't seem appropriate given the circumstances. She wondered what a real lady would do in this situation, but then, she thought despairingly, a real lady would hardly have gotten herself into this mess.

The woman returned, carrying the betty lamp. She, too, had taken the time to straighten her clothing. It was expensive clothing. A moss-green satin petticoat fell over a small far-thingale, and on top of it was a silver-brocade overskirt looped up on each side to draw attention to her hips. Pearly breasts rose from the low, lace-edged neckline of a richly embroidered bodice frosted with rows of gathered lace. The elegant ensemble was topped by a lofty headdress of a spangled turban mounted with ostrich feathers.

Gold hair and blue eyes, and fair, fair skin, with a single tiny, heart-shaped silk patch at one corner of her full mouth—oh, she was undeniably beautiful. But she was older than Delia had expected. Why, Delia thought with shock, she had to be close to thirty!

She was also unlike any whore Delia had ever seen before, certainly unlike the harlots who plied their trade at the Frisky Lyon and other such grog shops on the waterfront.

The woman set the lamp on a nearby chest. Delia, sprawled on the bed while they both stood looking down at her, felt at a decided disadvantage. She lifted her head and stared defiantly back at them, although inside she was wishing herself in a deep, deep hole somewhere on the other side of the world.

The woman wrinkled her dainty nose. "Really, Ty, I thought you had better taste."

"I assure you, Pris, I've never seen the wench before in my life."

Delia stared at his face. His darkly handsome features were finely cast, with a thin, straight nose, square jaw, and sharp cheekbones. Though his buff breeches and ruffled lawn shirt bespoke the gentleman, he was not wearing a wig. His thick hair was a rich, dark brown, and he wore it tied back with a simple riband. His black eyes glittered at Delia from beneath slightly flaring brows. She felt ensnared by those dark eyes though, strangely, she was not afraid . . .

Priscilla's strident voice broke the spell. "Perhaps I should leave."

"Yes. I think you should," he said.

This obviously was not what Priscilla wanted to hear. "Well, then . . . Stevens can certainly see me safely home in the shay," she said stiffly. "Don't bother showing me to the door."

Yet she stood still for a moment longer, looking at her man look at Delia, then she turned on her heel and marched from the room.

"You stay put," he told Delia before following.

Delia remained sitting obediently on the edge of the mattress until she remembered what he and the woman had been about to do in this very bed. *Why, he probably thinks he'll try me out next for a place in his bawdy house!*—and the thought brought Delia up fast onto shaky legs. Of their own accord, her feet carried her into the sitting room.

He stood by the door with Priscilla, who was wrapped up in a hooded red cloak. His hands rested on her shoulders and he was saying in a soothing, gentle voice, "She's probably here because of that damn advertisement. It's late anyway, sweet, and you should be getting home."

"Ty, if you take that girl to bed—"

He put his fingers against her lips. "Hush. You know I wouldn't do that to you. One of the reasons I came all this way to Boston was to see you, Pris."

She nodded, her full mouth parting tremulously. "And you're leaving tomorrow. It could be months, perhaps years, before I'll see you again."

His mouth quirked into an endearingly lopsided smile. "Somehow I don't think you'll lack for company in the meantime."

Laughing lightly, she flicked his cheek with a painted ivory fan. "Law you, Tyler Savitch, you've a wicked mind."

He brushed his lips across her cheekbone. "Goodbye, Pris."

"Take care, Ty," she answered, smiling still, but as she turned, fumbling for the doorlatch, Delia thought she saw the gleam of unshed tears.

Ty closed the door behind Priscilla. He did not look at Delia but went instead to the hearth. He moved with a fluid grace and his body was lean, like his face. And hard. The fine lawn of his shirt clung to the muscles of his chest and back as he moved.

He lifted an embroidered waistcoat off the back of the wainscot chair and shrugged it on, although he left it unbuttoned. Then he took a taper from the mantel and stuck it in the coals. He put the flame of the candle to a fresh torch of pitch pine held in a bracket on the wall. The torch caught, flaring and shedding a bright light on the room.

He turned. His face was set into hard lines, lips pressed together, a scowl drawing a crease between his brows. Delia had to stiffen her muscles to keep from squirming under his direct gaze.

"Come here," he said.

She swallowed hard and took two tiny steps into the room. He had promised the other woman he wouldn't take her to bed, but that didn't mean he hadn't lied. Or that he wouldn't strike out at her, like her da, should his temper get the better of him. She looked up into his face. His eyes weren't black. They were a very deep, dark blue.

"I suppose you're going to claim you wandered into the wrong bed by mistake," he said.

Color leaped to Delia's face as she remembered how she had sat in silence and watched him making love to Priscilla. Delia had thought herself wise to life, to love, but she hadn't known it could be like that between a man and a woman. So much . . . so much *passion*. She wondered why such a man, with his enticing good looks, felt the need to advertise for a wife. Perhaps he intended to test all the women who applied to see which candidate could please him best in bed before making his choice. The very thought caused her stomach to do a somersault.

"Well," the man said. His face was still stern, but his indigo eyes sparkled with repressed laughter. "What were you doing in my bed, brat?"

Delia's head came up as she pulled the folded newspaper from the pocket of her petticoat. "Are ye Tyler W. Savitch, M.D.?" she demanded, though she knew well by now that he was. She held the newspaper out to him, pointing with a dirty finger at the advertisement. "Then are ye denyin' ye're responsible for this?"

"You've got it upside down."

Hot color flooded her cheeks, but she thrust out her chin. "I know how t' read. Some. Anyways, the advert never said nothin' about knowin' how t' read."

"No, it didn't. . . . What's your name?"

"Delia. Delia McQuaid."

He beckoned to her with one languid hand. "Well, come closer, Delia McQuaid—"

Delia's whole body went rigid. "I don't know what ye're after, mister, but one thing ye ought t' know right off, I'm not intendin' t' lie with no man, leastways not till the 'I do's' are spoken.''

One brow flared upward, and his mouth twisted into a crooked smile. ''Thank you for warning me. Now come here so I can get a better look at you. Come, come. I won't bite.''

She came right up next to him.

A spasm of disgust crossed his face. ''Jesus, you reek like a distillery! When was the last time you bathed?''

Delia was mortally insulted. ''I'll have ye know, ye nosy bastard, that I bathe once a month!''

''We must be nearing the end of your thirty days then. Open your mouth.''

''Huh?''

He seized her chin and pried her mouth open.

She jerked it out of his grasp. ''Here now! There's no call t' be lookin' at my teeth. I'm no horse ye're thinkin' of buyin'.''

''At least your teeth are cleaner than the rest of you.''

He hooked the leg of the wainscot chair with the toe of his boot, pulling it around so that he could lean against the hearth with one foot braced against the seat of the chair, his shoulders pressed into the mantel, his thumbs hooked into his waistcoat pockets. He let his gaze move over her, studying her the way he had back in the bedroom. It made her uncomfortable to be looked at like that, yet she was acutely aware of his decidedly masculine pose and how he was making her heart thud loudly against her chest.

At last he drew in a deep breath, letting his foot fall as he straightened. ''Well, now, Delia McQuaid, you'll not thank me for it, but I'm afraid the—''

''Is it her—that Priscilla person? Is Priscilla the one ye've picked for the post of wife then?'' Not that Delia blamed him, for though the woman was perhaps a mite old for him, she was not only beautiful but also rich by the looks of her. And she obviously knew her way around a bedroom.

His laughter was a throaty rumble that brought another blush to her cheeks. ''I haven't picked anyone else. I was going to say I'm afraid the post—if you can call it that—is yours. If you want it. I've got to have somebody by tomorrow, and you're the best of a bad lot.''

Delia suspected she was being insulted again and her head jerked up with immediate defiance. "An' what's that supposed t' mean?"

"It means that you're young and hardy and your wits are all there, although how sharp they are remains to be seen . . ."

Delia's mouth fell open.

"And though your virtue is undoubtedly questionable, you don't appear to be suffering from the great pox yet, although—"

Delia's mouth fell open even wider. "Aooow!" she screeched, so loudly that he winced. "Ye filthy-minded bastard! I'll have ye know that just 'cause I work in a grog shop, it don't mean I'm a whore. I haven't said yes t' the post yet, no, nor will I now. Nay, not if ye was the last man on earth, would I marry ye, ye—ye—"

He looked taken aback. Then he threw back his head and let loose a hearty laugh. Delia searched the room for something to hit him with. Nothing appeared lethal enough, except perhaps for the fire poker . . .

"Delia, Delia," he said, laughing still. "Something tells me Merrymeeting Settlement would never be the same again with you around. And Nat would probably want to nail my hide to his barn door for landing you in his lap."

"I don't understand ye," Delia said through stiff lips. She wanted to burst into tears.

His laughter died down, but the amusement remained to give his eyes a mischievous glint. "I'm not the one in such desperate need of a wife. Heaven forfend."

"But ye said . . . The newspaper . . ."

"I placed that advertisement at the behest of a neighbor who lost his wife two months ago. With two young daughters and a farm to run, he needs a woman's help. But there's a sad dearth of eligible matrimonial material in The Maine," he said, naming the vast wilderness territory that lay northeast of the New Hampshire Colony. "I was coming to Boston anyway to hire a preacher for our settlement, and Nat prevailed upon me to find him a spouse while I was here. I told him he was off his fool head."

Delia felt a knot of sick disappointment forming in her

stomach. She should have known such a man as Tyler Savitch—so handsome and fairly oozing masculine charm—wouldn't need to stoop so low, nor would he ever be so desperate that he would advertise for a wife. What a wooden-headed fool she'd made of herself, first spying on him in that awful, shameful way, and now this . . . She imagined herself as he must see her in this moment, standing before him in all her ignorance and dirt, and she wanted to die.

She forced herself to meet his eyes. "What happened t' her, yer friend's wife?" She thought it probably behooved her to ask, for if she were to go gallivanting off to The Maine and marry a perfect stranger, it would be nice to know how the man's first wife had died. What if he had done the poor woman in?

Ty hitched his hip onto the edge of the desk. He looked down at the hands he had clasped in his lap. Delia looked at them as well. They were a gentleman's hands, long and fine-boned. There was no dirt under those nails.

He swung one long, booted leg back and forth restlessly. "She died of throat distemper."

"Oh." She swallowed, breathed, and wondered how things now stood between them. Did he mean to bring her with him into The Maine wilderness to be wife to his friend? Did she want him to? Nothing really had changed. She still yearned with an ache that was almost physical to get away from the misery of her life in Boston, to be given a fresh start somewhere, a chance to become respectable, to become a lady . . .

"An' how old are these motherless children?"

"One is nine. The other's three, I think."

"Oh." At least they weren't babies. Delia knew nothing about taking care of children, though she wasn't going to tell him that.

"What's he like then, this friend of yers?"

"Nathaniel Parkes is more in the nature of a neighbor than a close friend, but he's a good man, Delia. You needn't fear that. He owns over two hundred acres of timberland and farms another hundred and twenty acres, although he's only got about half of that cleared as yet. He's built himself a good-sized house. You'll have to work hard, but the Sagadahoc is a bountiful land and you won't lack for much."

"I'm not afraid of workin' hard."

"From what I've seen there doesn't appear to be much you *are* afraid of." He looked up at her and now his mouth twisted crookedly. She loved the way his smile transformed his face. His lips, she decided, did not go with the rest of his sharp, hawkish features. They were full and sensual, especially the lower lip. She wondered how it would feel to run her finger along it—

God, Delia, ye wooden-headed fool! D' ye think he'd ever let the likes of ye get close enough t' feel his lips, stinkin' as ye do of a distillery?

"Do ye live there yersel' then, at this Merrymeeting Settlement?"

"Most of the time."

She wet her mouth, her eyes shifting away from his. "An' are ye . . . are ye married?"

He said nothing at first and Delia cursed her flapping tongue. Then he pushed himself off the desk. It brought him right next to her, so close she imagined she could feel the heat of him. And smell him as well—leather and tobacco and something else that she couldn't really describe except as a certain manliness. Yes, that was it, a manly smell.

"I'm not married," he said abruptly. "But Nat Parkes does need a wife . . . if you're still willing."

For some strange reason his physical nearness had brought a rush of blood thrumming through her body, causing a rushing sound in her ears like breakers on a beach. She lifted her head to answer him and her eyes fell on his mouth, and the words died unspoken in her throat.

"I see you've changed your mind. I can't say that I blame you," he said. "It was a damn-fool idea anyway, and I told Nat as much on the day he hatched it. Still, I won't let you go away empty-handed." He thrust a pair of long, brown fingers into the pocket of his waistcoat. Reaching down, he took her by the wrist and pressed the coin from his pocket into her hand.

She looked down at the gold sovereign in her palm. It represented more wealth than she had ever in her life seen at one time, and it burned her flesh as if it were still molten from the coin press.

Her fingers closed around it, and she looked up at him. He was smiling at her, and she hated him. She hated him because she could use the money—oh, she could use it and now more than ever—and she hated him for knowing that, knowing she could use it, and for pitying her and thinking she'd be grateful. And she hated him because in some way that she only dimly understood she wanted him to like her, wanted him to want her, wanted *him*, and he could never be hers.

"I don't need yer charity, ye bloody bastard!" she cried, and she flung the coin at his face.

It struck him on the cheekbone and bounced to the floor. She stood looking at him, shocked at herself, at what she had done, and then she whirled to run.

He grabbed her waist. She cried out as his arm wrapped around her bruised ribs. Something sharp seemed to stab right through her lung and a wave of pain washed over her, so intense that her vision blackened. Swaying dizzily, she bent over, clutching her middle, and moaned deep within her throat.

He had let her go immediately when she first cried out, but now he touched her shoulder. "My God, Delia, what is it? Are you hurt?"

She sucked in a deep, shuddering breath. " 'Tis my ribs. I think they're busted."

"Here, can you straighten up?"

She nodded and straightened slowly, but the pain stabbed at her again and she gasped. He moved his fingers over her midriff, and she sucked in a sharp breath when he touched the sore spot.

"Has someone been beating on you?"

She bit her lip and nodded. "My da belted me a good one. He was the worse for drink."

"Take off your bodice—"

She gasped, backing away from him. "Oooh, ye men, ye're all alike, ye are. I hate ye all!"

"For God's sake, Delia, I'm a physician. I can't examine you properly with your clothes on. If your ribs are broken, they'll need to be bound up."

She had done it again, made a fool of herself in front of this man. More than anything she wanted to be away from here, from him; away, away, so that she could forget all this had ever happened.

But he was a doctor, and he wouldn't let her go until he was satisfied he had ministered to her needs. "All right, I'll take it off," she said reluctantly. "But ye have t' turn yer back whilst I do it."

His brows went up and she thought he was going to say something, but he didn't. Instead he turned his back on her, going over to the gateleg table where his physician's implements were laid out. He shook a few dried leaves from a jar and began to crush them in a mortar and pestle. As he worked, the muscles of his arms bunched beneath the thin shirt and his shoulders flexed, pulling the satin cloth of his waistcoat tight across his broad back.

"Take it off, Delia," he ordered, not bothering to turn around.

Delia started guiltily and flushed as if she'd just been caught with her fingers in the honey jar. Her hand shook as she unraveled the laces of her bodice and pulled it over her shoulders, letting it drop from her bare arms to the floor. Then she pulled her shift from beneath the waistband of her petticoat, drawing it over her head. This, too, she let fall to the floor. She stood in the middle of the room, naked from the waist up, and though the fire still burned brightly in the grate, her skin tightened and pimpled as if with a chill.

Ty turned around, taking a step toward her. Then his eyes dropped to her bare breasts and for the briefest moment his step faltered.

She tried to cover herself with her hands, but she was too well-endowed. She had never felt more naked in her life. And she *was* more naked than she had ever been in her life, for she always slept in her shift and bathed in it as well.

"Don't be embarrassed," he said with an easy smile. "We physicians are trained to remain unmoved by the sight of the nude female body."

"Ye weren't so unmoved by such a sight earlier this night," she said tartly, then instantly regretted it. Why did she want to go and remind him of *that* for?

Ty made a funny sound that wasn't quite a laugh, but she couldn't see his face for his head was bent and he was looking at her chest. He ran his hands over her flesh and bones, and she thought she had never been touched so gently. The brush of his palms and fingers across her skin seemed to soothe her pain. Goose bumps rose on her legs and arms, and a funny feeling danced down her spine. She actually had to clench her back teeth to keep from shivering. Then his forearm brushed her breasts and her whole body shuddered.

"Are you cold?"

"Aye." She gasped. The skin around her nipples had tightened, drawing them into two hard points. She prayed he wouldn't notice.

Ye wooden-headed fool! How can he help but notice, the way they're practically a-pokin' him in the face?

Ty touched an old bruise, yellow now and almost faded, just above her hipbone. He straightened and looked down at her, his brows drawn together in a frown. "Today obviously wasn't the first time he's used his fists on you."

Shame filled Delia, so bitter she thought she could taste it. She was ashamed to expose her weakness to a stranger. Oh, especially to him. She was ashamed of her da's drunkenness, but she was as much ashamed of herself. She was sure it was all her fault, that if she had managed to keep their home properly the way her ma had before she'd died, then her da would never have been driven to drown his misery in drink.

She couldn't meet Ty's eyes, so she spoke instead to the silver buttons on his waistcoat. " 'Twas all my fault. I got his dander up with my sass."

"Jesus Christ," Ty muttered under his breath.

She glanced up in time to catch the look of anger on his face and thought it was directed at herself, and the shame blossomed until tears filled her eyes. She turned her head aside before he could see them.

"Your ribs aren't broken," he said, his voice gruff. "But they're certainly badly bruised and they may well be cracked. To be safe, I'm going into the bedroom to get something to bind them up with. You won't run off?"

She sniffed and surreptitiously wiped at the tears. "Like this? Not bloody likely!"

Ty was gone for only a moment and he returned carrying a long piece of linen. He wrapped it around her ribs, pulling so tightly that Delia wondered how she was going to manage to breathe when he was done. And still, still his touch was so incredibly gentle. Tears, hot and warm, filled her eyes and a sweet ache pulled at her chest. Then his hand accidentally brushed her sensitive breasts and the sweet ache turned into a quivering hunger that was more than a hollow feeling in her belly. It was a yawning pain in the region of her heart.

She looked down at his bent head, at the dark, thick waves of his hair touched with gold by the torchlight, and she knew that what she was thinking was wrong, could never, never be; that she was a fool to wish it and a fool even to think of doing what she was going to do; and that she would do it anyway . . .

She had known this man for only a few minutes. He was a stranger in every way except one—she had felt the healing touch of his hands. And she knew, somehow she knew, that he alone in all the world could heal her soul.

She knew. And it was enough for her to want to be where he was, live where he lived. She wanted to wake up in the morning and know there was a chance, even if only a small one, that she would see his face sometime that day.

She swallowed and drew in a deep breath. "Dr. Savitch?"

"Um?"

"Can I change my mind again?"

"I've been told that's a woman's prerogative."

"Then ye'll take me to the Merrymeeting Settlement, to be wife t' yer friend?"

"If you wish. It's either you or no one because, frankly, I've run out of time and the inclination to interview any more desperate females." He tied off the binding with quick, deft strokes. "You can get dressed now."

While Delia put her clothes back on, he went over to a lowboy on one side of the hearth where a pewter pitcher and cups had been set out on a tray. He poured wine from the pitcher into one of the cups and carried it to the gateleg table. He spoke while he worked.

"Look, Delia, whatever you decide won't be irreversible, at least not until you and Nat actually marry. It's easy enough to catch a sloop at Falmouth going west, except during the winter months, of course, when the bay is frozen over. If once you get to Merrymeeting you decide you can't abide the place or you can't abide Nat, or he can't abide you, then you'll be shipped back to Boston. At my expense."

Delia made a face at his back. Lord, he made her sound like a piece of merchandise. *Returned due to inferior quality.*

Ty stirred the crushed leaves from the pestle into the cup of wine. He brought it over to her. "Drink this."

She eyed the cup suspiciously. "What is it?"

"Something to make the pain go away."

As she reached for the cup her fingers brushed his and she felt the jolt of it all the way down to her toes. But if he had felt anything as well, she couldn't tell by looking at him.

She drained the cup and handed it to him. She started to wipe her mouth on the back of her hand, remembering not to only just in time. "Well . . . ." she said, feeling suddenly awkward. "Uh, when—"

"Be here tomorrow morning at eight o'clock. That doesn't give you much time, I know, but we should have left two days ago. It's going to take us a good three weeks of hard traveling to get there."

Three weeks! Delia hadn't realized the place was so far away. Suddenly the thought of setting off for such a distant wilderness filled her with fear. But the lure was so tempting— the promise of a fresh start, a new life, a home of her own and a man to take care of her, a man who needed her and waited there for her, or someone like her—a lonely, desperate woman to be wife to him and mother to his two children. It all pulled her to Merrymeeting . . .

Her head was drawn up to meet the force of the doctor's compelling eyes. She remembered the feel of his hands on her flesh where he had touched her. *And him,* a small voice cried out inside her, a voice she tried without success to squelch. *Ye're going because of him.*

"Well . . . till the mornin' then," she said. She started for the door, but he stopped her by softly calling her name.

"What about your father? When you tell him you're leaving, will he . . . ?"

She smiled and waved a hand, as if brushing away his concern. "Oh, ye needn't think he'll come after me any more this night. Nay, he'll be flat out on his tick by now, a-flappin' the roof with his snores."

He smiled back at her, and she felt a strange flutter under her bound-up ribs. "Then I'll see you tomorrow morning," he said. "Don't bring any more with you than you can comfortably carry."

She laughed at that, feeling suddenly happy and wonderfully free. "Go on with ye, doctor," she scoffed. "I don't *own* any more than I can comfortably carry."

Chapter 3

Tyler Savitch grimaced at the trencher of food before him. Salt cod drenched in a sauce of butter and eggs and heavily spiced with pepper. It was supposed to be the specialty of the Red Dragon Inn, but after one look and one whiff, his abused insides had risen in revolt.

He looked around the empty taproom, seeking someone who could take it away and bring him something bland, such as a bowl of samp or a piece of toasted bread. He was just about to get up in search of a servant when his ears were assaulted by loud bangs and a terrible squawking noise coming from the hall.

"Aooow! I told ye, ye damn idiot, that he's expectin' me!"

This was followed by a husky voice sputtering a string of cuss words bluer than any Ty had heard outside of a Sagadahoc lumber camp. He recognized the voice. How could he not, since he had tossed and turned all night while it haunted his nightmares?

The door to the taproom banged open and Delia McQuaid strode through. She had one hand on her head, holding down a battered straw hat, and from the other hand dangled a lumpy grist sack. She still wore the same muddy, rum-stained clothes from the night before, except she had added to the ensemble a moth-eaten woolen cloak that looked as if it had been plucked straight off the rubbish heap.

She plopped down on the bench opposite Ty, dropping the grist sack at her feet. He supposed its contents represented all the chit's worldly belongings—it and the paltry rags she

34

wore on her back. He thought with a repressed sigh that the rum-stained bodice was probably the only one she owned.

Still, now that she was closer he noticed she had cleaned herself up from the filthy wretch she had appeared to be the night before. In fact, to his surprise, she was actually rather pretty. Beneath that grayish grime had been flawless skin, pale as snow flowers except for two pink blooms of color on her cheeks and a slash of bright coral that was her wide, expressive mouth. Her ablutions had even extended to her hair—what he could see of it beneath the floppy brim of the pathetic hat. Last night he had thought her hair to be the dull black of soot, but he saw now that it was shot with ruby lights, giving it a richness that seemed out of place on a tavern wench.

She sighed loudly, blowing a lock of hair off her forehead. "That damned porter. Ye'd think this was bloody Buckingham Palace the way he's a-guardin' the front door." She paused, looked at him for a long moment, then flashed a brilliant smile. "Mornin'."

Ty said nothing. He drained his tankard of ale and rapped it down on the table. His eyes automatically fell on her breasts, which were straining against the tight lacing of her too-small bodice. It wasn't only that damn sensual, husky voice that had haunted his dreams last night; those breasts had been in there, too.

It bothered him, this prurient interest he had in this girl's body, this wretched, pathetic waterfront brat. His *patient*, for God's sake. It was so unprofessional, so unlike himself. Hadn't he always prided himself on his self-control? He decided the fault was all in the fact that he had fallen into bed last night half-drunk and in a state of aching unspent lust. A state which was entirely the fault of the abject creature now sitting across from him.

He scowled at her from beneath the brim of his cocked hat.

"Ye look a bit bilious this mornin'," she said.

"A man of such refined tastes as myself," Ty intoned, "should never indulge in rum that has been debased with arrack, tea, and lemon juice."

"Huh?"

"I drank too much of that god-awful punch at the governor's assembly last night. My head feels like a pumpkin that's been kicked by a mule. And you banging around and yowling like a pair of fighting cats doesn't help matters any."

"Ye were lit last night?" She was staring hungrily at his trencher of salt cod, and Ty thought that if she were a dog she'd be drooling. "Ye could've fooled me, ye could, because ye certainly didn't show it. I can always tell when my da's had a tot or two, right off. Are ye goin' to be eatin' that?"

Ty shoved the trencher and spoon across the table to her. "Please. Help yourself. How do your ribs feel this morning?"

She smiled brightly at him. "Oh, ye've magic in yer hands, doctor! They scarce hurt at all anymore."

She sat, elbows akimbo on the table, and shoveled a heaping spoonful of the salt cod into her mouth, chewed once, swallowed, and shoved in another mouthful. Some of the sauce dribbled down her chin and she wiped it off with the back of her hand.

"So ye truly were drunk last night? Who'd have thought it?" She grinned at him, showing a mouthful of half-masticated cod. Ty's stomach stirred uncomfortably.

"Don't talk with your mouth full. And for God's sake chew the stuff a few times before you swallow it," he admonished.

The grin froze on her mouth, then her jaw snapped shut. Furious color flooded in a tide up her neck and over her face, and she swallowed—so hard he saw the movement of it in her throat. The spoon, clutched awkwardly in her fist, trembled slightly.

Then her chin came up. Slowly, she dipped the spoon into the trencher and carefully brought it up to her mouth. Her lips opened into the tiniest slit and she took a dainty piece of fish off the spoon. She chewed it very, very slowly, her eyes fastened on his face, and the silence stretched out long between them.

Christ, Ty thought with a shudder. What have I done? He drummed his fingers on the table. Had he really agreed to take this wretched tavern wench back with him to Merrymeeting to be Nat's bride and caretaker to those poor, motherless children? Stalwart, plodding Nathaniel Parkes, a man who was psalm reader at the Sabbath-day meeting, a man who had once shyly admitted to Ty that he'd known in the biblical sense only one woman in his life, and that woman was his wife of ten years, a wife dead a bare two months. Ty tried to picture Nat with the girl sitting across from him, a girl who had probably been turning two-shilling tricks since she was thirteen.

He swallowed a sigh. "This grog shop you work in—"

"The Frisky Lyon." More cream sauce trickled down her chin; she smeared it off with her fingers, then wiped them on her skirt. "Only I don't work there no more. Not since I poured a noggin of rum all over Jake Steerborn's head and flattened his fat nose with a tray—all 'cause he got t' feelin' a little too frisky." She laughed, spraying bits of soggy cod all over the table. Ty's stomach heaved.

"Christ, Delia, you have the manners of a pig!"

"Well, excuse me all over!" she snapped back at him. But her feelings had been hurt, for a moment later she dropped the spoon into the trencher with a clatter and stared down at her lap. Ty cursed himself.

"I'm sorry." He reached across and touched her hand where it lay on the table. Seeing her hand, so pale and insubstantial against the heavy dark wood, made Ty realize just how thin and frail she was. Jesus, he thought, the chit's half starved and you're railing at her about her table manners.

"When was the last time you got a good, decent meal inside of you?"

She shrugged. "Yesterday sometime. I had a collop of cold pork an' a slice of bread."

He nudged the trencher of salt cod. "Go on, finish that up. Or would you like something else?"

She shoved it back at him. "I've had sufficient, thank ye."

His lips twitched at the way she said it—*I've had sufficient, thank ye*—as if she'd practiced it for hours in front of a looking glass, hoping someday for the appropriate occasion to use it. He thought of that pugnacious chin of hers that came right up at the slightest provocation. Her pride amused and touched him.

Yes, she had pride, and a strange dignity in spite of her grimy, ragged appearance and her abominable manners. It was because of the pride and dignity inherent in the person of Delia McQuaid that he had picked her out from all the other whores and slatterns and desperate, downtrodden women who had come to him hoping for a chance at three square meals and a roof over their heads in return for slaving on a farm and warming a man's bed. Her pride . . . and later seeing the horrifying bruises on her body . . . had more than convinced him his decision was the right one. His face hardened with renewed anger at the memory. At least if he took her to Merrymeeting he would be saving her from her drunken bastard of a father.

He realized she had been speaking to him. "I beg your pardon?"

"I was askin' ye what the governor's assembly was like. I'll bet ye there was music an' dancing an' card playing an' everything!" She sighed. Her eyes, Ty suddenly noticed, were beautiful—a rich, tawny gold with a starburst of green in the centers. They shone brightly at him. "Oh, what I would give t' have been there!"

Ty had a sudden mental picture of the likes of Delia McQuaid at a governor's assembly and couldn't repress a smile.

She blinked, and the shining look left her eyes. They grew solemn and serious, and Ty found he couldn't look away. She stared at him for so long and hard that he began to grow uncomfortable. Then she said, "Do ye know ye've got a real nice smile? I like yer smile."

Ty felt strangely flattered. "Thank you."

"And ye've got a damn fine-lookin' arse, too."

"Jesus Christ!" Ty cheeks grew hot. He knew he was blushing and his embarrassment fueled his anger. "I realize, wench, that you are hardly a lady, so I can't expect you to behave like one. Nevertheless, I insist that while in my presence you refrain from using language more suited to a randy sailor. As I said, I am a man of refined tastes and I like to be surrounded by fine things."

Her face was florid with embarrassment. Nevertheless, Ty saw that rebellious chin jerk up, and he braced himself for the worse.

Then the chin quivered and fell. She looked down, clasping her hands tightly in her lap. "Oh Lord, Ty, I'm so sorry. When my tongue gets t' flappin', I forget t' think. It's all the time a-gettin' me into trouble." She looked up at him with pleading eyes. "Ye aren't going to change yer mind about taking me with ye, are ye?"

"Don't be absurd," he said gruffly, feeling like a brute. He shoved the bench away from the table, pushing himself to his feet. "Come on, brat, let's get out of here."

He walked across the taproom, heading for the door and not bothering to see if she followed. Delia almost knocked over the table in her haste not to be left behind. She snatched up her grist sack, anchored her hat firmly on her head, and hurried after him.

"Bloody pompous ass," he heard her muttering beneath her breath. "Him and his re-*fined* tastes."

Ty barely stopped himself from laughing out loud.

Delia had never been so excited in her life.

She had taken the ferry once across the river to Charles Town for the fair, and that had been a real adventure. And once with Tom she had ridden in a cart out to Mill Pond for a Sunday picnic supper. But never, never had she done anything so grand as to go riding in an honest-to-God coach.

The coach was painted black and trimmed in silver. It even had a crest painted on the doors, and it was pulled by two pairs of matching coal-black horses. The tall, dark-skinned servant called Jackie, who had come into the Red Dragon to get Ty, had climbed into a box in back, while another servant dressed in the same black and silver livery sat in front to do the driving. She had followed Ty inside the coach and plopped down right next to him on a seat of a leather so fine it was as soft as silk.

Sighing happily, Delia settled back, smoothing down her skirts and trying to assume what she thought was a dignified expression. She admonished herself sternly to remember to act like a proper lady, for she was riding across Boston in a fancy coach to meet Ty's grandfather.

Ty had been heading for the inn's front door, Delia close on his heels, when it had opened and a round, dusky-skinned face topped by an enormous yellow periwig had peered around the jamb. An earring made of a shoe buckle dangled from one black ear, swaying gently in the morning breeze, and a pair of big brown eyes searched the hall.

Ty stopped so abruptly that Delia plowed into the back of him. He groaned loudly. "Jackie . . . what the bloody hell are you doing here?"

The big brown eyes fell on Ty and the face broke into a wide grin. The head disappeared a moment, then the door opened wide and a tall man, wearing silver and black livery and a silver slave collar sauntered in.

"Here you is, Massah Tyler. Ah been sent wid the coach t' fetch you. Your grandfather wants t' see you and he's got his mad up. Lawd, yes, he's mad enuf t' chew nails."

"Bloody hell!" Ty had said again.

Delia would have liked to point out to Tyler W. Savitch, M.D., that all his "bloody hells" was hardly language befitting a gentlemen of refinement, but she refrained. There were currents of an almost savage restlessness beneath his hard, controlled exterior. She didn't know him well enough yet to dare to test the limits of that control.

So now she contented herself instead with rubbing her hands across the smooth seat and breathing deeply of the crisp leathery smell. While the coach rumbled through the traffic of gigs, carts, and sedan chairs, Ty stared out the window, wearing an angry scowl.

Delia couldn't believe her good fortune that Ty had decided to bring her with him. She knew he hadn't meant to do so at first. In fact, he had turned around and started to spew orders at her about staying put and out of trouble, when she had seen a wicked gleam suddenly come into his dark blue eyes.

"On the other hand, by God, I think I *will* bring you with me," he had said, letting out a short, harsh laugh. "Yes, by God, I believe I will!"

She was glad now she had gone to the trouble to wash herself off at the public well, even though it meant that for privacy's sake she'd had to get up long before dawn, shivering out in the open as the wind off the cold bay waters had whipped at her body, clad only in its thin shift. Lord, she was probably lucky she hadn't gotten herself arrested for indecency or given herself an ague and all to please *him*, though a fat lot of good it had done her for all the notice he'd taken of her new, cleaner self. Instead, he had found fault with the way she ate, likening her to a pig! Her face grew hot at the memory of how she had shamed herself before him, arousing his disgust. *I realize that you are hardly a lady,* he had said. Oh Lord, how she longed with her whole heart to prove him wrong . . .

Delia cast a surreptitious glance at his averted face. Last night she had thought him handsome. Now, studying him in bright daylight, she decided he was by far the finest-looking man she had ever seen. He didn't dress like a physician, however; for he was without the tightly curled wig, black suit, and gold-headed cane that normally denoted members of his profession. Instead, he was well-dressed in silk and snuff-colored mohair breeches, with what looked to be real silver buckles at his knees, and a dark blue coat with a lacy, high-necked stock folded over his linen shirt. The whiteness of the stock set off the stark contrast of his sun-browned face.

He was a man of contrasts, she thought. Such as the way he spoke—so posh and educated one minute and cussing up a blue streak like her da the next. And the perpetual scowl on his mouth that didn't go at all with the laugh lines around his eyes. He played the part of a gentleman rake, yet he had spoken so gently to his woman last night when they had parted; he had treated her with such respect. Delia knew it was hopeless to wish it, but still she longed for him to treat her so tenderly.

So respectfully.

No sooner had the coach rounded the town house toward Queen Street when it lumbered to an abrupt halt, nearly dumping Delia onto the floor. She saved herself by grabbing Ty's leg. The muscle of his thigh was warm and hard beneath her palm and she felt it tense through the thin material of his breeches. She left her hand on his thigh long after she should have—until he stared pointedly at the hand, then at her. Blushing, she removed it, unconsciously balling it into a tight fist on her lap.

Slowly, Delia became aware of shouting and screaming outside, and she leaned out the window to see what the commotion was about. A woman, stripped to the waist and tied to the tail of an ox cart, was being whipped around the town house square.

The man doing the whipping was going easy on the strokes, but even so the woman's naked back was criss-crossed with red weals. She had been branded as well, on her shoulder with the letter A. The significance of the brand made Delia think again of the woman who had been with Ty in his rooms last night.

"Seems to me yon whore is gettin' no worse'n she deserves," she muttered, loud enough for the man sitting beside her to hear. "A-lyin' in sin with a man not her husband . . ."

Ty looked away from the gruesome scene being enacted in the street and met Delia's accusing eyes. "I know what you're implying, Delia, and you're wrong. The woman in question—"

"Priscilla," Delia put in, just so there'd be no mistake.

"Priscilla," Ty admitted through gritted teeth, "is a widow. She's also kind, decent, honest to a fault, and one of the finest people I know. And why shouldn't she take a lover now and then if she so chooses?"

Delia sniffed. "There's many a God-fearin' folk in Boston who would argue with ye about that. An' what's more, ye ought t' marry her, Tyler Savitch, if ye're going t' do . . . do what ye've been doin' with her."

"If I proposed marriage to Priscilla, she would turn me down flat for she values her freedom as much as I do mine." He glared at her. "Jesus, why am I justifying myself to the likes of you? The entire matter is none of your damn business!"

Delia said nothing, although her breast rose in indignation at the hypocrisy of his words. Priscilla was a *lady,* rich and prominent, and therefore above society's censure no matter what her behavior, whereas a poor girl like herself couldn't work in a grog shop without being labeled a whore.

Ty had turned away, but he was not done with her, for a moment later his head snapped around and he growled at her some more. "And here's another thing. If that woman" —and he pointed out the carriage window—"*sinned,* as you call it, then there was a man helping her to do it. So why isn't he out there tied to that cart and taking his licks right along with her?''

Delia stared at him in surprise. That was one form of hypocrisy that had never occurred to her before. Yet for him, a man, it had.

She was still ruminating over this strange facet of Ty's character when the coach turned down Beacon Street and drew up before a manor house set well back on a tree-shaded lot. Only four houses stood on this side of the street, which ran into the base of Beacon Hill, where flags on the signal tower snapped in the wind, a wind that brought with it the cloyingly sweet smell of molasses from the rum-making distilleries on nearby Mill Pond.

The footman opened the carriage door and helped Delia to descend into the street. She looked up in wonder at the enormous mansion built of granite and trimmed with brown sandstone. It was three stories tall with a blue slate mansard roof and row upon row of large sashed windows. The front door was decorated with a frieze and flanked by columns and in the middle of it was a brass lion's head knocker with a ball in its mouth.

"Oh, Ty, I've never clapped sight of a house so grand!" Delia exclaimed. She looked at him with shimmering eyes. "Can I go inside with ye? Please. I promise I'll act like a proper lady, truly I will."

He smiled down at her. Then he actually took her arm and linked it through his, just as if she *were* a real lady, and Delia's chest swelled with pride.

But he spoiled it all by saying, "I don't want you acting like a lady, Delia, even if you are capable of such an impossible feat. I want you to be yourself."

Before Ty could knock, the door was opened by another servant—a woman large enough to stand eye-level with Ty's six feet. Her stiff apron crackled as she moved, and she had a gigantic turban balanced precariously on her pumpkin-sized head. She, too, wore a silver slave collar, engraved with the name of her owner. Her cheerful grin was so infectious, Delia couldn't help smiling back at her.

"Mornin', mistress," she said, nodding at Delia, whose wide-open eyes were taking in the long wainscoted hall and

the sweeping stairway with its elaborately carved balusters
and newel posts. "And mornin' t' you, Massah Tyler," she
said as she took Delia's cloak and grist sack, treating them
with the same reverence as if the cloak had been made of red
silk and the grist sack was a leather satchel. "A fine mornin',
isn't it? You be findin' Suh Patrick in his bedchamber, Massah Tyler."

Sir Patrick. Heaven preserve us, Delia thought, was Ty's
grandfather a bloody lord or something? Suddenly she wished
she'd waited outside.

"Thank you, Frailty," Ty said, and started for the stairs.
But Delia held him back by his coat sleeve.

"Yer grandfather's a *lordship?*"

Ty's glance automatically went to an oil portrait hanging
above a delicate walnut sideboard that stood along one wall
of the hall. Delia realized this must be the old noble gentleman himself. She had never seen a grander-looking person-
age—nor a meaner-looking one.

"Sir Patrick Graham . . . but he's not a lord," Ty was
saying. "In fact, he was born a Scottish crofter's son. He was
knighted by Queen Anne many years ago, after he discovered
a sunken Spanish galleon full of treasure off the coast of the
Bahamas." He gave her such a knowing grin that Delia
flushed. "He's a bit of a pompous ass and I'm counting on
you to bring him down a peg or two."

Frailty clucked her tongue and wagged her finger beneath
Ty's nose. "Massah Tyler, you oughta be 'shamed o' your-
self, usin' this po' gal t' get one back at your grandfather.
Don't you let him do it, honey," she said to Delia.

Delia took another careful look at the portrait of the hook-
beaked, stern-lipped old man. He didn't appear the sort who
would take kindly to having a tavern wench come sashaying
through the front door of his Beacon Street manor house with
a notion to put him in his place.

She swallowed nervously and tugged again at Ty's sleeve.
"What's your grandfather do now? I mean besides bein' a
knight."

"He's a slave trader."

As Delia followed Ty up the stairs, she glanced back over
her shoulder at Frailty, who still stood in the hall. Frailty

smiled encouragingly at Delia and made a shooing motion with her hands. Delia smiled back. A slave trader. Ty's grandfather was a slave trader.

Growing up as she had in the Boston waterfront slums, Delia was aware of the infamous triangular shipping trade on which so many New England fortunes were built—rum to Africa for slaves; slaves to the West Indies for molasses and sugar; molasses and sugar back to Boston to be distilled into rum. But not all the slaves went to the West Indies. Some were brought here, to New England, and many of the better sort had at least one or two dark-skinned servants to give prestige to their households.

Delia followed Ty up the stairs and down a long, broad hall lined with row upon row of portraits, some blackened with age. "Lord above us, I suppose these are all yer illustrious ancestors," she whispered, awed.

Ty emitted a short bark of laughter but said nothing.

He rapped once on a door at the end of the hall and opened it immediately. Delia followed after Ty, using his broad shoulders as a shield, but peering around them with unabashed curiosity.

Delia had thought Ty's rooms at the Red Dragon were the most magnificent she had ever seen, but they couldn't touch this room for pure luxury. With silk paper on the walls, a marble fireplace, and thick carpets scattered on the inlaid floor, it was almost too much to take in at once. Dominating the room was an enormous four-poster with carved and fluted pillars and cornices, and adorned with green damask hangings. It was even draped with a fine gauze curtain to keep the mosquitoes at bay.

And there, at the foot of the bed, wearing a flowing red silk banyan and matching felt slippers with curled-up toes, must be, Delia thought, Sir Patrick himself.

He was bent at the waist with a sheet draped over his shoulders and his face thrust into a paper cone, while a manservant shook white powder from a ball onto his bewigged head.

"Ty, is that you, boy?" came an old man's querulous voice, echoing within the paper cone. "You were going to try to sneak off without me knowing of it, weren't you?" He pulled the cone off his face and flapped it at his valet. "That's enough, damn you. Go on, go on, I'm done with you for now."

The valet took the sheet and cone and left the room on quiet feet while grandfather and grandson glared at each other.

"Well?" the old man demanded. "What have you got to say for yourself?"

Delia saw the telltale muscle tick along Ty's jaw. "When I was here three days ago you told me to get out of your damn sight."

"Aye, I did, but I was hoping in the interim you'd gotten some sense pounded into that thick head of yours." He turned and went over to a walnut dressing table and, bending stiffly, studied his reflection in the looking glass. He adjusted the wig a fraction. "This stubbornness of yours must come from your da's family. It isn't a Graham trait." He whirled around and fixed his grandson with a fierce glare. "I'm waiting, boy. I'm waiting to hear you tell me that you've changed your stubborn Savitch mind. That you're staying in Boston and you're taking over Graham Shipping, just as I've always planned for you."

Ty's mouth did have a stubborn set to it. "Then you'll be waiting till snow falls in hell. I'm a physician—I want to *heal* human flesh, not *trade* in it."

The old man released an angry breath, and fine white powder drifted like snow onto the shoulders of his long, voluminous banyan. The sight of the tall, stern-faced man fuming in the middle of the room in his blazing silk dressing gown reminded Delia of the fire-breathing creature on the signboard of the Red Dragon Inn.

"Well, don't stand there hovering in the doorway like a blamed fool," Sir Patrick scolded. "I've still got some things to say to you and, by God, for once you're going to listen!"

The old man stomped the length of the room, the robe flapping around his thin legs. At the fireplace, he turned, his hands locked behind him, his shoulders thrown back, and then his eyes fell on Delia. "Good God. Who's the wench?"

"I'm taking her to Merrymeeting with me," Ty said, a

mischievous smile on his face as he pulled a reluctant Delia into the room.

"Be damned you are!" the old man exclaimed, aghast.

Delia jerked her arm from Ty's grasp. She cast her eyes demurely downward and dropped into a wobbly curtsy. "How do ye do, yer lordship."

"Eh? Oh . . . it's a pleasure, mistress. A pleasure." Sir Patrick stared at her, and his eyebrows soared all the way up into his wig as he took in the sight of her ragged clothes and bare feet. But he said, "She's pretty, Ty. Right pretty."

Delia straightened and slid a triumphant glance in Ty's direction. He frowned at her.

Sir Patrick waved a thin, heavily-veined hand at a brocade chair. "Do sit down, mistress. Where's your manners, Ty? There's some hot mulled ale on the table over there. Bring some to the poor gel. Can't you see she's shivering from the morning chill?"

Ty cast Delia another scowl, but he went across the room to a tea table and poured a tankard of ale. As soon as Ty's back was turned the old man winked at Delia, and she had to bite her lip to keep from giggling. If Ty had planned to use her presence to bait his grandfather, it wasn't working.

"He does things to provoke me," he said to Delia as if he'd read her mind. "Don't think I don't know it. I sent him to Edinburgh University to read law and he came back with a degree in medicine instead. All done to irritate me."

Ty laughed. "Really, Sir Patrick, you flatter yourself if you think I arrange my life just to irritate you."

"What did you come around here this morning for, if it wasn't to irritate me?"

Ty turned from the table and bowed mockingly. "You commanded me, sir."

"Hunh! And why did you bother coming to Boston at all if you never meant to stay above a week—besides coming back to irritate me, aye, and turn up your nose at all the things I'm trying to do for you."

Ty shoved the tankard of ale into Delia's hands.

"Why, thank ye, Dr. Savitch," she said sweetly.

He lowered his voice and growled at her, "What happened to that blatting tongue of yours, brat?"

Delia gave him a demure smile and took a dainty, most ladylike sip of the ale. She would show Tyler Savitch she could behave like a proper lady if she put her mind to it.

"I came to Boston for the purpose of searching out a woman ornery enough to be a wife," Ty told his grandfather, grinning provokingly at Delia.

Sir Patrick's brows soared up again and his fierce gray eyes fastened onto Delia's blushing face, but he made no comment.

"Also, I've come to hire a preacher for the settlement. And I had heard about this new smallpox inoculation of Cotton Mather's," Ty went on amicably. "I wanted to see for myself the results of his experiments."

Sir Patrick snorted. "I don't hold with these inoculations. We mustn't interfere with God's handiwork. If God wishes to visit a man with smallpox, He must have His way."

"You'd feel differently if the disease came calling on you. The epidemic hasn't reached The Maine yet, and I'm hoping to convince the folks of Merrymeeting and the other settle—"

"Merrymeeting, bah!" The old man thumped his slippered foot on the floor. "Even the name of it sounds like a fool's paradise. That useless medical degree wasn't the only thing you acquired in Edinburgh. You picked up a taste for expensive things and even more expensive women. I can't picture you freezing your arse off in one of those miserable log houses during the winter and with no one to keep you warm at night but a squaw—" Sir Patrick cut himself off, his eyes straying to Delia. She smiled so sweetly at him, he blinked.

But Ty was oblivious of this exchange. He threw himself down into the chair opposite Delia's. Even then he couldn't stay still, crossing his legs to swing one foot back and forth, tapping his fingers on the chair arm. "I've managed to live quite happily there for two years now," he said. "And if you're worried about my expensive tastes, I'm the only physician from Wells to Port Royal and I'm well-compensated for my services."

"Well-compensated, are you? Ha!" Sir Patrick flapped his hand. "Do you live like this in that godforsaken settlement, eh? Answer me that."

Ty pushed himself back to his feet. "I don't want to live like this. Especially if the price is human bondage and misery!"

Sir Patrick's eyes followed his grandson as he paced the room, and Delia detected a note of desperation behind their glazed hardness. "Now you listen to me, Ty. I've let you sow your wild oats and I've given you a chance to get this fascination with the wilderness out of your system. But I'm not getting any younger, so you're going to stop all this foolishness this very day and you're going to take over the running of the company. I need you. You're all I've got and you owe me, boy."

Ty jerked around, his face dark and tight with anger. "I owe you nothing! Christ, what in God's great world makes you think I would agree to set one foot in Graham Shipping?" he bellowed at the old man. "Why can't you understand? I abominate what you do!"

Sir Patrick's head flung up and his hard, gray eyes blazed. "You dare to criticize me! You were nothing more than a naked, heathen savage when I found you that day ten years ago." He turned and flung out his arms, appealing to a wide-eyed Delia. "Why, he was no better than a slave himself!"

Ty's jaw clamped shut and he spoke through his teeth. "That's a lie and you know it. You had to *force* me back into your world. I had a family and a life and—"

"Aye, aye, right decent folk they were," Sir Patrick said, sarcasm oozing from his voice, and he spoke to Delia as if she were the one he had to convince. "Barely sixteen he was when I found him, and already he'd lifted his share of scalps. They had taken him captive, a boy of six, and made him one of them, made him into a bloody savage, and killed . . . killed . . ."

Sudden tears filled Sir Patrick's eyes, and he turned to look at the portrait above his head. It was of a delicate, ephemeral-looking young woman standing with her hand on the back of a chair as if she needed its weight to anchor her to the ground. She had hair so fair it looked almost silver and eyes the deep blue of the sea at dusk.

Ty's eyes, an identical blue, had gone to the portrait as well, and Delia saw the anger leave him. He sighed wearily and pushed his hand through the front of his hair. "I've told you and told you. They didn't kill her. She died in childbirth."

"After she had been raped and impregnated by one of your Abenaki savages!"

"He was her husband."

"Her *husband* was murdered!"

Sir Patrick came up to stand before Ty. They must have been the same height once, Delia thought, before age had stooped the older man. He stood nose to nose to his grandson now, trying to stare Ty down. But Ty's eyes met those of his grandfather's and held them steadily.

"How can you bear to go back there and live where it all happened?" Sir Patrick said, the pleading plain in his voice. "Where *they* are?"

Delia saw the movement of Ty's throat as he swallowed. "The Sagadahoc is my home. And I'm going back."

The old man blinked, and a tear fell from his eye to roll slowly down his cheek. "I thought I'd made an Englishman of you. I educated you, taught you how to dress and speak properly, but I never could touch your heart. Nay, at heart you're still one of them. You're still an Abenaki savage."

"I don't know . . . I don't know *what* I am anymore," Ty said, his voice strained, and in his eyes Delia saw the agony of a tormented soul.

But his grandfather was too hurt and too angry to see it. "Get out," he said, his voice low and harsh. "Go back there then, to your precious Abenaki wilderness. I never want to set eyes on you again."

A hundred questions danced on the tip of Delia's tongue as they were driven in the coach back to the Red Dragon—most having to do with savage, scalping Indians and their proximity to Merrymeeting Settlement. But there was such a forbidding look on Ty's face, she didn't dare voice even one of them.

At the inn, Ty jumped from the coach, leaving her to fend for herself. He disappeared inside and she thought about following, but she hadn't been asked, so she went down the street a ways, to the haberdashery shop next door, and leaned against the brick wall to wait for him. A few moments later she saw the ostler go around to the nearby livery stable and come back with a frisky Narragansett pacer and another sturdier horse equipped with a pack saddle. She knew Ty was preparing to leave. She shivered and drew her thin, ragged cloak around her, although it wasn't cold.

The front door to the Red Dragon opened wide and the porter emerged, staggering under three heavily-loaded haversacks, which he proceeded to tie onto the pack horse. A few moments later, Ty came out.

Delia barely recognized him. He had changed from his fine gentleman's clothes into a pair of worn buckskin breeches and a hunting shirt made of heavy linen dyed a butternut brown, with long fringes around the shoulders and down the sleeves. He carried his flintlock in one hand and from a beaded Indian strap across his chest hung a powder flask, a shot pouch, and an Indian ax. Only the costly fitted boots were reminiscent of his earlier elegance.

He looked tough and dangerous, his face hard and frightening. Certainly he seemed the sort of man who could live happily in the wilderness, even among the savages. Delia thought that if his grandfather had seen Ty looking as he did now, he would have realized how hopeless were his expectations.

Ty shoved the rifle into the saddle holster. He gathered up the lead of the pack horse and swung onto the pacer's back, digging his heels into the horse's side. It took Delia a moment to realize he was leaving without her.

She snatched up the grist sack at her feet and ran into the street after him. "Ty, wait! Wait for me!"

He whirled his horse around, and she saw by the look on his face that he had completely forgotten her.

"Delia . . ." His face softened and he even managed a smile. Leaning over, he held out his hand to her. "We'll have to pick up a horse for you later. For now we'll ride double."

Delia didn't move. She stood in the middle of the street, staring up at him. She wished he hadn't forgotten her. How *could* he have forgotten her? But then, what was she to him except a minor irritation, a package to be delivered and then dismissed from his mind?

"Come on, Delia," Ty said, impatient. "The reverend and his wife have been waiting for us at the Common for over an hour."

She approached the horse warily. "I don't know how to ride."

"Well, I haven't time to teach you!" he snapped. "Here, give me your arm, put your right foot on top of mine, and throw your left leg over his rump."

He tied her grist sack to the front of his saddle, then hauled on her arm, and she went flying up in the air to land with a hard jar, straddling the horse's rump. Its hide felt scratchy beneath her bare legs and her petticoat had been pulled clear up to her knees, but Delia had little time to think of that before Ty urged the horse into a fast trot. The sudden movement threw her against his broad back. She swallowed a nervous cry and wrapped her arms tight around his waist. Lacing her hands across the hard slab of his stomach, she pressed her cheek against his shoulder blade.

It didn't take long to make their way to the Common. Delia was just beginning to enjoy the wonder of being so close to Ty, close enough to feel his warmth, to hear his heart beat, when they turned onto Common Street and there, stretching before them, was a wide, muddy pasture dotted with grazing cows. At the very edge of the field waited an ox-drawn cart loaded with chests and furniture. A woman sat on the seat while a man paced at the team's heads, peering anxiously down the street.

Ty lifted his hand in greeting as they trotted up. He slid from his horse, causing Delia to tumble down after him, and he had to grab her arm to prevent her from sprawling in the dirt at his feet.

"Reverend Hooker," Ty said with a smile, releasing Delia to reach out and shake the young man's hand. "I'm sorry I'm late."

The Reverend Hooker was in his early twenties, with a thin, aesthetic face that seemed befitting to his profession. He was dressed in a plain dark broadcloth suit and a wide-brimmed hat with a low round crown. Even his stock was black.

He answered Ty's smile, then his solemn hazel eyes flickered over Delia. He smiled at her as well, a smile that slowly faded as he took in her bedraggled appearance.

"I'm Delia," she said. "I guess we all must be going to the Merrymeeting Settlement together."

The reverend looked taken aback. "Er, uh, I'm Caleb," he said, wiping his hand nervously against his leg. Then he cleared his throat and turned back to Ty, and when he spoke again it was in a preacher's voice, low and rhythmic. "I'm just glad you're here. We were starting to worry." He turned to the woman seated in the wagon. "Dr. Savitch, may I present to you my wife Elizabeth."

Delia looked with frank curiosity at the young minister's wife. Her neck was long and delicately bowed, like an egret's, her skin as white as fresh milk. Her nose and eyes were childlike but in perfect proportion above a small mouth that curled up on the ends like the petal of an iris. She, too, was dressed all in black, except for a white, undecorated bib over her bodice and a touch of white showing at the turned-back cuffs of her long sleeves. A calash covered most of her head, except for a few inches in the front where her hair showed pale, pale blond. In her lap she clutched a Bible bound in calfskin with a gilded clasp.

"Lizzie, this is the good doctor I was telling you about," the Reverend Caleb Hooker was saying, and the affection he felt for his wife showed in the gentle inflection of his voice. "The man who's going to take us to the Merrymeeting Settlement. And this is, uh, Delia."

The girl's gray eyes, as solemn and still as a dawn sky, glanced at them briefly before falling back down to the Bible in her lap. "I'm pleased to meet you, Dr. Savitch," she said in a soft, melodic voice.

Ty said nothing. It was this awkward silence that caused Delia to look from the young woman back to Ty . . . and at the expression on his face, Delia thought her heart would surely break.

For Tyler Savitch was staring up at the minister's wife with warm admiration in his eyes.

Chapter 4

~~~©~~~

hey took a flatboat ferry across the Charles River, sharing it with a stack of rum kegs and a herd of bleating goats. Elizabeth Hooker, fearful of either the river, the goats, or both, clung to the cart and shut her eyes. Ty hovered around her, looking manly and protective.

The sight of them together, the friendly admiration in Ty's eyes, was so painful to Delia that she wondered if she could bear it. How greedy is the human heart, she thought. Only last night it had been enough for her to be near him, to see his face. But already she wanted more. She wanted what she could never have.

Delia decided she could endure it more easily if she didn't have to see them together, so she went to the stern of the boat and watched the landmarks of her past slip away from her—the steeples of Boston's many meetinghouses sticking like thistles into the sky, the wharves jutting into the harbor, the sun reflecting off the copper roof of the lighthouse on Beacon Island, dazzling her eyes. She told herself she wasn't sorry to be leaving; it was only the bright sun that was making her blink away tears.

Oh, Da . . .

Her da must have passed out in a grog shop somewhere because he hadn't been asleep on his tick when she went home last night. She hadn't been able to tell him goodbye, but it was probably for the best. He'd be drunk for a day or two anyway, and he'd only have come after her with his fists.

But when he sobered up later he would miss her. Like as not he wouldn't even remember her taking a clout at him with

54

that piece of wood. He would search the waterfront for her, worry about her, and then figure out that she was gone for good, because he wasn't stupid, her da, leastways not when he was sober. And then he'd cry, because there was never one like her da for crying when he got to feeling sorry for himself.

Shame and guilt overwhelmed Delia. She promised herself she would have someone help her write a letter once she got to Merrymeeting, to tell him she was all right. At least then he wouldn't worry. Poor Da . . . Who would care for him now that she was gone?

And who would he use his fists on now when the drink got the best of him?

She shut her eyes, and her father's face came into her mind. But it was not her da as she'd last seen him—his eyes glittering with rage, his lips pulled back in a snarl. It was a dim memory of him on a day when he had seemed a god to her, so towering and strong to her little girl's eyes. They had stood on the end of the Long Wharf, just she and her da, as he pointed out the ships in the harbor to her. She could remember the strength of his large hand enveloping hers as they looked at the ships, the mysterious ships. She'd felt a scary excitement, thinking how wide and grand the world seemed. But mixed with that excitement was a warm feeling of security that her da was right there beside her to take care of her. She had looked up at him and he had smiled and said, "I love you, little puss . . ."

But then her ma had died. And the god had turned into a monster.

"Do you have family in the Merrymeeting Settlement?"

Delia turned and looked into the Reverend Caleb Hooker's thin face. He was smiling, and she noticed for the first time that his front teeth overlapped a bit. She liked that about him; it made him seem less saintly.

"I'm goin' to Merrymeeting t' be wed to a widower an' be a mother t' his two daughters," she replied, returning his smile.

"I see," he said, though he didn't sound at all as if he did.

Spoken so baldly, it sounded incredible to Delia's own ears.

She reminded herself that it was a new life she was going to.
A new life and respectability.

And to be near Ty, a niggling voice teased. But Delia ignored it.

Delia and the reverend looked at each other in silence, then
of one accord they turned toward the front of the ferry where
the reverend's wife sat in the ox cart and Tyler Savitch stood
beside her. His head was tilted up to her and he was saying
something that caused her to laugh. But only for a moment.
Then her eyes fell back down to the Bible she held in a white-
knuckled grip.

"My wife . . . she's frightened of the idea of journeying
into the wilderness," Caleb told Delia. "She's happiest
tucked up snug and warm inside with her spinning. She's
prodigious good with her spinning and her weaving." He
took off his hat and ran his fingers through limp seaweed-
brown hair. "This journey's going to be hard on her. But
once we get settled into the parsonage at Merrymeeting she'll
be fine," he added, sounding as if he were trying hard to
convince himself.

Delia gave him an encouraging smile. "Aye, I 'spect she
will."

They stood, smiling inanely at each other, then he said,
"Will you be joining the Meeting?"

"Well . . ." She blushed and looked down at her bare toes
sticking out from beneath the torn hem of her petticoat. "I
guess I've never been much of a one for churchgoin'."

The sound of soft laughter caused them to turn around.
Tyler Savitch stood tall before them, and the deep blue of the
river at his back matched the color of his eyes. His fingers
were hooked into the waistband of his breeches, his cocked
hat was tilted back on his head. The fringes of his hunting
shirt stirred in the breeze, drawing attention to the broad,
corded muscles of his chest. He was such a fine sight that
Delia felt a poignant ache in her breast.

"I'm afraid you won't be finding a big Community of
Saints in The Maine," Ty said. The mischievous twinkle was
back in his eyes again, the dazzling smile transforming his
face. Evidently the time spent in Elizabeth Hooker's gentle

company had restored his good humor, Delia thought unhappily, wishing *she* could have been the cause of that smile.

"But I was told my services had been requested," Caleb protested, oblivious to the misery that had crept into Delia's eyes. Ty wasn't even bothering to look at her.

"Massachusetts law says a settlement's got to have both a minister and a schoolmaster if it ever wants to be considered a proper town. But to be honest, Reverend, community funds are a bit strapped at the moment for us to take on the salaries of both. So it came down either to hiring you or taking on that schoolmaster, and you won by two votes." He pressed his tongue into the side of his cheek and stared out over the water. "Course, there's some say the election was rigged."

To Delia's surprise, the reverend burst into hearty laughter. She thought it a good thing that such a serious-minded man could also laugh at himself. She was glad to have the reverend's company on the long journey to Merrymeeting, and afterward, too. Aye, especially afterward. For Caleb Hooker seemed the kind of rare man who could be a friend to a woman. And Delia McQuaid had a feeling she was going to be needing a friend.

Once across the river, they were about to start out on the post road going northeast when Ty and Delia had their first altercation over the horse.

"I'm not ridin' on that beast with ye," she said, backing away from him when he started to put his hands around her waist to lift her into the saddle.

She made it sound as if it were the horse she feared. But it was he, or more precisely the dangerous and useless infatuation his nearness aroused in her. She knew she couldn't bear to ride for hours with her arms wrapped around that hard waist, her cheek pressed against that warm back, especially if *his* eyes were going to fall again and again on Mrs. Hooker.

"So what are you planning to do—walk all the way to Merrymeeting?" Ty demanded, not bothering to hide his exasperation.

"Aye!" she shot back at him. "Since I bloody well can't fly there!"

"Jesus Christ!" he bellowed, forgetting the presence of the reverend and his wife. "Why are you being so unreasonable? I'll buy you a horse first chance I get, but in the meantime—"

"I told ye afore, Tyler Savitch, I don't want none of yer charity."

"Oh, you want none of my charity, do you? And just who do you think is going to pay for your meals and lodging on this little jaunt?"

Hot color flooded her cheeks, but her chin jerked up in the air. "I'm no fool, Tyler Savitch. I know I can't make it all the way to The Maine without eatin' somethin' along the way, but I intend to pay ye back for whatever expenses I tot up"—Ty's brows arched, incensing Delia to further heights of aggravation—"but I'm not gettin' on that bloody horse with ye, nay, nor on any other horse or beast or method of conveyance that comes from yer filthy hands!"

Ty was laughing at her now. "Christ, what's got you madder than a wounded skunk all of a sudden?"

Delia whirled around and started down the road, calling him all manner of foul names under her breath.

"Delia, wait!" Caleb Hooker shouted after her. "We could probably find a place for you with us. I mean, well . . . it's a long way to walk."

Delia turned and looked back, first at Elizabeth Hooker, who regarded her husband with panic on her face, and then at the cart loaded to overflowing with a bedstead, chairs, chests, and two different kinds of spinning wheels—one for wool and one for flax. There wasn't *room* for her on the cart, even perched on the end of the tailboard, and even if the reverend's wife would have countenanced her lowly company.

She smiled at Caleb, shaking her head. "Thank ye just the same, Reverend."

"Well, if you're sure . . ."

"Now that we've got that settled, can we get started?" Ty said dryly. "I'd like to get to Merrymeeting sometime before the first snowfall."

Giving Delia an apologetic smile, Caleb hurried to scramble onto the cart. But as he picked up the goad, Elizabeth said, "Caleb, shouldn't you say a prayer before we begin?"

"Oh . . . yes, of course." He bowed his head. "May the will of Jehovah guide us on this journey, which we perform in humble service in this Thy name, O Lord. Amen," he finished with a rush, glancing up to give Ty a big grin.

Then he pricked the high ox with the goad, the cartwheel screeched in starting, and they were on their way to Merrymeeting Settlement, Sagadahoc Territory, The Maine.

It was slow going. The road was overgrown with skunk cabbage and jewelweed and full of boulders, stumps, and mudholes. They had to stop often to open gates as they rode through some farmer's pasture. Delia walked beside the reverend's fine red oxen. She enjoyed the company of the plodding, heavy-shouldered beasts. She found their lethargic tread oddly soothing, certainly easier on the nerves than riding on the horse with Ty would have been.

Ty, on the other hand, was so edgy he conveyed his feelings to the pacer, which danced along the trail, its ears flattened against its head, its tail flickering. Delia wondered at the cause of this restlessness and disquiet that were so much a part of Ty's character. No doubt it was due to his strange upbringing—ten years of living among the savages only to be brought back to civilization and made into an English gentleman. Perhaps a part of him had never quite been civilized, and that part didn't set too well with the gentleman physician he had become.

Delia pondered the enigma that was Tyler Savitch as they passed farms and tiny hamlets—five or six houses gathered together for company and protection. They went through gardens in small, irregular patches marked off with crude stone walls, and skirted newly planted mounds of Indian corn, their green tendrils of rolled leaves just piercing the earth. Once, they passed a couple of young girls drying flax over a pit on the hillside. The girls returned Delia's wave and she felt so happy, so carefree, she laughed out loud—only to look around and catch Ty watching her, a scowl marring his handsome face.

No doubt proper ladies didn't indulge in such vulgar displays of emotion, Delia supposed, and vowed to be more careful in the future.

Toward late afternoon they entered a stretch of salt marsh meadows and battalions of enormous, blue-colored flies that drew blood when they bit descended on them. Delia broke off a maple branch and switched the air above the oxen's heads to offer them some relief. But the insects were voracious, and Ty's horse's neck was soon swelling from the bites.

On the edge of the marshland, the road widened a bit and they came to a small village. Ty said they would stop there for the night, for when the flies got this bad it meant a rainstorm was coming. They'd have a wet day tomorrow, but at least the blood-sucking hordes would be gone. Delia didn't need the flies to tell her rain was coming, for her bruised ribs throbbed like rotten teeth.

Delia thought it a pathetic village, so small a body could spit from one end to the other. The meetinghouse lacked a steeple and the village green was just a muddy paddock upon which grazed a few scraggly cows. The last building in town was the only inn. Its signboard was a faded gray anchor suspended from a rusty chain that groaned in the wind. As they pulled up to the front door, they could smell the pigs and the necessary house from the yard out back.

The proprietor ambled out, scratching under his armpit and chewing vigorously on a quid of tobacco. His woolen breeches were unraveling at the ends and he sported "country boots"—simple leggings made from lengths of an old blanket, tied at the ankles and below the knees. A scraggly hound came trotting out of the door after the man, collapsing at his feet.

The innkeeper bobbed his shaggy head and spoke around the plug of tobacco bulging his cheek. "How ye folks doin'?"

Ty eased down off his horse. "Oh, fair to middling. You open for business?"

"Aye, that I am, esquire. This here is the Blue Anchor." He sized them up carefully, judging what the traffic could bear. "That'll be four shillings for the night's lodgin', esquire, an' that includes yer supper. Two shillings for the beasts."

Ty asked for some salt and water to rub on the pacer's

neck. The Hookers got down off the cart, and Elizabeth, looking wan and tired, hurried through the door. Delia was about to follow when Ty stopped her, putting his hand on her shoulder.

He looked pointedly down at her bruised, scratched, and bitten feet. "Let me see to you first."

"I can see t' myself, thank ye."

His lips tightened, but then he pulled in a deep breath and she knew he was battling his temper. She didn't enjoy making him angry, truly she didn't. But she was afraid that if she was the least bit nice to him, he'd see through her charade and guess that *he* was one of the things drawing her to Merrymeeting. And then he would pity her and her foolish dreams and she wouldn't be able bear that.

"At least now you'll have to admit that you were wrong and I was right and you're riding with me tomorrow," he stated.

"I'm not admittin' t' no such thing."

His hand slipped off her shoulder and around to cup her upthrust chin. She couldn't help shivering at the feel of his fingers brushing against her skin. He smiled at her and she wanted to burst into tears.

"What's the matter, brat?" he asked, his voice suddenly gentle. "What's got your dander up now?"

"Just leave me alone!"

She jerked away from him and banged through the dilapidated door, causing it to protest with a loud squeal of its rawhide hinges. Ty stood where he was long after the door had slammed in his face, struggling with conflicting desires—to haul the wench back by the scruff of her neck and shake some sense into her, and an equal compulsion to smother those pouting lips with his own and run his hands over those high, round breasts until he had her writhing in his arms. Instead, he did neither, but went to help Caleb Hooker unhitch the ox team, muttering to himself about women, horseflies, and other pesky creatures.

An hour later, the four of them sat at a rickety board table in the taproom while a slatternly woman passed around trenchers of stewed corn mush and noggins of rum.

Delia stared down at the food and felt her stomach rumble.

"Lord above us, I'm as hungry as sin," she said unthinkingly. She glanced up to find the others staring at her. Elizabeth looked shocked, Ty scowled, but the reverend actually laughed.

"You couldn't be any hungrier than I am," he said.

Delia laughed with him. She dug her spoon into the mush and had it halfway to her mouth when she heard the Reverend Hooker say, "For all we are about to receive, O Lord, make us thankful in Christ's name."

Cringing, Delia quickly dropped her spoon with a loud clatter. She glanced up from beneath her now respectfully lowered lids to see if anyone had noticed her mistake and discovered that, of course, Ty had. He frowned at her so fiercely that she squirmed on the bench, banging against the table and knocking over her noggin of rum. The liquid flowed like a wave across the table and splashed into Ty's lap.

"Je—" He cut the epithet off in mid-word, jumping up and rubbing with his napkin at the wet stain spreading on the crotch of his breeches. He looked up to catch Caleb grinning at him, and a blush of embarrassment spread across his high cheekbones.

He sat back down and leaned over to snarl into Delia's face. "I'll get you for that, brat."

" 'Twas an accident, Ty. Truly."

"Like hell."

Delia looked down at her bowl of food. She had intended to show Ty how she could eat properly, remembering not to talk or laugh with her mouth full and chewing carefully before swallowing, but already she'd made a literal mess of things by spilling her rum into Ty's lap. She looked over at Elizabeth, who was eating her corn mush daintily, dabbing at the corners of her small mouth with her napkin after each tiny bite.

I'll never be able t' do that, Delia thought with despair. I'll never know all the ways of actin' like a proper lady, and Ty will never find anythin' good t' like about me a-tall.

Her eyes stung with humiliation and she shoved the bowl of mush away from her, uneaten.

"Dr. Savitch has warned me, my dear, that we might not find ourselves welcome by everyone in Merrymeeting,"

Caleb said to his wife after they had been eating for a while in silence.

Delia watched in agony as Ty turned to Elizabeth and gave her a ravishing smile. "Oh, you'll be welcome, Mrs. Hooker, never fear. I only meant the reverend shouldn't expect to pack them in the meetinghouse right off. He's going to have his work cut out with some. We've got our share of lusty trappers in The Maine."

To Delia's disgust, Elizabeth actually blushed at the word "lusty."

"Timber beasts we call them," Ty said, his lips twitching in that adorable, teasing way that twisted Delia's heart. "Most of them are crazy as loons."

Elizabeth gave Ty a simpering, little-girl look, and Delia wanted to gag. "But what of you, Dr. Savitch?" Elizabeth said. "Will you be attending the Meeting?"

Delia wondered how Ty was going to talk himself out of that one, for he didn't strike her as the churchgoing kind. He was saved by the innkeeper, who spoke out from where he stood behind the taproom's sagging plank bar. "Aye, ye'll find yersel' lots of varmints up there in The Maine."

"What sort of varmints?" Delia craned her head around to ask the shaggy-haired, weathered old man.

"Oh, wolves an' panthers, of course. An' bears. Big as a mountain are some of them bears what roam the Maine woods. An' then there are the two-legged varmints, like pirates—"

"Pirates!" Delia turned to Ty, excitement lighting her face. "Do ye truly have honest-to-God pirates? Oh, maybe we'll run across some buried treasure!"

Ty laughed. "They prefer to call themselves privateers. And they spend their profits, they don't bury them."

"But the worst varmints are the Injuns," the innkeeper went on, a look of satisfied grimness on his beard-stubbled face.

Elizabeth Hooker sat up straight, alarm draining her already pale face. "Indians? But I thought the Indians were peaceful now. That a treaty had been signed. Caleb, you said—"

"Never been an Injun borned that cared squat for treaties," the innkeeper said.

"I heard tell that if ye're unfortunate enough t' be captured by the savages, why then they spit ye on a sharpened pole and roast ye over a slow fire. Just like a Christmas goose," Delia said, and saw Elizabeth Hooker go even whiter. She hid a smile.

"Yep, you heard that a-right," the innkeeper agreed happily, enjoying the turn the conversation had taken. "But the roastin' part—that only comes after they do other dastardly things, like tearin' at your flesh with hot irons an' slicin' off pieces of you—"

"An' then eating them afore yer very eyes!" Delia finished with relish.

Elizabeth Hooker jumped up so abruptly that the bench skidded across the floor. She pressed her hand to her mouth and fled the room, tearing up the wobbly stairs to the sleeping loft above. A door banged above their heads.

Ty stood up and Delia thought he was going to run after the reverend's wife, but instead he grabbed Delia by the arm and hauled her to her feet and out the taproom door into the front yard before she could even open her mouth to protest.

Once outside, he whipped her around to face him and Delia cringed at the fury in his eyes.

He gave her arm a rough shake. "I ought to take you out to the woodshed and shingle you proper!"

"I was only carryin' on a friendly conversation with the innkeeper. 'Tisn't my fault that every little thing winds up scarin' yer precious Elizabeth."

"Elizabeth Hooker is a frightened young woman and you aren't stupid, Delia. You sensed her fears and preyed on them out of pure spite or meanness or whatever the hell it is that's motivating you to behave like a spoiled brat!"

What did he have, the insides of a clock? Delia wondered. Couldn't he see what was the matter with her? Couldn't he see she was dying with love for him, when to him she was but a nuisance? And a brat.

Her chin went down and she stared at the ground. "I'm sorry, Ty," she said softly.

He let go of her. "It's not me you should be apologizing to."

"I'll tell her I'm sorry. Later. But maybe ye should be doin' some apologizin' yersel'. T' the reverend, after the way ye been sniffin' around his wife like a breed bull."

"What!" Ty's head snapped up and his nostrils actually flared, just like a bull's, Delia thought. She would have laughed if she hadn't been so close to crying.

"Ye think it's not noticeable, the way ye were a-stickin' t' her all day like a snail t' its shell, lookin' at her all moony-eyed. It was disgustin'—"

Ty clamped her arms with a pair of strong hands, lifting her off her feet. He shoved his face into hers. "Get your mind out of the gutter, Delia. A man can be polite and friendly, even admire the looks of a woman, without wanting to bed her."

"Ye can't deny ye're lustin' after the reverend's wife!"

"I *do* deny it—"

But Delia tore away from his grasp, whirling and running down the road that led out of town. She heard him call after her, but she didn't look back. Tears bathed her face. Sobs choked her throat.

She veered off the road and ran into a hillside forest of red and white pines and dark green spruce. The trees shaded the late afternoon sunlight, and it was cool beneath the ceiling of intermeshed branches. Her feet made no sound on the thick carpet of brown needles. Before long she stopped running, but she kept walking, following a deer trail.

It was beautiful in the forest. The tears dried on Delia's cheeks, and the heavy, hollow feeling left her chest. She looked in wonder around her. At a flicker drumming on a dead trunk, searching for beetles and grubs. At a soft brown butterfly with yellow circles on its wings that flitted along beside her, as if looking for company. At a bed of toadstools lined up in neat rows around a cinnamon fern, resembling a company of militiamen on parade.

She continued down the path until she found the way blocked by a blowdown caused by a past storm. She hesitated a moment. Perhaps she ought to go back; she didn't want to get lost and give Ty something else to shout at her for. Besides, as beautiful as it was, there were probably varmints in these woods, too. Panthers and bears. Wolves . . .

At that very moment, something rustled the brush behind her and she whirled, her heart jumping into her throat.

She peered through the heavy thicket of trees but saw nothing. It seemed in the last few minutes to have grown suddenly darker, as if something had swallowed up the sun. She decided she would definitely go back now; she didn't want to be out in these woods after nightfall.

She did an about-face and followed the deer trail back in the direction she had come . . . until it forked into two paths, one going left and one right.

She took the path on her right, but after a moment her steps faltered. Nothing looked familiar. No, that wasn't true. Everything looked the same; all the trees and ferns looked alike. Then a scattering of yellow flowers caught her eye. It was a bed of goldenrod. She was sure she would have remembered seeing that splash of bright gold.

She decided she must have taken the wrong trail.

She turned back, but now instead of coming to a fork with two choices, she had three paths to pick from. Suddenly, the forest seemed honeycombed with paths, all running in circles and crisscrossing one another—

The brush rustled behind her. A twig snapped in two.

Delia took off running. She leaped over a bracken fern, brushed a bough of green spruce out of her way . . . and stepped into space.

She saw the ground rushing up to meet her and instinctively tucked in her head so that when she landed she turned a somersault. That was what saved her life. For a huge log fell in after her and would have crushed her skull if she hadn't rolled out of its way at the last second.

As it was, the log fell across her leg and she cried out in pain. Dirt and needles and leaves rained down on her. Then all was silent.

She looked up. She could see bits of blue sky and green branches overhead. Way overhead. The hole she had fallen into had to be at least eight feet deep and still she might have been able to claw her way out if the heavy log hadn't been lying across her leg, pinning her to the ground.

"Help!"

She didn't like the way her voice echoed back at her, as if she were the only thing left in the world. The only human . . .

Delia strained her ears, sure she had heard that rustling sound again. Yes, there it was. She clenched her jaw shut to keep from screaming and pushed at the log. It didn't budge. The bushes rustled again, closer this time.

Then she heard breathing, heavy breathing. And a low growl.

"Oh, Lord above us . . ." It was a wolf. She was sure of it. Did wolves eat people? If they were hungry enough, she reasoned. She hoped this one wasn't hungry, merely curious. It would be getting dark soon. The bits of blue were fading to gray. The tree branches looked like black fingers stretching across the shadowy sky.

Dirt and leaves slithered down the side of the hole at her back. Slowly, Delia craned her neck around and looked up . . . into a pair of yellow, glowing eyes and a snoutful of snarling teeth.

She screamed, and the eyes and teeth disappeared. She heaved at the log, straining her arms, the cords standing out on her neck with the effort, but to no avail.

Falling back with exhaustion, she looked up again . . .

"Well, well," came a familiar drawl. "Seems we've caught ourselves a varmint here."

Chapter 5

H e stood looking down at her, leaning on his rifle, his
chin resting on his wrist.

"Get me out of here," she said.

"Why?"

"Because . . . Oooh! Ye can be so damn infuriatin'. D'
ye expect me t' spend the night in this pit? Get me out!"

"So that you can frighten poor Mrs. Hooker with more
fanciful tales of murderous Indians?"

"I told ye I was sorry—"

"So that you can bedevil me by spurning all my efforts to
be nice to you?"

"Nice t' me! Hunh! Ye call this bein' nice t' me?"

He heaved a deep, sad sigh, but Delia wasn't fooled. She
could tell by the ragged catch in his voice that he was enjoying a good laugh at her expense.

Rays from the dying sun penetrated the canopy of trees,
shining directly on him, bathing his face with a golden glow
and bringing out the bronze lights in his rich dark hair. As
always she was struck by the sight of him—he was such a
marvelous figure of a man. She doubted he could really see
much of her, thank goodness, the way she lay sprawled in
the bottom of the black pit, her petticoat pulled halfway up
around her waist, and covered as she was with dirt and pine
needles.

"I'll help you out, but there's a condition attached," he
said.

"I'm not ridin' that bloody horse with ye!" Delia cried,
anticipating his condition.

"Fine then." He disappeared from sight.

"Goddamn ye, Ty!" When he didn't come back right away, she screamed louder. "Ty, come back! Please! I'll do what ye say, everythin' ye say, only please come back. Ty!"

He came back. He squatted down to sit at the edge of the pit, his legs dangling over the side, the rifle resting across his lap, as if, Delia thought, grinding her teeth with frustration, he had all bloody day.

"Be dark soon," he said cheerfully, squinting up at the needly bower overhead.

Delia ground her teeth some more.

"Aye . . ." He blew his breath out in a soft whistle. "I reckon we'll be getting some rain 'round about midnight."

"Ty, there's a wolf a-roamin' around loose up there." Her voice began husky-sweet but took on an edge as it grew in volume. "I hope it eats ye. It would serve ye bloody right!"

Ty laughed. "I doubt it was a wolf you saw. Not this close to the village. Must have been the innkeeper's old hound dog."

Delia began to have a horrible premonition. "How . . . how far away do ye figure we are from the village?"

"Oh, about fifty rods."

Delia's cheeks felt warm. She was glad of the darkness within the pit so that Ty couldn't see her embarrassment. She had thought herself hopelessly lost, deep in a wilderness forest, and here she was only fifty rods from the village!

Ty startled her by leaping gracefully down into the pit with her. He groped his way to her side and then she heard him swear as he felt the log lying across her leg. "Christ, why didn't you say something?"

"I thought ye knew."

"How could I possibly—" he began, then cut himself off. He wrapped his arms around the thick log, grunted, heaved, and suddenly she was free. "Don't move," he ordered as she started to sit up.

He felt all along her leg, even up under her skirt. The leg had been throbbing with pain, but at the first touch of his fingers, the pain faded. Delia's eyes fluttered closed and her flesh seemed to melt beneath his soothing hands . . . gentle, gentle, so very, very gentle. A warm heat began glowing in the pit of her stomach, spreading outward, making her skin feel on fire. Her throat grew tight and dry.

His voice came at her from far away. "It's not broken, but you'll be sporting another fine-looking bruise. You were lucky you weren't killed. This is someone's old deadfall trap and that log was meant to come crashing down on whatever prey stumbled into it. It could have split your head like a squash."

Delia shivered. Then she shivered again as his strong hands went around her waist and he helped her to her feet. "Can you put your weight on it?"

She tested the leg. "I think so. Aye, I can," she said, or tried to say. Her voice wasn't working properly any longer.

His hands lingered at her waist; his chest pressed up against her back. She was more than ever aware of the nearness of him. It was as if he generated a melting heat, like a blacksmith's forge. Suddenly, it seemed so quiet she could hear his breathing. And feel it as well, rising and falling within his chest, rising, falling, rising—

His breath caught. He took a step back and his hands fell away.

"I'll kneel down and you get on my shoulders. Then I'll boost you up," he said. There was a rough edge to his voice. Delia thought he was probably angry with her again. What a wooden-headed fool she was for getting herself into this predicament. Real ladies, she was sure, didn't get into a snit and go running off into the woods to get lost and then fall into a pit so that they had to be rescued.

Ty knelt in front of her. She hesitated a moment, for she really didn't want to touch him. There were things she wanted to do to Tyler Savitch, although she was only vaguely aware of the nature of those things. She just knew that once she started touching him she wouldn't be able to stop herself.

He gave an impatient grunt. "Let's go, Delia . . ."

Drawing in a deep breath, she wrapped her arms around his neck. He reached behind him and grasped her legs, pulling them around his waist and standing up in one fluid motion. The top of the pit was now only a couple of feet above Ty's head and it would be a simple matter for her to let go of his neck and pull herself out.

But she didn't move. She was aware of the pulse in his

neck beating against the flesh of her arms; of his lungs expanding and contracting beneath her thighs; of her womanly mound pressing against the hard, warm muscle of his back. And the smell of him—leather and tobacco and pure man.

Unconsciously, she put her cheek to the back of his head, rubbing it against his hair.

"Are we going to stand like this all night?"

Delia came to with a start. She must be heavy, clinging to him like this. Perhaps that was why his voice sounded so strained. With shaking hands, she let go of Ty's neck and reached up. Digging her fingers onto the flat earth above, she pulled herself up and over Ty's head and out of the pit. At the last moment he put his palms on her bottom to give her a boost, and the shock of his hands touching her so intimately caused Delia to groan aloud.

"Are you all right?" she heard him say.

She scrambled up on her hands and knees and looked down into Ty's upturned face. There was a light film of sweat on his forehead, although the evening air seemed suddenly to have grown cool. His lips were pressed together into a tight, hard line. She saw the movement of his throat as he swallowed.

"Give me a hand up," he said.

She stretched her hand down to him, and he wrapped his fingers around her wrist. Bracing against her weight, he crab-walked up the slightly sloping side of the pit. He came up over the lip of it faster than she expected, and the sudden release of the pull of his weight caused her body to react like a spring, recoiling backward. She landed on her back and he fell on top of her, his elbows braced on each side of her shoulders.

Their faces were inches apart, so close she could feel the warm moistness of his breath and notice herself reflected in the dark, dusky blue of his eyes. The sun had set by now, but there was still enough light to see the sweep of his lashes as his lids drifted closed and the gleam of his teeth as his lips parted open.

Those lips touched hers, lightly at first, brushing back and forth across the soft, swelling fullness of her mouth. Then his mouth pressed down harder and her lips moved, opened

beneath his. Her arms went around him, pulling him down
onto her. She dug her fingers into the muscles of his shoulders and felt him shudder. He ran the edge of his tongue
along her teeth, slid it deep into her mouth. It was hard and
slick and strangely, mysteriously evocative of something,
something that made the hollow, burning place low in her
belly ache to be filled.

She arched, rubbing that aching, empty place against the
hard bone of his hip, rubbing until he tore his mouth from
hers and exhaled sharply, "Christ, Delia."

He kissed her again, soft feathery kisses, flicking his tongue
back and forth over the swell of her lips, delving in and out
between them quickly, teasingly. Moaning, she put her palm
against the back of his head and boldly pressed his open
mouth down over hers.

She explored his tongue with her own and then put her
tongue full into his mouth. It was hot and sweet and tasted
of rum, and nothing, nothing in her entire life had tasted or
felt so fine. She knew this kiss was only the beginning. There
was more, oh so much more, and she wanted it, all of it. She
wanted him.

He shifted his weight onto his side, and his hand came
between them to tug at the laces of her bodice. He tangled
the fingers of his other hand in her hair, pulling her head
back. His mouth released her lips to slide along her jaw,
down her neck. Oh God . . . the feel of his lips on her neck,
so moist and warm, pulsating to match the hard rush of her
blood. Her whole body tensed and arched, and one breast
came free to fill his hand. His fingers twisted the nipple until
it almost hurt, but not quite, and her muscles drew up tighter,
her toes curled, and she stopped breathing.

His hand released her breast and drifted down the length
of her. Her petticoat and shift had both ridden up around her
thighs, and his fingers touched her bare flesh at the same
moment that his mouth closed around her taut nipple. Her
body jerked as if he'd seared her with fire—

She gave a mighty heave, pushing him off her and rolling
away from him, sitting up. He lay motionless on the ground
for a brief moment, braced on his elbows with his head

bowed, breathing heavily. Then he, too, pushed himself up to kneel before her, his hands resting on his thighs.

He glared at her. "And what am I supposed to do now, Delia-girl? Do you like to be forced? Or are you expecting me to pay for it first?"

She pulled back and delivered a walloping slap across his face, rocking him on his heels and snapping his head back.

Anger darkened his face. "Why, you little—"

His hand shot out to grab her, but she skittered away from him, jumping to her feet. He stood up more slowly, a hard smile tautening his lips. His cheek bore the red imprint of her palm, and a muscle twitched beneath the mark.

Delia backed away from him, one fist pressed to her breast where her bodice gaped open. "Don't ye touch me, ye bastard!"

His lips curled into a sneer. "Why not? If you didn't want to be touched, you sure as hell gave a good imitation of wanting it."

She whirled around, but she had barely taken a step before his arm wrapped around her waist, hauling her back against him.

She jabbed an elbow into his midriff, so hard he grunted. He pressed his mouth against her ear. "I'm bigger and stronger and meaner than you, and there's no way you can win, Delia-girl, so don't make me prove it."

"Go t' hell, ye . . . ye . . ." She called him the foulest names she knew as she flailed against him, trying to kick his shins with her bare feet.

"Shit!" He panted as her nails raked across the back of his hand. His arm tightened around her bruised ribs, and a sharp pain jabbed her, so fierce it made her scream.

Ty instantly relaxed his grip. She stumbled away from him, her hand pressed to her side, her breath sawing in her throat.

"Delia . . ." He touched her shoulder, but she flinched away, so he let his hand fall.

She drew in a deep, sobbing breath. Her lips, her breasts, her whole body burned. She wiped at her mouth with the back of a hand that trembled so badly she might have had a fever. "Oh, I hate ye, Tyler Savitch. Truly I do."

A nerve jumped once in his cheek, then his face relaxed

and he shook his head in mock sorrow. "I know. You hate me and my kisses obviously disgust you. But is that any reason to try to beat the bloody bejesus out of me?"

"I'll not have ye slakin' yer lust on me, Tyler Savitch." Her voice shook as she jerked the laces of her bodice back together. "Not when it's Mrs. Hooker ye're really hankerin' for."

He grimaced with exasperation, flicking his tousled hair out of his eyes. "Are you back to harping on that subject? How many times must I tell you that I haven't the least desire—"

"Don't think I care about you an' her, 'cause I don't!" Hateful tears spilled from Delia's eyes. She brushed them angrily away. "It just isn't right for a man to be kissin' one woman when 'tis the other one he's a-wantin'."

"You're wrong. I don't want Elizabeth."

Her chin trembled. "Ye d-do."

"I don't."

His hand cupped the side of her face, his head dipped down, his warm breath flooded over her. And Delia stopped breathing again.

"Delia, my Delia," he whispered, and his voice was a caress that sent her heart pounding like a kettledrum in her breast. "It's you I want. It's you . . ." His lips hovered over her open mouth.

She jerked her head to the side. "I want to go back to the inn now, Ty," she said stiffly.

He straightened, backing up. "Then go. I won't try to stop you."

But Delia didn't move. She was concentrating hard on not looking at any part of him because her eyes kept wanting to drift down . . . to the prominent bulge at the crotch of his breeches. She had felt it while struggling against him, his hardened manhood pressing against her buttocks. She knew what it meant when a man got like that. She had worked too many years at the Frisky Lyon, and gone a little too far a few times with Tom Mullins, not to know.

Lusting after her . . . He had practically admitted as much. But that wasn't what frightened her. What frightened her was her own heart thrusting heavily in her breast and the yawning

ache in the pit of her stomach. What frightened her was the
knowledge that *she* lusted after him.

Delia whipped around and started back down the trail,
swatting so hard at the needles and leaves on her skirt that
she was stinging her thighs, as if she could swat some sense
back into herself.

He had to call out to her twice and even start after her
before she would turn around.

"You keep going long enough in that direction," he said,
"and you'll soon find yourself back in Boston."

"Oh . . ." Embarrassment warmed her cheeks. She still
couldn't look at him. "These damn trails—they all look alike.
Ye'd think somebody'd put up signposts or somethin'."

Ty laughed, shaking his head. "God, Delia, you're a
strange one." He took a step back and sketched a mocking
bow. "After you, m'lady."

They walked back to the inn side by side, not touching,
not speaking. They passed out of the forest onto the road.
Their faint shadows stretched out long before them in the
dusky twilight, side by side, yet apart.

Through the oiled-paper pane of the dormer window, Elizabeth Hooker looked at black spires of trees silhouetted
against a silvery gray sky.

Right now back in Boston, in the parsonage of the Brattle
Street Church, her father would be lighting the betty lamp on
his desk as he prepared to work on his mid-week sermon.
Her mother would be sitting on the settle before the fire,
carding wool for tomorrow's spinning. Her two younger sisters would be working on their knitting, chatting between
themselves, perhaps about the new silk ribbons they had
bought that afternoon or the cakes they would bake for next
Saturday's church social.

Elizabeth closed her eyes, picturing the scene as she had
seen it so many times. The reflection of the firelight flickering in the silver tea service. Smoke curling up from her father's pipe to form a halo around his head. The swinging
pendulum of the lantern clock filling the room with its steady
ticking and blending with her sisters' soft voices . . .

Her lids clenched and her lips twisted. "I want to go

home!'' she cried aloud, her voice breaking the empty silence of the inn's tiny, shabby room. "Oh, Caleb, please take me home." But Caleb wasn't there to hear her.

After a moment she drew in a deep, shuddering breath. She opened her eyes to the forest beyond the window. She hated it already, and she was sure she would hate Merry-meeting just as much. Everything was so rough, so dirty. Her head throbbed and every bone ached from the constant rattling of the ox cart. Her throat felt parched from the incessant dust. The skin of her face and neck and hands—every part of her that hadn't been protected by clothing—was covered with red weals left by the sucking flies.

The treetops swayed against the lowering sky and she thought that, even through the window, she could hear the lonely sigh of the wind and smell the coming rain. Her stomach knotted as she remembered what that odious innkeeper had said about the savages and their heinous tortures. They could be out there right now, she thought, lurking in the forest, waiting for dark to fall and the storm to come before—

With a hand that trembled so badly she could barely control it, she pulled the shutters closed over the glazed window and pushed home the bolts. The pounding in her head subsided somewhat, but it only brought to the forefront of her consciousness the itching of the welts on her neck.

She balled up her fists to keep from engaging in a bout of furious, unladylike scratching. Turning away from the window, she looked around the shabby room with its low, sloping ceiling. There was a small jack bed built into the corner, its ticking filled with rags and cornhusks. The bedding was no doubt infested with lice and nits, Elizabeth thought with a shudder. At least she was prepared for that, her mother having warned her to pack within handy reach her own clean things.

She went to the chest that Caleb had earlier taken from the cart. He had placed her Bible on top where she would be sure to find it. Kneeling, she ran her palm across the tooled leather binding. Caleb was a good man, kind and thoughtful. Yet there had been times during this long and terrible day when she had thought she hated him for uprooting her from her family and dragging her with him into the wilderness, making her endure the ox cart and the dust and the flies. But they made her feel guilty now, those feelings of hatred that she had harbored against her own husband.

Elizabeth pressed her lips together. She would do better by him tomorrow; she would endure it better tomorrow. It was only because today was the first day that it had seemed so hard.

She stripped the bed and remade it with her own sheets and blankets. She herself had spun and woven the wool and the linen cloth they were made of, and she was proud of their quality. They were part of her trousseau when she had married two months before. She had shown them to her husband on their wedding day, and he had claimed no man could have been more fortunate in his choice of wife than the Reverend Caleb Hooker. She often wondered if he still felt the same—now that he knew her better.

She smoothed the blanket flat, tucking it under the ticking. The combination of the lengthening shadows and her thoughts of Caleb brought on a sick feeling of dread in the pit of her stomach and she felt sweat bead on her forehead. Once, she had welcomed the coming of darkness as a quiet time, sitting around the fire with her family. But since her marriage she experienced such fear as the day ended and night fell, the dread of whether this night Caleb would want to exercise his husbandly rights on her.

She always submitted, when he insisted, for it was her duty. And she was grateful to Caleb for not asking too often because she suspected he derived pleasure from their coupling, although he had never said so. It wasn't right to take pleasure from it. The Book was clear on that. Although it was necessary, of course. Necessary to procreate mankind, and a wife must submit. The Book was clear on that as well.

Her mother, on the night before she married, had warned her about a little of it and had told her she would hurt and bleed some. Although the bleeding had stopped after the first two or three times, it still hurt; it hurt dreadfully. Oh, there were parts of it she actually liked. He would always kiss her once and stroke her a few times before he mounted her. Afterward, he usually whispered that he loved her. But she hated the penetration. Oh God, she hated that. It hurt so and she felt so invaded . . . yes, that was the word. Invaded.

She hurried to get undressed and into her nightrail before Caleb came up. She had just sat down on the room's only chair to pull the bone pins from her hair when the door opened and he came in with a cool draft of air.

"I brought a light," he said. His cupped palm protected a sulfur wick and he lit the tallow dip with it. He turned and smiled down at her.

She smiled back at him and said before he could ask, "I'm all right now, Caleb."

He took the hairbrush from her hand. "Here, let me do that for you."

She leaned against the chair's ladder back. Caleb lifted the fall of her fine, silver-blond hair and pulled the brush through it. She closed her eyes and sighed.

"What do you think of Dr. Savitch?" Caleb asked.

"He's a good man," she answered readily. Good and kind like Caleb. He had charming manners, and she sensed he had gone out of his way to put her at ease. But for all his civilized ways he seemed too much like the wilderness he came from— beautiful to look at, but savage underneath.

"That Delia is something else again though," Caleb was saying. "A real scrapper. It's going to take a lot of praying on our part to get that girl to see the light of our Lord." He stopped brushing Elizabeth's hair and came around to kneel before her, placing his hands on her lap to gaze up into her face. "She's been hurt, I think, Lizzie. Hurt badly. She's going to need a friend."

"I like Delia," Elizabeth said, and found as she said it that it was true. But she envied Delia as well. She remembered the way the girl had walked beside the oxen that day with her fearless, long-legged strides, the way she had taken such delight in all they had passed. The dust and the flies had not seemed to bother Delia.

Elizabeth got up from the chair and went to the bed. She slid beneath the covers and scooted over to the far edge of the ticking against the wall. As she watched Caleb undress, the dread within her grew.

He brought the tallow dip over and set it on the floor by

the bed. Its flickering light threw his shadow up huge against the wall in back of her.

"Lizzie . . ." He cleared his throat. "How are you feeling tonight?"

She knew what he was really asking and her whole body tensed. She swallowed, wet her lips. "I'm very tired tonight, Caleb."

She saw his disappointment plainly in his face. But then he said, "Yes. Of course. It's been a very tiring day for you." She felt relief as the tension eased from her.

He got into bed. He lay stiff beside her in silence for a moment, then groped for her hand. "This is hard on you, Lizzie. Don't think I don't know how you hated to leave Boston and your family. How much you'll miss them . . ."

Elizabeth heard the doubt in her husband's voice. He didn't understand, not really. She had him now and he thought that should be enough.

"You'll be fine once we get to Merrymeeting," he went on. "Ty says the folk there have already built us a parsonage right next to the meetinghouse and we're to have our own plot of land. There'll be neighbors and you'll make new friends." He squeezed her hand. "It's my duty to go and minister where I'm called. You understand that, Lizzie, don't you? It is God's will."

"Yes. God's will."

Caleb, hold me, she wanted to say. But didn't for fear he would think she wanted the other, the coupling.

Rolling away from her, he snuffed out the candle. He was silent for so long she thought he had fallen asleep. Then he spoke into the dark. "Lizzie? Do you think we could be having a baby soon? You'd like that, wouldn't you, a baby of our own?"

She stiffened, sure now that he would turn to her and roll up her nightrail.

"Lizzie?"

She forced out her pent-up breath. "Yes . . . yes, of course, Caleb. A baby would be nice."

He sighed. After a while she heard his soft snoring and she relaxed, for she knew that he slept.

* * *

Tyler Savitch didn't give Delia a chance to argue with him about the horse the next morning. He grabbed her and tossed her into the saddle while she was still stretching and rubbing her back and complaining loudly, and profanely, to the innkeeper about the condition of the ticking she had been forced to sleep on.

She clung to the saddle pommel with both hands and looked down on Ty with surprise at first, and then he could see the coming explosion building on her face.

"Don't you say a word," he warned. "Not one word."

Her mouth had fallen part way open, but she shut it with a click of her teeth. Then she smiled. "I was only goin' t' say good mornin'."

Ty's answer was a growl.

He was not in a good mood. For the second night in a row he had gone to bed sexually frustrated, to be beset by nightmares filled with a husky voice and a pair of full, high breasts. It was bad enough to find himself attracted to the little tavern wench, but that she had actually spurned his lovemaking . . . he couldn't believe it! He had thought she'd taken a fancy to him, that she wanted one last bit of fun before she settled down to married life. Naturally he had assumed—hell, up until the second before she'd slapped his face, he'd have staked his last shilling that she wanted to have that bit of fun with him.

It had rained during the night, and now low clouds clung wetly to the sky. Water dripped from trees and the roof eaves to form pools in the muddy yard. Water dripped down Ty's back as he settled the innkeeper's tally. Elizabeth already clung to her perch on the cart, waiting for Caleb to finish yoking up the team. There was a mulish set to her mouth as she hunched her shoulders and drew the collar of her cloak beneath her chin.

Caleb motioned Ty over to the cart after he had finished with the innkeeper. "How far do you figure we have to go today?" he asked. He stood next to his wife's legs, one hand on the seat rail, the other holding up the goad.

"I'd at least like to get across the Merrimack," Ty said.

Caleb threw a glance at Elizabeth, then turned back to Ty. He let go of the rail, scratched the back of his neck, shuffled his feet, cleared his throat. "Yes, but how long will we be on the trail? Elizabeth is, uh . . ."

Ty repressed a sigh. At this rate they would be all summer getting to Merrymeeting. "We'll take it easy today," he said.

Caleb visibly relaxed. He patted his wife's knee, giving her a cheerful grin. "See, it won't be so bad today, Lizzie."

She looked up at the soggy blanket of clouds overhead. "It's probably going to rain all day."

Caleb's smile faded only a little. "Well, at least we won't be bothered by the flies."

Ty went back to Delia and the horse, and as he approached she smiled at him. The way her incredible eyes shimmered like golden coins did a funny thing to his chest, so that for a moment he found it difficult to breathe. If he hadn't caught himself just in time he would have smiled back at her.

He scowled instead. He tied her grist sack to the cantle of the saddle, then took the pacer's reins to lead him onto the road.

"Ye're not ridin' along up here with me?" Delia asked.

Ty snarled a negative reply as he tried to imagine how long he'd last with her riding double, rubbing those magnificent breasts against his back, breathing hotly against his neck, her hands clinging to his waist, pressing into his stomach, drifting lower and lower until—

Christ! Just the thought of it made the sweat start out on his face, and his groin begin to swell uncomfortably. He'd be having to stop every other mile to take a dip in a cold creek.

It was, in fact, a river that brought their journey to an abrupt halt early that afternoon. The Merrimack was too deep and wide to be forded by an ox cart. There was no ferry in sight, but a bell hung from a pole at the landing. Ty gave it a hard yank. When no one came after five minutes he hallooed across the water, but he knew it was hopeless. The old rascal that ran the Merrimack ferry did so at his own whim and on the basis of whether the fish were biting well that day.

"Looks like we'll have to camp out on this side of the river," Ty told the others. The remains of old campfires strewn along the grassy bank attested to the fact that they were not the first to have to spend the night on the west side of the Merrimack.

Delia slid off the horse onto wobbly legs. She rubbed her bottom and sighed loudly. "Lord above us, I think I've worn blisters on my arse . . ."

Her husky voice trailed off and she blushed. Then she looked down, sucking on her lower lip, and Ty thought about how it had felt to kiss that lip, to taste it. He had some salve in one of his haversacks, but he didn't say anything. The mere thought of rubbing it on that pert little bottom of hers almost made him groan aloud.

Ty jerked his rifle from the saddle holster. "I'll scout around and see if I can rustle us up some supper. Delia, make yourself useful for a change and gather some wood for the fire—"

"I'll do it," Caleb said hastily. "I feel the need to stretch my legs." He helped Elizabeth down from the cart as Ty disappeared into the woods. "Remember that feeder stream we passed a few yards back, Lizzie? I noticed it formed a pool by that patch of hemlocks. I was thinking maybe you might like a wash-up."

Elizabeth looked around her, swallowed, nodded. "Yes, I would. A wash-up sounds nice, Caleb."

Delia saw Elizabeth start back along the road and she ran after her. "Mrs. Hooker, wait! I thought maybe I'd go down t' that crik along with ye."

Delia fully expected to be rebuffed, but instead Elizabeth smiled brightly at her. "Oh, yes. Please . . . But you must call me Elizabeth," she said as Delia came running up.

They found the grove of hemlocks easily. The shallow pool looked cool and inviting, and Delia immediately sat down on the bank to soak her feet. Last night's storm had broken up and blown away, and now the sun was out. The air smelled fresh and green from the rain and drops still occasionally splattered onto their heads from the sodden trees.

Kneeling on a mossy slope before the pool, Elizabeth rolled up the sleeves of her frock and splashed water over her face and arms. "I should have brought some soft soap with me," she said. "It would be nice to have a bath."

"I took a bath early yesterday mornin'," Delia said, feeling smug about her new, clean self. "I even washed my hair."

Elizabeth dried off her face and hands with her petticoat. "Well, of course. But after the dust yesterday, and the flies, I was dying for a bath last night." She smiled shyly at Delia. "But can you imagine asking that horrid old innkeeper at the Blue Anchor for a tub of hot water?"

A startling thought occurred to Delia. "How often do ye take a bath, Elizabeth?"

"Oh, at least twice a week, sometimes three in the summer."

"Twice a week!" Delia gaped at her in disbelief. "But that's not healthy!" Why, as frail-looking as she was, Elizabeth Hooker was lucky she hadn't sickened of the lung fever and died long before now.

But then Delia remembered how Ty had complained about the way she had smelled the other night. Perhaps bathing once a month or so wasn't enough. She stifled a sigh. Evidently she was going to have to take a bath twice a week, in spite of the risk to her health, if she was going to make herself into a proper lady.

Elizabeth sat down on the bank, wrapping her arms around her folded-up legs. She glanced around nervously, and Delia couldn't help doing the same. But all Delia could see was a patch of bloodroot blooming nearby and a brown frog corpulent with Mayflies sunning itself on a rock.

"It's pretty here, don't you think?" Delia said.

"Yes . . . nice and peaceful."

That reminded Delia of the promise she had made to Ty.

"Elizabeth . . ." Delia paused and searched for the right words. This wasn't going to be as easy as she had thought. She drew in a deep breath. "I'm sorry about what I did last night, tryin' t' scare ye. 'Twas mean of me and, well . . . I'm sorry."

Elizabeth looked down at her hands resting on her bent knees. "Please, it doesn't matter." She forced out a smile. "I know I must seem like such a scared little rabbit, but until now the most adventuresome thing I ever did in my life was to take the ferry over to Charles Town for the fair."

"Oh, but I did that too, once!" Delia leaned forward eagerly, pleased to have discovered this common ground between herself and Elizabeth, who was a real lady. "My da took me t' the fair when I was seven. I ate too many persimmon tarts that day and got sick all over his Sunday-go-to-meeting suit.''

Delia chuckled at the memory, and after a moment Elizabeth started to giggle softly. Then a man's hearty laughter joined them.

Startled, they looked up and across the creek. An Indian stood on the opposite bank, grinning at them.

He wore a battered cocked hat made of beaverskin, with a single white gull's feather sticking straight up from a hole in the crown. The European jacket he had on was much too small and didn't quite reach around his bare chest, which glistened bronze in the sun. The bottom half of him was dressed in more traditional Indian clothing—leggings and a kilt of doeskin that flapped around his knees. He carried an old, rust-pitted French musket in the crook of his arm.

Delia glanced sideways at Elizabeth. She was white around the mouth and sweat beaded her forehead. ''Don't act like ye're scared,'' Delia whispered, standing up slowly and carefully.

''Good day, Englishwomen,'' the Indian said in a thick, guttural accent.

Delia swallowed and tried to dredge up some spit so that she could talk. ''Good day . . . sir.''

The Indian grinned and nodded. Delia grinned and nodded back at him. She could hear Elizabeth's shallow breaths coming out of her in a high-pitched keen.

''I think he's friendly,'' Delia said from the corner of her mouth. And she grinned and nodded some more.

The Indian tossed the musket onto the ground and took a step into the pool, and Elizabeth jerked to her feet with a piercing shriek.

''Don't run!'' Delia cried out, but it was too late, for Elizabeth was already running, crashing headlong through the trees and underbrush, her shrill screams piercing the still air.

The Indian stood in the middle of the pond and spat a bunch of guttural Indian words at Delia. He motioned at her with his hand, a wide grin on his face. ''You come,'' he said and smiled some more. ''You hungry? We fish.''

''Fish?''

He nodded vigorously. ''Fish.''

Don't act like ye're scared, Delia reminded herself. *Oh, Lord above us, what if he's not as friendly as he looks . . .*

She stepped into the pond.

The Indian grinned again and nodded. "Come?"

She stopped when she was still a good three feet away. This close to him she could see now that he was quite old. Scores of lines crisscrossed his face, and the hair beneath his floppy hat was streaked with gray. He bent over and pointed at the bottom of the pool. Delia took a step closer and bent over as well. A half dozen good-sized trout drifted among the smooth, mossy rocks.

The Indian rolled up the sleeve of his jacket and extended his arm into the water. Slowly, he slipped his hand under one of the trout and held it motionless. Then suddenly there was a flurry of flapping tail and fins as his fingers closed around the fish's gills. He stood up holding the wriggling trout in his hand.

He grunted and grinned. "Fish!"

Delia laughed and clapped her hands with delight. "Why, isn't that something else! Can ye show me how t' do that?"

The screams brought Ty running back to the campsite with his rifle primed and ready to fire. He found Elizabeth sobbing hysterically on Caleb's chest. There was no sign of Delia.

"What's happened?"

Caleb looked at him helplessly. "I don't know. I can't get her to stop crying."

Ty pried Elizabeth loose from the stranglehold she had on her husband's neck. He shook her gently at first, then a bit more roughly. "Elizabeth!" he shouted, and her sobs quieted some. "Easy, easy, take a deep breath. . . . Now tell us what happened."

"S-savage. He . . . he . . ."

"Where's Delia?"

"I don't know. I ran. She . . . I don't know."

Ty was barely able to stop himself from shaking the poor woman again. "Where? Where did you leave her?"

"P-pond. At the pond."

"They went down to that pond we passed a ways back,"

Caleb said. "The one by the hemlocks. Elizabeth wanted to wash up—"

"You let them go down there alone? My God, man, what the hell were you thinking of?"

Caleb paled. "I didn't know it wasn't safe—" he began, but Ty was already running back up the trail.

When he got close to the pond, Ty slowed and approached it quietly, glad he had put on his moccasins that morning in anticipation of having to walk all day. He heard them first— Delia's throaty laugh, joined by a man's deep chuckle. He straightened from a half crouch to lean against one of the broad hemlock trunks, his rifle uncocked and cradled in the crook of his elbow, and watched for a moment.

Delia and an old Indian stood together in the middle of the pond. She was bent at the waist, her petticoat clinging wetly to her slim legs, her arm trailing in the water.

Suddenly she jerked upright, holding a squirming fish tight in her hand above her head. "I got one!" she cried. "I got one!"

Ty felt a warm feeling of pride welling up in his chest. By God, she was incredible, his gutsy little tavern wench.

There was something else as well, mixed in with the pride. But Ty, who had never experienced such a feeling before, wasn't able to recognize the emotion for what it was. To him it merely seemed an odd sense of possession—she was *his* gutsy little tavern wench.

He stepped out from behind the hemlock trunk. The Indian saw him first, and the grin slid off the old man's mouth. Delia, who had been looking at the Indian, turned around. Then she spotted Ty, and a bright smile blazoned across her face.

She held the trout out to him. "Look, Ty. I'm a-catchin' us some fish for supper!"

Chapter 6

Chattering and twitching their fat, striped bodies, the chipmunks gathered in a semicircle around Delia. Ty watched, unconsciously scowling, as she fed them crumbs of johnnycake. Sunlight glinted off the ruby lights in her ebony hair and her tawny eyes glowed brightly. There was a smile of delight on her wide mouth and her breasts swelled gently with silent laughter.

Never had Ty known anyone to take such unbounded joy in the simple act of living as did this one girl. The strange thing was, her exuberance seemed to be infectious, for he had found himself smiling and laughing along with her countless times during the last two days, and missing her when they were not together—

Cursing beneath his breath, Ty uncorked a small horn brandy flask and poured a good portion of the fiery contents down his throat. So the girl was uncommonly pretty, with a sensual body that made a man think automatically of bed. She was also, he reminded himself, nothing but a lusty tavern wench, schooled in the ways and means of enticing men. *She's got you horn-mad for her, Savitch, and there's no great mystery about that.*

He scowled at her again. "You might as well give it up, Delia, because it bloody well isn't going to work."

She tossed the last of the crumbs to the chipmunks, dusting off her hands, and turned to him with a smile so dazzling it made his breath catch. "Did ye say something, Ty?"

He stared at her for the longest moment, unable to speak,

unable to breathe. "Never mind," he finally growled, taking another deep pull from the brandy flask.

A pair of thick logs had been rolled up across from each other next to the campfire; Ty and Delia sat on one, the Hookers on the other, reading together from their Bible. They had just finished a supper of Delia's fish and the johnnycake—a flat bread made of cornmeal and baked on a scoured wooden shingle. Since they'd camped so early, there was still an hour or so of daylight left to while away before sleep.

Lost in thought, Ty watched the Hookers at their Bible reading. Then he edged a piece of charred wood away from the fire, kicking dirt over it to cool it. Taking a square of birchbark paper from his haversack, he used the piece of charcoal to draw three concentric circles.

Delia leaned into him as he worked, her knees pressing against his thigh, her breath stirring his hair where it curled around his ear. "What are ye goin t' do with that?" she asked.

Ty was very much aware of Delia's leg rubbing against his. It was making his breath go shallow and causing a definite and uncomfortable reaction within the tight confines of his breeches. She leaned closer, flattening her full breast against his shoulder, and Ty clenched his jaw.

"What does it look like I'm doing?" he snarled at her. Her body felt warm, alive, inviting, and if she didn't move that damn breast off his shoulder he was going to drag her into the woods by the hair and do things to her she'd only dreamed of. "I'm making a target."

Delia straightened and Ty let out his breath. "A target?" she asked brightly. "Are ye going t' shoot at it?"

"No, you are."

Pressing her fingers against her breast, she reared back, her eyes rounding in disbelief. *"Me?"* She cast a glance over her shoulder as if there had to be somebody standing behind her. "But, Ty, I don't know how t' shoot."

"When I'm through with you, you will." He raised his head, speaking across the fire. "You too, Reverend."

Caleb jerked with surprise, then he exchanged a look with his wife. He rubbed his palms over his bent knees before getting slowly to his feet and ambling over.

He cleared his throat. "I admit such a skill would be useful where we're going, for hunting game and such. But I could never bring myself to shoot at another human being, Ty. Not even a savage."

Ty stared at Caleb, incredulous. He could understand a man finding it difficult to kill another human being, but the Community of Saints were great ones for preaching that the only solution to the Indians' heathen threat was to slaughter them in mass. It had been the settlers, after all, not the Indians, who had first devised the gruesome practice of taking scalps as proof of an enemy's death. The Boston Public Treasury still offered a ten-pound bounty on Abenaki scalps, even though a peace treaty had supposedly been in effect for the last few years.

Of course there was no such thing as real peace. Not with France and England constantly at each other's throats and bringing their battlegrounds into the New World, with each side forming alliances among the native inhabitants. The Abenaki, for instance, already indignant and frightened over the seizures of their hunting and fishing grounds, were actively encouraged by the French Jesuit missionaries to take up the hatchet against the English settlers in The Maine. In turn, the Indian warriors' hit-and-run method of waging war, the torture and taking of captives, the killing of women and children, had nurtured a spirit of revenge among settlers against the Abenaki Nation.

It was a vicious circle of war and death that had been going on for the last fifty years, and the Puritan church of New England had always been right in the thick of it. Ty just didn't have the Reverend Caleb Hooker figured for a hypocrite.

"I thought killing Indians was part of your religion, Reverend?"

Caleb's jaw took on a proud jut. "I am my own man, doctor."

The anger faded from Ty's eyes, but his mouth remained grim. "You also have a wife, Caleb." He lowered his voice so that Elizabeth wouldn't hear. "You ever see what a woman looks like after she's been scalped? Do you know how it's done? You wrap her hair around your fist and you take your scalping knife and make a deep incision around her temples.

Then you give a good hard jerk and the scalp comes right off in your hand like a bloody glove. It leaves a big gory hole in the top of her head.''

Caleb's skin had turned pasty and Ty regretted having to be so brutal. But if the Hookers were going to live in the wilderness, then they had better learn fast how to survive in it.

"If the picture I painted disgusts you, Reverend," he said, keeping his voice cold and hard, "then I suggest you prepare yourself in the best way you can from ever having to see it for real. If you're ever attacked by Indians, then you'd better damn well be able to kill them before they kill you. Or Elizabeth.''

Delia, Ty noticed, hadn't even flinched during his vivid description of how to take a scalp. Caleb, on the other hand, trembled slightly, but his mouth set in resolution. "Yes . . . yes, I realize now that you're right.''

Elizabeth had bent her head back over the book in her lap, but she looked up sharply at Caleb's words. "But, Caleb, surely you aren't—''

"I am, Lizzie,'' he said firmly. "It's a necessary thing to know, for self-protection. The Indians—''

"But that Indian was friendly!'' She looked with wide, nervous eyes at the dense, encroaching forest. "Isn't that what you said, doctor, that the Indian was friendly?''

"He was friendly, Mrs. Hooker. But the next one might not be.''

Ty got up and walked off fifty paces. He wedged the target into the V of a tree branch. Sauntering back, he stopped to pick up his rifle from where it leaned against the log. Elizabeth had come to stand by Caleb, her hand resting on his arm. She frowned at Ty, disapproving of what she obviously considered his corruption of her husband's principles.

Ty ignored her. Giving Delia and Caleb each a hard, pointed look, he said, "Now you watch carefully how this is done. You have to know how to load as well as fire. And when there are fifty whooping warriors breathing down your neck, you have to be able to do it fast.''

Taking a paper-wrapped cartridge from his bullet pouch, he tore the end of it open with his teeth. He half cocked the

weapon, snapped open the frizzon, poured a little powder
from the cartridge into the pan, then snapped the frizzon
shut. He set the rifle on its butt on the ground, poured the
rest of the powder charge down the muzzle, and dropped in
the bullet. Balling up the paper wrapper, he rammed it down
the muzzle with the rod.

Squaring off to the target, he brought the rifle up to his
shoulder, drew the hammer back to full cock, and pulled the
trigger. There was the flash of a spark, a puff of acrid black
smoke, and the crack of the shot bouncing off the trees.

Before Ty could stop her, Delia dashed out in front of him,
heading for the tree to inspect the target. "Bull's-eye!" she
whooped with delight. "Ye hit the bull's-eye, Ty!"

Ty waited with his teeth clenched until she came back,
then he flung out one hand, grabbing her by the arm and
hauling her up against him. He shoved his face into hers. "If
you *ever* run out into the line of fire like that again, Delia-
girl, I'll whale the stuffing out of you!"

She was startled by his anger and then contrite, her lips
forming a soft pout that looked so delectable it quashed Ty's
rage. He wanted to cover that mouth with kisses. Hot, hard,
tongue-thrusting kisses that went on forever.

Instead, he let her go, backing off. He gripped the stock
of his rifle so hard that his fingers whitened.

"I'm sorry, Ty," she said, rubbing her arm where he'd
grabbed her.

Ty struggled to get hold of himself. "Never mind. Just
don't do it again."

"So can I try it now, Ty? Can I try it first?" she pleaded,
excitement making her contralto voice dip down so low and
husky it caused the muscles deep in Ty's stomach to flutter.

"All right then." He shoved the unloaded rifle into her
hands. "Let's see if you were paying attention."

To his amazement she primed and loaded the rifle perfectly
the first time and without any prompting. But when she went
to lift the gun up to her shoulder, the end of it wobbled a bit.
Ty stepped behind her and wrapped his arms around her
shoulders, putting his left hand under hers to help support
the rifle's weight. His chest was now pressed flush along her

back and the bulge of his manhood brushed against the curve of her bottom.

For a long moment they stood frozen as the air sizzled and crackled between them. Ty's heart was thrusting heavily within a chest that suddenly seemed too tight and small. She felt fragile and vulnerable within the circle of his arms. He felt hard and powerfully male.

At the same time they both became aware that Caleb and Elizabeth were watching them. "Wh-what do I do now, Ty?" Delia asked in a breathy voice.

Ty sucked on his cheeks, trying to dredge some moisture back into a mouth that had suddenly gone dry. "Pull the cock back all the way." He guided her fingers into drawing the flint-carrying hammer back to full cock. "Now, sight your eyes along the barrel . . . and squeeze the trigger, nice and slow."

The rifle fired, slamming her back against his chest and ramming her bottom against his crotch that was now full to bursting with his hard and thickened manhood.

Ty let out a strangled oath and let go of Delia so fast he stumbled back a step, but he was still careful to keep her body between himself and the Hookers, who wouldn't have been able to miss seeing the severe case of lust that had seized him.

Delia craned her head around to give him a brilliant smile. "Did I hit the bull's-eye, Ty?"

He laughed shakily. "Christ, Delia, you didn't hit the *tree*."

Her face fell.

He lifted her chin with his curled finger. "Come on, we'll do it again. Only try keeping your eyes open this time."

When she managed to nick a piece off the bottom corner of the target on the fourth try, he told her that was enough for now. He didn't think he would be able to bear any more of being so close to her without doing something to ease the incessant ache in his breeches, and damn the consequences.

He turned with evident relief to Caleb. "You ready now, Reverend?"

Caleb looked miserable, but he nodded that he was ready.

The young reverend turned out not to be nearly as adept a

pupil as Delia. The closest he came to the target was to shoot
the branch off a tree five feet away. But Ty also knew that a
man's aim tended to improve considerably when the lives of
his wife and children were at stake.

The sun set, and it quickly became too dark for target
practice. Subdued by Ty's reminder of the dangers inherent
in their future home, the Hookers retired with their bedrolls
across the fire. Ty dropped back down on the log and began
to oil and clean his rifle. Delia sat cross-legged on the ground
beside him, her back braced against the log. She watched his
every move with a frown darkening her brow.

As the silence dragged out between them, he glanced up
at her from time to time, until finally he said, "You got
something to say, Delia, then spit it out."

"Did ye really take scalps when ye lived with the Indians?"

He had expected this question sooner or later. Women,
when they found out about his ten years with the Abenaki,
were often more titillated than horrified. To Ty's cynical
amusement, his wicked, savage past had gotten him into more
beds than charm and manners ever would.

"Yes, I've taken scalps," he finally said, expecting to see
her eyes go limpid and round with horror and her mouth
tremble seductively with shock.

They didn't. "A white woman's scalp?" she asked matter-
of-factly.

"A Yengi woman."

"What?"

"Yengi is what the Abenaki call the white race. It means
the silent ones." At her perplexed look, he laughed. "It's an
Abenaki joke, Delia. Most whites don't know when to shut
up."

"Oh . . . An' did ye scalp a Yengi woman then?" she
persisted.

He gave her a see-what-I-mean look and for a long moment
he didn't answer. He watched her from beneath carefully lowered lids. He saw no disgust or horror or even titillation on
her face, but rather confusion, as if she had already accepted
what he had confessed and was merely trying now to recon-
cile this murderous savage to the gentleman physician she had

thought him to be. He was suddenly possessed with an overwhelming desire to have her like him—*both* parts of him, Abenaki and Yengi.

Ty scowled, looking away. Why the hell should he care what this little tavern wench thought of him? Had she cared what her customers at the Frisky Lyon thought of her when she'd let them sample her charms for two shillings a time?

But the truth was, he did care . . . He reached down and lightly stroked her cheek with the backs of his fingers. "Delia . . . I've never killed a woman."

"But ye've killed men. Ye've lifted their scalps."

"Yes. Not Yengi though, but only because by the time I was old enough to be a *sannup*, an Abenaki warrior, and go on a raiding party, my tribe wasn't doing much raiding of the English settlements. Instead, we had a big war going on with the Erie tribes, mainly the Mohawks. It was a war, Delia, same as any other war, and in war men kill their enemy—" He realized he was justifying his Abenaki self and so he cut off the words. He had promised himself long ago that he would never again feel shame for those ten years spent as an Abenaki. "It wasn't long after that I came to live with my grandfather."

"But what was it like—"

"Sssh . . ." He pressed his finger against her lips. "No more talk, brat. Go to bed now. You need your sleep." Her lips felt warm and moist and so incredibly soft beneath his finger, silken as a dewy rosebud. Her mouth parted open, inviting his kiss. But the warm pressure against the front of his breeches warned him he would never be able to stop with just a kiss.

His instincts told him he could take her by the hand, lead her into the forest, and she would go with him willingly. But after what had happened the last time he'd tried making love to her, he no longer trusted his instincts. The last thing he wanted was to get into another wrestling match while the Hookers witnessed the whole thing from the other side of the fire.

"Go to sleep, Delia," he ordered. For once, and to his frustrated disappointment, she obeyed him.

* * *

Ty leaned back on the hind legs of the chair and drew deeply on his short pipe. "You got yourselves a nice spread here," he said around the bit in his mouth. It was two days later and they were another fifty miles closer to Merrymeeting.

"You know, I think I can almost smell salt water," Caleb said from the chair beside him.

Their host, a farmer by the name of Silas Potter, beamed and nodded. "Ocean's just right beyond that rise over yonder." The rise was covered by a stand of firs that blocked out the last rays of the sun and cut off all view of the nearby Atlantic. But if he strained his ears, Ty thought he could just pick out the low boom of the surf.

The farmer sat beside Ty on the front stoop of his hewn-log cabin. He had just started clearing the land and the spring corn had been planted in a field of girdled trees. Already the branches of the trees were dying, letting in the sunlight. That fall, after the corn was harvested, he would burn down the dead trees and haul out the stumps.

The cabin at their backs only had one room, but the farmer had built himself a fine barn with the help of some neighbors and he had offered to let Tyler Savitch and his party bed down there for the night.

"What about you?" he said now to Ty, raising his voice a bit over the sudden chir of the crickets. "You got some land up there on the . . . what was the place? The Merrymeeting Bay?"

"Some." Ty gestured with his pipe at Caleb, who sat with his chin on his chest looking sleepy-eyed. "The reverend here is going to be our parson. We're going to be an honest-to-God township now, thanks to him."

Caleb grinned. "I thought we still lacked a schoolmaster."

"Oh, we'll get around that some way."

From behind the men came the sound of feminine chatter and the clatter of crockery. A rush lamp spilling from the open door cast a wavering light onto the stoop. Silas and his wife, Betsy, had just fed them well on a hearty meal of hard cider, sausage, and cornbread, and now the women were clearing up the dishes while the men were outside for an after-supper pipe.

Silas had taken down a pair of ladder-back chairs—they were kept hanging from pegs on the wall when they weren't being used—and set them out on the stoop. Then he poured off three tankards of spruce beer from the brew-kettle in the corner. He had offered the chairs to Ty and Caleb and settled himself on the overturned barrel. The farmer appeared glad for their company; they didn't get many travelers along the post road this far east.

Delia poked her head out the door. "Mrs. Potter wants to know if you fellas want some more pone with jam," she said to them all, although her eyes lingered on Ty.

And it was Ty who grinned at her and said, "Not me. I'm full as a stuffed goose."

Delia gazed at him for a moment longer, a slight smile on her face, her hands clutching nervously at her petticoat. Then she realized both Caleb and the farmer were staring at her, so she went back inside.

Silas Potter nodded to the now empty doorway. "That li'l gal of yours, mister, she reminds me sorely of our daughter Jenny. They's both about the same size—long and slim as trout. She died last winter, our Jenny. She was sixteen."

"I think Delia's a bit older," Ty said, frowning.

The farmer sighed. "It was a bad winter."

Caleb cleared his throat. "Our Lord's ways are often hard to—" he began, but Ty cut him off.

"Do you still have any of your daughter's clothes?"

The farmer nodded. "My Betsy couldn't bear to throw them out."

"I'd like to buy a few from you if I might."

Caleb's head jerked up in surprise, but Ty carefully avoided meeting the young reverend's eyes.

The farmer stroked his chin and shook his head reluctantly, but his eyes had grown shrewd. "Well, I don't know . . . What can you pay with?"

"Hard money," Ty said and knew he had himself a sale. He might not have been able to barter with anything less than his horse, and he probably couldn't have given away the Massachusetts shillings he had in his purse. But good hard English silver bought just about anything in the wilderness.

* * *

Early the next morning, Delia was kneeling stark naked in the middle of the horse stall where she had spent the night, trying to wash herself from a big bucket of well water, when the stall door burst open and Ty stepped through.

He froze in mid-stride and his eyebrows soared upward. His shoulders jerked slightly as if he would turn away, but in the end he was as incapable of moving as she was.

Delia had bolted upright. She stared at him, while his eyes went from her face to her breasts to the triangle of black hair between her thighs and back to her breasts again. His eyes darkened from dusky blue to stormy gray. She saw hunger in his face, hot and raw, and it brought her heart slamming up into her throat.

He took a step forward and that snapped her back to her senses.

She flung her arms across her breasts. "What the hell d' ye think ye're doing?" Her eyes searched the stall frantically for her clothes, but she'd tossed them into a corner out of reach. She glowered at him. "How dare ye come saunterin' in here, bold as brass, and then proceed to . . . to . . ."

Ty flashed an unrepentant grin. "Morning, Delia," he said, although his voice was more of a hoarse growl. He had one hand behind his back and now he brought it around in front of him. From his fingers dangled a bundle of clothing tied up with twine. "I bought you a present."

Delia didn't look at his present. In fact she barely heard what he said. All she could think of was that she was kneeling naked at Ty Savitch's feet and she didn't want him to leave. She wanted to stand up and press her naked body flush against the hard length of him and let him do to her what his eyes were promising.

"I see you're having a bath," he said, laughter now in his voice. "We must have entered another new month."

"Get out," she said through clenched teeth.

He tossed the bundle of clothing down beside her. "Aren't you going to thank me for the present? Why not put them on for me now. Let me see how they fit."

"Get out."

"You know, brat, for such a scrawny little thing, you sure do have an almighty fine pair of—"

"Get out!" Snatching up the bundle of clothes, she reared up, swinging for his head.

Laughing, Ty threw his hands in front of his face and ducked quickly out the stall. Delia stood still, her flesh tingling where his eyes had caressed her. She felt disappointed, relieved, and frightened—all at the same time.

If he had touched her just then she would have died.

Never in her life had she more wanted a man to touch her.

Slowly she looked down at the bundle in her hand. She untied the string that held the clothes together. She found a heavy linsey-woolsey petticoat and a blue-striped calico short gown. There was a calico bonnet with a wide brim to match the short gown, along with a pair of brown worsted stockings and a shift made of soft, light linen. And lastly—and the sight of them brought tears to Delia's eyes—a pair of calfskin shoes with pewter buckles and fancy red heels.

She ran her fingers over the smooth, supple leather, sighing with awe. Never had she owned anything so fine. They were a real lady's shoes, she was sure of it, for they were not laced but fashionably buckled, and the red leather heels were over an inch high. With careful reverence, she slipped one on over her bare foot to see if it would fit, terrified it wouldn't. It was only a little big.

Hurriedly, she finished bathing. She had borrowed a small dab of Elizabeth Hooker's soft soap last night and she used it to scrub her skin until it tingled. The soap, scented with sassafras, left her smelling sweetly of laurel. She drew more water to wash her hair, rinsing it until it squeaked. She wanted to be really clean when she put on her new clothes.

They fit almost perfectly, as if they'd been made for her, except for the bodice that clung a bit too snugly to her full breasts. She ran her hands over the front of the short gown, down over the petticoat. Lastly, she put on the new shoes. She tried them out, gliding back and forth across the stall, feeling tall and graceful, like a princess.

Suddenly she laughed aloud and twirled around, hugging herself. She felt so pretty. She wished she had a looking glass so she could see how smart she looked.

She stopped dancing and squeezed her eyes shut, thinking she might just cry for pure happiness. No one had ever bought her clothes before. And the shoes! It had to mean Ty felt more for her than mere lust, in spite of what he had said. A man didn't up and give a girl such a personal thing as a pair of shoes if he was only lusting after her.

Buying a girl things—surely a man didn't do that unless he cared for her.

Chapter 7

A light drizzle fell the next afternoon as Ty leaned against a paddock fence and cast a dubious eye at the small sturdy bay mare grazing on a scattering of hay. A fly bit her on the rump and she kicked up her heels.

"I don't know," he said. "She looks a bit too frisky to me. I was hoping for something with a sweet disposition." To balance out the disposition of the wench who'll be riding her, Ty thought with a smile.

The man who owned the horse was desperate for a sale. "Sweet as maple sap in March," he said.

Ty grunted. "I'll need some tack."

"She comes outfitted with a saddle and bridle. I'll give you the whole kit and caboodle for two pounds."

Ty pushed himself off the fence. "I'll think about it." He turned and headed off toward the docks.

"One pound ten!" the man called after him, but Ty kept going. The mare would still be there later.

The town of Portsmouth was a bustling hive of water-powered sawmills and shipyards sprawling on the mouth of the Piscataqua River. It was a prosperous town, as evidenced by the activity on its crowded docks. Just to get to the ferry landing, Ty had to walk around piles of weathered hoops and oak staves, which would be shipped and then assembled somewhere into barrels and hogsheads. There were stacks of other lumber as well: clapboard for houses, shingles for roofs, and the tall white pine masts meant for the King's ships—masts that were all over a hundred feet long.

Dozens of pinnaces and shallops rode at anchor in the harbor, and small rowboats and canoes dotted the river's gravelly beaches. It was a busy town of little high-posted houses with sharply pitched gables, narrow brick chimneys, and tiny leaded casement windows, all crowded together on dirt streets. It was a noisy town, too, with clanging hammers, the grate of saws, the squeal of the hogs running wild on the wharves.

On the Maine side of the wide mouth of the river, across from the Portsmouth docks, was the settlement of Kittery—smaller and more spread out. The place had a more rugged look to it, with its two-story garrison houses built of sturdy, hewn logs. In Kittery, a man walking down the street felt he could flap his elbows without knocking someone else to the ground. It was here that Tyler Savitch had spent the first six years of his life.

He couldn't remember much of those years. Later events had crowded out those scraps of memories. But he always felt a poignant loss, a sad sense of what might have been, whenever he first looked across the Piscataqua after a long absence and saw the piers, the garrison houses, the sawmills and shipyards of Kittery.

"Ty . . ."

He whirled around, irritation darkening his face. "Christ, what do you want now?"

Delia took a step back, her hand drifting up to her breast. "I'm sorry. I was only . . . I'm sorry . . ."

She started to run off, but he grabbed her arm. She whipped back around and that damn proud chin jerked right up into the air—but he couldn't miss the hurt in her eyes.

"I didn't mean it, Delia . . . Don't go." He realized it was the truth. He had thought he wanted to be alone, and he had deliberately left the others back at the inn. But now, seeing her, he suddenly felt this strange need to have her with him.

"Don't go," he said again.

"I only came t' see if ye were hungry."

"I'm not. But I still don't want you to go."

He released her arm and let out a relieved breath when she didn't run off. Her head was turned away from him, and she clutched the folds of her ragged old cloak, pulling it together across her breasts. As usual, Ty's eyes were drawn to those breasts, prominent beneath the threadbare material. Dammit, why hadn't he thought about buying a cloak from that farmer when he'd picked out the other things?

The blue-striped calico bonnet he had bought hid her face and hair from him. He didn't like the thing. He tugged at the strings beneath her chin. "Take this off. It doesn't suit you."

"But, Ty, it's raining."

She tried to still his hands, but he persisted. She had found some pins to bind up her hair, and he pulled those out as well. Clean raven tresses fell over his hands and a sudden beam of sunlight broke through the clouds, glinting off ruby highlights and making it shimmer like dark wine in a silver goblet. He had to fight a compulsion to bury his face in it. It was so silken, so soft. It was also slightly damp, and he realized she must have just washed it again this afternoon. He suspected this sudden fascination with cleanliness was because of him, and the thought made him scowl. He didn't want her changing to please him. In his experience when a woman did that, she next started making demands, expecting *him* to change to please her.

He let her hair trickle through his fingers. "That's better," he said. "It's stopped raining anyway."

He had dropped the bonnet to the ground, but now she bent and snatched it up. "Oh, damn ye, Ty, here I've been tryin' so hard t' be a proper lady and proper ladies don't run around with their bloody hair flying about their face and— oh, hell!"

To his amusement she clapped her hand over her mouth and her eyes squinted up in laughter. "I don't suppose proper ladies run around a-cussin' up a blue streak neither, do they?"

"Never mind. I like you with your hair flying about your face. And I'm getting used to that foul tongue of yours."

Her mouth quirked up into a big grin. "Hunh! An' you with yer re-*fined* tastes."

Laughing, he held out his hand to her. "Come on, brat."

She regarded his hand so suspiciously that he wanted to laugh again. But it made him sad as well, that she didn't trust him not to hurt her.

Then she smiled and slipped her fingers around his.

He walked at a fast pace back along the wharf and down to the riverbank, keeping her hand in a tight grip. The feel of her hand, so small and slender enveloped in his own, made him feel strong and protective. He had to chuckle at himself. Tough, gutsy little Delia McQuaid would certainly have laughed if she could have read his thoughts.

She had to run to keep up, but he didn't slow down. "Where are we going?" she said, panting slightly.

"Across the river."

"Why didn't we just take the ferry?"

Ty didn't answer. When they got to the river's edge he flipped over a birchbark canoe and slid it into the water. Seizing her by the waist, he lifted her into it.

She looked around nervously. "Ty? We're not stealin' this thing, are we? I don't want to wind up in the Portsmouth gaol."

"We're only borrowing it for an hour or so." He got into the canoe with her. Leaning over, he cupped her face in his hands. "Delia, I'm going across the river and I want you with me, that's all. No other reason. I just want you with me."

He surprised himself with what he had said, for until the words came out he hadn't known his need was so desperate. Perhaps it was a simple matter of wanting her company—he was feeling lonely and restless, and she could always make him laugh.

His words had surprised her as well. Her eyes widened until they filled her face. She half stood up, and for a moment he thought she was going to scramble out of the canoe, then she sat down again. She dipped her head, refusing to look at him.

He paddled the canoe as he had been taught, the Abenaki way, holding his lower arms straight and using his whole upper body, rocking forward in a pushing, sculling motion. The paddle made a soft sucking sound as it left the water at the end of each stroke. He enjoyed the physical exertion of his muscles. Inside, he felt like the string of a lute tuned so tightly it was about to break.

A light breeze brought with it the sharp fragrance of balsam and cedar. The clouds were breaking up, and late afternoon sun tinted the water a tawny gold. The tall, deep green trees that crowded in at the river's edge were reflected on the rippling surface. Green-streaked gold . . . the color of her eyes.

Even as he thought of her, she turned her head to look at him and smiled.

He didn't go directly across to Kittery but upriver instead. They rounded a bend and surprised a doe drinking at the bank. Her head jerked up and she stared at them, her eyes wide and unblinking, then she disappeared into the trees with a flip of her white tail.

Ty sent the canoe toward the bank where the doe had been. There was only a tiny strip of beach and stands of spruce and balsam fir encroached right down to the water line. The rain-wet branches dripped onto their heads as they came ashore.

Ty paced the length of the small beach. He kicked at a rotting log that had been tossed up by the tide, his abrupt movement scaring a nearby sandpiper that had been picking among the pebbles.

Delia watched him, a small frown at the corners of her mouth. "This is a pretty spot, Ty," she said tentatively when the silence had drawn on too long.

"My father was killed here."

"Oh, Ty . . . I'm so sorry."

He had turned his back on her to look across the river. She came up beside him. He had been feeling cold, but then to his surprise she slipped her hand into his, intertwining their fingers, and it made him feel warm inside. Less lonely.

"By the Indians?" she asked softly.

"They were Pequawkets. Led by Frenchmen." Queen Anne's War it had been called, France against England, and the New World had merely been one of many battlegrounds. The existence of the war, the reasons for it, had meant nothing to a six-year-old boy living in a small clapboard house in The Maine on the edge of the wilderness. He still wasn't sure what it had been about.

"There had been talk all that fall about the Indian threat," he said. "About how the French had them stirred up by offering bounties for English scalps. Lots of folk left the settlements and went back to Boston. But my father had a business—he owned a shipworks and it was just starting to turn a profit. I can remember him and my mother talking about it, about how the business would fail if he had to abandon it, even for a year.''

Ty paused, surprised at the vividness of the memory. Perhaps he remembered the scene so clearly because his mother had shouted at his father and she so rarely raised her voice. It had been his mother who was so dead set against leaving Kittery and the shipworks.

"Once winter came we all breathed easier,'' Ty went on. "But then one night we woke up to see a red glow in the sky from the other settlements burning upriver. It was a night in February and it had snowed again only that morning. We never expected to be attacked in the middle of winter with so much snow on the ground.''

Ice had crusted the snow, and it crunched under their feet as they ran. The moon was out. Everything glittered silver, and little ice crystals danced on the wind. He kept falling down, and his father grabbed him by the arm, lifting him so high off the ground that his feet pumped in the air. He laughed aloud with excitement, too young to know he should have been afraid.

"There was a garrison house over in Portsmouth and the river was frozen solid. All we had to do was run across the ice and take shelter there.'' His eyes, dark with pain, scanned the narrow bank. "This was as far as we got.''

They had seemed to come flying right out of the trunks of the trees, whooping their war cries. His mother screamed and his father fired off his musket once and then his mother screamed again. A hard arm wrapped around Ty's throat and he saw the flash of the tomahawk. Although he kicked and struggled, even his child's mind at last understood that he was about to die. Then his mother flung herself against the man who held him, and although others came and dragged his mother off, the moment was over and Ty knew he wouldn't die after all.

But it was too late for his father. They had stood right at this spot, he and his mother, while the Pequawkets danced around them, chanting their triumphant battle songs. A pool of bright scarlet darkened the white, white snow beneath his father's head, and icy crystals swirled around the bloody, gaping flesh where the dark brown hair had been.

Later, when Ty was fourteen and an Abenaki in every way but blood, he had gone on his first war party against the Mohawks to the west, and he had taken three scalps of his own. He had felt so proud and brave and lusty that day, and he had danced in triumph over his victims' deaths just as the Pequawkets had danced around his father.

Suddenly, Ty's legs began to tremble. Heedless of the wet ground, he sat among the rocks, settling Delia between his thighs. She leaned against his chest and wrapped her arms around her drawn-up legs. Ty thought that he liked having her there, just the feel of her within the circle his body made on the bank. A sense of calm and peace stole over him, perhaps the first he had felt in years . . . since that day he had been torn from his Abenaki family and brought back into the Yengi world.

They sat in silence for a long time. Then she stirred and rubbed her palm across his bent knee, and when she spoke he knew she had been thinking about him, about what he had told her, and he wished now that he hadn't done it. He felt suddenly embarrassed to have revealed himself in that way.

"They took you and your ma captive," she said. "What a terrible thing t' happen t' a boy of six."

He wanted to tell her it hadn't been so terrible. But then it probably had and he'd only made himself forget. "They loaded us down like beasts with packs," he said. "Stuff looted from the houses they had burned. And they marched us four hundred miles, all the way to Quebec. The French were paying ten pounds apiece for English prisoners, ten pounds for scalps, too, so if you couldn't keep up you got beat first—"

"But surely not ye! Ye were just a little boy."

"I was big enough to walk." He twisted a lock of her hair around his finger and pulled it behind her ear. "After a while the beatings stopped making an impression. You got so tired and cold you didn't care what they did to you anymore, and so you just laid down right there on the trail. That's when you got the tomahawk. We started out from Kittery with twenty-six captives, all women and children, and only ten of us made it to Quebec.''

"I would've hated them," she said fiercely. "I would've wanted t' kill them all."

Ty thought that maybe not for himself, for he had been too young, but for the others it might have been hate that had kept them alive.

"What happened then?" Delia asked. "What happened once ye got t' Quebec?"

"The Pequawkets are a tribe of the Abenaki nation," he said. "Chiefs from all the Abenaki tribes had gathered that winter at Quebec for a powwow, a war council. One of them was Assacumbuit, a grand sachem from an Abenaki tribe known as the Norridgewocks. One night, the Pequawkets put on a big bragging show, with singing and dancing, all about the raid they had pulled off. They paraded us captives before the others. Assacumbuit saw my mother and decided he wanted her. He offered the Pequawket warrior who owned us fifty beaver hides for us both—a king's ransom. So instead of going into a French prison, we went back into The Maine with Assacumbuit and the Norridgewocks. And you might think her a coward, but she didn't hate him."

Delia's hand tightened on his knee. "Oh, no, Ty. She must have been so very brave t' endure all that. So strong."

"Not that strong. She died having Assacumbuit's child."

"Yet ye loved him," Delia said, uncannily guessing at the reason for his torment. "In spite of what they did t' ye an' yer ma, ye loved yer Indian father."

"Yes . . ." The admission felt torn from him. "Yes, I loved him."

"So why did ye leave him? Why did ye come back?"

"He made me," Ty said, but now he didn't want to talk about it anymore. Instinctively, she seemed to sense it, for she asked no more questions. She fell into a silence with him, leaning against his chest, and that strange sense of peace stole over Ty again, in spite of the memories.

No one, especially his grandfather, had understood why Ty had so hated being brought back into his parents' world. They couldn't understand that after ten years Ty *was* Abenaki; he could remember little of his earlier life and only a few words of his native tongue. He had a family, a man who had made him his son, and a stepbrother they called the Dreamer, who was both friend and rival, another boy to hunt and fight with. Yet when he was sixteen, a peace treaty had been signed between the Abenaki and the English that called for a repatriation of all captives, and so Assacumbuit had turned him over to the garrison at Wells.

That particular peace had lasted all of six weeks, but by then Ty's grandfather had sailed up from Boston to get him. Sir Patrick immediately set about making an Englishman of Ty, usually by flogging him with a cane whenever he lapsed into Abenaki or reverted to his Indian ways. In the Norridgewock village, Ty had been a *sannup,* a respected warrior, and to find himself being beaten like a slave or a woman had been a shameful experience.

He had endured the beatings in stoic silence, because he'd been raised in the Abenaki way to be respectful to his elders. But he reminded himself over and over that he had done nothing wrong, that he was proud to be Abenaki, to be Assacumbuit's son. Yet inevitably the doubts had crept in. Before long he felt neither Yengi nor Abenaki. He belonged nowhere, cared for no one. He had spent the last years of his youth lonely, confused, and very, very bitter. At times he wondered if he had ever outgrown those feelings, especially the loneliness.

Ty stirred, jerking his mind back to the present by an act of will. Unconsciously, he rubbed his cheek lightly across the top of her head. "It's time we were getting back," he said.

They drifted downriver with the current. Delia sat between Ty's legs, and he showed her how to paddle the canoe in the Abenaki way. He held her arm, directing the pull of the stroke. He was surprised at the strength he could feel in her firm muscles as she flexed them. Her flesh was warm and she smelled of sassafras and of the piny forest they had left behind. The wind whipped a tendril of her hair across his mouth; her breast brushed against his arm. And in spite of his melancholy mood, his groin stirred and tightened.

Before, it had always been small, ephemeral blondes who would catch Ty's eye, icy women who had to be wooed and conquered first, then bedded. He had never thought he could be attracted to a girl like Delia, with all her rough edges and easy ways. A tavern wench who belonged only to the last man to have her. Yet she had dignity and pride, and something, something . . . Was it that she could be wooed and bedded but never conquered? he wondered. The thought disturbed him.

She craned her head around and looked up, and Ty was captivated by her lips as they smiled and parted. Her breasts rose and fell in time with the water lapping against the side of the canoe. The wind lifted her hair; it spread and fluttered like a raven's wing. Their eyes met, held, then flashed apart.

He watched her breasts lift as she drew in a breath and her mouth part open as she spoke. "If the Abenakis adopted ye, they must have given ye a name. What did they call ye?"

For a moment Ty was so bedazzled he couldn't think. "What?"

"Yer Abenaki name."

"Bedagi."

"Beda—" she started to repeat after him, but he put his hand across her mouth.

"The Abenaki believe you shouldn't use a person's name too often, or its power gets used up."

She nodded, her eyes serious. Still, he kept his fingers across her mouth for a moment longer and when he finally did let his hand fall, she wet her lips with her tongue, and Ty's breath caught. He shifted his weight to ease the pressure of his breeches tightening across what had become an iron-hard erection.

Her eyes held his and he felt himself being sucked like a twig into a whirlpool, drawn helplessly into those green-tawny depths. "Can ye say what it means in English—without usin' up its power?" she asked, her voice low and seductively husky.

Ty had to swallow before he could speak. "It means Big Thunder."

Delia burst into loud laughter.

"What the hell's so funny, brat?" he demanded, disappointed—or was it relieved?—that the spell had been broken.

"Oh, Ty . . . Ty!" Delia exclaimed between whoops. "Big Thunder—how it suits ye!"

"You've missed the whole point," he said, laughing now as well, although the tight swelling in his breeches remained.

Then the laughter left her face and that serious, beckoning look came back into her eyes. She had turned to face him, sitting back on her heels, but now she straightened and leaned forward to put her hands on his thighs. Before he could even guess what she was about to do, she brought her sweet mouth up to his.

The shock of her lips on his sent excitement surging back into Ty so hard and fast it rendered him momentarily dizzy. The canoe rocked dangerously, but he didn't notice. He clutched her shoulders and pressed his lips down savagely hard onto hers, plunging his tongue into her mouth. She fell backward, bringing him with her. He shuddered violently at the feel of her warm, pliant flesh, but in that same instant, the force of their weight slammed into the birchbark hull. The canoe rolled.

Ty kept his hands locked on Delia's shoulders as they were dumped with a splat into the water, but the canoe flipped over on top of them, landing a glancing blow on his brow. He blacked out for several seconds. When he came to, Delia was no longer in his arms and he was being pulled beneath the river surface by the force of the current.

Thrusting up with a hard kick, Ty tossed the streaming hair from his eyes, coughing up what he had swallowed while unconscious. He tread water, looking for Delia and fighting down a seizure of panic when he didn't spot her right away. The overturned canoe was drifting away from him downstream, and for a moment he had the terrifying thought that she might be trapped beneath it. Then suddenly her head and one arm bobbed up a few feet away and he relaxed with relief, only to see her black hair go down again and her thin, white hand disappear from sight.

He dove down after her. The snow-fed river was freezing and inky black; he could see nothing. He groped, feeling for her, and the fear and the cold squeezed the air from his lungs. His chest began to burn and the frigid water stabbed at his eyes. Just as he thought he would have to surface again, his hand brushed her cloak. He tangled his fist in it and surged up, dragging her with him.

She hadn't lost consciousness yet and he expected her to fight him from panic, but instead she lay limp within the cradle of his arm. He was easily able to swim the few dozen yards to the bank and haul her up onto its gravelly slope.

He helped support her as she struggled to push herself half upright, bracing on her straight, outstretched arms. She retched and coughed the water out of her stomach as her heaving lungs fought for air.

Finally, her stertorous breathing calmed. Pushing the wet hair out of her face with a shaky hand, she turned her head, giving Ty a weak smile. "I've never been too good at swimmin'."

"Jesus, Delia!" he shouted at her because he had been so damn scared. Then he noticed that her lips were blue and shivers rippled along the surface of her skin, and he got scared all over again.

Ty had never built a fire so fast in his life, at least not without a tinderbox. Gathering up bits of fibrous bark and small twigs, he laid a pile of kindling. Then he found a dead dry stick about the width of a thumb-span and flattened it on both sides with his jackknife so that it would lie firmly on the ground. He notched it, and then, taking a slender dry branch, he sharpened one end and set it into the notch of the larger stick. He twirled the spindle rapidly between his palms. After what seemed an eternity a thin line of smoke appeared.

He blew on the spark and then used larger branches and logs to build up the fire, and as the wood caught he scolded her. "You are the most damn helpless creature it's ever been my misfortune to lead into the wilderness. You can't ride and you can't swim. You fall into pits and go wandering off by yourself and stumble across old Indians that you're just damn lucky don't take your scalp. You can't hit a standing barn with a rifle and I don't suppose you've even the remotest idea how to go about setting a snare."

"D-don't know," she said through chattering teeth, inching up so close to the fire she was practically sitting in it. "I've n-never tried t'."

He took off her sodden cloak and wrapped his arms around

her, drawing her up to his chest, trying to impart some of his own body's warmth to her as well. "Well then, what the hell good are you?"

"I c-can catch fish with my bare hands."

He laughed. "I'd forgotten about that."

"An' I can make ye laugh, Ty. I've gotten real good at that."

"Ah, Jesus, brat . . ." He hugged her tightly to him and, unconsciously, because she was so close, he pressed his lips into her hair. He held her like that for a long while, until she stopped shivering.

She sighed and rubbed her cheek against his chest like a cat seeking a pat. But the next moment she pushed and squirmed away from him. "Ye're a most perplexin' man, Tyler Savitch," she said, tilting her head back to look up at him solemnly. "A man of contradictions."

"I'm perplexing?"

"Aye. Ye're like one of those tails on a clock—"

"Tails on a clock?"

She settled against him again, her back to his chest. "Aye the tail, ye know. That part that wags back and forth. Tick, ye're yellin' at me for this an' that an' every little thing. Tock, ye're kissin' me so hard we fall out of the canoe."

"Pendulum," Ty said, repressing a smile. "And you kissed me."

Delia waved her hand, dismissing this minor detail. "Tick, ye're braggin' on yer refined an' gentlemanly ways. Tock, ye bloody ogle me when I'm caught bare-arsed with nothin' at hand t' cover myself."

Ty's chest rumbled against her back. "I couldn't help ogling. Never had I seen a more fetching sight."

Delia preened like a jay bird, but she said, "A gentleman would have turned his back."

"A gentleman would have," Ty agreed.

Stretching her feet out before the fire, she wriggled her toes, pleased to have this chance to freely dissect his character. "Tick, ye care about people so much ye take up doctoring," she went on. "Tock, ye—oh, bloody hell!"

She jumped up and ran back down to the river so fast she

was already up to her knees in the water by the time Ty grabbed her.

"Delia! For God's sake, what are you doing?"

The wet, mossy rocks beneath his moccasined feet were slippery, and she fought him so hard she sent him sprawling onto his butt, bringing her down with him. He cursed as the icy water lapped around his most sensitive parts, but he didn't dare let go of her, even after she punched him in the chest.

"My shoes, Ty! I've lost my shoes in the river!"

"Delia!" He wrapped his arms around her so tightly he knew he was practically squeezing the breath out of her, and still she fought him. He had to shake her roughly. "They're gone! I'll buy you another pair. I'll buy you a dozen pairs."

She stopped struggling. She twisted around and looked up at him, tears streaming down her cheeks. "But they were the *first* that ye bought me, Ty. An' there can always only be one first."

"Aw, Delia." He held her, rocking her in his arms as she sobbed against his chest. "Don't cry, honey. Don't cry . . ."

They were only a pair of shoes, Ty thought, and it would be a simple matter to replace them. He couldn't understand why they were so important to her. Yet she cried as if their loss broke her heart.

Chapter 8

Delia stood on the inn's front porch and peered through the driving rain at a small bay mare tied to the hitching post. "Oh, Ty, ye've gone an' bought me a horse!" She looked up at him, her eyes glowing, her smile wide.

Ty stared back at her, his brows drawn together, as if he were trying to decipher the meaning of the look on her face. Instinctively, Delia ducked her head, afraid he would see too much.

"I got tired of walking," he finally said, sounding almost angry, but she was getting used to his morning grouchiness, and it no longer bothered her. "Besides," he added, "I told you I would."

Heedless of the pouring rain, Delia leaned out from beneath the shelter of the porch roof to give the mare a pat on the muzzle. The mare blasted air out of her nose, and Delia snatched her hand back. She expected Ty to laugh at her, but he didn't.

He squinted against the rain as he looked down the road where a boy walked, driving a cow with a stick. "I wasn't able to find you any shoes though. The only cobbler in Portsmouth is so busy he said it would take him at least half a day before he could get around to sewing you up a pair. We really don't have time to wait, Delia. I'm sorry."

"Oh, that don't matter t' me, Ty," she said, although every time she thought of the shoes lost forever at the bottom of the river, she felt so sad. It was as if she was never meant to have them, just as she was never meant to have Ty's love. And the sadness swelled inside her until she felt she would choke on it. "I don't need shoes, Ty. Especially now that I've got my own horse t' ride."

Ty didn't seem to hear. He had bent over to rummage through the haversack at his feet. "I thought in the meantime you could wear these," he said offhandedly, and he held up a pair of soft white deerskin moccasins intricately decorated with colorfully dyed porcupine quills and shell beads. They were so beautiful Delia didn't dare reach out to take them. Tears pressed behind her eyes, making them ache.

"Oh, Ty . . ."

He pushed the moccasins against her stomach. "Well, aren't you going to take them?"

She raised her eyes to his face. His mouth was set in a hard, taut line. But his eyes blazed with a turbulent emotion she didn't understand, though it had the power to make her heart thunder crazily in her chest.

The porch suddenly seemed too small to contain them both. She made a tiny movement as if she would dash out into the rain. His hand fell heavily on her arm and she jumped.

"But, Ty, I can't," she protested.

"Yes, you can. Sit down," he ordered gruffly, gesturing behind her at a bench that leaned against the wall next to the inn's front door. "I'll put them on for you."

Delia gathered her cloak beneath her and sat. The rain overflowed from the gutters, splashing into the muddy yard, but the porch was snug and dry. Ty knelt at her feet. He bracketed her legs with his widespread thighs, his position pulling his buckskin breeches tautly across his hard muscles. His hunting shirt was open at the neck, revealing an expanse of brown skin and a V of curling dark chest hair. Nestled within the hair was a small deerskin pouch hanging from a thong around his neck.

She touched it with her fingertips. "What's this?"

He looked up. His eyes were shadowed, brooding. "It's just a bag."

"But what's in it?"

He sighed. "A totem . . . a symbol. Of my manitou, my guardian spirit."

She stared at the bag where it rested against his chest. She wondered how it would feel to twist her fingers in that soft, curling hair. Or to press her lips there, in the hollow in his throat where his pulse throbbed steadily.

"Ye actually believe in those Indian things? In guardian spirits?" she asked to break the heavy silence, and her voice quavered shamefully.

He didn't answer. "Give me your foot," he demanded instead.

His hand encircled her ankle, and the touch of his fingers on her bare skin sent an exquisite shiver up her leg. Her stomach went all fluttery and her heart all skittery, and she shuddered.

"See there, you've probably already caught a chill," Ty grumbled. "Running around barefoot in this weather." He shoved on the moccasin almost roughly. "Give me your other foot."

"These are a lady's moccasins, Ty. How did ye come by them?" she asked, and then immediately cursed her flapping tongue. For they probably belonged to an Abenaki girl who had been his lover, or perhaps still was.

She didn't think he was going to answer her, but then he said, "They belonged to my mother."

Delia gazed down at the bent head of the man kneeling at her feet. Her heart was filled with so much love for him it hurt. "I promise I'll be specially careful with them, Ty," she said softly. " 'Cause I know ye'll be wantin' them back."

"They're a gift, Delia. I don't want them back."

The other moccasin was on now, but Ty didn't let go of her foot. He rubbed his thumb over her toes, smoothing the moccasin's supple leather, then his hand moved up her calf, sliding beneath her cloak and petticoat to the back of her knee. Delia's whole body jerked.

He looked up at her, and his face was transformed by a gentle smile. "Are you ticklish, brat?"

"Aye," she gasped, bereft of breath. She held her whole body stiff, not daring to move in case she tempted his hand to wander further. And yet, yet . . . there was a sweet, burning spot between her thighs that ached for him to touch her there.

Instead he trailed his hand lightly down her calf, his fingers lingering on her ankle before letting it go, and all the while his eyes were fastened on hers. His intense look melted her, as if she were a crock of butter left in the broiling sun.

"Come to me tonight, Delia," he said, his voice low and as compelling as his eyes. She found herself leaning into him, as if he had spoken too softly for her to hear, when in fact his words seemed to sear into her flesh the way his touch had earlier. "Will you come to me tonight?"

"What?" To Delia's horror her voice squeaked like that of a mouse caught in a trap.

He gave her a brilliant smile, relaxed and easy, almost wicked. "I'm asking you to come to my bed tonight. I want to make love to you, Delia."

The door creaked open and they both jerked around, Delia blushing guiltily. The Reverend Caleb Hooker came onto the porch, followed by his wife. He gave Delia a conspiratorial wink and then looked out at the driving rain. "We're going to be miserable riding in this all day. What are you doing kneeling at Delia's feet, Ty? You wouldn't by any chance be propos—"

"Don't be an ass, Caleb." Ty got up fast, then bent over to brush imaginary dust off his knees, flushing under Caleb's knowing smirk.

Delia held her feet out straight before her, showing off the moccasins. "Lookit what Ty's given me."

"Why, they're beautiful!" Elizabeth had been staring morosely out at the weather, but now she stepped up to Delia and a smile hovered on her dainty lips. "Aren't they beautiful, Caleb?"

Caleb's face lit up at the sight of his wife's smile. "Yes, indeed."

"Hell, let's get started," Ty growled, bending over to snatch up his haversack. "I've never known a group of people for dawdling away a morning. At this rate I'm going to be an old man by the time I make it back to Merrymeeting."

"Don't pay attention t' him," Delia said. "He's always ornery as a weasel in the mornin's. Come noon he'll have growled himself out of it."

The Hookers laughed and Ty scowled at her. She gave him an impish grin in return. *I want to make love to you, Delia.* Had she really heard him say that?

They took the ferry across the river to Kittery. From there they would follow the King's Highway, which ran parallel to the sea all the way up to Falmouth, deep in Maine territory. As Delia rode beside the Hookers' cart, she looked around the small settlement with curiosity, for this was where Ty had been born. Born and brought up within a loving family until that February night when he had been snatched away by the savages and made into a savage himself. Yet eventually he had been found and brought back—*forced* back, was the word Ty had used—and made again into someone else, an English gentleman.

Delia's heart ached for Ty, the boy. Three times in his early life he had suffered wrenching losses of those he loved—his father, his mother, and then a father again. Delia, who herself had lost a mother to death and a father to drunkenness, could well understand the agony in Ty's eyes as he had stood within his grandfather's luxurious bedchamber and said, *I don't know what I am anymore.*

How she longed to be able to wipe away his pain and loneliness. She thought that if only he would let her, she could heal him with her love. And he could heal her with his.

As they passed a palisaded garrison house in the center of town, they saw a pair of Indians shooting with bows and arrows at a target painted onto the spiked wooden wall. A group of rowdy, bearded men stood around, betting high stakes on the outcome.

Delia glanced over at Elizabeth, hoping she wouldn't start screaming the way she had the last time they had come across an Indian. But Elizabeth was too busy being miserable to be frightened. She sat hunched in the ox cart, the hood of her cloak pulled over her head. Just then the wind changed direction, dashing rain hard into their faces. Caleb turned solicitously to his wife, helping to draw her cloak tighter around her. Elizabeth glanced up briefly at her husband, but the look she gave him was not one of gratitude.

Caleb turned his head aside, and Delia saw a sigh puff his lips. She pitied the reverend, for it was obvious he loved his wife dearly, wanted only her happiness, but all his efforts were being met with rebuff and failure.

Delia tried to think of some encouraging words to offer Caleb when Elizabeth drew her attention by pointing to their left and exclaiming, "Why, look at that!"

Delia followed the direction of her finger and saw a sagging, dilapidated clapboard building.

It looked as if it had been abandoned long ago. The front door leaned drunkenly from one hinge. Weeds and a pair of scraggly pines had thrust up between the boards of the stoop. The diamond panes of the few windows were long gone, and furry moss covered the clapboards on the building's north side. Incongruously, braced on a pedestal that was fastened to the wall near the door, stood a ship's figurehead.

She was a mermaid, and she must have been painted bright jewel colors once—ruby-red for her hair, jade-green for her tail. Her upper torso was unclothed except for a trailing sapphire-blue veil. Her bared breasts, their tips still rosy, must have once been the color of luminescent pearls. But the paint was cracked and peeling now, and sooty streaks marred her siren's face, looking like tears. It made Delia indescribably sad to see this mythical sea creature abandoned on land to be battered by the wind and baked by the sun, forever alone.

Delia squinted, trying to make out the faded black words on the signboard that ran across the length of the building, and cursed her ignorance, for the sign was a mere jumble of letters to her. "What is it? What does it say?" she asked Elizabeth.

"Savitch and Son, Shipworks," Caleb answered for his wife, surprise in his voice, and they all glanced toward Ty, who had increased his lead ahead of them. He wasn't looking at the clapboard building that bore his name but instead out to sea. If he heard what they were speaking of, he gave no sign of it.

Caleb opened his mouth, but Delia forestalled him. "Ty's da was a shipbuilder here in Kittery," she said hastily. "Afore he was killed by the Indians years ago. That building must be where he had his business."

"Oh . . . I see," Caleb said as his light brown gaze sadly followed Ty's rigid back.

Delia's eyes were pulled back toward the sign. Savitch and

Son. She wondered about the man who'd had that sign painted, already eagerly anticipating the day when his young son would work by his side, building ships. Ty's father had died so young and violently and had left so much—a business that had faded without him, a wife who had died bearing his enemy's child, and a son. A son who had survived and grown up tall and strong. And lonely.

"Was Ty the only one of his family to survive the massacre?"

Delia looked down at Caleb in the cart. It took a moment for his voice to penetrate her thoughts and for her to make sense of the words. "What? Oh, no . . . Ty an' his ma were taken captive. But she died later."

Caleb's sympathetic eyes were again drawn to Ty's back. Elizabeth sat whey-faced and rigid beside him, the talk of Indian massacres reviving all her fears of the wilderness. To Delia's relief, they all lapsed into silence as the last of the settlement of Kittery fell away from them.

But she couldn't silence her thoughts. *I want to make love to you, Delia.* She hadn't wished it out of his mouth; he'd actually said it. But what did he *mean* by it? Delia knew well how a man could take his pleasure from a woman without feeling an ounce of love. It was an urge men got, and the girls at the Frisky Lyon had charged two shillings to ease it. Was what Ty felt for her nothing more than an urge?

At first they passed yokes of oxen dragging logs back for the Kittery mills, but before long they were the only ones on the road. It was, in fact, being charitable to call it a road. It wound along the coastline almost at the very edge of the sea and was more a pair of deep ruts which the rain had turned into a sucking quagmire. Three times the ox cart got stuck and they all had to get down and push it free, and before long they were covered with the slimy mud, even Elizabeth. The rain poured down and the surf boomed and crashed against the rocky shore, dashing them with salty spray that left a sticky film on top of the mud that coated their hair, faces, and clothes.

Come to my bed tonight. I want to make love to you, Delia.

Yet now he barely glanced her way and he never once spoke to her except to issue orders in a curt voice that set her teeth on edge. He furiously shouted at her when she insisted on taking off the precious moccasins so they wouldn't get ruined by the wet and the mud.

I want to make love to you. He'd been on his knees as he said it. On his knees, as if, Delia thought with a tiny shiver of excitement, as if he had been about to propose . . .

Delia, ye wooden-headed fool! The word "marriage" never passed the man's lips. Lord, but she would have to be careful. She loved him so much, wanted so desperately for him to love her. If she wasn't careful she'd be putting words into his mouth and feelings into his heart, feelings that weren't there.

Because of the weather and the condition of the road, they made little progress that day. They stopped for the night at York, a small settlement that stretched for several miles along the eastern bank of the Agamenticus River. The place was too small and isolated to support an inn or a tavern. But it did have an ordinary house—a house that had been converted into a way station for travelers, in this case by a widow whose husband had been killed during the last Indian war.

Beneath the steep, sloping roof of the house was a sleeping loft divided by thin partitions into narrow cubicles. The beds were merely pallets on the white pine floor and the loft was reached by a ladder through a trap door just inside the keeping room, where the cooking and eating were done. At Ty's request, and at the cost of a copper penny, the widow allowed him the fill a tub in the linter with hot water. The women used it first and then the men, and for the first time in her life, Delia had two baths in as many days.

The supper hour passed too quickly, and before Delia was at all ready, she found herself sitting alone on a settle before the fire in the keeping room, while the Hookers climbed the ladder to the loft and their bed. Ty was out checking the animals, but soon he would come back and he'd expect her to climb up that ladder with him, to get into his bed, to let him—

"Delia!"

Startled, Delia looked up into Ty's face. His hair was slightly damp and he'd brought the smell of rain in with him. His lips slanted into a teasing smile. "What were you thinking so deeply about, brat? I thought I was going to have to bellow at you through a peddler's horn to get your attention.''

She felt a warm blush creep up her neck. ''Nothin'. I . . . I wasn't thinking . . .''

His smile faded, and he seemed to rivet her with his eyes. There was no mistaking the look of hunger in those dark blue depths. ''Come to bed, Delia.'' It was distinctly a command.

She moistened her lips, tried to swallow, and choked instead. She stumbled to her feet, backing away from him. ''I . . . I got t' use t-the necessary house.''

''Don't be long,'' he said, his voice a rough burr.

Delia's feet swished through rain-wet grass as she hurried across the dark yard toward the privy, but she didn't go inside for she'd used the facilities only a half hour before. It had merely been an excuse to delay going up that ladder and into Tyler Savitch's waiting arms.

Tilting her head back, she gazed up at the night sky. A brisk wind was scattering the storm, and stars peeked in and out from behind the fleecy, scudding clouds.

Will you come to me tonight? Oh Lord above us, did she dare? The love she felt for him was so powerful, so consuming. She wondered if it was possible to love this much and survive it. Hugging herself, Delia stood outside alone in the cool spring darkness, torn by conflicting feelings of desire and fear. When she went back inside five minutes later, she was no nearer to deciding what she would do.

Ty was waiting for her at the top of the ladder.

She froze at the sight of him so that he had to reach down and haul her up through the trap door. He slipped his arm around her, leaning into her. Instinctively, she wrapped her arms around his waist and felt the supple muscles of his back flex beneath her hands. The entire lengths of their bodies were pressed so tightly together, Delia thought surely he could feel her heart thudding against her chest.

''Christ, Delia, I thought this day would never end.'' He sighed and his hot breath stirred her hair.

Somehow they had wound up with one of his legs between hers, and he rubbed it against the folds of her skirt, pressing until she felt the hard thigh muscle grind against her mound, even with all their clothing in between. Her chest began to

burn, and at first she thought it was because of the painful
hammering of her heart. It wasn't until she sucked in a gasping lungful of air that she realized she had forgotten to
breathe.

"Ty," she protested. Only it didn't sound like a protest,
but rather an invitation.

"You got me so damn hard for you, Delia-girl, I'm about
to burst," he whispered, his voice deep and rough. Taking
her hand by the wrist, he pressed it against the front of his
breeches. Delia felt dizzy with the shock of what he was
doing, of what she was letting him do. Yet a part of her was
curiously aware of what she felt—a stiff, thick, pulsating
warmth that seemed alive beneath her palm.

He nuzzled her neck with his chin and Delia trembled,
biting back a groan. He tilted her head up and nodded toward
one of the flimsy partitions that divided the sleeping area.
"You've been put in there," he said, still keeping his voice
low, "and I'm right next to you. Luckily, the Hookers are
bedded down clear at the other end. But I'll wait until they
get good and settled before I come to you—"

Delia's heart came slamming up into her throat. "No! I'll . . .
I'll come t' you, Ty . . ."

He kissed her hard and fast and wetly on the mouth. "All
right, but hurry. Oh, Christ, but I want you, Delia." His
hand dropped from her waist to caress her bottom as he let
her go.

Delia lay on her pallet in the darkness. The minutes ticked
away and the night deepened and Tyler Savitch waited for her
on the other side of the partition. If only, she kept saying
over and over to herself, tossing and turning until her head
ached and she felt almost feverish, if only she could be sure
it was love he felt for her.

But he didn't love her. If he did he would have said so,
wouldn't he? Of course, men weren't always blatting the word
about the way women did. And he had given her things,
hadn't he? First the fancy red-heeled shoes and then his
mother's moccasins . . .

Still, he was bringing her to Merrymeeting to be another
man's wife. If she went to his bed tonight, what would he do
afterward? Would he marry her himself, or would he just give

her another present and a final kiss and turn her over to Nathaniel Parkes without another thought? Delia's heart, already aching with love for him, might as well be wrenched from her breast, so painful would that be.

He doesn't love ye, Delia scolded herself as she flopped over on the lumpy cornhusk pallet. She punched her balled-up fist into the pillow. *He doesn't love ye an' if ye go to him this night ye'll be no better than the slut yer da always named ye.*

And what of Nat Parkes and the obligation she owed to him? He was expecting a wife, a mother for his daughters. *Oh, Delia, look at the mess ye've made of things. Fallin' in love with a man who's never goin' t' love ye, and all the while promised to a man ye've never laid eyes on.*

Delia turned on her side, facing the partition behind which Tyler Savitch lay, waiting for her. She would give up a lot for love of Ty—her virginity, easily, and even her honor by breaking the promise she'd made to Mr. Parkes. But only if she was sure he loved her. Only if she was sure . . .

And so although the man she loved waited for her throughout the long night on the other side of the partition, Delia lay awake as well, thinking of him, wanting him, but not going to him after all.

Very early the next morning, Delia descended the ladder from the loft and slipped into the keeping room, hoping to put a kettle on the fire and have a nerve-soothing cup of tea before the others awakened. But Ty was there before her, sitting at the board table, his bent head resting on his clasped hands. He looked up at the sound of her footstep.

She tried a bright smile. "Mornin', Ty."

He glared at her with bloodshot eyes.

Delia sidled around the table and headed for the door to the linter, the small added-on room that housed the pantry and led to the outbuildings in back.

Ty jumped up, sending the bench skidding across the floor, overtaking her in two steps. Whirling to run, Delia tripped over a sack of cornhusks used for kindling. She was back on her feet in a split second, but Ty snagged her arm. He hauled her around and slammed against her, pinning her to the wall between the hearth and the linter.

"Ye're crushin' me!" she cried, more angry than afraid. Somehow she knew that Ty, unlike her da, would never use his fists on her no matter how hard she pushed his temper.

Ty eased his weight off her, but he kept her trapped by placing his hands on either side of her shoulders. "Where were you last night?"

"Let me go."

"No."

"Ye're always such a bastard in the mornin'."

"Where were you last night?" he asked again.

"I never said for sure I was comin'. Ye just assumed it."

"Christ!" He pushed himself away from the wall, turning around and shoving his hand through his hair. Then his head jerked back around to her. "Why are you *doing* this to me?"

"I'll not fall into bed with ye, Tyler Savitch, just 'cause ye've gone an' snapped yer fingers beneath my nose."

His brows came down, his eyes narrowed, and his thin nostrils flared, and Delia, who was coming to know him well, tensed because she saw real anger now, deep and cold and dangerous.

Then she realized she didn't know him so well after all, because an instant later he threw back his head and laughed. "You're a funny one, brat," he said. "If I remember correctly, my bed was the first place I found you."

Her chest tightened and her eyes filled with tears as he lifted his hand and stroked her cheek with his knuckles, moving them up into her hair, then down a heavy ringlet, following the length of it where it curled around her breast.

"Delia," he began, but she didn't wait to hear more. She pushed against him and ran from the room, through the linter and into the yard.

She did not stop running until she was sure he wasn't following her.

There was smallpox in Wells.

The epidemic had already run its course, leaving its victims dead and mutilated. Only two, an old woman and a child, were still in the throes of the disease, and neither was expected to last the night. Ty and his party had meant to spend the night in this small town that was scattered for seven miles along the Maine coast, but when they learned of the epidemic, they rode straight through and set up camp on the beach five miles farther down the King's Highway.

Ty didn't wait to eat supper. He was all set to ride back to the beleaguered town when Delia tried to stop him.

She grabbed his arm as he gathered up the reins, preparing to mount. "Ty, ye can't go back there! What if ye was t' get the disease yerself?"

He dipped his head and planted a kiss on her nose. "I won't, Delia-girl. I've been inoculated."

These were the first words he had spoken to her since they had argued that morning—argued about sharing his bed. A part of Delia was relieved he was no longer angry with her, another part remained furious with him. His temper was quickly ignited and just as quickly doused, whereas Delia's temper tended to smolder. She tightened her grip on his arm. "That's a lot of horse feathers, those inoc— those things. Sir Patrick said so." In truth, she had no idea what the word even meant.

Ty pried her fingers loose. "When you and Sir Patrick can show me your degrees from Edinburgh, perhaps I'll give some credence to your learned medical opinions." He mounted, but he paused to look down into her worried, angry face. "Delia, I'm a physician. I can't ride off and leave a person in need."

"But if they're goin' t' die anyway—"

"I can help them die easier." He pulled the pacer's head around and rode off down the road, leaving her shouting after him.

"Ye're a wooden-headed fool, Tyler Savitch! If ye get the pox, don't come expectin' me t' nurse ye back t' health!"

His laughter carried back to her in the still evening air. Delia watched him go, loving him, worried for him. In so many ways, she knew, it was the very qualities that caused her to love him that made her so afraid . . . afraid of losing him.

Ye're the wooden-headed fool, Delia taunted herself. *How can ye lose what ye never had in the first place?*

Much later that night, Delia stood at the very edge of the ocean, letting the tide come to within inches of her toes. She breathed deeply of the sharp sea smell of kelp on wet rock. A tangy breeze caressed her cheek, as gently as a lover.

The Atlantic stretched wide before her, shimmering dully like a flat pewter tray and reflecting the golden bowl of a full moon. Behind her was the forest. It grew right up to the scattering of brine-washed boulders and this sliver of a sandy beach.

The flickering shadows of their campfire danced on the sand to the right of her. She could see the glow from the flames but not the fire itself, for it was sheltered by a lichen-covered ledge and hidden within the sickle curve of the beach. Delia could hear the low drone of Caleb's voice as he read to his wife from their Bible. Then she heard the crunch of footsteps on the sand.

She tensed, but she didn't turn to look at him, not even when she felt her cloak land heavily over her shoulders. His hands lingered at her neck, then fell away.

"I thought you might be cold," he said.

When she said nothing, he came to stand in front of her, heedless of the salt water that now lapped around his boots. He tucked a sprig of sea lavender into her hair and gave her a boyish, lopsided smile. "You aren't angry with me, Delia. Not really. So quit pretending that you are."

Oh, but he was an engaging rascal. He could charm the clothes off a bishop's wife, and probably had.

The thought made her smile, but she said, "I suppose ye think all this bein' nice to me now will make me forgive ye."

He laughed, shrugged. "Hell, so far I haven't done anything to be forgiven for."

"Hunh," she protested. Still, she reached up and touched the flowers he had put in her hair. It was too dark to read the expression on his face, but she could feel the intensity of his eyes boring into her.

It only took one step to bring his body right up against hers and he took it. She did not back away. As if from a far distance, she could hear the sea lapping and sucking at his boots.

So slowly it seemed an eternity, his lips descended. But

his mouth hovered provocatively over hers and his breath, warm and moist, bathed her cheek as he spoke.

"You want me, Delia."

The word barely made it out of her constricted throat. "No."

"Yes."

"I—"

"Yes. I can make you want me."

His mouth crushed down on hers, forcing her lips apart in a fierce, hungry kiss. Her protest had dissolved with the first touch of his lips on hers.

He pressed his palm against the back of her head so that he could hold her mouth in place while he thrust his tongue in and out of it rhythmically. Then his tongue slowed, stayed, filled her mouth, and he turned his head back and forth, slanting his lips across hers.

She made a tiny whimpering noise in the back of her throat. It seemed the only thing keeping her upright was his hand on the back of her head. She reached up and clung to his arms, her fingers digging into the tense, rigid muscles.

He broke the kiss, pulling away from her. She saw the flash of his teeth as he smiled at her. "You want me, Delia-girl. But I think maybe next time I'll make *you* do the asking."

He left her there, standing on the beach, wanting him. Just as he had said he would.

Chapter 9

The tiny settlement on Falmouth Neck smelled steamily of soft soap.

It came from the front yard of an old fortified log house that stood directly across from the Neck's main pier where it hooked out into Casco Bay. A woman and a small boy were stirring a boiling mixture of grease and wood ash lye in a fat iron kettle that hung from a lug pole over a big fire.

The woman paused in her work to look up as Ty rode in, the others following. She wiped the stringing wisps of hair from her sweating face and then her mouth broke into a huge smile.

"Ty!" she cried and, dropping the stick, started to run. Ty slid off his pacer and met her halfway. They threw their arms around each other and Ty lifted her off the ground, kissing her long and hard on the mouth.

Delia sat on the horse Ty had given her and watched them with a sick little smile on her face. This one was like all of Ty's other women, fair and delicate and, since she was in the middle of boiling up a big pot of soap, probably clean as a saint on Sabbath day as well.

The woman clasped Ty's arms and stepped back, studying him up and down. "Oh my, but you're lookin' fine." Her hands fluttered up to her hair, then she wiped them on the skirt of her faded Holland frock. "Darn you, Tyler Savitch, why do you always manage to catch *me* looking such a mess?"

"You look beautiful, Suz," Ty said.

The Hookers had gotten off the ox cart, so Delia dismounted as well, but she hung back while the introductions were made. The woman's name was Susannah Marsten and she was a widow who ran the trading post in Falmouth. She had a five-year-old son called Tobias. He stood with Ty's hand resting lightly on his head. Susannah Marsten leaned close enough to Ty that their shoulders rubbed and she was smiling so happily. Delia thought the three of them already looked like a family and she felt almost nauseated with a hot, burning jealousy.

"You sure are a welcome sight in these parts, Reverend," Susannah said to Caleb as they were introduced. "You too, Mrs. Hooker."

Caleb's wide, charming smile revealed his overlapping teeth. "To hear Ty talk, I only got hired so that Merrymeeting could call itself a proper town."

"Oh, you mustn't take Ty seriously. He loves to tease." Susannah laughed and looked up at Ty, her eyes shining. They were as bright a blue as cornflowers, Delia thought enviously.

"And this is Delia. The girl I've brought for Nat," Ty said. He motioned at Delia. "Come over here, brat. Since when have you turned shy as an old maiden aunt?"

Delia lifted her head and stepped forward. "I thought I was bein' polite. Giving two old *friends* a chance t' get reacquainted an' all."

This brought on one of Ty's scowls. Susannah looked Delia over carefully and then her eyes went back to Ty. Delia was glad to see a worried frown crease the woman's fair, smooth brow.

"You folks thirsty?" Susannah asked after a long awkward moment, while Ty glared at Delia and she glared back at him.

Ty jerked his eyes away from Delia. Slipping his arm around Susannah's waist, he gave it a familiar squeeze. "I'm dry enough to make a hen quack."

Susannah laughed. "Then come on in. All of you. I'll broach a hogshead. There's someone inside you need to look at, Ty." Moving with an unconscious grace, she led them across the yard to the front door of the large, hewn-log building. "That old timber beast, Increase Spoon, came down to trade some peltry. He brought his squaw with him. She's powerful sick.''

They entered a long room with a fireplace at one end around which were grouped a settle and a couple of chairs. In one far corner stood a table and opposite it a maple cupboard, displaying a set of blue glassware. Beside the cupboard, a musket hung muzzle-down by its trigger guard from a pair of deerhorns. Four copper-bottomed pots swung over the mantel tree above the hearth.

The commercial part of the room was separated from the living area by a hip-high partition with a swinging door in the middle. Along one wall of the store ran a counter, behind which were shelves filled with everything imaginable—from buttons to stockings, ax helves to lamp oil.

The floor was covered with larger items such as rum kegs and crocks of applejack. Bales of beaver and bear fur and blankets and beads for the Indian trade were all arranged in neat rows. A path about two feet wide had been cleared through the stacks of trade goods, running from the front door along the counter to the living quarters in the rear.

Two figures huddled before the fire. One, a man, stood up as they came in. He was dressed head to toe in buckskins that were stained with grease and stiff in spots with dried blood. His graying hair hung long about his face, becoming entangled with his beard where it grew past his neck. He watched them come toward him with eyes that were as small and dark as olive pits.

Someone lay on a pallet at his feet. As they got closer, the reek of blood and feces emanating from the blankets was so strong Elizabeth made a small gagging sound in the back of her throat.

"Lizzie, perhaps you should wait outside." Caleb said.

To Delia's surprise, Elizabeth almost snapped at her husband. "Nonsense, Caleb! The poor girl might need our help.''

Delia thought it was Ty's help the poor girl needed most. As he knelt beside her, the girl gazed up at him with sunken eyes that were huge in her thin, sallow face. She had black straight hair and a small pointed face, and she couldn't have been older than fourteen.

Susannah Marsten shoved aside a jar of bear grease and a pot of bean seeds to clear a space on the counter. "Here, put her up on this, Increase. Where the doc can get a better look at her." Then she came back to stir up the fire, raking the glowing embers to one side to put a kettle on to boil. Elizabeth hurried over to help her.

Ty picked the girl up off the filthy pallet and laid her carefully on the countertop. He said something to her in her own language. It startled Delia, hearing the guttural syllables coming so naturally out of Ty's mouth.

He unlaced the front of the girl's deerskin dress and slipped his hand onto her chest, then moving down to her stomach. The girl smiled; she had lost a good part of her teeth and her gums were bloody. But her smile was bright and Delia could almost see the pain visibly leave her face.

He has magic hands, she thought, and felt a jumbled mixture of pride and admiration and possessiveness as she looked at Tyler Savitch's sharp profile. He was smiling at the Indian girl, with gentleness and hope, and Delia loved him more in that one moment than she would have ever thought possible.

The old trapper shuffled over. "What's she got, Doc?"

"She has a disease that comes from improper diet, Increase. You two have to eat more than salt meat and biscuits for months on end." He said something else to the girl in Abenaki and she nodded seriously. "Boil her up a mess of fiddleheads this afternoon and make her eat every bite. And then get her to drink a couple of tankards of spruce beer. Can you do that?"

"Aye. She gonna live?"

"If you start feeding her right. Spruce beer, greens and vegetables, almost every day, Increase. Berries and apples when they come into season, and preserve them so you'll have them to eat come winter. Right now I've got something in my pack for you to brew into a tea for her. It'll help stop the purging."

The old trapper nodded. He picked the girl up and followed Ty back outside into the yard without another word.

Susannah looked after them, sighing and shaking her head. "He's crazy as a backhouse rat, is Increase. Poor girl. Although I think deep down he really is quite fond of her."

She sighed again and then turned to give the Hookers, who were standing side by side in front of the hearth, a bright smile. "Well, I've got to get dinner started. You all are stayin' at least the day and the night, I hope?"

"I sure hope so," Caleb said, with a sigh. They had endured two weeks of hard traveling since leaving Wells and they were all exhausted. "Ty mentioned something about having to get us a ride on a schooner going the rest of the way to Merrymeeting. I guess there isn't a road."

"The road ends right here in Falmouth. There's a deer trail that runs around the bay, but that's too rough even for a horse let alone an ox cart. That old pirate Cap'n Abbott has a schooner anchored out in the stream. He'll take you over tomorrow. He owes Ty because he got the chest consumption winter before last and Ty pulled him through it."

"How far away is Merrymeeting from here?" Delia asked, even though Susannah was studiously ignoring her.

"Not far. If the tide is right, about a day going by ship, which is the way most folks do it . . ." She stroked the towhead of her son, who had been hovering at her skirts looking shyly at the activity around him with wide-open blue eyes. "Toby, why don't you run up to the attic and bring down a bunch of corn ears. We'll pop some corn before dinner and drink a flip or two. It's one of Ty's favorite things."

She laughed almost girlishly and glanced back down the length of the room, and Delia saw that Ty had come back inside, ducking his head to avoid banging it on the low door. "The flip, I'm talkin' about. Not the popped corn," Susannah added and laughed again, for Ty had flashed his slanted smile.

A day's ride by ship, Delia thought. That meant by tomorrow they would be in Merrymeeting and Ty would deliver her to Nathaniel Parkes. She would be married to a man whose face she had yet to look upon. She would live in the same place as Ty. She would see him from time to time at bees and raisin' parties, and maybe on the Sabbath day if he bothered to come to the Meeting. When she got sick he would come and smile at her and touch her with his magic hands. And if she had babies . . .

Every morning when she woke up there would be the

chance that she would see his face sometime that day. It was
what she had thought she wanted. But, oh Lord above us,
what had ever made her think that would be enough?

Susannah Marsten mixed a batch of buttermilk biscuits,
whipping the spoon so vigorously it thudded against the side
of the wooden bowl. Delia sat across the table from her,
perched on a grindstone, her legs spread wide, while she
snapped beans in her lap. The pop of the beans and the thud
of the spoon were the only sounds to disturb the heavy silence.

Except for the boy Tobias, who turned the spit where a
haunch of venison roasted over the fire, Delia and Susannah
were the only ones in the room and Delia thought the other
woman was feeling uncomfortable because of it. Delia had
to admit she was a bit unnerved herself.

After munching on the popped corn and drinking a couple
of flips—a potent concoction of beer sweetened with molasses, thickened with an egg, and strengthened with rum—Ty
and Caleb had felt about as relaxed as cats stretched out nap-
ping in the sun. It was only with considerable difficulty that
Ty was able to force himself up and out of the house to try
to track down Cap'n Abbott to see about getting passage
tomorrow or the next day. Caleb went with him, wobbling a
bit on his long, thin legs.

From time to time Susannah would glance at the closed
door of the inner room where she and her son slept at night,
and where Elizabeth Hooker had retired an hour ago, claim-
ing the need to rest before dinner.

"Is Mrs. Hooker ill?" Susannah finally asked, when the
uncomfortable silence had dragged on too long.

Delia shrugged. "I don't think so. She's just a bit weary
from ridin' in the ox cart. She's used t' an easier life, ye see,
her da bein' minister t' Brattle Street Church back in Boston."

Susannah sniffed disdainfully and Delia realized she had,
without intending to, put Elizabeth in a bad light. Guiltily,
she tried to make up for it by adding, "Mrs. Hooker's always
been real nice t' me," which only caused Susannah to sniff
harder.

Susannah set the biscuit dough down on the hearthstone to rise while the oven got hot. She touched her son's shoulder. "Toby, go out to the spring house, please, and fetch me that jug of milk."

Delia watched the little boy scurry to obey. "Your boy sure is good, but he don't say much."

"He's shy at first. By tonight he'll be chewing your ear off."

Susannah straightened, wiping her hands on her apron. Since Ty had left she had taken the time to change her clothes, putting on a linsey-woolsey petticoat and calamanco short gown that showed off her uptilted breasts. She had covered her head with a long, checked kerchief that fell over her shoulders and was tucked into her apron. With her hair pulled back off her face, her delicate features of tiny, bow-shaped mouth, upturned nose, and small, pointed chin stood out in classical relief.

She's beautiful, Delia thought, dismayed. And Susannah couldn't look more different than herself.

As Susannah turned from the hearth, Delia glanced quickly down at the beans in her lap. She could feel the woman's eyes on her questioning and evaluating just as she had been doing, and unconsciously Delia's spine stiffened. She drew her feet up, pressing them against the side of the grindstone as if to give herself support.

"Those are pretty moccasins," Susannah said, forcing a smile.

Delia's head came up and triumph flashed in her eyes. "Ty gave 'em t' me. They were his mother's."

A shadow crossed Susannah's face and Delia's moment of triumph grew. "Oh . . . how nice of him," Susannah said.

Delia decided she would have no peace if she didn't know the truth, and the only way to get at the truth was to ask for it outright.

"Are you an' Ty sleepin' together?"

Susannah's thin shoulders jerked and a dark flush stained her fair skin. "Of course not! And how dare you even imply such a wicked thing!" she exclaimed, which Delia took to mean that if she hadn't done it yet, she had certainly thought about doing it, and more than once, probably.

After a moment of heavy silence, Susannah asked, "So you've come to Merrymeeting to marry Nathaniel Parkes?"

"Aye . . . if we suit." Another long silence passed before Delia added, "How come ye don't marry him?"

Susannah snatched a bean pot off the table, then set it down again with a sharp rap. Her face was the deep purple color of overripe apples. "He hasn't asked me."

Delia hid a smile. "I didn't mean Ty. I was talkin' about Mr. Parkes. Since ye lost yer husband, and he's just lost his wife, it would seem only natural the two of ye would think about hookin' up. These beans're done."

Susannah stood stiff, with her mouth partway open. Then she snapped her jaw shut with an audible click. "The eating things are in the top drawer of that cupboard. Should you want to set the table."

Delia dumped the beans into the pot on the table, then went to the maple cupboard. In the drawer was pewterware and linen napkins, all very refined-looking. Ty would be pleased.

"As a matter of fact, Nat did ask me," Susannah said to Delia's back. "He's a good man, but we don't suit."

Which meant, Delia thought, that she was holding out for a better offer. From Tyler Savitch.

Ty ate three thick slabs of the roasted venison and eight biscuits smothered with gravy.

After dinner and after the plates were cleared, Susannah picked up a grist sack and announced that she and Tobias had planned to go down to the mill that afternoon. She looked at Ty as she said it, but although he smiled at her, he made no offer to accompany them.

Caleb and Elizabeth sat down side by side on the settle, which had been drawn up to the light of the fire, and Caleb began to read from the Bible in his mellifluous voice. Ty sat farther away from the heat, on a chair made from a barrel with a sealskin seat. He cleaned and oiled his flintlock, his pipe forgotten on the floor. Delia perched beside him on the grindstone, as close to him as she dared to get without being obvious about it, and watched him from beneath sleepy lids.

She felt jealous of the way he ran his long, slender hands over the gun, so gently, as if he stroked a woman's flesh.

Once, he glanced up and met her eyes, but she couldn't read the look on his face. She wondered if he would spend the coming night in Susannah Marsten's bed.

Caleb had just started reading Delia's favorite, the Twenty-third Psalm, when he was interrupted by a sharp rap on the door. Ty set his rifle on the floor and got to his feet, but the latch string had been left out and so a second later the door opened and an enormous woman came bustling through. She paused on the threshold and her eyes raked the room, settling on Ty.

Ty's eyes widened at the sight of her. "Oh, shit," he said beneath his breath, and looked behind him as if hoping there had suddenly appeared a second door out the back.

The woman advanced and Ty retreated, going around behind the barrel chair. She stopped halfway down the path along the counter and pointed a fat finger at him, wagging it menacingly. "You can't escape from me, you riphell, though you might think to try. My sister said she'd seen you skulking into town early this morning."

"I rode in quite openly, if I remember, Sara Kemble," Ty told the formidable-looking woman. "Hello, Obadiah." He nodded to a small, thin man who hovered behind her. The man had a white mustache stained yellow at the ends and edges and small, pale pumpkin-seed eyes with heavy drooping lids. Ty gave him a quick smile. "What are you folks doing over here in Falmouth Neck?"

Obadiah Kemble opened his mouth to answer, but his wife did it for him. "We're visiting my sister, but never you mind about that. I didn't come here to talk about my affairs."

Sara Kemble advanced, banging the swinging door open with her hip, stopping just inside the living area. Her husband slunk behind like a puny shadow.

She wore a heavy quilted petticoat and a white mobcap with trailing ribbons, and the whole effect when added to her bulk reminded Delia of a ship under full sail. She put her fists on her broad hips and looked around her. Her eyes passed over Delia, pausing only briefly on the Hookers. Caleb had risen politely when she first entered the room and now he offered her a tentative smile, which she ignored. Then her narrow, short-lashed eyes fastened back onto Ty. "Well, where is he? What have you done with him?"

Ty had attempted to arrange his features into a look of pure, cherubic innocence. "Done with whom?"

"Don't you play dumb with me, Tyler Savitch. We sent you to Boston to bring us back a parson and I don't see him anywheres. Knowing you, I suppose you drank and wenched away your time there, instead of seeing to the business at hand."

Ty's eyes were now brimming with laughter, although Delia noticed he still kept the barrel chair between himself and the awe-provoking woman. "You just looked right at him."

Sara Kemble's two chins snapped around and she peered again at Caleb, only more carefully this time, starting with the round crowned hat on his head and going down to his square-toed shoes.

Caleb swallowed so hard that his Adam's apple bobbed. "How do you do, uh . . . Mrs. Kemble."

Sara's eyebrows disappeared into her cap and her small mouth formed a perfect circle as she drew in a deep breath. "Why, he hardly looks old enough to be out of hanging sleeves!"

"He's old enough to have earned a divinity degree from Harvard," Ty said, grinning at Caleb.

"Harvard!" Sara Kemble sniffed and her whole—and considerable—body trembled. "We're simple folk at Merrymeeting," she said to Caleb. "God-fearing folk. We don't hold with fancy, educated ways."

"Yes . . . Well, I . . ." Caleb cast an imploring look at Ty, which he ignored.

Sara Kemble's fists went back on her hips. "Haven't you got a proper tongue in that head of yours? You can't expect to preach a decent sermon if your tongue ties itself in knots every time you open your mouth to use it. Didn't they teach you that at Harvard?"

"I, uh . . ." Caleb swallowed noisily and pulled at his collar. Reaching behind him, he yanked Elizabeth off the settle and gave her a slight push forward. "Uh, this is my wife. Elizabeth. Elizabeth Hooker."

Having thus been thrown to the lioness by her fearless mate, Elizabeth handled herself quite well, Delia thought, feeling proud of her new friend. First, she met and held Sara Kemble's eyes until the older woman was the first to blink, then she dropped into a polite but restrained curtsy. "How do you do, Goodwife Kemble," she said, using the old-fashioned term of address for a woman of the middling sort, a respectable craftsman's or farmer's wife, and most effectively relegating Sara Kemble to her proper place in the order of things.

Sara's dirt-colored eyes looked Elizabeth over carefully and she nodded her approval. "Well, then. At least your missus appears to have her wits about her." Then she rounded on Ty again. His grin slid off his face. "And that reminds me . . . Did you get that wife for Nathaniel like you promised?"

"As a matter of fact—"

But Sara Kemble's scathing gaze had fallen onto Delia. "So this is she, is it? You there, girl, stand up."

Delia stood up slowly and her chin automatically went up into the air.

"Law you, Tyler Savitch, anyone with a dab of sense can see she's nothing but a tart!"

Delia jerked as if she'd been slapped.

"Now, Sara, you can't expect—" Ty began.

"What I expected was that you'd have had the wit to bring Nathaniel back a decent woman to be wife to him and mother to those poor girls of his. Instead you bring the likes of this one and she no better than she ought to be. This is a fine state of affairs and I blame you for it, Tyler Savitch. I told Mr. Kemble you should never have been entrusted with the errand." Seeking his confirmation, she turned to her husband, who still lingered outside the partition. "Didn't I, Mr. Kemble? And you can see now how I was right."

Obadiah cast an apologetic look at Ty. "Yes, m'dear."

Ty spared a glance for Delia, who stood stiffly beside him, her face so drained of color that it reflected the flickering light from the fire like a windowpane. "Nat asked me to do the best I could for him. Just because Delia's worked in a tavern, she's—"

"We all *know* what she is. And you're a lazy man, Tyler

Savitch,'' Sara Kemble scolded. ''Where did you look? Not far beyond the tavern she worked in, I vow. You can hardly expect me to believe this little tart was the best you could turn up with the whole of unmarried female Boston to choose from—''

''Aooow!'' Delia snatched up Ty's rifle, holding it like a club. ''If ye call me a tart one more time, ye old bawd, I'll wrap this flintlock 'round yer fat an' wrinkled neck!''

Sara Kemble's jaw flapped open as if it had become unhinged. She backed up two steps, her hands fluttering up to her heaving bossom. ''Oh, my Lord have mercy. Somebody *do* something. She's threatening to shoot me!''

''Aye, shoot ye and worse!'' Delia lifted the flintlock into the air. ''If ye don't take back those things ye said about me, ye old lard-faced witch.''

Sara gasped and her bossom swelled to alarming proportions. ''Witch!''

''Aye, back in Boston we hang women like you. If somebody were t' give ye a birch broom, why I bet we would see that ye can fly!''

Sara Kemble whirled around and hit the swinging door at a lumbering stride. She tottered down the length of the store so hard the puncheon floor shook beneath her feet. Fumbling frantically with the doorlatch, she craned her head around to keep a wary eye on Delia.

She flung the door open, but when she saw Delia wasn't coming after her she stopped and whipped around. Her doughy face was mottled with anger. ''You'll rue this day, my fine hussy. And you, too, Tyler Savitch. The pair of you will come to rue this day.''

She slammed the door shut behind her, then flung it open again immediately. ''Mr. Kemble!'' she bellowed. ''Are you coming?''

Obadiah Kemble glanced back once at Delia, a look of pure wonder on his face, then shuffled down the room and out the door.

The place now seemed suddenly quiet. To Delia's surprise, Elizabeth Hooker ran up and flung her arms around her. ''Oh, Delia, I'm so proud of you for standing up to that awful woman.'' She gave Delia a hard hug, then bestowed on both

Caleb and Ty a withering glare. "And with no help from the other tongueless wonders in this room."

Caleb smiled sheepishly at his wife, and then suddenly he bent over and began to whoop with laughter. "Criminy, Ty, did you see the look on that old battle-ax's face when Delia threatened to wrap the flintlock around her fat neck?"

Ty's mouth was contorted with the effort not to laugh, but he couldn't keep it in and it burst out of him in a deep, rumbling chuckle. "She was huffing and puffing so hard I thought she was going to bust a gut!" Ty exclaimed, slapping Caleb on the back as if congratulating *him* on their mighty vanquishing of the formidable Sara Kemble. Only Delia wasn't laughing.

"For years, folk in Merrymeeting have been edging up to the nerve to put old Sara Kemble in her place," Ty said, laughing some more. "Wait until this gets around. The old bitch won't be able to poke her head out her front door without—"

"It isn't funny," Delia said.

They all stopped laughing and looked at her.

"It isn't funny," she said again. She tossed the flintlock at Ty so hard and fast he barely flung up a hand in time to catch it. "She called me a tart and then I just went an' proved her right, didn't I?"

"Aw, Delia-girl . . ." Ty stepped over and put his arm around her, but she stiffened and pulled away from him.

"A proper lady wouldn't never have done what I did, an' ye know it." She looked at Elizabeth and Caleb. "Ye all know it."

She didn't start crying, although she wanted to. She did turn jerkily around and walk stiff-legged down the long length of the room and out the door. But unlike Sara Kemble, who had gone before her, she didn't look back.

Chapter 10

Delia stood on the very edge of the tiny spit of land and gazed longingly over the broad expanse of water. The bay was lumpy with dozens of islands that resembled a flotilla of ships on parade.

Leaning over, she peered down at the narrow strip of beach filled with tidal pools and kelp-covered rocks. A lone conifer clung to a ledge just at the tideline, and a pair of gulls rode the wind currents below her, cawing noisily at each other. She wondered if they were quarreling lovers.

"Delia! Come away from there!"

She spun around. Tyler Savitch stood among the charred ruins of what must have once been the stockade of an old fort. Even from this distance she could sense his tenseness, as if he feared she would jump. For some reason that made her laugh. The wooden-headed fool. As if she'd come all this way just to throw herself into the sea when she could have done the same in Boston and saved herself a lot of heartache in between, not to mention blisters on her arse from riding that damn horse.

She abandoned her perch on the ledge and walked back toward him, stopping when they stood face to face, close enough to touch. He had his hands hooked on his waist, legs spread, hips tilted slightly forward. The pose was intimidatingly manly; it made her smile.

The wind snatched a piece of her hair and plastered it across her mouth. He pulled it away, smoothing it behind her ear, and a rush of blood pulsed through her body at the gentle touch of his fingers.

"Are ye in love with Susannah Marsten?"

He looked startled at her question, then color spread across his cheekbones. He forced out a laugh. "Jesus, Delia. One of these days you're going to trip over that tongue of yours."

"Are ye?"

Their eyes clashed, then his mouth crooked into a mocking smile. "Now don't go getting your dander up again, Delia-girl. Susannah and I are just good friends."

Ye're more than that t' her, Delia thought, but she didn't say it. What she did say was, "She's pretty though."

"She's pretty, yes . . ." He picked up her hand, pressing his lips to her palm, and his eyes glinted with a teasing challenge. "But so are you."

To Delia's unbounded delight, he kept her hand as they walked together back through the ruins. She seemed such a part of him, walking like this, hand in hand. She could feel his strength as his fingers wrapped around hers, in the flexing sinews of his wrist as he helped her over a fallen timber. His flesh was warm, invigorating, and his strength made her feel protected, cherished. They breathed in harmony and she wondered if their hearts also beat as one. She could do this forever, walk like this with Ty, hand in hand.

"This used to be the site of old Fort Loyal." Ty waved at the remains of a palisaded wall and a crumbling blockhouse. "It was destroyed during the last Indian war and the unit was abandoned, though it never was much use in the first place."

A single cannon had been left behind, its barrel turned orange with rust. The cannon pointed not out to sea as one would expect, but down the slope toward the part of Falmouth Neck where the rows of flakes stood. Flakes were wooden racks used for drying the ocean cod which would later be salted and put into barrels and shipped around the world. Several men and women and a scattering of children walked rapidly among the flakes, turning the fish over. The briny smell of cod filled the air in spite of the wind that whipped off the bay.

Ty stopped and leaned against the cannon, pulling Delia in front of him until their stomachs brushed. He laced his hands behind her back and her hands settled naturally to span his waist. The wind flapped his sleeve against her arm and billowed her skirt around his legs. He pressed his linked hands into her back, pulling her closer. The heat of his body seared her, and she felt the burning fever of desire in the sudden dryness in her throat, the lack of air in her lungs.

To calm her knocking heart, Delia looked toward the bay and the ocean beyond. "I used t' wish I could go t' sea. I used t' dream about sailin' t' somewheres excitin', like the Indies. Or even England." She laughed softly. "And here I am about to set sail on the morrow for some place called the Sagadahoc Territory, which is so foreign I'd never even heard of it afore that night we met, and I'm not excited a-tall. I'm scared." Her eyes sought his face. "What did ye used t' wish for, Ty?"

His chest rose and fell, and for a long moment he didn't answer. Then he said, "I've never wasted my time on wishes." But she had a feeling the words were a lie.

Her eyes were on his lips as he spoke. She remembered the first time she had seen him, how she had wanted to run her finger along that sensual lower lip.

She did so now.

His lip moved beneath her fingertip. "You ran off like that from the trading post, hoping I would follow you."

"Aye," she admitted. "An' ye did."

"Yes. I did." He straightened, cupping her bottom with his widespread hands, jerking her hard against him. "And you damn well know why," he growled.

"Why?" she asked, meaning, Show me why. And he did.

His arms tightened around her, his head dipped down. He smothered her mouth with his.

There was a desperation to his kiss, almost a savagery. He forced her lips open, invaded her mouth with his tongue. She didn't stop him this time; she prayed he wouldn't stop himself.

She plunged her hand into his hair, damp with sea spray, twisting her fingers in it, pulling his head back to press her mouth into the hollow of his throat. She felt the erratic beat of his pulse, and his low moan was a vibration against her lips. His splayed hands cupped her buttocks harder, fingers digging in, and he ground his hips against her. He was hard for her and he wanted her to know it.

They kissed again, long, tongue-filled kisses that seemed to go on for eternity. Delia's heart thundered in her ears. It seemed as if the crash of the surf below had entered her blood. Their choppy, gasping breathing rivaled the soughing of the wind through the trees. The sun beat down upon her head and the earth tipped and swayed, undulating in waves beneath her feet.

She flung her head back, rubbing her breasts against his chest, and she opened her eyes to the wide blue sky spinning crazily above her. He laid his open mouth against her neck.

"D' ye love me, Ty?"

"Oh, my God, Delia . . ." she heard, felt him say.

Her knees were trembling so violently they couldn't support her, and she started to sink to the ground. "No, not here," he said, pulling her back to her feet. "It's too rocky." His fingers fastened around her wrist, and he dragged her off into the forest. It was darker beneath the thick canopy of trees. The air was still, the quiet dense and pervasive.

She watched his hands as he undressed her, lean, brown fingers dispatching with laces and buttons until the short gown parted open. He massaged her breasts through the thin linen of her shift, drawing her nipples into taut, hard points. She stood before him with her hands resting on his shoulders, her head flung back, while he made love to her nipples with his thumbs and to her neck with his lips, and it was ecstasy.

He crooned love words into her ear as he slipped his finger along the waistband of her petticoat until he encountered the laces in back. He found one loose end and tugged, causing it to snarl into a knot.

"Damn," he said, laughing, his breath hot and ragged against her cheek. "Turn around."

He gathered up her hair and draped it over her shoulder so that he could smother her neck with kisses while he picked at the knot. But he became too distracted licking at the line of hair that ran up behind her ear and nibbling at her tender earlobe, and eventually Delia had to work her petticoat around so that the laces were in front where she could untie them herself.

At last the knot came loose and she pushed the skirt down over her hips. Ty was much more adept at dispensing with her shift. He wisked it off over her head. The air felt cool and soft against her bare skin.

He stood behind her, his hands on her shoulders. His lips brushed the nape of her neck. "I've been wanting to get you naked for a long time, Delia-girl." He rubbed his pelvis against her bottom. "Do you feel that, Delia? Soon . . . soon you will feel it inside you."

"Soon . . ." she echoed, and her heart skittered and leaped at his words.

His hands drifted down her back to cup her buttocks, kneading them gently, then moved up the flare of her hips to span her waist. He turned her slowly around. His hands lingered at her waist, and then he stepped back to look at her.

She started to cross her arms over her breasts, but he reached out and stopped her, taking her wrists and pulling her hands down, pressing them flush against her sides.

"No, my sweet Delia. I want to look at you."

Her glance flickered up. She saw the heat of desire burning bright in his eyes and she quickly looked down again. But her eyes were caught by the bulging hard ridge that pressed against his smooth leather breeches. *Soon . . . inside me soon . . .* Her skin felt tight all over, too small for her body; she thought she would burst apart when he touched her again.

He slipped out of his shirt and spread it like a sheet on the ground at their feet. Boldly, she ran her palms across his naked chest—muscles, skin, hair. Man. She felt a heady triumph as his skin shivered uncontrollably, like the wind suddenly causing a ripple on a calm lake. She could feel his heart beating, hard and fast, and knew it beat for her.

His hands fell on her shoulders; his head came down. Slowly, mouths locked, they sunk together to their knees. He pressed her backward, and she landed partly on his shirt and partly on a bed of ferns and needles and dried, decaying leaves that rustled softly.

He stretched out beside her and stared down at her breasts. Her nipples drew up, hardened. "I've dreamed about your breasts," he murmured. "Ah, Christ, but they are beautiful."

She wanted to tell him that she had dreamed of him, but words were impossible.

He rubbed his knuckles against first one nipple then the other, then he began to knead her breasts almost roughly, pulling and lifting them up to his hungry mouth. He took a nipple between his teeth, biting it, slavering it with his tongue. Throwing her head back, she whimpered from pleasure that was almost unbearable, wanting him to stop because the feeling was too exquisitely wonderful, wanting him to go on doing it forever.

He released one nipple and went to the other, and she almost screamed from the delightful shock of him drawing it deep into his mouth, as if he would swallow it. The other nipple, now abandoned and left wet by his mouth and tongue, puckered up tightly as it was bathed by a cool draft of air.

His hands began to stroke the length of her, feeling ribs and belly, hips and thighs. His mouth fastened onto hers, his tongue delving in deeply, tasting of her. He sucked and nibbled on her lips, and his hands . . . his hands were everywhere, stroking, caressing, making her skin burn. Branding her.

He groaned against her mouth, "Ah, Delia . . . Delia . . ."

Shifting to make a space between them, he trailed his fingertips across her stomach, moving lower and lower still until they drifted, swirled, became enmeshed in the fine hairs between her thighs, and she shuddered uncontrollably. She felt embarrassed being touched in so intimate a place and she opened her mouth to ask him to stop. But what came out was, "Oh, Ty, please . . ."

He traced the outer edge of the triangular nest, following the folds of her skin where her legs joined. Instinctively, her legs fell apart, inviting him to explore further.

He did so suddenly, thrusting his fingers into her inner wetness, and her hips rose off the ground from the shock of pleasure that stabbed her. He slid his fingers in and out of her, again and again, until she thought she would go mad from the sizzling jolts of hot feeling. Her whole world became one hard, throbbing point that he rubbed and teased with his thumb. Incredible sensations lashed through her, causing her to push upward against his hand and draw her legs tightly together as pleasure shuddered through her, pulling a hoarse cry from somewhere deep within her.

Rolling over on top of her, he pressed down, grinding the hard bulge in his breeches against her pelvis. He grabbed a handful of her hair and pulled her head back, bringing his face close to hers. "Do you want me now, Delia?"

"Oh, God . . ."

"Say you want me now."

"Now . . . I want you . . ."

He straddled her, his knees pressing into the earth on either side of her hips. He straightened and she looked up—and the magnificent sight of him robbed her lungs of breath and caused her heart to wrench in her breast.

His buckskin breeches were pulled tautly against the lean muscles of his thighs, outlining their contours and making his confined manhood so very, very evident. His stomach was flat and smooth, though pumping a little from his harsh, panting breaths. Copper nipples stood out in the light mat of dark brown hair that covered his chest. She reached up, running her fingers through it, curling them around his totem bag, rubbing her thumbs against his nipples. She felt him groan against her palms. Sunlight, filtering down through the trees, sharpened the bones of his face. His eyes glowed at her like twin indigo moons.

Delia stared fascinated as he unlaced his breeches and peeled them down over his buttocks. His sex seemed to spring out at her, rising up so thick and long from the dark nest of hair below his belly. The enormity of what was about to happen now frightened her. If she had been capable of speech she would have told him to stop.

"Touch me," he said.

She didn't move. She didn't even breathe.

He took her hand and wrapped it around his hard length. She was surprised by the heat of it and the slick softness of the skin around the huge, thick rigidity. It filled her hand and he moved her palm up and down on it. Instinctively, her fingers tightened their grip, squeezing him, and he made a low groaning sound, like an animal in pain.

His hands, dark on the white of her thighs, spread her wide. He moved between her legs and pressed the round, smooth tip of his erect manhood against her moist, inner folds. His eyes fastened onto hers as he drove into her.

Delia cried out, arching her back against the pain and driving him deeper inside her. He tensed as he felt the barrier and his eyes, which had started to flutter closed, opened wide. But it was too late to stop. He had already torn through her virginity. And so after a moment he gave another harder thrust, embedding himself deep inside her, and this time he smothered her cry with his mouth.

He moved his lips gently across her cheek. "Sssh, Delia-girl. It's all right. It'll be all right."

He lay quiet a long moment, thick and hard within her, and then he began to move. His stroking was slow, yet sure, and all that had gone before, all that had seemed so wonderful was nothing to the sensation of this—of him filling her, man in woman, two bodies joined so intimately that he had become a part of her and she had enveloped him.

His stroking grew in speed and intensity, and it began to hurt again so that she tensed. But then he cupped his hands beneath her buttocks, lifting her to absorb the shock of his thrusts and to lance her deeper. He arched his back, taking his weight off her chest, and as he stroked the inner core of her with his thick length, he slid one hand between their joined bodies until he found again that knob of pleasure. He rolled his thumb across it, almost sending her shooting out of her skin. Rolling, stroking, thrusting, on and on, until the whole world was reduced to the place deep within her belly that he speared and the throbbing point beneath his thumb. Shudders racked her body, driving her mindless with the feeling, the feeling, the exquisite, unbearable feeling . . .

She opened her bemused, glazed eyes onto his face. Ty's head was thrown back, his eyes squeezed tightly shut, his jaw clenched, and his mouth contorted as if in pain. Suddenly he gave one last mighty heaving thrust and his whole body shuddered, tearing a groan from between his pressed lips. He pumped into her, filling her.

Love for him exploded inside of her with such force, Delia was surprised she didn't die of it.

Ty lay stretched out on the ground on his back, his breath coming in heaving bellows. His whole body felt leaden, as if he'd been beaten with something thick and heavy. He didn't even have the strength to open his eyes. *Jesus,* he thought. *Oh, sweet Jesus.*

He felt her stir beside him and reached out blindly, meeting her elbow and moving down her arm until he found her hand. Her hand always felt so damn small. It brought a tight, poignant ache in his chest. Mortified, he realized he was close to tears and he didn't understand why.

He summoned the strength to roll up onto his side. He looked across at her and smiled.

She lay still and silent as her gaze wandered over his face. Then she traced his lower lip with her finger. "I love ye, Tyler Savitch."

He dipped his head, avoiding her eyes, uncomfortable with the depth of emotion he saw revealed in those tawny depths. He inched his lips closer and kissed her nose, and because that felt so good he kissed her cheek and then her mouth. She sighed and her lips moved with his, warm and moist and easy, as if they had been created by God just to give him pleasure.

He pulled away from her. Hitching his butt up, he yanked his breeches over his hips, fastening them. Her words hung in the air between them as if they had taken shape. *I love ye, Tyler Savitch.* Christ, he didn't want that.

He turned around to look at her. She lay sprawled on the ground, gloriously naked, looking wanton and abandoned and oh so damn desirable. Their eyes met and they shared the memory of what had passed between them. Suddenly, she sat up, snatching at her petticoat. Covering her breasts, she tucked the folds of the skirt securely beneath her arms. Her face was shiny red with embarrassment, and it almost made him smile, this belated sense of modesty.

"Delia, why didn't you tell me you were a virgin?"

Her eyes closed a moment and he saw her swallow. Her cheekbones were still bright red, but the skin around her lips had turned white. When she opened her eyes he saw they brimmed with tears. "I told ye that first night we met that just 'cause I worked in a grog shop, it didn't make me a whore. I knew ye didn't believe me."

Ty couldn't deny it, but he didn't want to spoil the pleasure they had shared so he slanted his lips into a teasing smile and stroked her cheek, tilting her face up. "I should have figured it out though, what with all that virginal resistance you put up every time I went near you. Do you have any idea of the hell you've made me suffer these past weeks?"

She laughed, sniffled. Her lower lip trembled and he couldn't resist flicking his tongue across it, sucking it into his mouth. But she pulled her head back out of his reach. "It wasn't all that pleasurable for ye, was it? Me bein' a virgin and not knowin' what I was supposed t' do."

"Aw, Delia . . ." He cupped the back of her neck, giving her a gentle shake as he smiled down into her solemn, beckoning eyes. Poor brat . . . Here she was worried about whether she'd pleased him, when it could hardly have been a very satisfying or pleasurable experience for her. "I'm the one who made a mess of things," he said. "It probably hurt like hell—"

She shook her head. "Oh, no, Ty—"

He put two fingers across her lips. "It hurt. I know it did." He drew her to him, pressing her head against his shoulder. "Christ, but you were so small and tight. I shouldn't have gone thrusting into you like that, like some damn lusty bull."

She made a muffled protest against his chest. "It only hurt at the beginning. Afterward, I liked havin' ye inside me, Ty. Oh, it felt so fine!"

"It felt fine being inside you, too," he said, and realized the words were a puny way of expressing the sensation of filling her hot, tight wetness. Fine? My God, it had been the other side of ecstasy.

He tangled his fingers in her hair, pulling her head back so that he could look into her eyes. "Out by the cannon we were so hot for each other. I thought you'd want it hard and fast and now."

"But I did want it that way, Ty. Just the way ye said. Hard an' fast an' now." The way she said it, in that rough, throaty voice of hers, was so erotic it caused a feeble stirring of his exhausted manhood. Hot wasn't the word for what it had been like between them, what he had felt for her. He had been ravenous.

He kissed her again, a light, teasing kiss that just started to turn into something more before he ended it. "Next time

I make love to you, I'm taking it slow and easy, the way a man should make love to a beautiful, willing virgin.''

''Next time . . .'' Joy blazed out of her face, bright and intense. ''Oh, Ty, does that mean ye'll be wantin' me again?''

He drew her tightly against him, nuzzling her neck with his lips. ''Hell, yes, I'll be wanting you again. And again and again and again . . .''

Smiling with delight, she fell back on the ground, drawing him down with her. ''Now?''

Laughing, feeling wonderfully happy, he kissed her hard on the mouth before whisking away the intruding petticoat. ''Greedy brat. A man needs some time in between. We have the rest of the afternoon and all night. But in the meantime I can begin to get you''—his lips moved down and captured a nipple, drawing it immediately into a hard point—''ready. And teach you how to make me''—he released the nipple, trailing his tongue around the underside of her breast, licking her and tasting salty sweat and crushed pine needles and a little of himself—''ready.''

She sucked in a sharp breath and tangled her fingers in his hair. ''Ty, what are we goin' t' do now about Mr. Parkes?''

His tongue drifted lower down her stomach and he felt his manhood begin to stiffen. Perhaps he wouldn't need to wait quite so long after all. ''Um?''

''Mr. Parkes. What are we goin' t' tell him?''

But Ty had forgotten all about Nat and he certainly didn't want to think about him now, not with the delectable Delia warm and fast becoming ready in his arms. ''. . . won't tell him,'' Ty mumbled, delving into her belly button with his tongue.

She squirmed, twisting her hips sensuously, and he smiled to himself. Perhaps he hadn't been such a failure after all in initiating Delia McQuaid into the joys of lovemaking.

''But we got t' tell him *somethin'*, Ty,'' she said, panting a little. The skin beneath his mouth quivered. ''Won't he be angry with ye when he finds out it's you who'll be marryin' me now, 'stead of him?''

Ty's tongue stopped in its downward journey. Suddenly it was so quiet he could hear the wind-tossed cry of a gull and the distant sound of someone shouting below on the wharf of Falmouth Neck. The breeze felt cold against his naked back.

Rolling off her, he sat up. He forced himself to meet her startled eyes and felt a sick clenching of self-disgust deep inside his gut. The pressure in his chest was so fierce he could barely breathe.

Reaching down, he drew her up so that they were sitting across from each other, knees touching. In this position she seemed so small and vulnerable, barely older than a child. Hell, she *was* barely older than a child, a girl—although no longer a girl in one very important way, thanks to him.

He could see the fear building behind her eyes. Steeling himself, he drew a deep breath. "I'm not marrying you, Delia."

She jerked her head back and forth, once, and her mouth slanted up in a funny, twisted way. "But ye said ye loved me."

"I never said that."

"But ye did! D' ye think I would have let . . . Oh, God!" She pounded her thighs with her fists. Tears filled her eyes and spilled over. "D' ye think any of this would have happened if I hadn't believed ye loved me? But ye gave me things—the clothes and the horse. An' the moccasins, Ty. Y-yer m-mother's moccasins."

"Delia—"

"And out there by the cannon, ye said ye loved me. Otherwise I wouldn't never have let you, I wouldn't have, I wouldn't have . . . But I love *ye*. So much, don't ye see? And ye said ye loved me."

Had he said those three damning words in the heat of the moment? He was sure he hadn't.

She was crying now, choking, heaving sobs, gulping in drafts of air. He couldn't bear it, but at the same time he felt suffocated by her emotions, trapped. "I'm sorry this happened. I never set out to hurt you, please believe that—"

"Liar!" He reached for her, but she twisted out of his grasp, jerking to her feet. She snatched up her shift, pulling it over her head. Ty stood up now as well. The sickness in his gut had spread to his limbs, making them feel heavy, and he swayed a little on his feet.

He held his arms out from his sides. "It's just that I'm not ready for marriage now. My God, what I think I want out of *life* changes depending on which side of bed I roll out of in the morning. How can I be expected to know what I want in a wife?"

She clutched her petticoat in a fist in front of her. Suddenly she dropped it and fell to her knees before him, wrapping her arms around his thighs. "Oh God, Ty, don't do this to me. I love ye so much an' I will be so good t' ye, Ty. The best wife ever—"

He reached down and pulled her back on her feet, shaking her. "Damn it, Delia, stop it! I'm not marrying you!"

Her sobs ended suddenly, as if someone had choked them off. She shuddered once and pushed her hands up over her face, through her hair. "I'm sorry . . . I didn't mean t' embarrass ye. Or shame myself."

She moved away from him and finished dressing. He felt he should do something, say something, explain . . . "If I had known you were a virgin and that you fancied yourself in love with me, I would never have allowed things to go so far—"

She whipped around and it was the old Delia back—proud, angry, fighting him. "Is that what ye think it is I feel for you—a fancy?"

"What else could it be? We barely know each other."

She finished lacing her short gown and came to stand before him, uncomfortably close. She stared hard at his face until he wanted to look away. "I guess ye figured ye knew me well enough for beddin' though. Or is it a game t' ye—seducing poor innocent girls?"

"Innocent!" He laughed once, hard and harsh. Then he closed his fingers tightly around her scalp and brought her face close to his, close enough that he could see his own breath stir the dampened wisps of her hair. "Virgin or not, you knew damn well what you were doing, Delia-girl. And if you think now you're going to use the loss of your precious maidenhood to trap me into marrying you, think again."

Her chest jerked with her efforts not to sob, although she couldn't stop her eyes from becoming brimming golden-green pools of hurt. Or her lips from trembling open. He came within a hair's-breadth of crushing his mouth down over hers. Never had he wanted to kiss a woman more in his life and he almost hated her for it. That she could make him want something so badly, and so beyond his control . . .

"I d-didn't d-do that, Ty," she choked out. "I didn't t-try t' trap ye, I swear—"

"Didn't you?" He let her go so abruptly that she stumbled back a step. "Christ, just look at yourself! You were nothing but a ragged, filthy tavern wench the night I found you . . . *in my bed*. Nobody would ever blame me for thinking you were just a two-shilling tart all hot for a little roll—"

Guilt and fear had sent the lacerating words spewing from his mouth, but he shut them off at the sight of what they had done to her. The blood had drained completely from her face, as if he'd torn open her heart. Her eyes fluttered and she swayed. He reached out a hand to steady her.

"Ah, God, Delia. I didn't mean—"

She shuddered violently. "Let go of me," she said, her voice hoarse and strained.

He dropped her arm. *Jesus, Savitch, what kind of bastard are you?*

Ty made himself face her, feeling low and small and mean. He wished she had hauled off and slapped him, or screamed that she hated him. But he could tell by the way she let her gaze roam unselfconsciously over his features, as if she were etching them onto her heart, that she didn't hate him, no matter how much he deserved it. She loved him and the knowledge terrified him. He didn't want such power over another human being and he certainly didn't want to give someone that power over him.

"I never set out to hurt you, Delia."

Her hand started up to his face, but she let it fall without touching him. "Oh, Ty, I know ye didn't. The whole thing was all my fault, wishing for somethin' I couldn't have an' lettin' myself believe . . ."

Oh, Jesus. "Delia, don't—"

"That first night when I saw ye an' ye touched me, I thought there never was anythin' in this world more wonderful than you. I fell in love with ye then, Tyler Savitch. But I shouldn't have given up my honor t' ye like that. I shouldn't have let ye take me like a whore.''

She turned then and walked away from him, and he came so close to calling her back, to begging her to forgive him, even, for Christ's sake, to promising to marry her. But although he thought he would do almost anything to wipe the torment from her face, he knew that in the end calling her back would only hurt her worse. For what she wanted from him was love, and that he couldn't give.

He stood in one place for a long time after she had gone. Then, slowly, he bent and picked up his shirt. He started to put it on when he saw that it was stained with blood. Her blood.

He walked out of the forest, down the long path, around to the sea. He knelt in the sand beside a tidal pool and immersed the shirt. He watched the bloodstain seep out of the cloth and mingle with the water, becoming steadily weaker until it had dissipated altogether. Somehow, it seemed that with her virgin's blood he was washing away something within himself, something that had been such an integral part of him he hadn't even known it was there until now, when he missed it.

Then he realized what it was. It was joy. For the last three weeks, since she had burst upon his life, he had felt unbounded joy just on waking up in the morning and knowing he would see that impish, smiling face, hear that husky voice. She had made him laugh and she had made him angry, but above all she had made him glad to be alive. She had made him want her with a hunger unsurpassed and still—damn her and that damn consuming, sensuous body of hers—unsatisfied. Yet he couldn't find within him the courage to let himself love her, and so he cast her aside.

Taking his joy with her.

Chapter 11

❧ ⁀⁀

The pretty, beaded moccasins lay on top of his haversack, looking forlorn, the toes touching and the heels slightly apart. Ty squatted and reached out to pick them up. For a moment his hand hovered as if he couldn't bring himself to touch them, then with a snarl of anger he snatched the moccasins and shoved them deep inside the haversack and out of his sight.

"Goddamn you, Delia McQuaid."

He stood up, draping the haversack over his shoulder, and walked out of the trading post and into the bright morning sun. Susannah Marsten was in the yard waiting for him.

"I wish you could stay longer," she said, blushing slightly as he walked up to her.

He shifted the pack on his shoulder, met her eyes, and then looked away. After edging up to it for months, Susannah Marsten had finally invited him into her bed last night. He'd at least had the decency not to take her up on it. Still, not going had turned out to be almost as hurtful to her as his going would have been. Within the last twenty-four hours he had managed to hurt two fine women, and all in all Tyler Savitch wasn't feeling particularly good about himself this morning.

"I'm going to have to turn right around and come back again next week," he said. "There's a woman expecting over at Cape Elizabeth. She's so tiny it's going to be pure hell for her and I promised I'd be on hand in case something went wrong."

157

Susannah twisted her fingers in her skirt. "Well, then . . . you're welcome to stay the night here. On your way."

Ty managed to nod noncommittally, while saying nothing.

They stood beside the big black kettle in her yard. The fire was out; the soap lay half-congealed in the pot. They looked down the slope toward the pier where Delia and the Hookers watched while the oxen were being coaxed up a gangplank onto the schooner that would take them to Merrymeeting. Caleb pointed out something to Delia and they heard her delighted laughter carried to them on the morning breeze.

"Are you thinking of marrying that girl yourself?" Susannah asked, trying for teasing nonchalance and failing miserably.

Ty's eyes had been on Delia, but now he pinned them on Susannah and they darkened with sudden anger. "I have no intention of getting married. Not now. Not ever."

Her face paled and the fingers she had tangled in her skirt trembled. Ty regretted the blunt cruelty of his words, but he didn't regret saying them. He wanted no repetition of what had happened yesterday.

He clenched his jaw, glowering at the dark-haired slip of a girl on the dock, the real cause of all the turmoil, frustration, and guilt he was feeling. Dammit, take a woman to bed, even *think* of taking a woman to bed, and the next thing you knew she was talking about marriage and humming lullabies.

Delia would have had to turn around to see that Ty watched her. But she didn't need to do so for she could feel those intense, dusky blue eyes boring into her back. The throbbing ache between her thighs, though fading now, reminded her of what had happened between them yesterday—as if she could ever forget! She knew she would have to face him eventually, talk to him . . . But not, please God, just yet.

Delia felt something brush her arm and she turned to look into Elizabeth Hooker's concerned face.

"Delia, are you all right? You look as if . . . well, as if you've been crying."

"I guess I'm a little homesick," Delia lied. "An' maybe a little nervous, too. About meetin' Mr. Parkes today an' all."

That certainly wasn't a lie. Letting herself fall in love with one man while promising herself to another, giving herself to Ty like that, so wantonly—Delia was sure her shame was etched in letters on her face for all the world to see. She had thought Merrymeeting would be a new beginning for her, a life of respectability. She didn't deserve such a life now, and poor Nat Parkes and his daughters, they hardly deserved the likes of her.

Caleb boarded the schooner to ensure his precious oxen were properly secured in the hold. Elizabeth watched her husband walk across the deck and disappear down a hatch, then she took a step closer to Delia, lowering her voice. "Are you sure you should be marrying Mr. Parkes? What about Dr. Savitch? It seemed you and he . . . well, that you two were . . ."

Delia bit her lip and looked out over the water, blinking back fresh tears. It should be impossible for there to be any tears left in her, but they seemed to be springing up from a bottomless well. And there was such a big lump in her throat. It felt as if she'd tried to swallow an egg whole and it had gotten stuck in there.

"I asked Ty t' marry me, Elizabeth. He wouldn't have me."

"Oh, Delia . . ." Elizabeth looked back toward the trading post where Ty and Susannah Marsten stood talking by the big soap pot.

Delia's chin went up. " 'Course no doubt there'll come a day when I'll look back on all this and consider myself lucky things turned out as they did."

"Oh, Delia, I'm sure you're right," Elizabeth said with heartfelt enthusiasm. "He's a good man, but I don't think Dr. Savitch would make a particularly good husband."

Caleb leaned over the bulwarks and called out that it was time to come on board. Elizabeth started cautiously up the gangplank, but Delia lingered on the shore for a moment longer.

Her eyes burned from the tears she had shed the previous night and her throat was raw. There was a cold, hollow feeling in the pit of her stomach and an ache in her chest that she didn't think would ever go away. She hadn't gone back to the trading post last night. She had spent the hours instead huddled beneath the cannon in the burned-out ruins of the old fort, weeping until she thought the weeping would kill her.

Oh, God, Ty, but I love ye so!

But he doesn't love ye, Delia. He'll never love ye.

So why, knowing that, couldn't she stop loving him? *Pride* . . . Oh, she had been so *proud* once of her pride. But what pride was there in loving a man who spurned you? He had thought her a two-shilling girl, and so he had taken her, and she knew she ought to hate him for it, but how could she hate him when she loved him so much?

When she thought of what they had done together, instead of feeling shame, all she could think of was the ecstasy . . . oh, the feel of his hands, his lips, his tongue, the wondrous joy of him loving her. When he had spilled his seed inside her, it had been as if the hand of God had touched her, giving her life. How could you hate a man who made you feel like that?

"Delia . . ."

Delia's heart stopped, then started up again, slamming hard in her chest. Slowly she turned, steeling herself to look into his face without letting her feelings for him show in her own.

His step faltered and then he came on, although he paused when they were still a good two feet apart. He studied her and she knew by his frown that he was noting her swollen lids and reddened eyes. A corner of his mouth twitched with a spasm of regret.

"Good morning, Delia," he said gently, tentatively.

Delia's eyes stung with relief. After all that had passed between them she'd been afraid he wouldn't even want to talk to her. She gave him her brightest smile. "Mornin', Ty."

They stood in silence, looking at each other. Finally, Ty drew in a deep breath and blew it out in a sigh. "I want to apologize again for what I . . . for what happened yesterday. Especially for the things I said—"

"Oh, Ty, I reckon most any man would've reacted the same when faced with a hysterical female throwin' herself at his feet."

"Delia, stop blaming yourself, damn it!" Although he had shouted the words at her, he thrust his fingers through his hair, a gesture she knew he made when he was more upset than angry. "It . . . it just happened, that's all, and—"

"No, Ty. It didn't just happen." Pride kept her head up and the tears at bay. "I'm not ashamed of lovin' ye. But I promise I'll never speak of it again. Nor will I embarrass ye by throwin' myself at ye the way I've been doing. But I would like yer friendship, Ty. I really don't know how I could bear it if I thought we couldn't at least be friends now."

His throat worked, as if he were having a hard time pushing the words out. His eyes moved from her face to the bay at her back. "I would value your friendship, Delia."

Joy filled her. He would still be hers. Not in the way she wanted him, but still a part of him would be hers, and since she couldn't have more, she would make it be enough.

The joy was short-lived.

"You realize there's a very real possibility that you're pregnant," Ty said, his voice now clipped and hard.

Delia was barely able to speak around the clot of emotion in her throat. "N-no . . ." she protested, unwilling to accept the awful possibility that she could be with child.

"Yes," he pursued relentlessly. "And I want your promise that if you discover you are, you will tell me."

"An' would ye marry me then? If I was t' be havin' yer baby?"

He said nothing for the longest moment, then snapped, "I suppose I'll have to, won't I? You might have been willing, but you *were* a virgin."

The lump in her throat was in danger of choking her. He hates it, she thought. He hates the very idea of marrying me.

She started to brush past him, but he stepped in front of her. "I'd like your promise, Delia."

"Well, ye won't be gettin' it," she said, spinning on her heel and walking away from him without a backward glance.

Cap'n Abbott of the coastal schooner *The Sagadahoc Maiden* did not look at all the way Delia imagined a pirate should look. He wore lace at his wrists, his hair fell about his shoulders in long blond locks, and he had a smile charming enough to flutter even the coldest of virginal hearts.

But then Cap'n Abbott wasn't quite a pirate in the strictest sense. Rather he was what folks in The Maine called a *contrebandier,* an intermediary in the profitable but illicit trade with the French settlers in Acadia. Of course, if from time to time *The Sagadahoc Maiden* came upon a lost or wallowing merchant ship, Cap'n Abbott was not above helping to lighten the merchantman's load.

"An act of charity, you see," he had told Delia with a delightfully wicked smile, while openly eyeing her bosom.

The light morning air fluttered the rising sails as they cast off into Casco Bay. The schooner was a smelly, bouncing vessel, but Delia barely noticed, so thrilled was she to be sailing off to the wide horizon—even if the horizon was only up the coast. She loved the sounds, the creak of the rigging and the swish of water at the bow; and the smells, fish and salt and wet canvas; and she loved the feel of the wind whipping through her unbound hair.

Elizabeth Hooker had an entirely different reaction to the rolling waves and the undulating shoreline with its stretches of rocky crags and stands of fir and pine. Caleb had taken one look at his wife's white, sweating face and tightly pressed lips and asked the captain if they might retire to his cabin.

As they sailed across the wide mouth of Casco Bay, Cap'n Abbott pointed out the landmarks to Delia. The bay was filled with hundreds of islands and they all, it seemed, had names. A few were inhabited with old hewn-log or stone houses, and the shore was dotted here and there with fishermen's nets and more flakes for drying cod.

Once, Delia spotted a seal swimming beside them, his sleek body cutting the waves and his head bobbing up and down on the surface. Cap'n Abbott sent one of his sailors to the stores below for some pieces of dried cod. He gave them to Delia, guiding her hand as she cast the fish out over the bulwarks to the seal in the water. Neither of them noticed Ty leaning against the gunwale, his arms folded across his chest, scowling at them. They were too busy laughing together at the seal who had rolled onto its back, flapping its fins and barking its thanks for the treat.

It took most of the day to cross Casco Bay. A large peninsula of towering pines and granite ledges marked the eastern boundary. Around the cape of the peninsula was an estuary, a broad gray channel divided by dark green islands, that stretched for seven miles into the crescent-shaped Merrymeeting Bay.

The setting sun was turning the sails crimson as the waters of the estuary began to broaden around them. Here, dozens of seals frolicked around the ship, but it would have been pointless to toss them dried cod for they were already gorging themselves on schools of salmon and sea bass so tightly packed one could have dipped them up with baskets.

Delia stood at the bulwarks and stared in wonder at the stunning vista that surrounded her. "Oh, but it's beautiful," she said softly to herself.

She felt a movement beside her and thought it was Cap'n Abbott, but when she turned her head she saw that it was Ty. A warm flush crept up her neck and her heartbeat quickened.

"There's a myth," he said, "that somewhere in The Maine there lies a city made of gold. A city called Norumbega. Many have set out to look for it, but it's never been found."

The water was as turquoise and as clear as the sky above it, so that one seemed to be a mirror of the other. Dusky blue hills rose in the distance, but here the land sloped gently to the shore, a thick, rich carpet of dark pines, spruces, cedars, and maples. The beaches were broken up by dozens of inlets, green with wild rice and marsh grasses that rippled in the breeze. Five rivers, including the mighty Kennebec, started high in snow-packed mountains and, fed by hundreds of streams and lakes, flowed down to spill into this beautiful inland sea.

" 'Tis here," Delia whispered. "This is the city of gold." When she turned to Ty again, she caught a look of almost worship on his face.

"Merrymeeting Bay . . ."

He loves it, she thought. He loves this place. And she was glad for him, glad there was a place where he could be so happy. A place he could think of as home.

Ty shook himself slightly as if waking from a dream. "The Abenaki call it the Quinnebequi. It's the same name they give to the river spirit. They believe he dwells within these waters. It's a sacred place."

A cold shiver slithered up Delia's spine. "Is he a friendly spirit, this Quinnebequi?"

"Of course." He smiled and waved his arm in a broad arc, as if drawing all that surrounded them—the bay, the trees, the rivers—unto himself. "Do you think evil could be at home among such beauty? This land here, the Kennebec basin, used to be the fishing and hunting grounds for my peo— for the Norridgewocks."

"Used t' be?"

A spasm of pain crossed Ty's face. "The Yengi live here now."

"But you're . . ."

She had started to say, "But *you're* Yengi. Your blood is English." But she knew that although Ty's blood was all English, within him there had been created two souls, or perhaps it was that his soul had been torn in two. And she suspected that here, at the hunting grounds watched over by the river god Quinnebequi, there dwelled easiest the part of Ty's soul that was Abenaki.

There was a flap of sails as *The Sagadahoc Maiden* came about, heading for the mouth of the Kennebec River, and Delia got her first view of what was to be her new home—the Merrymeeting Settlement.

Her first impression was of a short, broad wharf covered with barrels where tall white pine masts were being winched into the hold of a ship. Overlooking the area was a tidal sawmill for turning logs into timber and planking and, beside the mill, a fine red brick manor house with a gambrel roof.

Delia could catch only glimpses of simple, framed clapboard houses among the thick stands of trees along the shore. To the left, on the high ground, stood a palisaded log blockhouse, two stories tall, with loopholes in the walls and a spy loft in the sodder roof, equipped with an alarm bell. It was a grim reminder that although Merrymeeting might have a mill and a meetinghouse, and though it might call itself a town, it was still an uneasy oasis in the middle of a wild and hostile wilderness.

The Sagadahoc Maiden maneuvered around a string of gundalows tied together stern to bow, then tacked toward an open pier. The Hookers emerged on deck. Delia was glad to see that although her face was still unnaturally pale, much of Elizabeth's seasickness had abated as they approached land.

"Look," Elizabeth said, pointing to the mast landing. "They're expecting us."

Delia narrowed her eyes against the glare of the setting sun. A handful of people stood together on the pier. Most were men and she supposed one of them must be Nathaniel Parkes. One beamy figure in quilted skirts, mobcap ribbons snapping in the breeze, stood at the forefront of the group like the blunted point of an arrow. Sara Kemble.

Beside her she heard Ty swear.

"How do you figure she got here ahead of us?" Caleb asked, a worried frown marring his thin face.

"Her brother-in-law's a fisherman," Ty answered. "She probably made him bring her over last night in his sloop. Damn the gossiping, malicious bitch."

Shame brought a stain of color to Delia's cheekbones and although her chin automatically came up, it quivered a little. All of Merrymeeting now knew that Ty was bringing back with him from Boston a foul-mouthed, slovenly tavern wench to be wife to Nathaniel Parkes and mother to his two girls.

As the passengers from *The Sagadahoc Maiden* debarked, a man and a woman separated themselves from the group and came forward. Delia could tell immediately by the man's dress that he was the local gentry. He wore a fine cloth coat lined with scarlet satin, silver buckles at his knees and shoes, and a high-crowned beaver hat over a light-colored bobwig. His rotund and dimpled face with its patched, florid complexion gave him the strange appearance of a scalded apple.

The gentrified man walked toward them with a swing of outthrust elbows. The woman who accompanied him, Delia took to be his servant, for she was dressed in a spotted bodice with a kerchief beneath, a striped apron, and a heavy wool skirt. Her faded brown hair had been pulled severely off her face and flattened down against the sides of her head before being covered with a white cap. She was so thin her high shoulder bones poked through her bodice and she jerked awkwardly when she moved, as if her joints were held together by twine.

The gentleman spotted Caleb and stuck out his hand while

he was still a good five feet away. "You must be the Reverend Hooker! Welcome. Welcome to Merrymeeting."

Ty performed the introductions while Delia hovered nervously at his side. She scanned the few remaining people for a man who could be Nathaniel Parkes. The gentleman, she heard Ty say, was Colonel Giles Bishop, mast agent and commander of the local militia, and the thin woman Delia had taken for the man's servant was his wife, Anne. Just then Delia spotted a tall, rangy man with hair the color of straw standing within the shadow of the mast house. He was flanked by two little girls. Their eyes met for a moment, then they both looked quickly away.

The man took the girls by the hand and started toward her.

Ty slipped his arm around Delia, casually caressing her waist as he drew her forward. It was the first time he had touched her since they had made love. The shock of his palm, warm and hard, pressing against her back caused Delia to stumble and her breath to catch in her throat.

Ty mistook Delia's reaction for fear and gave her a gentle squeeze. "Nat's a fair man," he said, keeping his voice low even though the Hookers and the Bishops had slipped into an animated conversation about mutual acquaintances in Boston. "He won't have judged you before he meets you."

But Delia thought Sara Kemble must have given Nat an earful, for he wore a worried frown as he approached them, and he looked at Ty with a question in his eyes.

Ty pulled Delia in front of him, his hands clasping her arms. She wished he wouldn't touch her like that. Somehow she didn't think it right to be greeting her future husband while her heart beat wildly for another man.

"Nat, this is Delia McQuaid of Boston," Ty said, trying to reassure all concerned with his dazzling smile.

Delia met the man's assessing gray eyes squarely. He was dressed simply, in drab homespun breeches, a jersey coat with no cravat, and an old felt hat cocked up in back. He was as tall as Ty, perhaps even a little taller. But whereas Ty's body was all muscular leanness, Nat's was thin and rawboned, with big hands and feet, giving him an awkward look. His face could by no stretch be called handsome, for his ears stuck out from the sides of his head like the handles of a butter crock and his nose was flat and slightly crooked. He had a wide, loose mouth with creases at the corners that gave the impression he had once smiled a lot, although he wasn't smiling now.

At last Ty's hands left her arms and she realized he had turned back to rejoin the Hookers, giving her and Nat some privacy.

"I'm the one who answered yer advertisement for a wife," Delia stated, breaking the silence between them.

Nathaniel Parkes nodded sharply, then cleared his throat. "It was good of you to take pity on my situation."

"It wasn't yer situation I took pity on, Mr. Parkes. 'Twas my own."

Nat blinked in surprise. He started to smile, but thought better of it, giving her another nod instead. "Well then, it seems we have come to each other's mutual rescue." He looked down at a young girl of about nine who clung to his right arm. "This is my elder daughter, Margaret. We call her Meg."

"Hello, Meg." Delia smiled at the girl. Meg's little pointed chin jerked up into the air and she scowled ferociously back at Delia, as if challenging Delia to find anything the least bit lovable about her. Delia responded to the challenge, loving her instantly.

How like her I was at that age, Delia thought. Awkward and gangly with limp, dark hair twisted into braids that curved out like commas from her thin face. She was outgrowing her clothes so fast that a good portion of her skinny, scratched, and bitten legs stuck out from beneath the hem of her petticoat. Delia could guess exactly what Meg was thinking: *She won't like me, so I'll get even right off by not liking her.*

"And this is my baby, Tildy," Nat said, pride coloring his voice. Tildy truly was adorable, a chubby toddler with a head of curly blond hair and dimpled cheeks. She wore a pinner over her petticoat and hanging sleeves—extra sleeves that hung down the back to assist a child in learning how to walk and were usually worn by custom until the age of six.

"I'm three and a half," Tildy stated.

"My, three years old!" Delia exclaimed.

"And a half!"

Delia laughed. "And a half even."

Tildy clutched in her arms a cornhusk doll that was tied with vines and dyed with berry juice. She held it up for Delia's inspection.

Delia knelt before the little girl and took the doll's tiny straw hand. "An' who is this?"

"Her name's Gretchen," Tildy announced proudly.

"How d' ye do, Gretchen. What a fine an' pretty lady ye are."

Tildy laughed with delight and looked up at her father. "She likes Gretchen."

"Indeed she does," Nat said. He had a solemn and deliberate way of speaking that Delia found disconcerting.

Tildy turned back to Delia, two round dimples the size of shillings indenting her fat cheeks. "Are you going to be our new ma?"

"She can't!" Meg put in harshly. "Even if Papa does marry her, it doesn't mean she's going to be our ma. Not just because our real ma died!"

"Meg—" Nat began, but Delia interrupted him before he could scold the girl.

"Of course I won't be takin' the place of yer ma," Delia said matter-of-factly as she stood up. She didn't smile, although she did look carefully down into the girl's worried dark brown eyes. "I'll be yer da's new wife an' that's a different thing altogether, isn't it?"

The girl said nothing and the hostility remained on her face. She'll not be won over easily, Delia thought, and loved her all the more for that stubborn pride.

"You'll be staying with the Bishops for the time being," Nat said. "I'll see you settled there." He looked around the pier. "Where are your things?"

Delia realized she had left her grist sack with its pathetic contents on board *The Sagadahoc Maiden*. Perhaps Ty would see it was brought to her later, but even if he didn't the few rags it contained would hardly suit her now. Of course there was the mare he had bought her. But that she would insist he have back.

So she gave Nat a brilliant smile, holding her hands out from her sides. "I come as ye see me, Mr. Parkes."

Delia's smile slowly faded as he stared at her, a faint mark of disapproval on his face. Evidently what he saw didn't please him in the least.

"I suppose you'd better call me Nat," he finally said.

"Nat," Delia repeated obediently, her voice throaty and pitched low with nervousness.

Nat continued to stare at her, a crease deepening between his brows, until Delia had to stiffen her muscles to keep from squirming. Finally he released a sigh. "Well . . . the Bishop place is this way."

They began to stroll slowly down the wharf toward the brick manor house, the two girls between them. They crossed in front of the lumber works. Walking this close to him, Delia realized Nathaniel Parkes moved stiffly and with a definite limp. He wore large heavy leather sea boots that flapped against his calves and thudded unevenly on the wooden wharf.

In spite of Nat Parkes's less than enthusiastic welcome, Delia's blood began to sing with excitement as she looked around her. This was going to be a new beginning for her, a new life, and she couldn't have picked a more beautiful place.

The air was filled with the fragrance of freshly cut pine and cedar mixed with the more pungent aromas of fish, tar, and sea slime. On the hills in the distance, the spruce and fir looked black and soldierly among the tall and slender white pines. The setting sun gilded the surface of the bay and river waters. From the lumber yard came the steady thunk of someone riving clapboards.

They passed a couple of men working a piece of timber, who paused to stare openly at Delia. They waved and called out to Nat. One of the men was squaring the timber with a broadax while another followed behind, dressing it with an adz.

Meg pointed to the man with the adz, but her relentless brown gaze was fastened on Delia. "That's how our papa lost his foot. Doing that."

Delia glanced at Nat with surprise, for although she had noticed his limp, she hadn't thought it possible for a man to walk with only one foot. "Ye've only got the one foot?"

His eyes shifted away from hers. "Didn't Ty tell you? I used to work from time to time at the yard here, whenever my Mary—'' He stopped, coloring slightly. "Whenever we needed a little extra something around the house. It happened a year ago last March. Just a year before my Mary . . .''

His voice dwindled and Delia suspected he had been about to say the accident had occurred a year before his wife died. Obviously, he still missed her so deeply he couldn't bear to mention her name, and Delia wondered if perhaps it was a mistake for Nat to be taking a new wife so soon. But then she looked down at Meg's thin, pinched face and she understood.

"The adz slipped," Nat went on, "and I cut across the tops of my toes. The wound putrefied and Ty said the foot had to come off. But Obadiah Kemble, he's the joiner here in Merrymeeting, he carved me a new foot out of walnut. You needn't worry that I won't be able to provide for a wife," he finished stiffly. "I still work my timberland and farm as good as most."

"Lord above us, ye've got yersel' a foot made of wood!" Delia exclaimed. "Can I see it?"

Nat looked appalled at the very idea and Delia cursed her flapping tongue. Nat Parkes wasn't taking much of a liking to her as it was and if she weren't careful she'd find herself back on *The Sagadahoc Maiden* and on her way to Boston before her dust could settle here.

"I hardly think it would be appropriate—'' Nat began, but he was interrupted by Meg tugging on his sleeve.

"Show her, Papa."

"Show her, Papa," Tildy parroted.

Nat absently rubbed his nose and for the briefest moment the creases alongside his mouth deepened into a smile as he studied his daughters' upturned, eager faces. "Well, I suppose I could . . .''

"Oh, no, please," Delia protested, thoroughly embarrassed now.

But Nat had limped over to drop down onto a keg of nails beneath the eaves of the mast house. He kicked off his big boot, peeled off his home-knitted stocking, and thrust out his leg before Delia. Suddenly, he smiled at her, a full, genuine smile, and Delia got a glimpse of the man he had been before tragedy had blighted his life.

"See there, he's got a wooden foot," Meg stated, giving Delia a hard, assessing look, obviously hoping Delia would shrink from her father in horror.

Curious in spite of herself, Delia leaned over to get a better look at the appendage. It was a wonderful replica of a foot, even down to the five individually carved toes. A hinge had been put at the joint so that it could bend almost as good as a real ankle. It looked so real in fact that Delia almost touched it, as if to reassure herself it was wood, not flesh.

"Oh, Nat, it's marvel—"

"Really, Nathaniel Parkes, you ought to be ashamed!"

Delia jerked upright and whirled to face a huffing Sara Kemble, who had fists on her ample hips and fire in her squinting eyes. Delia hadn't realized it, but the Hookers, the Bishops, and Ty had been walking behind them. Now they, along with Sara Kemble and her perpetual shadow, Mr. Kemble, had all stopped at the sight of Nathaniel Parkes taking off boot and stocking in public to show his wife-to-be his wooden foot.

Delia smiled at Obadiah, ignoring Sara Kemble, which wasn't easy as the woman seemed to be looming over her, breathing fire like a dragon.

"Mr. Kemble, Nat's been showin' me the foot ye made for him," Delia called out. "I don't know when I've seen a finer piece of workmanship."

Sara Kemble puffed a loud harrumph from her fat cheeks. "Mr. Kemble is a joiner, the *only* joiner east of Wells. He had no call to be wasting his skills on such outlandish—"

"I 'spect most any man can come t' make a table or a chair," Delia said. "But I didn't think no one but God could make a foot."

"Did you hear that?" Sara Kemble flung her arm out to the Reverend Hooker, who jumped in alarm, causing Elizabeth to stifle a giggle with her hand. Sara pointed a quivering sausage-shaped finger at Delia. "Did you hear the blasphemous words this creature just uttered?"

"Shut up, Sara," Obadiah said in his mild-mannered voice.

Sara Kemble's mouth fell open, then she drew herself up to her formidable height. "Just who do you—"

"Your husband, that's who. And if I say shut up, then, by golly, you'll shut up!"

Sara's massive jaw snapped closed and she ground her teeth, reminding Delia of a cow chewing its cud. Then she whirled on her heel and stomped back down the wharf, shaking the pilings. Obadiah followed, but not before grinning and winking at Delia.

Delia met Ty's eyes, which were brimming with amusement, and a big smile crossed her face. "Mr. Kemble's gone an' put his foot down. Lord above us, who'd have ever thought it!"

Ty started to laugh and then his eyes focused behind her and the laughter vanished from his face. She turned to find Nathaniel Parkes glowering at her from his perch on the keg of nails. Tildy stood between his spread knees and Meg leaned alongside of him, her hand resting on his arm, a look of triumph blazing from her face.

Furious color suffused Delia's cheeks and she lowered her head, twisting her hands in her petticoat. *Ye wooden-headed fool. Ye're not at the place above ten minutes afore ye're mortifying the poor man who's now stuck with ye for a wife.*

A broad shadow fell over her and a long, brown hand landed lightly on her arm, pulling her around. Slowly her head came up. Their eyes met and held.

A lazy smile lifted the corners of Tyler Savitch's mouth. "Welcome to Merrymeeting, Delia-girl."

Chapter 12

"We were raided by timber pirates while you were gone, Ty," Colonel Bishop said, setting down his soup spoon and wiping his mouth on the white table napkin he had tied around his neck. "A gang of about fifty came down in sloops from Boston. They cut and made off with some of our best trees."

"We sure could have used that sharp-shooting flintlock of yours, Doc," Anne Bishop added. She had a tart voice, like vinegar, which seemed to go with her angular face. But the smile she gave Ty revealed her fondness for him. "Rifle shot and a couple of your blood-curdling Abenaki war whoops would've scared them off plenty quick."

Ty mumbled something about maybe next time. Delia could feel his eyes on her, and she knew that familiar scowl was meant for her as well. She glanced around the table at the other diners and her eyes met those of Nathaniel Parkes, who regarded her with a puzzled expression, as if he couldn't quite remember the reason for her being there. The dim candlelight etched the lines of grief deeper into his face, and his gray eyes were dull with sadness. Delia knew instinctively he was comparing her to his dead wife and finding her lacking.

For propriety's sake, Delia was to stay with the Bishops until the banns were posted and the wedding could take place. This first supper at Merrymeeting was supposed to be a festive occasion. The Hookers had been invited, and Nat of course. But his daughters had been banished to eat in the kitchen with the servants. Delia thought that if the girls had

173

been at the table, her own lack of sophistication wouldn't
have been so obvious and Ty wouldn't be scowling at her.

Repressing a nervous sigh, she looked down at the delftware bowl of creamed pumpkin soup. Taking a deep breath,
she picked up the pewter spoon. *Now don't ye dare spill
none, an' don't ye start slurpin' it up like a half-starved
hound,* she admonished herself, which made her so nervous
she immediately set the spoon down again.

The soup looked delicious and she was famished, but Delia
was terrified of making some terrible blunder, as she had
done that first morning with Ty when he had accused her of
having the manners of a pig. It seemed there were hundreds
of rules that were part and parcel of the proper deportment
of a real lady, and she despaired of ever mastering them all.
She could feel Nat Parkes's eyes solemnly watching her every
move. She wanted so badly for him to like her. Lord above
us, if she were to marry the man, he at least should *like* her.

Delia had never eaten off delftware or pewter before. Nor
had she known the luxury of a separate dining room even
existed; she'd always taken her meals in a kitchen or a taproom or bought them off a vendor in the street. The Bishops'
dining room was furnished with a fine black cherry table and
delicate chairs that seemed to creak every time anyone shifted
a muscle. The room smelled cloyingly of dried violets and
snuff, which wafted in thick clouds from the person of Colonel Bishop.

Aware suddenly of the overpowering smell of the snuff,
Delia felt an irresistible urge to sneeze. The harder she fought
it, the more imminent the sneeze became, until it exploded
out of her, sounding louder than the discharge of a cannon.

Blushing furiously, Delia covered the lower half of her face
with her napkin. "I-I'm sorry," she mumbled. Never had
she felt more bitterly ashamed. No wonder neither Ty nor
Nat wanted to marry her; *she* wouldn't want to be married
to her disgusting, ill-mannered, boorish self.

"It's the snuff," Anne Bishop stated. "Really, Giles, you
should be more considerate."

The colonel's heavy-jowled face deepened a shade. "Yes,
of course. My apologies, Mistress McQuaid."

Delia stole a look at Ty, expecting a scowl, but instead

caught the glint of laughter in his eyes. He gave her a sudden, blinding smile. Thoroughly confused, Delia looked away.

Ty had never appeared more handsome than he did this night, and the sight of him brought a poignant ache to her chest. He had disappeared for a while and returned wearing different clothes—a coat with stiffened, buttoned-back cuffs and a pinched waist that showed off his splendid physique. Beneath the coat was a velvet waistcoat, and the snowy gorget around his neck set off his dark skin and the vivid hue of his eyes. On his head he had worn a gray hat decorated with an indigo-blue ribbon that matched those eyes.

In fact, everyone except Delia had dressed for dinner. Elizabeth Hooker had added a white kerchief to her usual black dress, enhancing her pale, ephemeral beauty. The reverend had acquired a daring touch of color with his clover-green drugget coat. Even Anne Bishop had changed out of her spotted bodice into a violet silk polonaise gown, although the color did little to enliven her sallow complexion.

While everyone else spooned their soup and talked about timber pirates and lumbering, Delia took the opportunity to study the colonel's wife. In her late forties, she seemed older than her husband, weathered and twisted, as if her life had been much harder than the relative luxury of the manor house would suggest. There seemed to be an aura of sadness around her, almost of deep misery, yet there had been an underlying kindness in the few words she had spoken thus far to Delia. Delia noticed a large death's-head mourning ring on the woman's right hand, which was thin and bony with swollen knuckles. Perhaps the reason for the ring explained the sadness.

"I noticed all those masts on the wharf were marked with an arrow shaped like a crow's foot," the Reverend Hooker said, as a servant passed around a voider and the soup plates were cleared from the table. "Does the mark have some special meaning?"

"The King claims all masts measuring over two feet in diameter for the use of his Royal Navy," the colonel explained. "As mast agent I'm supposed to see that white pine trunks of this size are carved with the King's mark, the 'broad arrow,' thus reserving them for the King's use." He smiled wistfully. "I'm afraid that makes me unpopular with some folk around here."

Anne Bishop made a sharp, grunting noise. "That's because most folk can get a better price for their masts in Lisbon or Cadiz than they can from the King. I'm afraid you'll find we're not all loyal, law-abiding subjects here in Merrymeeting."

"Now, I wonder why that doesn't surprise me," Caleb said.

Everyone laughed and Delia began to relax. Colonel Bishop went on to explain how the King's masts had to be perfect, not broken or warped, while the servant set before them plates filled with thick slabs of roast pork, steamed cabbage, and slices of pone slathered with apple butter. Beside the plate the servant placed an eating knife and something in an open leather case that Delia had never seen before.

Actually, she had seen something *like* it before—a cooking tool with a large handle and two large tines called a fork, which was used to hold down a roast while it was being carved. But this fork was small, the width and length of an eating spoon. It had a bone handle and three slender metal tines.

Delia's stomach rumbled with hunger, but she dreaded having to eat with this strange implement. She watched Ty from beneath lowered lids. He held the meat down with the tines, sliced off a piece, then lifted the food to his mouth. Delia watched him do it a few times before she tried it herself.

To her delight, she actually managed it without doing something embarrassing such as missing her mouth or dropping the food on her lap. But she looked askance at this newfangled eating ware. It seemed a lot of bother; she would rather have used her fingers.

Still, she had done it! She was sitting in a real dining room, eating at a fine table, not off a plank board. She was using a fork, or whatever the newfangled thing was called, eating off delftware and drinking from a pewter cup. She had done it.

So ye grew up in a shack on the Boston waterfront. Ye had a drunk for a da an' ye worked in a grog shop since ye was fourteen. But that don't mean ye can't change. Ye've never been so stupid that ye couldn't learn better. So's there's no reason why ye can't learn to dress genteely and muzzle yer flapping tongue. To act like a real lady's supposed to act.

She looked up and met Ty's eyes. He was scowling at her again and her chin jutted up. *I might not be good enough for yer company now, Tyler Savitch, but one day I will be. Just ye watch an' see.*

One day Tyler Savitch would look at her and she would see admiration reflected in those dusky blue eyes.

Admiration, and regret.

Later that night, Ty and the Hookers left the manor house together. Ty walked them back to the parsonage, leading his pacer, his rifle resting against his shoulder, one hand wrapped around the stock to hold it in place.

In the dark the encroaching forest seemed menacing to Caleb, full of barely fathomable dangers. He kept expecting to see glowing red eyes, to hear the sudden whoop of an Indian war cry. He glanced at his wife, at her tense mouth that was a tight slash in the pale oval of her face, and knew she felt it even more keenly than he did: the lurking danger lying beneath the beauty that was Merrymeeting.

They stopped in front of the new parsonage. "Stay a moment," Caleb said to Ty. "I'd like a word."

Ty looped the pacer's reins loosely around the porch rail as Elizabeth disappeared inside, taking the whale-oil lantern with her. They could see her shadow moving across the sashed windows before she pulled the shutters closed, leaving the two men alone with the sound of the crickets for company and only a pale light of a waning moon to reveal their faces.

"I must admit I'm a mite disappointed," Caleb said.

"What disappoints you? Doesn't the missus like the house?"

Caleb took off his hat and ran his hand through his light brown hair. He flashed his crooked-toothed smile. "Oh, the parsonage is fine and soon as Lizzie gets all her doodads arranged just the way she likes, it's going to seem as if we've lived here our entire lives." And the windows all have shutters, Caleb thought irrelevantly, so she can shut out the wilderness and the town that she's already made up her mind to hate, shut out everything, including me, and spin and spin and spin . . .

Caleb's throat closed around a sigh. He wondered sometimes how he could expect to minister to others when he couldn't help Elizabeth, or himself.

"No, it's just that during those long nights of studying at Harvard," Caleb said, "whenever I sat back and pictured my first ministry, the meetinghouse always had a tall steeple. With a weathercock."

Ty looked at the silhouette of the squat raw clapboard meetinghouse next door. "No steeple," he agreed.

"I suppose that should be a lesson to me," Caleb went on carefully, "not to attach too much importance to wishful dreams."

"There's nothing wrong with dreams," Ty said, but he didn't sound as if he truly believed it.

Caleb let the silence between them grow. He and Tyler Savitch had shared some long conversations on the journey to Merrymeeting and, if asked, he would have said they'd become fast friends for all that Ty was a difficult man to get to know. But Caleb was finding it hard to broach the subject he wanted to discuss.

He decided to try a direct approach. "Are you sure you should allow Nathaniel Parkes to marry Delia?"

"Nat should consider himself lucky to be getting Delia!" Ty snapped, letting Caleb feel the bite of his quick temper. "She's going to make him a fine wife."

"You misunderstand. I think Delia would make *any* man a fine wife. But especially you, because anyone can see that she loves you so very much . . . and I suspect you love her," he added after Ty said nothing.

"I don't love her, damn it all! Just because I—" Ty kicked at the step with the heel of his boot. "Hell, Caleb, I don't know what the emotion means, what it is I'm supposed to feel. Maybe I'm just plain not capable of feeling love."

"Oh, I think you're capable of it, and more so than most men. That's why you're fighting it so hard. Perhaps you feel love weakens you, or makes you vulnerable to pain—"

"Bullshit."

"Fine. Be mulish and pig-headed and stubborn!" Caleb shouted, waving his arms, his own temper rising now, along with his voice. "But remember this. Once she marries Mr. Parkes, Delia is lost to you. Forever."

There. He'd gotten out what he wanted to say. But would Ty take his warning to heart?

Balling his hands into fists, Ty stuffed them in his coat pockets. He had stepped down off the stoop, turning his back, but now he spun around again.

The moonlight cast harsh shadows on the sharp bones of his face. "What would you have me do, Reverend? Offer to marry Delia in Nat's stead on the off chance that I might be in love with her and not know it? Christ, I'm so damn confused at this point it's lucky I remember how to put my breeches on in the morning, let alone distinguish the fine line between lust and love." His lips twisted into a bitter smile. "I can hardly take her as my mistress while I decide which it is, can I? I doubt you would approve. And knowing Delia, she'd slap my face for even suggesting it."

"Yes. I can see your point," Caleb said, feeling sad for them. For himself. "But love—gentle, shining, spiritual love—it comes so rarely between a man and a woman and if—"

Ty barked a laugh, flinging his arms out from his sides. "I want to swive the wench, not marry her! What the hell is spiritual about that?"

Caleb swallowed hard and looked away.

Ty took a step forward. "I'm sorry, Caleb. I didn't mean to offend you."

"I've heard the word before." His mouth quirked into a tiny smile. "Even used it once or twice myself. I might be a man of God, Ty, but I'm still a man."

Elizabeth . . . Caleb thought. Always, always, there was the fear and the disgust on her face on the nights when his physical appetite couldn't be staved off, when he took her, knowing how she hated it. In which of them was the love lacking? *A man, a man, I'm only a man* . . .

He turned and looked at Ty. There was a genuine pain on the young doctor's face and Caleb knew it reflected his own expression.

"I am sorry," Ty said again.

"No, no. I shouldn't have brought it up."

"Has Delia said some—"

"No, nothing. It's just that with Delia her emotions are so transparent—happiness, anger . . . anguish. You can't miss what she's feeling."

A corner of Ty's mouth twisted downward. "She's better off with Nat."

"Yes. I expect you're right."

Ty left the reverend standing on the front stoop of his new parsonage. He rode past the mast house and lumber works, the grist mill and blacksmith forge, the handful of houses and businesses that made up the tiny settlement of Merrymeeting. He rode along the Kennebec River toward the welcoming solitude of his cabin isolated deep in the Sagadahoc woods.

He thought about the nature of love.

He didn't love Delia. At least not if you went by the Reverend Hooker's definition because there sure as hell was nothing gentle or spiritual about the way his manhood would thicken and harden at the mere sight of her, or the way the sound of that damn husky voice of hers could send the blood rushing hot through his veins and make the sweat start out on his face. That was lust, not love, and he should have had the sense not to tangle with her in the first place. Either that, or he should have gotten her into his bed sooner. Then he might have been able to assuage his lust. As it was . . .

All right, he still wanted her. He could admit that. But there was no reason to go upsetting the berry basket just because he had an itch between his legs that still needed satisfying. Delia would marry Nathaniel Parkes. Nat was a fine man; he would be good to her, provide for her, and she would be happy. And Dr. Tyler Savitch would remain free—

Free to do what? a niggling voice asked him.

But Ty ignored it.

Delia stood on the wharf within the black shadows cast by stacks of lumber and masts, and looked at the inky waters of the Merrymeeting Bay. Pale moonlight gave the smooth surface a silvery sheen, as though it were a looking glass. No breeze rippled the water or stirred the pine boughs, and the heavy air smelled of wet grass and salt.

She tilted her head back. The sky was a shade blacker than the bay, and the stars were so close they seemed to dance on the air, twinkling like cinders. But although the sight before her was beautiful, a wave of misery engulfed her and heavy tears built up to clog the back of her throat. For a moment she couldn't understand where this lonely sadness came from and then she realized . . . Ty was gone.

He had left with the Hookers, walking with them to the new parsonage. Delia had stood at the door watching him go. He had even smiled at her and said, "Good night, brat." She had felt a warm happiness at the smile and the familiar teasing tone of his words. But now, standing seemingly on the edge of the world, she felt so alone. It could be days before she saw him again, and although she knew she was going to have to make herself get used now to a life with only occasional glimpses of him, she wondered how it would ever be possible.

He would probably go out of his way to avoid her. Although this morning they had spoken of being friends, there was a tension when they were together now, so palpable it was as if a bow string had been drawn tautly between them. The strain came not from her side but from his. For all his pretensions at being a rakehell, he was not the sort of man to feel pleasure at seducing a virgin. Every time their eyes met she saw his shame and guilt over what had happened yesterday in the Falmouth Neck woods. Which in turn made him angry with her for making *him* feel so miserable.

Delia smiled sadly to herself in the darkness. Beneath that gruff, temperamental exterior of his, there beat a soft heart that Tyler Savitch worked very hard at hiding, even from himself. She had lost her virginity, but Ty was the one experiencing the regrets.

She heard a footstep behind her, creaking on the wooden boards and, because she had been thinking of him, she whirled around, expectation lighting her face—

"You should be in bed," Anne Bishop said, in a voice as tart as lemon juice. "The sun comes up early here in The

Maine. Do you have everything you need?'' she added as Delia took a step forward to meet her.

"Oh, aye. 'Tis a lovely room ye've given me.''

For the first time in her life Delia was to sleep in her own room, in a four-poster bed with a feather mattress. The room even had an oak chest-of-drawers to put her clothes in, although she had no clothes except the ones on her back. She had her own fireplace, with a chair and a crocheted rug on the floor in front of it. As a little girl she had often imagined such a room. It seemed so strange to find it in this wilderness outpost.

Anne touched Delia's arm. "Come along, girl. The mosquitoes are feeding tonight. They'll soon be thicker than fiddlers at a fair.'' And, indeed, just then Delia felt the sharp sting as one bit into her neck. She slapped it.

Anne snorted. "What did I tell you? They'll suck you dry, will Maine mosquitoes.''

They walked toward the manor house. A veranda fronted the side that faced the bay. The benches that flanked the open door were hulking shapes in the darkness, but light shone from the windows upstairs. It was a comforting sight, Delia thought, the yellow glow of lamplight shining through a window that was home. Of course the Bishops' manor house was not home to her, merely a way station on her quest for a new home of her own. When she married Nathaniel Parkes, she would have a house, land, children. A man. But when she closed her eyes to picture this idyllic scene, it wasn't Nat Parkes she saw standing at her side.

They stepped from the veranda into the long hall that divided the house. The wooden floor was painted an odd black and white diamond pattern that made Delia dizzy if she stared at it too long. A staircase with spiral balusters of oak led to the rooms upstairs. Delia started to mount the stairs, but she paused with her hand on the newel post. Flickering candlelight spilled from an open doorway and Delia caught a glimpse of a carved recessed china cabinet. But what was strange about it was that, instead of kitchenware, books and folios were crammed together on the shelves.

Intrigued, Delia stepped off the stairs and went into the room, not thinking that she should have waited to be invited.

"It's a second parlor, but I call it my library to give myself airs," Anne Bishop said, following behind her.

"My!" Delia exclaimed. She ran her hand reverently across the spines of the books. "Do all these belong t' the colonel then? He must be an educated man. Like T—" She caught his name on the tip of her tongue and changed it at the last moment. "Like Dr. Savitch. D' ye know he went t' Edinburgh University? It's where he learned so much—all those fancy words and how to dress like a gentleman and be a physician."

Anne emitted one of her characteristic snorts. "Now when it comes to putting on airs, that Tyler Savitch has got me beat. That man is gorgeous enough to break the heart of a grindstone and he knows it. He can act worse than a turkey cock at times too, strutting about with his feather ruffs all fanned out and expecting the overwhelmed females within miles to throw themselves at his feet." She snorted again. "Which they all do, myself included."

Delia laughed at Anne's description of Ty. He *was* like that at times.

"As for my Giles," Anne went on, "he would rather spend his leisure slogging about the marshes and seeing how many ducks and geese he can slaughter in one day . . . No, these books are mine."

Delia looked at her in surprise. "Ye've read these? All of them?"

"I have. Many several times over, although it galls Giles when he catches me at it for he feels it's a waste of a woman's time. Most men, I vow, would have it that a woman with book knowledge is about as useful as last year's crow's nest."

"My da's the same. He's always a-tellin' me women are of little use t' a man outside the kitchen and the bed—" Delia stopped, appalled that she had said such a thing. A real lady would never have alluded to the intimacy that went on between a husband and wife. When, oh when, was she going to learn to think before speaking?

But Anne Bishop didn't appear offended. Instead she broke into an odd-sounding cackle that Delia supposed was meant to be a laugh. "If a man can be ruled though, Delia, then that's where it's done—either the kitchen or the bedroom.

And most often I swear it's the kitchen. My mother's cooking could put whiskers on a man's feet and the result was she never had to take a lick of sass from my father. But then, you'll find all this out soon enough once you're married, if you haven't got it figured already. The kitchen and the bedroom. That's our kingdom.''

She patted Delia on the shoulder as if she were a child and for the briefest moment a smile stretched her thin lips. ''Now you must get yourself on up to bed, girl. You mark if your Nat isn't here first thing in the morning, wanting to drag you out and show you that farm of his that he's so button-busting proud of.''

My Nat . . . Delia thought.

Again Anne Bishop smiled at her. But although Delia tried hard, she just couldn't dredge up a smile in return.

Chapter 13

Nathaniel Parkes twisted the broad brim of his felt hat in his hands. "I thought you might want to ride out this morning and see the farm," he said to Delia, although he aimed the words at his feet.

Delia felt a moment of panic—what if Ty were to come while she was gone? But that was ridiculous. Ty probably had no reason to visit the Bishops, having just spent several hours last evening in their company. And the last thing he'd do would be to stop by especially to see her.

Ashamed of herself and her useless yearnings, she gave Nat a smile so bright that he blinked. "That would be real fine, Nat."

She followed Nat out to his cart where it stood in the yard. The mare, who had been drowsing in the shafts, woke up with a snort as Nat helped Delia into the seat. She felt the strength of his fingers clasping her arm and waited for the shiver that would have come if it had been Ty touching her even in so casual a manner, but she felt nothing.

As if to make up for it, she gave Nat another big smile as he climbed up beside her.

The settlement of Merrymeeting was arranged in the shape of a horseshoe, with the new meetinghouse and the blockhouse at either end, and the wharf and lumber works fronting the bay. In the center was a village green that was truly green, covered with marsh grass, wild rice, and clumps of rosemary and hawkweed. A lone white pine had been left in the middle of the green, and on top of it perched a weathervane. Anne Bishop had told Delia, with the hint of a smile crinkling her eyes, that the first thing a body did on waking every morning in Merrymeeting was to look outside and see which way the wind was blowing.

Right now a mild, damp breeze came in directly off the water. It plucked at the tendrils of Delia's hair, pulling them from beneath the blue and white calico bonnet Ty had bought for her and then claimed to hate. She hoped he would see her riding with Nathaniel Parkes on the cart, see her wearing the bonnet he hated. While Nat drove in silence, Delia searched in vain for a glimpse of dark hair and a sharp-boned face.

Nat guided the cart along the rutted road that ran along the edge of the village, following the curve of the riverbank. Smudge from the blacksmith forge drifted into the air and Delia could hear the clatter of the wheel rackets in the nearby gristmill. A couple of young boys were sweeping up sawdust and shavings from among the stacks of lumber products outside the mast house. The wharf was loaded with pine boards, oak timber, hogshead staves and, of course, the King's masts.

The main part of Merrymeeting was soon past them. The cart rattled over a corduroy road made of logs laid crosswise, so necessary during the Sagadahoc's wet and muddy springs. Myriad brooks, creeks, and ponds all drained into Merrymeeting Bay and were forded by a succession of crude bridges, nothing more than tree trunks laid together across the roadbed. Before long the road had dwindled to mere cart tracks between the farms. Here and there a clapboard house could be spotted in a clearing among the trees. Delia wondered what sort of a dwelling Ty lived in, and if he would always want to live in it alone.

"Does one of these houses belong t' Dr. Savitch?" she finally asked, unable to stop herself.

"No, Dr. Ty's cabin is much farther up river. Out beyond my place." He fixed solemn gray eyes onto her face. "Tyler Savitch is about as independent as a hog on ice. Like most folks in The Maine, he likes his privacy. You'd do well to remember that if you're going to live out here among us."

"I will." Stung by the reprimand, unsure of what she had done to deserve it or what he meant by it, Delia fell silent. At last Nat turned the cart away from the river and they bounced over deep ruts for a few hundred yards, winding through the dense forest of spruce, fir, pine, and maple. Then he hauled on the reins. Suddenly it was so quiet Delia could hear the drum of a cock grouse and the click of grasshoppers.

"Here it is," Nat said unnecessarily. She could feel his eyes on her, gauging her reaction.

The house stood in an unshaded clearing, surrounded on three sides by hilled rows of Indian corn. It faced the river, and although she couldn't see the water through the trees, she could hear it—a faint rushing sound like wind whipping through tall grass. The house was made of riven clapboards, one story but with a high sleeping loft. A pair of dormer windows poked out a cedar-shingled roof that had a steep pitch to it to shake off the snow. In front lay the kitchen garden and farther away a small apple orchard. The barn had been built into the gentle slope of a hill and far enough away from the house not to be endangered by sparks from the chimney. A woodshed and smokehouse were connected to the house by way of the linter.

Delia gave Nat a bright smile. "I don't claim t' be an expert, but we passed a good lot of farms 'tween here an' Boston and this is the finest I've ever seen."

She thought he would be pleased by the compliment, which was heartfelt, but his tightly drawn mouth didn't relax a bit. "It requires a good lot of hard work to keep it up," he said curtly, and Delia knew it was meant as a warning—she was not to expect life here to be easy.

"I told Dr. Savitch when I answered his advert that I wasn't afraid of workin' hard."

"But then that depends," he said, pinning her with his eyes, "on what you consider working hard."

Delia could feel the heat rise on her cheeks. Nat noted her embarrassment and looked away, nodding as if it confirmed his worse suspicions of her.

"Nat, whatever Sara Kemble told ye about me, I want ye t' know—"

"Later. We'll discuss it later. The girls are waiting for us inside. Meg's fixed us dinner. That is, if you're agreeable to staying."

Delia gave him a subdued smile. "Why, dinner would be nice, Nat. Thank ye."

Nat helped Delia down from the cart and led her toward the house. She held back a moment to look around her again. It truly was a beautiful farm. I could be happy here, she decided. If only, if only . . . But she wouldn't think of that.

Beyond the cleared acreage, in the widening circle, was an expanse of deadened, girdled trees, and among the trees had also been planted corn and beans and pumpkins in the Indian fashion. The corn stalks served as bean poles and gave shade to the pumpkin and squash vines.

"The soil is fertile," Nat said, "but it's the devil to harrow and plow because of the rocks. I swear, they mate and breed over winter, under the snowfall."

The tinkle of a bell caught Delia's attention. "Oh, look," she cried, clapping her hands with delight. "Ye've got a billy goat!"

Nat managed a laugh at that. It was the first laugh she had heard from him and she liked the sound of it, warm and soft, billowing out of his chest like a pan of dough.

"I can see you don't know much about livestock," he said. "That's a she-goat." The goat was tied to a stake within munching distance of the corn shocks stacked against the side of the barn. "She's a fine provider of milk and cheese, but when she gets loose in the garden it looks like a plague of locusts passed through. My wife . . . that is, M-Mary got so mad one time she threatened to make a stew out of that old goat . . ."

Nat's voice trailed off and he looked away. Delia stood in silence, waiting until he had collected himself.

When he turned back to her, all traces of his earlier laughter had faded and his face was etched again with pain. "I'm pleased you like the place, Delia."

"Oh, I do, Nat. Truly I do." She had put all the enthusiasm she could muster into her voice, hoping to wipe away some of the sadness in Nat's eyes. But the sadness remained.

Nat stepped aside and pushed the door to his house. It opened into a small, enclosed vestibule that abutted one wall of the hearth's granite chimney. Next to the chimney, a ladder of pegs led to the sleeping loft. To the left of the porch was the back wall of a small inner room, or bedroom, and to the right was the keeping room. The tiny porch was filled with farming tools—hoes, axes, rakes—and seasonal clothing such as snowshoes, golo-shoes, and oilcloth coats. A musket rested on branch hooks over the door.

Delia ducked her head and passed into the keeping room.

Tildy Parkes sat at a table of milled plank, chewing on her tongue as she laboriously copied letters from a hornbook onto a thin sheef of birchbark with a piece of plummet lead. Meg was bent over stoking the fire, and as Delia entered the room she straightened and greeted Delia with a fierce frown.

"Look, it's our new ma!" Tildy exclaimed. She jumped off the bench and, clutching the birchbark in one dimpled fist, tottered up to Delia. "See. I've been learning my ABC's."

Delia examined the piece of bark with genuine interest. "Why, how smart you are."

"She's not our new ma!" Meg protested angrily. "They aren't even married yet."

"Meg, don't start again," Nat warned. Meg said nothing more, but Delia saw the girl give her father a defiant look that he couldn't have missed.

Meg turned away from them and started to lift a cauldron of stew off the hearth and hang it from the lug pole over the fire. The cauldron was heavy and the tendons on her thin arms stood out from the strain. Delia stepped forward to help her.

"I can manage it myself!" Meg said fiercely.

Nat stepped between them, grabbing the cauldron from his daughter's hands. "I've had enough of these shenanigans, Meg! If you don't find your manners real quick, I'm going to find and peel myself a willow switch."

Meg's thin face paled and her lips tightened. Tears welled up in her eyes, but they didn't fall. "I'm going outside. I got chores to do. Come on, Tildy."

"Don't want to," Tildy said. But Meg grabbed Tildy's hand and hauled her sister out of the room. They could hear the little girl's screams of protest even after the front door had slammed shut behind them.

Nat gave Delia a sheepish look as he looped the pot handle

over a trammel hook. "I'm sorry, Delia. I don't know why she's acting this way." His face hardened. "But I promise you this is going to stop."

"Oh, please don't punish Meg on my account. Give her a little time. My ma died, too, when I was Meg's age. A girl's old enough then t' understand about death, about how it means forever, an' it leaves her feelin' real scared." Unconsciously, Delia put her hand on Nat's arm. "Please don't punish her."

Nat stiffened, pulling away from her, and Delia's hand fell awkwardly to her side. He stared at the floor, his mouth pursed, then he lifted his shoulder in a quick shrug. "Oh, well, I doubt if there's a willow tree within miles of here."

Delia laughed, and Nat even managed a tiny smile, which quickly faded as the grief crept back into his eyes. "But my Mary would not have tolerated such rudeness from Meg."

There was nothing Delia could say to that, so she remained silent. She wiped her sweating palms on her skirt and turned in a slow circle, looking around the room. The granite hearth had a fair-sized spit and a well-drawing chimney equipped with an oven. The inner walls had been sealed with pine boards, and cheerful print cotton curtains were strung on cords across the room's two windows. Most of the kitchen furnishings were plain, except for a maple dresser decorated with scalloped moldings. A set of six earthenware plates was arranged on top of the dresser, flanking a white china teapot. The room smelled deliciously of bayberry candles.

Delia's eyes fell on a framed silk and linen sampler hanging on the wall opposite the hearth, and she crossed the room to examine it more closely.

"My Mary did that," Nat said with pride.

" 'Tis pretty, Nat."

The picture in the sampler was of a barn and a horse and a man mowing hay. There was a saying at the bottom, but Delia couldn't make out the words.

Nat read it aloud for her:

This work is mine, my Friends may have
When I am Dead and Laid in Grave.

Delia shuddered at the morbid sentiment, wondering about the woman who had stitched it. For a moment she was assailed by a vivid, poignant memory of her own mother working on a sampler, though a much cheerier one with the alphabet and a border of flowers. She could hear in her mind her mother's voice crooning to her as she named the stitches—the petal stitch, the satin stitch, the loop. She thought her mother might even have taught her how to do all the different stitches that day, and she had been only a year or so older than Tildy. But if so, the skill had long ago left her.

Beside the sampler and above a wool spinning wheel hung a lantern clock. Delia studied it as well. It was a fine one, made of polished brass and cherry wood, and its quiet ticking gave the house a homey, cozy sound.

"That was my wedding present to Mary," Nat said, his voice strained. "I couldn't decide whether to get her a cow or the clock. I decided on the clock. Afterward, she said I should have gotten her the cow. She was always such a practical-minded girl, was Mary."

Delia thought she would much rather have had the clock, but of course she didn't say so. She looked around the room again, at the pretty curtains, the dishes on the dresser, the spinning wheel in the corner, the sampler. Mary Parkes had unmistakably left her stamp on her house and on her family.

She glanced at Nat's averted face. He was staring at the clock, his lips compressed, his eyes haunted. Mary Parkes had left her mark on her man as well. An indelible mark. Delia realized she had never completely considered the enormity of the task she was undertaking. Repressing a sigh, she ran her finger along the whorl of the spinning wheel, setting it in motion. What had ever made her think she could come to Merrymeeting and step into another woman's place?

"Mary always claimed she could get a first-rate tone out of that wheel," Nat said.

Delia turned and met his eyes. She drew in a deep breath. "I'll be honest with ye, Nat. I know all there is t' workin' in a grog shop, but I never set foot on a farm afore I left Boston. I 'spect someone's goin' t' have t' teach me how t' do most everythin'."

Nat's eyes wavered and his mouth turned down sourly. "I

can't pretend I'm not disappointed, Delia. Well, you must know the reason I sought a wife was to relieve me of the burden of caring for the girls and the house, and to have the extra pair of hands in the fields. It wasn't . . . I have no use for a woman otherwise.''

Delia wasn't sure what he meant by that remark. No use for a woman otherwise? She felt empty, so very, very alone.

"Perhaps ye can teach me the things I'll need t' know,'' she said, hating the note of desperation in her voice. "I'm a fast learner.''

"Perhaps.'' Nat stopped the whirling wheel with the heel of his hand. "But I can't teach you women's things.''

"Oh, Elizabeth Hooker's a prodigiously good spinner, or so Caleb says. Maybe she'll be agreeable t' teachin' me.''

They looked at each other in strained silence. Then Nat cleared his throat. "It's not much, but would you care to see the rest of the house? The girls sleep in the loft and Mary and I—'' He cut himself off and a dark flush suffused his face. "That is, the b-bedstead's in the inner room.''

The doorway to the inner room was between the hearth and the linter. It was only large enough to hold the bedstead, a calfskin chest, and a small pine dresser. But it had its own fireplace, which shared a chimney stack with the hearth in the keeping room. The bed was painted a fanciful red, and the sight of it made Delia nervous. Nat, she noticed, held his whole head stiff so he wouldn't even accidently look at it.

This room, too, had a small, narrow window, and Delia stepped up to it. She leaned her palms against the wooden frame, which was sanded smooth and felt warm from the sun. A noon mark had been cut into the sill to indicate the time of day, and she ran her finger along it.

She saw Meg weeding among the regularly spaced hills of corn with their entwining bean vines. From time to time the girl would pause to glance back at the house, a mixture of anger and fear on her face. Tildy sat in the dirt at the end of one of the corn rows, playing with her doll Gretchen. Delia could hear her chirping voice singing: "Lucky Locket, lost her pocket . . .''

Nat cleared his throat. "I'd like to be told the truth now, Delia. About Boston and the life you led back there.''

She turned away from the window, facing him. "My da was a toper an' I worked in a grog shop t' support him an' myself. Since I was fourteen. I might've done some things ye don't approve of, but I never sold my body. Not once. I'm no whore, nor never was I."

He stared hard into her face, his brow wrinkled. "I think I believe you," he finally acknowledged. "As for myself, I'm a good provider in spite of my gimp leg. And I'm an abstemious man by nature." He waved at the window. "You've seen the place and I believe we now understand what's expected of each other, so I see no reason not to go through with it, if you're still agreeable."

"Are ye sayin' ye feel inclined to marry me?"

Nat nodded, his expression serious. "Aye, I'm so inclined. Delia McQuaid, will you consent to being my wife?"

For a moment Delia simply stood there, unable to move, unable to speak, for this wasn't how it should be. So cold, so meaningless. A voice in her heart cried out, *Oh, Ty, Ty, why isn't it you?* so loudly that for a moment Delia thought the words had come bursting out of her mouth.

She couldn't marry Nat, not when her heart, her soul, belonged to another man. But Ty didn't love her. And although Nat didn't love her either, he did at least need her, and his daughters needed her. Especially Meg, poor hurt, frightened Meg. They needed her and she had never been needed before—except by her da, who only wanted money from her to buy the drink.

There were other considerations, too. Now that she was here in Merrymeeting, how was she going to support herself? There were no grog shops to offer her a job. Ty had said he would send her back to Boston if she and Nat didn't suit, but what was waiting for her there? A drunken, abusive father, a wretched existence that would inevitably have led to whoredom.

But in Merrymeeting . . . Already she loved it here. She would be a married woman, a respectable woman. She would have a home and a family, a man to care for who would in turn take care of her. She could never have what she wanted most, Ty's love, but she could have Merrymeeting and the new life it represented.

There was one final consideration she didn't want to admit, not even to herself. Ty's cabin was right up the river, so there would be a chance that she would see his face sometime every day. All she had to do was walk up the river . . . and he would be there.

"Aye, Nathaniel Parkes," Delia said, and if the smile she gave him was not completely real, only she knew it. "I consent t' being yer wife."

Nat let out his breath in a loud, sad sigh. "That's settled then. I suppose the town will expect some sort of frolic so the sooner it's done, the sooner we can get on with more important things. We'll have the haying to do in a couple of weeks and there won't be time for frivolities then."

"No, I suppose not . . ."

"I'd best ask the new reverend to tack the marriage banns on the meetinghouse door right away. And I'll pay Jack Tyson—he's a fisherman, when he's not trapping—to take his sloop down to Wells and bring back the magistrate to do the officiating."

Delia nodded, swallowing around the lump in her throat. Inside, she felt cold and numb. She'd hardly expected Nat to fall in love with her, but she'd have liked him to feel at least *something*. He approached the matter of their marriage as if he were acquiring a bonded servant and she expected him at any moment to produce indenture papers, asking her to sign away her life to him. *But then ye are,* she thought. *Ye are in a way signin' yer life to this man.*

"Ye're not overly fond of the rum, are ye?" she asked in a sudden fit of panic.

Nat had already turned toward the door, but he stopped to answer her in his deliberate way. "I told you I'm abstemious by nature. I never touch the devil's brew."

Delia released a fluttery breath. "How long d' ye think it'll take—the banns and such?"

He shrugged his rangy shoulders. "No more than ten days, I should think."

Ten days. Delia's eyes drifted over Nat's shoulder, to the bed in the corner. Ten days.

Later, after dinner, when Nat went outside to hitch the mare up to the cart so that he could take Delia back to the manor house, Delia spotted Tildy's hornbook on the settle by the hearth and asked the little girl if she could borrow it during the coming week.

"You can take it," Meg answered for her sister, a sneer on her face. "I bet you don't know how to read or write, do you? Tildy's only three, but already she knows all her letters, don't you, Tildy?"

Tildy looked up at Delia with wide-open eyes. "Sort of."

"She's going to be starting on the primer next," Meg said, then added when she noticed the color suffusing Delia's cheeks, "My ma could read and write everything and she taught me, and now I'm teaching Tildy and I don't see why Papa has to marry you. We don't need you and you don't know anything anyway."

Delia said nothing, but she took the hornbook with her. She thought of the shelves of books and folios she had seen in Anne Bishop's "library." Perhaps Anne would be willing to teach her how to read and write. She told herself she wanted to be a better wife and mother. But she knew she was lying to herself.

She wanted to impress Dr. Tyler Savitch. And maybe she wanted to show him just what sort of woman he was letting slip through those magic hands.

A noisy crowd was gathered before the manor house on the edge of the village green when Nat and Delia drove up. Delia immediately spotted Ty standing on the steps that led to the Bishops' front door. He was shouting something, and several people were yelling back at him.

Anne Bishop stood on the porch behind Ty, leaning against the wall with her arms folded across her flat chest. Delia skirted the edge of the crowd and ran up the steps.

Ty spared a glance for her, but he called out to someone in the crowd. "You there, Agnes Cartwright, are you going to stand by and watch your five little ones get the smallpox just because you're too damn stubborn to see sense!"

"What's happening?" Delia asked Anne. "Why is everyone so angry?"

"Oh, Doc's come up with some foolish notion that injecting cowpox pus into a person can keep him from getting the smallpox.''

Delia remembered Ty talking with his grandfather about the famous Cotton Mather's experiments. There had been a word for it, she remembered . . . ''But they're a-doin' that back in Boston now,'' she said.

Anne snorted. ''As if *giving* a body one disease can keep him from *getting* another one.''

She had said the latter loud enough for Ty to hear and he did. He whirled around to growl at her, ''You haven't been listening to a bloody word I've said!''

''My ears never do work right when somebody shouts into 'em.''

Delia giggled and Ty turned his scowl onto her. ''Where've you been all bloody day?''

''With Nat. Lookin' at his farm. Ye can do it t' me, Ty. I don't mind.''

Ty's eyebrows went up and he smiled suddenly. ''That's a rather suggestive remark, brat. Do what to you?''

She gestured at the physician's bag on the railing beside him. ''The experiment with the cowpox. Maybe when everyone else sees I've survived it, they'll agree t' be lettin' ye do it t' them.''

Ty didn't hesitate. He opened the bag and took out his set of lancet blades and a vial of something wrapped in linen whose contents Delia didn't want to think about. The crowd had gone abruptly silent.

''Give me your arm, please,'' Ty said. The anger had left him. He spoke softly to her now, and his touch as he lifted her arm was gentle. Foolish tears tickled her eyes and she had to look away from him.

''I suppose it *is* better if you don't watch,'' he teased. ''You aren't the fainting type, are you?''

''Not bloody likely.''

''I'm going to have to puncture your arm a little.''

''I won't holler.''

He grunted. ''Good. I doubt my reputation could stand it if you were to let out with one of those God-awful yowls of yours.''

"I sure hope you know what you're doing," Anne Bishop said.

" 'Course he knows," Delia retorted. She turned to look at Ty, her faith in him showing plainly on her face.

The inoculation took only a minute, the crowd watching intently. Delia didn't even wince. Afterward, Ty wrapped a piece of linen around the small puncture wound in her arm.

"You'll actually get a very mild form of the cowpox disease so you might feel a bit of a fever in a couple of days," he said. "And the scrape I made on your arm will fester some. Anne, why don't you take her inside now and brew her a cup of sassafras tea?"

Anne sniffed. "You and sassafras tea. You'd think it was a magic elixir the way you're always prescribing it for just about every ill imaginable."

Ty smiled. "It is a magic elixir." He stared down at Delia, then caressed her cheek. "Delia, I . . . never mind. Just . . . thank you."

She gave him a lopsided grin. " 'Twas nothin', Ty." She raised her voice so all could hear. "An' if I'm not dead by the end of the week, ye can be sure I'll be shoutin' yer success all over Merrymeeting."

While Ty had been inoculating Delia against smallpox on the front porch of Anne Bishop's manor house, Nat had been waiting patiently for an opportunity to get Ty alone. He caught the doctor half an hour later, waking across the green toward the new parsonage.

"I want you to tell it to me straight, Dr. Ty. Back in Boston, where you found her, was Delia a whore?"

Ty paused and shifted his physician's bag from one hand to the other. He didn't know how he was able to meet Nat's eyes, but he did. "No, she wasn't. I know for a fact she wasn't," he said, grateful that he was able to give Nat the truth.

Nat's eyes clinched shut. "She told me as much and I believed her, but then I got to thinking . . . I could never bring a whore into my Mary's house, and there are my girls to think of. So I had to be sure."

For a moment Ty felt an unexpected sense of relief so

strong it made him smile. "Nat, as I told Delia back in Boston, if you two should decide you don't suit—"

"No, no. It isn't that." Nat sighed and pushed a hand through his yellow hair. His clear gray eyes grew suddenly solemn, like a winter sky clouding over. "It's just that when I saw her getting off that schooner yesterday . . . she was so darn different than what I'd expected. I think I foolishly hoped deep inside myself that the woman you would bring back to be wife to me would be m-my M-Mary in the flesh."

"Nat—"

"Ah, Doc, it's not your fault. Or the poor girl's either. How can I blame her for not being Mary? I think yesterday was the first time I finally admitted to myself that Mary is dead. She's *dead*, Ty." His voice caught on a sob. "But it's just so blasted hard. God, I miss her so much . . ."

Ty said nothing. There was such anguish in Nat Parkes's eyes. For a moment Ty's mind was overwhelmed with his own stark memory of his mother lying on a bed of furs, her life's blood pooling around her, Assacumbuit—that proud, indomitable warrior—kneeling above her while the tears flowed in silent rivers down his chiseled cheeks. Ty had watched while his Indian father had wailed the mourning song and rent his flesh with his hunting knife, his blood dripping off his bronze chest to splash onto the still, white skin of his dead wife's face . . .

Ty wrenched his mind back to the present by an act of will, but he thought immediately of the woman on Cape Elizabeth, great with child and too damn small to be likely to survive the birthing of it, and her husband near beside himself with fear. A man would have to be a fool to love a woman so much that he risked such pain at the losing of her. Especially when every time he even acted on that love, he chanced planting the seed that could kill her.

No, no, Ty thought, his resolution hardening. Better not to love so deeply, better not to care so much, than to suffer having the few things that come to matter to you in this life snatched away from you.

"I don't want you to think I don't appreciate what you did, Dr. Ty, bringing that girl all the way up here," Nat was saying earnestly. "Although she's a mite young and I wish she were less . . . well, rough and ignorant. I know you did the best for me that you could," he added hastily. "It's just that Delia's so different than my Mary. Mary was as solid, as easy to understand as this earth." He kicked a tuft of marsh grass with the toe of his boot. "But Delia is like a will o' the wisp. She's constantly surprising me and it makes me . . ." He let out a shaky laugh, rubbing a big hand over his mouth. "To tell you the truth, I'm not sure I can handle her."

"Maybe you ought to postpone the marriage," Ty said, the odd sense of relief he had felt earlier returning. "Give yourselves a chance to get to know each other better."

Nat shook his head, wiping out Ty's strange relief with one gesture. "There's no time for that. I got to get my hay in and the garden's choked with weeds. Anyway, we wouldn't be the first to marry ignorant of each other's ways and peculiarities." He clapped his hand on Ty's shoulder, giving it a hard squeeze. "No, as long as you swear she's no whore, then there's no reason to wait. In fact, I'm on my way to see the Reverend Hooker now, to have him post the banns."

Ty stood in the middle of the Merrymeeting green and watched Nathaniel Parkes drive away in his cart. He gave a short, bitter laugh. Two days ago she had said she loved *him*. Now she was agreeing to marry another man, and wasn't that just typical of a woman! They all felt compelled to be married, and it didn't matter a hoot who the man was as long as he had a strong back and was on the young side of sixty.

Still, Delia sure as hell could have waited a while longer before saying yes to Nat Parkes, at least long enough for him to decide . . . to decide what? Did he—no, by God, he didn't love her! It was only her body he craved. She wanted a husband and the last thing in this world he wanted was a wife. What he wanted was simple enough. He wanted her to share his bed for one sweet summer. One sweet summer, that was all. No marriage, no babies, no love everlasting.

He turned and, looking back toward the manor house, thought he saw a curtain move in one of the upstairs windows. He was sure it was Delia.

Damn you, Delia, he cried out to her silently. *Why won't you let me go?*

Chapter 14

Delia's dark head was bent over a slate that rested on her thighs, and the chalk squeaked across the stone as she wrote. Anne Bishop paused within the doorway of the veranda to look at the girl, a smile softening the harsh lines of her face.

After a moment, she came to stand behind Delia, peering over her shoulder. Delia held the slate out so they both could see it better. "I've been writing my name," she said. "And yours and the colonel's as well."

"And Tyler Savitch's too, I see."

Bright color flooded Delia's cheeks and she hurriedly wiped the slate clean with a wet rag. When she finished, she turned on the bench and smiled. "It's kind of you, Anne, to teach me my letters."

For the past week and a half, Delia had been taking care to articulate her words properly, lapsing back into her old patterns of speech only when she became nervous or excited or angry. Anne felt a fierce pride at the rapid progress of her pupil; Delia McQuaid was a tavern wench no longer.

"I'll have you reading *Pilgrim's Progress* by the end of the month," Anne said, meaning it. The girl truly was as smart as the crack of a rifle. And Tyler Savitch was a fool.

Anne walked around to the front of the veranda and looked out at the enamel blue bay. "It'll soon be time for you to get dressed. Your Nat was here a while ago, making more of a nuisance of himself than a wet pup. I told him no less than three times yesterday that he wasn't to come around here until a half hour before the ceremony."

200

The marriage between Delia McQuaid and Nathaniel Parkes would take place that afternoon. Already Anne's servants were setting out trestle tables on the village green, preparing for the feast that was to follow. "I've never seen that poor boy so scared. His knees were clacking together louder than the batten on a loom."

Delia heaved a huge sigh. "Lord above us, Anne, my knees are all a-wobble, too. I've never been married before."

Anne burst forth with one of her cackles. "Well, it's hardly the sort of thing that gets easier with practice."

Delia set the slate on the floor, standing up just as a servant came through the wide double doors, wheeling a tea cart. "Take that back, Bridget," Anne said, waving a hand. "And bring us both a glass of sack."

Delia joined Anne at the front of the veranda. Anne could feel the girl looking at her, her open face full of affection. Strangely, for she was not a demonstrative person, Anne longed to wrap her arms around Delia and hold her close. The yearning was so fierce it brought tears to Anne's eyes. The tears surprised her; she hadn't cried in years and years.

The tidal wheel turning in the sawmill next door filled the air with a soothing, tinkling sound that was in sharp counterpoint to the raucous cries of the herring gulls swooping overhead. The early afternoon sun shone on the waters of the bay, making it gleam like a field of marigolds, and sunbeams danced among the high treetops of the white pines. A gentle breeze brought with it the smell of sweet fern and bayberry.

Delia breathed a soft sigh. "It's so pretty here."

"Oh, Merrymeeting is truly the most beautiful spot on earth," Anne said. "But it isn't paradise. Never, never mistake it for paradise." *And I ought to know*, Anne thought. *For haven't I buried one husband and three children on this land?*

Bridget came back with the sack in two slender pewter chalices. Anne took a large swallow of the tart white wine and felt its coolness flow down her throat into her chest. She turned and held her glass up to Delia in a silent toast. "It's a beautiful day for a wedding and a frolic."

A sadness came over Delia's remarkable golden eyes. "If anybody bothers to come."

"Why wouldn't people come?"

"Sara Kemble. She's told everyone that back in Boston I was a . . . that I would lie with any man for the price of a tallow candle. All of Merrymeeting's talking about it. They do it loud enough so's I can hear."

Anne snorted. "It doesn't matter a hang what that gadder Sara Kemble's been saying. Some people always manage to get the wrong pig by the ear and Sara sure is one of them." She leaned close to Delia and lowered her voice. "Sara's problem is she's homelier than a basket of eels and barren as a bedpost. She's jealous of a young and pretty thing like you."

Delia's lips trembled into a smile. "To the devil with Sara Kemble then." She took a sip of the wine, then choked. "Ugh!" She looked down at the glass in her hand, screwing up her mouth in distaste.

"Ladies drink sack, Delia," Anne said. "You must acquire a taste for it."

Delia nodded and dutifully took another sip of the wine, trying politely not to show her dislike, and Anne smothered a smile. The girl was so damn strong. Strong enough to do whatever she must, to face whatever life demanded of her— and life would demand a lot, Anne knew. Life could demand everything you had, and more. So much more. For a moment Anne envied Delia her strength and her youth. For years and years, it seemed, Anne had felt so tired. So very tired and so very old.

"I haven't seen Dr. Savitch around this past week," Delia said, oh so very casually, and Anne felt an empathetic ache in the region of her heart that she thought had long ago hardened into stone.

"He sailed his skiff across to Falmouth Neck on Wednesday."

"Oh . . ." Delia swallowed hard and her fingers on the stem of the chalice tightened.

"To deliver a baby of a woman at Cape Elizabeth."

"Oh, a baby!" Delia exclaimed, relief plain in her voice.

"It's showing rather badly, my dear."

Delia's eyes dropped down to her bodice in alarm. "What's showing?"

Anne laughed. She set her wine on the veranda railing and cupped Delia's cheeks between her rough, bony hands. "Your love for Ty Savitch. It shows in your face, in your eyes, in the very way you say his name."

Delia pulled away from her, turning her back.

"I have to admit I'm a little in love with him myself," Anne said. "I doubt there's a woman in Merrymeeting who isn't. That man is as good to look at as a mountain in dogwood time."

Delia whipped back around and her chin came up. "I would love Tyler Savitch if he was scarred by the pox. I'll love him when he's old and stooped and toothless. I'll still go on loving him long after I'm dead and buried and my flesh has rotted and my bones have turned to dust!"

Anne let out a loud snort. "Never mind that romantic nonsense, girl. What about tonight, after you are *married* to Nathaniel Parkes? Surely you know about what goes on between a man and his wife, the intimacy of the shared bed . . . ?"

Delia's face was so pale it looked siphoned of blood. "I know," she said, her throaty voice so strained it cracked. "I know, and I swear to you that I'll be a good wife to Nat for he's a fine man and he deserves no less. And it isn't as if he's in love with me, for he still loves his dead wife. So I won't be taking something away from him by loving Ty deep inside the secret part of myself that Nat will never see."

"Oh, Delia, that could very well be true now, but things change—"

Delia reached out, clutching Anne's hands. "Oh, Anne, don't you see? I love Ty, but he doesn't love me. And there's a tender side to him, a hurting side, although I think sometimes he hates that part of himself. But he knows how I feel about him, how deeply I love him, and it makes *him* feel so uncomfortable and guilty and—"

"He should feel guilty!"

Tears welled in Delia's eyes. "No, no, you don't understand. He touched me with his magic hands and I fell in love and he couldn't help that any more than he can help breathing. But if I marry Nat, Ty can stop feeling so bad about me, about me being in love with him." Her mouth twisted into a watery, rueful smile. "And when the day comes that Ty marries, I'll rejoice for him, aye, for he'll be happy then. He's not happy now. He's lonely, lonely and sad.''

My God, Anne thought, to be loved like that. Tyler Savitch was no fool after all. To be loved like that . . . No wonder he was frightened.

Suddenly Anne Bishop saw a familiar figure sauntering toward them down the wharf. ''Speaking of the devil . . .'' she said, but Delia was already turning as if some extra sense had alerted her that Tyler Savitch was near.

Silently, Anne picked up the two pewter chalices and left the veranda. As she did so she thought about life, about how there was always so much pain. So much loss.

Delia stood on the veranda, one hand wrapped around a post, leaning into it. At the sight of her his step quickened. When he became aware of it, he made himself slow down.

Still, he ran up the steps two at a time and almost pulled her into his arms. He stopped himself just in time. Their eyes met and his breath caught. He hadn't remembered her being quite so beautiful.

But she also seemed different in a way that didn't please him. Her hair, that glorious wine-colored hair, was hidden beneath a cap. The bodice she wore had long sleeves with stiff white turned-back cuffs that covered her slender wrists, and her petticoat came down to the tops of her shoes. She looked fresh-scrubbed and pure and innocent, and he wasn't sure he liked it. He wanted back his waterfront wench.

''How are you, Delia?''

''Oh, I figure I'll make out.'' She said the words teasingly and her smile shone from her face like a blazing sun. Her love for him glowed in her tawny eyes and he felt it as a caress on his face. To his shame he realized he had been waiting for that look, needing it.

He took her arm. She jumped and tried to pull away from him, but he held it fast. He unbuttoned the cuff at her wrist.

''What are you doing?'' she cried. There was a breathless note in her voice, and when he looked into her eyes he saw the pupils were wide and dark. For a moment he stared into those eyes, not moving, saying nothing. His fingers where they touched the bare flesh of her wrist felt on fire.

He saw her lips move and her voice came at him from a long way away. "Ty . . . let go of me. Please."

Ty jerked his eyes off her face. He could feel her pulse; it was racing abnormally fast. "There's no need to fly into a fit," he said gruffly. "I only want to examine the inoculation."

He rolled up her sleeve. The pustule had scabbed over and was healing well. "Have you been feeling all right? Any fever?"

"N-no . . ." She bit her lip. He could feel the tremors rippling through her whole body. He released her arm and she immediately backed away from him, pressing her spine along the length of the veranda post. She rolled down her sleeve and refastened it. "It itched some."

Ty nodded. "And have you settled into life at Merrymeeting, then?"

"Oh, yes, yes. I love it, Ty!"

He smiled. "Well, that's good . . . I'm glad."

A heavy silence fell between them. Their eyes met and held. Ty felt an overwhelming urge to kiss her, but he fought it down. Today was her *wedding* day, for Christ's sake. Her wedding day . . .

She suddenly spoke, and in spite of all the armor he had tried to wrap around himself, her words warmed him. "I've missed you, Ty. I've missed seeing you."

"I've been gone."

She nodded. "Yes, I know. You went to birth a baby."

"You're well informed." His eyes fixed on her face. Not only did she look different, she sounded different as well. Almost, by God, like a real little lady. The thought made him smile.

"The mother and child, are they well?" she asked, oh so very refined and politely. His smile deepened.

"It was bad, but they survived it."

"And did you visit Susannah Marsten while you were at Falmouth Neck?"

Now that, he thought, with a startled mixture of amusement and exasperation, was more like the old Delia. Damn her, but she could still disconcert him. He could feel his face coloring and it infuriated him that she could do this to him.

"Yes. I saw her," he said, knowing what she would think and knowing it would hurt her.

"Did you take her to bed?"

Jesus . . .

He hadn't taken Susannah to bed. He hadn't because he had spent every damn minute of the past week thinking about, dreaming about, hungering for the silky feel of those heavy round breasts filling his hands and the sound of that soft, husky voice caressing his ear, saying *I love ye, Tyler Savitch . . . love ye . . . love ye . . .*

No, he hadn't slept with Susannah Marsten and he probably never would now. His silence, however, was as good as saying that he had. As he knew it would be.

"You ought to marry her," Delia said.

"I might consider it." Ty's smile showed a good part of his teeth and he leaned closer, so close their breath commingled, so close he could smell her. Sassafras soap and bayberry candles and a musky, erotic smell that was all hers and made him think of sex. It brought his manhood to instant hard and trembling life. He thought he just might hate her for being able to do that to him.

Her lips parted open as she took in a breath and he considered smothering her mouth with his. Instead he said, "Have you taken up matchmaking, brat? Now that you're going to be a happily married woman yourself."

She actually laughed! He was deliberating trying to wound her and she was *laughing*. For a moment he fantasized wrapping his hands around that slender neck and throttling her. She was driving him crazy!

"Why won't you marry her?" Delia asked.

"Damn it!" He slammed his hand on the post, inches from her face. She didn't even flinch. "What is this obsession that you have with marriage?"

"She's a nice person, Ty. And she's in love with you."

"Well, that's too bloody bad because I'm not in love with her!"

He hadn't meant to say that, but once said he had thought the admission would at least please her. Instead she frowned. "Hasn't there ever been a woman you loved, Ty?"

"Why are you *doing* this?"

"Doing what?"

He leaned close to her again, so close this time that their lips almost touched. Hers parted open again as she sucked in a sharp breath. "This is all some kind of a trick, isn't it?" he said, his voice low and hard. "You and Nat Parkes and this bloody ridiculous marriage. You think I won't let you go through with it, that I'll stop it at the last minute—well, I've got a surprise for you, Delia-girl . . ."

He seized her arms, giving her a rough shake, and continued to shake her as he shouted into her face. "I don't love you, Delia, and no amount of wishing and conniving on your part is going to convince me that I do! And there is nothing, *nothing* you can do that will make me love you!"

He flung her away and stepped back the better to survey the damage he had done. He was hurting inside, confused, and, to his shame, frightened. He blamed her for it and so, like a child, he had wanted to hurt her back. He got his wish. Her face was white and frozen, as if sculpted of ice, her eyes two black, bottomless holes, and he couldn't bear it.

He came within a second of enfolding her in his arms and telling her that it was all lies, lies, lies. Not only was he afraid that he did love her, but he thought he was probably damned to love her the rest of his life. And if he let himself do that, let himself love her, then he would inevitably lose her. And if that happened just one more time, he wouldn't be able to bear it, it would certainly kill him, and still . . . still, he almost gave himself away.

But then she thrust out that proud, defiant chin and her eyes flared wide. "Are ye done shoutin' at me, Tyler Savitch?"

"No, by God—"

"Because I don't have the time t' listen t' it. I'm supposed t' be gettin' dressed. For my weddin'."

She brushed past him, heading for the open doorway.

"Delia!" he shouted after her.

But she didn't stop and she didn't look back.

Nat Parkes climbed the sloping hill behind the barn, his wooden foot dragging through the green wheat. The hill had been the first of his land that he had cleared and planted the year he bought the farm. He did it first because it backed up to the house and he feared the murdering, heathen savages could sneak up too easily on them through the dense trees and underbrush.

Mary had worked right alongside him to clear the hill, until she realized she was carrying Meg. Then she slowed down on the heavy work, and chopping down brush and pulling stumps was indeed heavy work. Perhaps it was because they had worked this hill together, but whatever the reason, it had always been Mary's favorite spot. She often would come up there alone, "to have a conversation with myself," as she would say.

And so it was the place he had chosen to bury her.

After two months the freshly turned black earth had dried to brown. But the marker still looked new. He'd had a stone carver in Portsmouth hew it for him. It was etched with a death's-head on top, and below that the words: *Here lies the body of Mary Parkes born 1693 aged 28 years.* He'd wanted to have *Beloved Wife and Mother* in there somewhere, but the stone carver had run out of room.

He knelt and traced the letters of her name.

Mary . . .

It's happening today, Mary. I'm marrying that girl. I guess I told you already her name is Delia McQuaid. I'm not sure you'd approve of her much. She's a bit ungodly, I'm afraid, and I suspect she can be notional too, at times. He gave a weak laugh. *You always said a man should steer clear of notional women . . . Trouble is, Mary, she's what Dr. Ty brought back with him from Boston, so I suppose she's the one it has to be. I haven't the heart to go looking for another.*

His head fell back and he gazed up at the sky, his throat working to suppress the tears. He squeezed his eyes shut.

I wish now you hadn't asked me for that promise, Mary. I suppose you were thinking of the girls and you knew I'd never marry again if left to my own will. And I wouldn't have. There can never be one to take your place, Mary. Never—

His shoulders jerked and hunched, and he pressed his palms hard into his face to stifle a sob.

Aw Lord, Mary . . . What did you want to go and die on me for?

* * *

Anne Bishop wound a wreath of goldenrod and daisies through the shining black coils of Delia's hair. Her hand lingered on the single curl that had been left to fall over Delia's shoulder, her rough fingers snagging in the silken tresses.

Anne stepped back and Delia looked down at herself, running her palms over the smooth bodice of her new linen short gown. She lifted the folds of the calico petticoat, marveling at its light softness. It was the shade of an apple tree in full bloom, with tiny green dots. Her short gown was the color of forest moss with ruffled elbow-length sleeves. Her skirt rustled when she walked and brushed against her legs, feeling like the soft strokes of a hundred goose feathers. It was a practical outfit for a wilderness wedding—too fine for wearing to work in the fields, but not so extravagant that it wouldn't do for a typical Sabbath-day meeting.

Laughing suddenly, she twirled on the toes of her new leather slippers. "Oh, Anne, I feel so pretty!"

Anne rubbed at the corner of one eye with her knuckle. "You look as beautiful as a Kennebec swan."

Delia stopped dancing. She smiled into Anne's pinched and weathered face. Faded brown eyes looked back at her, unblinking, but with a warmth that brought a soft glow to Delia's chest. During the past ten days she had grown to love this strange, irascible woman. In many ways Anne Bishop had become for Delia the mother she had lost when she was nine.

"Oh, Anne . . . How can I ever thank you for all you've done for me? For making me these new clothes and giving me the lessons. And the fine hospitality of your beautiful house." She looked around the bedroom that had come to feel so much like home to her, the home she had always dreamed of. A wistful sigh escaped her lips. "I'm going to miss living here with you and the colonel."

"But you'll be coming back three mornings a week to continue with those lessons," Anne said, her voice vinegar tart. "I didn't spend all those hours teaching you to read and write and speak properly only to see you stop at this rudimentary level. I intend to educate you, girl, if I have to do it with the end of a switch."

Delia laughed. "Afore long I should be able to recite aloud that Pope fellow's poems you're so almighty keen on while I'm out doing my milking. Nat's she-goat should be mightily impressed!"

Anne pretended to snort with indignation. Then she picked up a silk-wrapped package from the chest and handed it to Delia. "I thought you might like to wear these. They were a gift from my mother to me and I wore them for my first wedding. I want you to have them, Delia."

Delia looked at Anne in surprise, for she hadn't known the woman had been married once before. She hesitated to pull open the silk material; the wrapping itself was more valuable than any gift she'd ever received before. Except, she thought with a sudden stab of pain, for a certain pair of calfskin shoes with red heels.

"Well, don't just stand there frozen like a hunter in a blind," Anne said. "Open it, girl."

Delia pulled apart the folds of silk. Inside was a pair of delicate white lace mitts intricately embroidered with tiny seed pearls. She gasped at the wonder of owning anything so fine. "Oh, Anne, they're beautiful. But I could never . . ."

"Nonsense. You can and you shall." She stroked Delia's cheek with one bent, rough knuckle. "I never had a daughter of my own to give them to."

Tears oozed from Delia's eyes and she brushed them with the heels of her hands. "Oh, Lord above us . . ." The two women shared watery smiles and then fell into each other's arms, exchanging fierce hugs.

Anne stroked Delia's back. "Be happy."

"I will," Delia said, her mouth against Anne's bony shoulder.

But inside she felt an ache of disappointment so strong she wanted to cry. Every girl dreams of this day, her wedding day, when she will be joined for life to the man she loves. But the man Delia loved didn't love her and the man she was marrying loved his dead wife.

The only person likely to be happy on this day, she thought, was Tyler Savitch—who would at least be rid of his bothersome tavern wench and the guilt-filled memory of a warm and windy afternoon in the forest on Falmouth Neck.

* * *

Delia walked slowly down the stairs, her lace-covered palm trailing lightly along the banister. Nathaniel Parkes waited for her in the hall, twisting his hat in his hands. He looked up, took a step forward, and then paused. She saw surprise cross his face, the creases alongside his mouth deepening with an involuntary smile.

"Why, you look dreadfully pretty, Delia!" The words had burst out of him, startling himself as much as her, and a vivid blush immediately suffused his face.

"That's the nicest compliment anyone's ever paid to me," Delia said, wanting to put him at ease and wishing it wasn't necessary for her always to have to be so mindful of what he was thinking or feeling.

Her efforts failed to get the desired result anyway, for instead he frowned and, although he took her arm to lead her down the hall and out the front door, his fingers barely touched her. They walked with their bodies so far apart her skirt didn't even brush against his leg. His limp seemed worse today, the wooden foot scraping across the boards of Anne's diamond-patterned hall.

A thick lump, like soggy dough, formed in Delia's throat and she could barely swallow around it. *Quit being a wooden-headed fool. Just what did you expect to find on walking down these stairs—Tyler Savitch standing here in Nat's place, waiting for you with undying love in his eyes? Nat Parkes needs a wife and you need a home, and few marriages begin with love anyway and even fewer wind up with love at the end of them, so quit wishing for the moon. Marry the man and have done with it.*

The short marriage ceremony was to take place in front of the manor house on the village green. It was a good excuse for a frolic and everyone in Merrymeeting was already gathered on the green, waiting for the marriage to be over with so the fun could begin. When the front door to the manor house opened, everyone stopped what he was doing or saying and turned of one accord to look at the bride and groom.

Tildy Parkes sat astride the hitching rail in front of the manor house, pretending to ride a horse, kicking her legs and tossing her head and making high-pitched neighing noises in the back of her throat. When the front door opened and Delia and her father emerged, it so startled her that she fell off the rail to land with a hard jar on her hands and knees. She thought about crying but changed her mind when she remembered the wonderful thing that was about to happen.

She pushed herself up, bottom first, and ran toward them, chubby legs pumping hard, a big rip in her new pinter. "Papa, Papa, is it happening now? Are we gonna be getting our new ma?"

She flung herself against her father's legs, reaching up to grasp the edge of his hip-length coat. He bent over and brushed the dirt off her pinter, fingering the tear. "Matilda Parkes, you promised me you would try to stay neat and clean, and where in heaven's name are your shoes?" he scolded, or tried to—for there was more amusement than anger in his voice. He grinned apologetically at Delia. "I was hoping she would manage to stay put together for at least the five minutes it will take to see us married."

Laughing, Delia scooped the little girl into her arms, settling her down on one outthrust hip and heedless of the dusty smudges Tildy's bare feet were leaving on her own skirts. "Yes, little puss," she said, kissing Tildy's fat cheek. The soft, sun-warmed skin felt smooth against her lips. "It's happening now. Your da and I are getting married."

Tildy let out a delighted squeal that rattled Delia's eardrum and made her laugh.

Carrying Tildy in her arms, Delia stepped out onto the green. As she did her eyes scanned the crowd for a certain face. She didn't see him at first and the disappointment she had been feeling deepened into a hollow, aching pain in her chest. Tears hovered so close to the surface they were making her eyes burn. He hadn't even bothered to show up. Did she matter so little to him that he could treat her marriage to another man with such indifference?

And then she saw him—at the back of the crowd, leaning nonchalantly against one of the trestle tables loaded with food for the feast afterward. His hip was hitched onto the corner of one of the plank boards, his long booted legs crossed at the ankles, his arms folded over his chest. Their eyes clashed and held, but she could tell nothing from the expression on his face, although his lips did wear that perpetual scowl. Delia looked away.

Nat, too, was searching the crowd. "Where's Meg?"

"Meg's angry," Tildy said. She had wrapped one arm around Delia's neck, panting against Delia's cheek. Her breath smelled of milk and corn mush. "Meg don't want a new ma."

Nat heaved a sigh, a crease of worry appearing between his brows. "I'm sorry, Delia. I don't know what to do about her."

"She'll come around, Nat, if you let her be."

Delia had already spotted Meg hovering in the shadows between the apple cider press and the mast house. She, too, was wearing a new dress in honor of the occasion, but it hung lankly on her thin frame, its drab brown color blending in with her hair, making her look like a scrawny grouse chick.

Just then a stranger stepped forward, blocking Delia's view of Meg. He was a diminutive man with a small, flattened nose from which dangled precariously a pair of spectacles. Nat introduced him as Isaac Deere, the colonial magistrate who was to conduct the ceremony. Oddly enough for a society in which religion played such a strong part, in the Massachusetts Bay Colony marriages were deemed civil, not religious, affairs.

Nevertheless, the Reverend Caleb Hooker was on hand to give his official blessing, for Nat had insisted on having their vows receive religious sanction as well. Caleb came up to them now, wearing such a wide smile that his upper lip seemed to catch on his overlapping front teeth. "You look lovely, Delia. Wonderful day for a wedding, Mr. Parkes."

Flushing, Nat tugged at the kerchief tied around his neck and mumbled something to the ground.

"Thank you, Caleb," Delia said. She thought about what a true friend he had turned out to be for her—he and Elizabeth. Delia hadn't realized how few friends she'd had in her life before now and she searched out Elizabeth, who had just set a pot of baked beans on one of the tables and was walking toward them, moving with that smooth, ladylike grace that Delia so admired and despaired of ever being able to achieve.

Elizabeth's greeting was more subdued, although her

cheeks were dusted with a light color of rose, like a bloom just fading. She took Delia's hand and gave it a hard squeeze. "May God keep you, Delia. May God keep you and Mr. Parkes."

Delia's smile widened to include all those who had started to gather around for the ceremony—Anne Bishop and the colonel; Obadiah Kemble, who grinned and winked at her; even nasty Sara, who glared back at Delia, expressing her disapproval by drawing her pinched lips tightly together like a stitched seam.

Delia looked at all the folk of Merrymeeting who had come together on this warm and breezy summer afternoon to see her and Nat married. Most were still strangers to her, but soon these people would be her neighbors and perhaps someday her friends. The gristmill owner, Constant Hall, and his wife, Charity. Samuel and Hannah Randolf—Sam, with his fiery red hair, was the village blacksmith, and they had seven children with another on the way. Guy and Nancy Sewall, who owned the farm closest to Nat's . . .

And Ty.

Their eyes locked again and Delia's smile faded. She felt the old familiar ache in her heart.

Ty was the first to look away. He walked off, his boots cutting a swath through the grass as he strode rapidly toward the blue bowl of the bay. He didn't look back, not even when the magistrate cleared his throat and said loudly, "If we might begin . . ."

Isaac Deere pushed his drooping spectacles back onto the bridge of his nose and stared pointedly at Tildy, whom Delia still held in her arms. Delia set the little girl down, but she kept hold of her hand. It was sticky with sweat, yet Delia drew comfort from it. And courage.

She glanced at Nat. He stared straight ahead, his gray eyes cloudy and brooding and focused on something in the distance. As if, Delia thought, he expected—no, as if he *prayed*—that his Mary would come walking out of the wilderness forest and save him from this terrible fate.

"Nat," she said softly, oblivious to the magistrate, who couldn't help but hear, "it's not too late to change your mind."

He swallowed, squeezed his eyes shut, and his head swiveled loosely back and forth on his neck, as if anchored by a peg that was coming loose. "No, Delia . . . No. It must be done."

Aye, Delia thought. It must be done.

Yet she, too, yearned to be saved. She had to stiffen her spine to keep from whirling and crying out to Ty with all her heart to come back, come back and stop this marriage, come declare his love and save her from what she was suddenly sure was a terrible mistake.

But she didn't turn around and Ty didn't come back and the magistrate began speaking the words of the marriage ritual, droning them in a bored voice that almost obscured their importance. Nat and Delia gave the correct responses automatically, because if either of them had thought about what they were saying, their throats would have seized up, capturing the words like birds in a cage.

Then, of a sudden, Delia heard Isaac Deere say, "By the laws of God and this commonwealth, I, as magistrate, pronounce you man and wife."

Chapter 15

The Merrymeeting frolic was in full swing and Meg Parkes was sulking—although she preferred to think of it as simply keeping to herself.

She was whipping her new top on a patch of packed earth in front of the Bishops' manor house, competing against herself to see how long she could keep it going. She leaned over and started it spinning with a quick twist of her hand. Stepping back, she lashed it with the eelskin thong just as three boys, who were part of a game of whoop-and-hide, ran past her, deliberately jostling her arm and almost knocking her over. One of them was Daniel Randolf, the blacksmith's oldest boy, whom she destested more than anyone in the whole world.

Daniel stopped to jeer at her. "Whyn't ye give it up, Meg Parkes? Ye're never going t' be able t' whip a top right."

"I'm already better at it than you, Daniel Randolf." It was a slight exaggeration. She was as good as he was, not better.

Daniel barked a cocky laugh. "Whoever heard of a *girl* bein' any good at whippin' tops?"

"Whoever heard of a *girl* being any good at anything?" his younger brother chimed in.

Meg tried to think of a particularly devastating remark, but all she could come up with was, "Your mother chews tobaccy," and she'd already used that one on the Randolf boys before. She settled for sticking out her tongue and shouting, "Go to hell, Daniel Randolf!"

Daniel and his brother merely laughed and ran off, hooting

like Indians and generally showing off, to Meg's supreme disgust.

"He's wrong, you know. There's no reason why a girl can't whip a top good as any boy."

Meg spun around at the sound of that husky voice, a grimace of dislike already plastered on her face, for she knew who it was: Delia McQuaid, her father's new wife. But *never,* she reminded herself, never would the woman be her mother, marriage or not. Nobody, not even Papa, was going to force her to admit otherwise.

She put on her best sneer. "What do you know about it?"

Delia smiled down at her, but there was a nervous quiver in her voice. "I was the champion top-spinner of Ship's Wharf for five years. And I retired undefeated. I know a trick or two that'll set those lads to spinning on their ears. Would you be wanting me to show you?"

"No. And it's no use your trying to make friends with me because I'm never going to see my way to liking you."

"Aye? That's as may be. But then, my da always said I'm as stubborn as a hen at roosting time. So I'll keep on trying if you don't mind."

Meg shrugged her thin shoulders. She pretended to ignore Delia. She looked instead toward the trestle tables set out beneath the lone white pine with its weathervaned top. A pair of greedy, noisy whiskey jacks were trying to steal the food. Mrs. Bishop shrieked at them and flapped her apron, and the other women laughed.

Meg nodded her small, pointed chin toward the tables. "Shouldn't you be over yonder, helping the others to set out the food?"

"I offered," Delia said, sounding wistful, "but they don't seem to want my help."

Meg smiled to herself. She had already seen the other women shooing Delia away just as they had the whiskey jacks. Except for Mrs. Bishop and the new preacher's wife, the other women liked Delia not at all. Sara Kemble said she'd done bad things back in Boston. For a moment Meg felt sorry for Delia because the other women didn't like her. She tried to harden her heart, telling herself such treatment was no worse than Delia deserved.

But she couldn't stop herself from holding the whip out to Delia begrudgingly. "I suppose you can show me how to whip the top. Were you really champion spinner?"

"Aye!" Delia exclaimed, her strange-colored eyes sparkling so brightly that Meg began to regret her slight unbending. "I kept one going for a good hour once," Delia said. "It broke all records . . . well, at least all the records that I know of."

Meg watched while Delia set the top up on its apex. She started it spinning with a hard jerk of her wrist and then began to stroke the toy with deft flicks of the whip, prolonging the spin. She got the top going so fast it was just a blur to Meg's eyes and Meg laughed with delight, forgetting for a moment that she didn't at all like her father's new wife.

Delia's eyes flickered up at Meg, and the smile she flashed stretched her lips wide, showing even, white teeth. "It's all in the stroke, you see. You've got to do it lightly, lightly, as if you were trying to brush a pool of water with a feather without causing a ripple. Lightly, lightly . . ." she crooned, and the top went on spinning.

Daniel Randolf and some of the other boys had drifted back to take a look. Meg could tell they were mightily impressed with Delia's skill. She was whipping the top faster and already longer than any Merrymeeting boy had ever managed to do and Delia was a girl, well a woman, but a female at least, and Meg doubted any *man,* not even her papa, could whip a top any better.

She thumped Daniel Randolf in the side with her elbow. "She's going to teach me how to do that."

Daniel's eyes widened. "Honest to gosh? Can ye teach me, too, ma'am?" he called out to Delia.

Meg stiffened, holding her breath. Delia's eyes flickered up at her again and then back down to the spinning top. "I'd like to, young Daniel, truly. But I'm afraid I can't. It's a secret only us girls are allowed to know."

The boys all looked crestfallen and Meg's face lit up with a triumphant grin. "I challenge you to a top-spinning contest next Sabbath day, Daniel. I'll wager you a penny I can keep mine going longer than yours."

But Daniel had turned on his heel, stalking off. "I don't spin against girls!" he threw back over his shoulder.

Meg stared after him, fists on hips. "Oooh! I hate boys!"

"It's in the nature of them," Delia said. She had let the top spin itself out and bent over now to wind the whip around it. "Cocky, arrogant fellows every one of them. And they don't improve much with the aging."

Rich baritone laughter filled the air. Meg had been watching Dr. Ty approach them from the direction of Colonel Bishop's stable, leading a pretty bay mare. But Delia had her back to him and at the sound of his laughter, she straightened with a snap and spun around as fast as any top, her hand pressed to her breast as if she was trying to keep her heart from flying right out of it.

"Damn ye, Tyler Savitch, how dare ye sneak up on me like that!"

Ty draped the horse's reins over his shoulder and hooked a thumb into the waistband of his breeches, thrusting his hip out. "I didn't sneak up on you. I walked up quite brazenly. And don't believe a word she says, Meg honey." He smiled down at Meg, tugging on one of her pigtails, but a second later his eyes, glinting with mischievous lights, were fastened back onto Delia's face. "We're not all cocky, arrogant fellows. Take me, for instance—"

"Ha!" Delia exclaimed, her face turning berry-red. "Why, even Anne Bishop thinks you're worse'n a turkey cock with all your strutting ways."

Dr. Ty looked hurt, but Meg could tell he was only pretending because of the way the corners of his mouth twitched. From Delia's flushed face and angry eyes, Meg got a distinct impression that the woman didn't much like the doctor. But before she could ponder the reason for this she noticed her father, with Tildy by the hand, standing alongside the trestle tables and waving her over. People were crowding around the tables, sitting down on benches, stools, and chests. Already the plates of food were being passed around, along with jugs of spruce beer and apple cider.

"Hey, we're eating dinner now!" she announced. The two grown-ups seemed too busy glowering at each other to notice, so after a moment she shrugged, picked up her top, and ran off.

Delia took a step after the girl, but Ty stopped her by placing a hand on her arm. As usual his touch brought the blood rushing hot to her face and shortened her breath. What had ever made her think that becoming another man's wife would change how she felt about this one? She would always love him, but from now on she would have to take care not to let it show, not even to him. Oh, especially not to him.

Averting her head, she pulled away from him. "Ty, don't . . . Nat's probably waiting . . ." she faltered, unable to look at him.

"In a minute," he said. "I'd like to give you your wedding gift first."

That brought her head around and her chin up. Her eyes went from his mocking smile to the bay mare he had by the lead. The mare tossed her head and blew air out her nose, and Delia recognized her as the horse he had given her once before—that morning in Portsmouth when he had first said the words: *Let me make love to you . . .*

She sucked in a sharp breath. "I gave that horse back to ye once already an' ye can bloody well have it back again—"

Delia's chin had started to come up even higher and he gripped it between his thumb and finger. "The horse is for *both* you and Nat. And don't keep throwing my gifts back in my face, brat. It isn't polite."

Delia jerked free of his grasp. The skin burned where he had touched her and she had to quell an impulse to rub it. "You won't mind, though, if I'm not overcome with gratitude. I've learned, you see, not to put a whole lot of value into the meaning of your gifts."

Ty's face tightened, his nostrils flaring, and Delia instantly regretted her hurtful, nasty words. She felt small because of her churlish behavior. Before long he wouldn't even want her for a friend.

She swallowed hard and summoned her courage to meet his eyes directly. "I'm sorry, Ty. I *was* being rude. She's a beautiful horse and a valuable gift and I thank you for it."

For a moment longer his mouth stayed pressed into a tight line, his eyes boring mercilessly into hers. Then his fury left him along with his pent-up breath. "Aw, Delia, I didn't mean to anger you by giving you the horse. You seemed so excited the first time you saw her. I thought she would please you."

"She does please me, Ty, truly. And Nat'll be pleased, too. She'll be useful to us on the farm, because Nat's only got the one horse now and she's a mite old."

A delighted, boyish smile lit up Ty's face, bringing happiness surging within her. "Actually, the truth is Nat's already seen her. He's planning on riding her this afternoon in the race."

Ty stepped over to the Bishops' hitching post, looping the mare's reins around the rail. He leaned back with his arms straight, his palms braced against the rough wood. He had discarded his coat somewhere, and his shirtsleeves were rolled up to his elbows. Sunlight glinted off the golden brown hair on his tanned forearms. Yet even in this relaxed and masculine pose he seemed tense. Delia was drawn to come stand beside him. She wrapped her hands around the rail and leaned backward, locking her knees and swinging back and forth on her heels. They could be friends now, she was sure of it. Lord above us, but it felt so fine just to look at him.

"What is this horse race you mentioned?" she asked when the silence between them began to feel too intimate. "Seems I've heard nothing but talk of it all afternoon."

The breeze snatched a lock of his hair, blowing it across his forehead, and he tossed his head back, just as the mare had done a moment ago. "It's a tradition at all Merrymeeting frolics."

"I suppose it's you who always wins."

"You suppose wrong. But then I don't compete."

"Afraid of losing, are you?"

His lips quivered with repressed amusement. "No, brat. I don't compete in the race because *I* am the prize. Or rather the prize is a free baby."

"What!" Delia exclaimed, laughing. She let go of the hitching post, straightening to look at him.

"Whoever wins the race, I help deliver his next kid free of charge. It's a valuable prize because my services aren't cheap. And what with the long, cold winters we have up here, folk in Merrymeeting are always having babies."

Unaware she was even doing it, Delia's eyes roamed his face lovingly. "Oh, Ty," she blurted out. "You are truly the most remarkable, wonderful man!"

The laughter fled his face. He looked away from her, out at the thick wilderness forest that stretched into the hills. His eyes had darkened to the color of an autumn sky at dusk. "Not so wonderful . . . Delia, I'm sorry about those hurtful things I said to you earlier. I don't know what—"

"Don't, Ty. Don't let's speak of it. It's over and done with and I'm . . . I'm married now." Delia's heart felt as if it would crack in two.

Their eyes met, then pulled apart. When he turned back he touched her again, this time squeezing her shoulder in a brief, almost impersonal caress, and yet it brought her heart thudding up into her throat. "I hope you'll be happy, Delia," he said, a roughness in his voice. "I wish you and Nat all the happiness in the world."

She nodded jerkily, unable to speak and hoping he couldn't hear her heart thumping so heavily in her breast. Or see the tears pooling in her eyes.

"Well . . ." His hand fell from her shoulder, brushing against her arm, and she had to set her jaw to keep from shivering. "We'd better get something to eat while there's still some left."

He walked off, leaving her. She followed him with her eyes, aching for him, aching for herself. And still wanting what she would never have.

Delia bunched her skirts into a wad between her knees, revealing the shapliest ankles Ty had ever seen. Grinning, he watched as she hurled the ball at the wicket—in this case a three-legged stool. Daniel Randolf swung his stick bat through the air so hard his momentum curled him around on his toes. But the ball sailed past him untouched, bowling the stool over.

"Ha-ha!" Meg Parkes bellowed, cupping her hands around her mouth. "You missed, Daniel!"

Daniel whipped around to glare at her. "Ye just shut up, Meg Parkes!"

Ty glanced down at the girl's dark head. "I thought you and young Daniel were sweet on each other."

"Ugh!" Meg screwed her face up into such a grimace of disgust that Ty laughed. "I hate him! He's mean as a rabid coon and he's uglier than a stump fence to boot."

Ty glanced at the lad in question. In truth, Daniel Randolf was a fine-looking boy, with a lithe, athletic body and hair so golden it outshone the sun. Give them another couple of years, Ty thought, and they'd be trading kisses instead of insults.

Tildy Parkes sat cross-legged on the ground in front of Ty, leaning against his legs. She removed her thumb from her mouth long enough to pipe up, "Dr. Ty? Girls can play stool-ball just as good as boys. Delia says so!"

"She appears to be right," Ty said. He laughed again as another Randolf boy took a good cut at Delia's bowled ball, only to miss.

She was a delight to look at. The sun glinted off the ruby lights in her hair, and the wind caught it, fluttering wisps like feathers against her face. Her cheeks glowed as fresh as dew-wet peaches. But especially intriguing was what the motion of throwing the ball did to her full breasts. As she pulled her arm back, they rose, pointing skyward. Then, as she flung the hand with the ball forward, they dipped down, pressing together to form a deep crease of cleavage, only to come up again, bouncing provocatively on the followthrough—

"Delia's my new ma," Tildy stated proudly.

Ty's head jerked up like a startled stag's. His chest felt pinched and he sucked in a deep, shuddering breath. Christ, what was he doing—lusting after the girl like this? Delia wasn't his little tavern wench any longer. She was another man's wife.

"Delia!"

Nathaniel Parkes crossed the green, walking so fast his wooden foot put a big hitch in his stride. At the sound of his voice, Delia tossed the ball to one of the boys and, letting her skirts fall, ran forward to meet him. She was slightly out of breath and her breasts rose and fell quickly within the tight confines of her bodice. Ty had to force himself to look away.

Nat didn't seem to have any trouble resisting his new wife's charms. "What were you doing?" he demanded angrily.

"I was just showing the girls how to bowl—"

"I saw that. I meant why would you make such a spectacle of yourself?" He flung his arm out from his side. "For the love of heaven, everybody's watching!"

It was a slight exaggeration. Most of the women were still bustling around the trestle tables, clearing away the empty plates and platters, and the men had gathered at the end of the green, getting ready for the start of the horse race.

Delia looked up at him, her forehead creased. "But what harm—"

"Harm! Did you give no thought to what people will think? And furthermore, Delia, I will not have you encouraging my daughters in this sort of hoydenish behavior. My Mary would never have countenanced such actions, let alone engaged in them herself."

Delia reacted as if he'd slapped her, hunching her shoulders and dipping her head down. "I'm sorry . . . I didn't think."

Anger washed over Ty and he opened his mouth to come to Delia's defense, then promptly shut it. If Nat Parkes didn't want his wife playing stoolball, it was certainly his place to forbid it. Slowly, Ty let out his breath and relaxed his fists. But he was left surprised and shaken at the burst of protectiveness he had felt for Delia.

Nat patted the top of Delia's head as if she were a cowering dog he'd just whipped. "Never mind. I know your intention wasn't to shame me."

Just then Colonel Bishop began whacking on a triangle, summoning everybody for the start of the race. Meg, who had been watching Delia's humiliation with a triumphant smirk, slipped away from Ty's side and trotted up to her father. "The race is about ready to start, Papa. You don't want to miss it."

Ty helped Tildy lurch to her feet and she, too, ran up to her father. Nat swung her up in the air, settling her down on his shoulders. "Let's go then, girls." He smiled at Ty. "Thanks to the doc's wedding gift, this is one race I think I'm going to win."

Delia watched her new husband walk off with his daughters, her face tight and drawn. She turned to look at him, and Ty saw her breasts heave once as she fought down tears.

"Lord above us, I'm such a wooden-headed fool for even thinkin'—think*ing,*" she corrected herself through gritted teeth, "that I'm capable of acting like a proper lady."

"Aw, Delia-girl . . ."

Ty's heart ached for her, for he knew exactly how she must feel—shame and pride all tangled together until it became a knot in your gut that wouldn't go away. There had been countless times in that first year after he'd been dragged back to the Yengi world when he'd slipped up and inadvertently done something that marked him as an "Abenaki savage." He had felt a bitter, frustrated shame at the looks of horror and disgust on the faces of those around him. But he had felt a traitor as well. As if by turning his back on the Abenaki ways, he was denying the man who for ten years had raised and loved him as a son.

Ty wanted to wrap his arm around Delia's shoulders and pull her against him, to kiss the tears from her eyes. But of course he couldn't. He started to take her hand before he realized he shouldn't be doing even that anymore. His hand clenched into a fist. "Come on, brat. Let's go watch the race."

She nodded, wiping at a stray tear that had escaped to meander down her cheek. "All right, Ty," she said, giving him a brave smile that broke his heart.

Ty went back to the manor house to pick up the starting pistol and was crossing the green when the Reverend Caleb Hooker joined him.

Caleb flashed his engaging smile. "I've been told the prize for this affair is a free baby."

Ty grinned. "That's right, Reverend. Aren't you going to compete? A prize like that—it should be coming in handy for you and Elizabeth before too long."

Caleb flushed. His eyes drifted over to Elizabeth, who still sat at one of the trestle tables, talking with Anne Bishop and Hannah Randolf, the blacksmith's pregnant wife. For a moment, a moment so brief Ty wasn't sure if he had imagined it, the young minister's face darkened with anguish.

But when he turned back to Ty the crooked-toothed smile was back in place. "It appears as if Mrs. Randolf's the one in most imminent need of the prize."

"With Hannah Randolf such a need is *always* imminent. If you want to ride, I've got a horse I can loan you."

Caleb laughed, shaking his head. He glanced wistfully at the men who were doing some last minute adjusting to saddles and stirrups before mounting up. "Somehow I don't think my superiors back in Boston would approve of one of their ministers riding hellbent for leather in a horse race."

Ty wondered if the young reverend knew that there was some heavy betting being done on the race's outcome. He probably did, Ty thought, but judiciously chose to ignore it.

Merrymeeting horse races traditionally covered five miles. They started at the weathervaned pine tree in the middle of the green, looped around the mast house and lumber works, dipped down to the new meetinghouse and parsonage, and then followed the cart track out to the farms. Here, out of sight of witnesses, the race always turned into a free-for-all, with each contestant using every dirty trick to jockey his horse into the lead. What man couldn't unseat, the thick and savage wilderness could. Four miles later, the race wound up back at the settlement, circling the blockhouse and finishing up at the lone pine tree. The winner was usually the horse and rider who had simply hung on to survive it, and Dr. Savitch had treated many a broken bone and abrasion following a Merrymeeting horse race.

It was also Ty's task to signal the start. He took his place beneath the pine, the women and children in a semicircle around him, and raised Colonel Bishop's old pistol above his head. Ty was acutely aware that Delia had drifted over to stand beside him. For some stupid reason his heart was knocking against his rib cage and he kept forgetting to breathe.

His voice cracked as he called out, "Gentlemen, take your marks!"

There wasn't exactly a starting line, so the riders pushed

and shoved against each other for the best vantage, growling and swearing good-naturedly.

Ty cocked the pistol. "Get set."

"Hey, Doc!" somebody yelled. "Fer Chrissakes, git on with it!"

Laughing, Ty pulled the trigger. The crack of the gunshot bounced across the water, its echo drowned out by yells and the thundering of hooves across the green.

Delia, her earlier humiliation forgotten, jumped up and down with excitement. As the horses and their riders rounded the meetinghouse, heading for open country, Nat was in the lead, and Delia clutched Ty's arm, whooping in his ear.

"Look, Ty, look! Nat's ahead. Oh, I hope he wins!"

Her fingers pressing into his arm sent a jolt through Ty, drawing his head around to look into her laughing face—and the ramifications of what she had just said finally struck home, as if an angry giant had balled up a fist and landed a blow smack in the middle of his gut. The prize was a free birthing of the winner's next child . . .

And Nat's next child would be by Delia.

Nat won the race.

The bay mare burst out of the forest on the stockade side of Merrymeeting, with Nat clinging to her neck and one foot dangling from the stirrup. They still had to circle the palisades before galloping to the finish, but the mare was a good three lengths ahead of the closest rival and with plenty of wind left in her. The only question was whether Nat could manage to hang on until they reached the tree.

At last Nat and the mare careened around the pine. He hauled desperately on the reins and the mare skidded to a stop, spraying up divots of marsh grass and dirt. He fell out of the saddle, wobbling a bit as his entire weight landed briefly on his wooden foot. There was a jagged rip in one sleeve of his Sabbath-day suit and a pair of gashes on his forehead trickled blood, but his face bore a triumphant grin.

Delia scooped up Tildy and, with Meg at her heels, ran up to Nat. She was so excited she flung her free arm around his neck, kissing him on the mouth. "Oh, Nat, Nat. Ye've won!" Nat stiffened and set her away from him, but the action went unnoticed for Meg had thrown herself against her father, wrapping her arms around his waist, chattering excitedly and hopping up and down.

"Papa won! Papa won!" Tildy cried, her voice shrill.

"Aye, that he did," Delia said, laughing and handing the little girl into her father's arms.

"Gosh," Meg said, her thin face blazing with pride. "He's never won before."

Nat's laugh was low and bubbly as he rubbed the top of his daughter's head. "Hush, young'un. Don't throw all my past failures up in my face."

The others gathered around to congratulate the winner as the stragglers made it back to the finish line. The blacksmith, Sam Randolf, slid from his horse alongside Ty, lightly thumping Ty on the shoulder with his fist. "It 'pears like ye'll be settlin' up this prize long about nine months from now, eh, Doc?"

He'd said the words loud enough for all to hear and everybody laughed. A couple of the men cracked more ribald jokes about the wedding night to come. Nat blushed furiously, but then his eyes met Delia's and his mouth creased into a slow smile. He slid his arm around her waist, pulling her against him.

"Papa, are you going to be shooting your mettle tonight?" Tildy asked loudly from her perch on her father's hip, innocently picking up on a not-so-innocent comment one of the men had made.

Nat quickly covered his daughter's mouth with his hand. "You hush now, Tildy," he said, grinning bashfully at Delia. "Remember good little girls are seen and not heard."

Ty watched it all—the blushes and shared smiles, the proprietary caresses—and knew for the first time in his life the searing pain of a bitter jealousy. An image flickered across his mind of Nat covering a naked Delia with his large body, thrusting into her hot, tight wetness, and of Delia's head falling back, her face suffused with passion and fulfillment.

Ty shuddered violently, squeezing his eyes shut. *You asked for this, Savitch, you big damn idiot. You wanted her safely married off where she couldn't drive you crazy arousing feel-*

ings you weren't ready to handle. Now how are you going to manage to handle this?

It didn't matter that Nat felt no love for Delia. Theirs was a marriage of convenience, but it was still a marriage.

And tonight Delia would sleep in Nat's bed.

The somnolent feelings generated by the large meal and the warm sun had been banished by the excitement of the horse race, and a note of frenzied merriment entered into the frolic. A few of the settlers who were musically inclined put together an ensemble of fiddles and a Jew's harp.

Even if he'd been able to manage with his wooden foot, Nat Parkes, as a strict Congregationalist, eschewed dancing. Delia stood beside her new husband with a forlorn smile on her face, watching the other couples romp through the spirited country dances.

Ty couldn't bear seeing her unhappy. Cursing himself for making what he knew was a mistake, he approached her, performing a courtly bow. "Would you dance with me, Delia?"

She cast an apprehensive glance at Nat. "Well, I . . ."

"You know I don't hold with dancing, Dr. Ty," Nat said. " 'Tis the devil's handiwork."

Ty's mouth stretched into a tight smile. He nodded toward the circle of whirling couples that included a flush-faced Elizabeth and a laughing Caleb. "If the reverend perceives no danger in it, I should think your wife's soul is probably safe from corruption." And before Nat could argue further, Ty slipped his arm around Delia and pulled her into the ring of dancers. For a few seconds she moved stiffly, but soon she gave herself over to the joy of the music. Their bodies joined together and parted as they moved through the intricate steps.

He tried to shut his senses off to the look, the feel of her, but it would have been like trying to hold back the sunrise. The wind flicked tendrils of her hair against his neck, sending chills rippling along his skin. There was a damp spot between the hollow of her breasts that fluttered with her panting breaths. She smelled sweetly of rosewater and muskily of woman. He knew how she would look naked and beneath him.

He wanted her naked and beneath him.

She whirled away from him and her expressive mouth laughed, her golden eyes beckoned, beckoned . . . He thought of the wide, fur-covered bed in the loft back at his cabin. He was hard and empty and hungry for her. Oh God, how he longed to take her home this night and lay her across that big, wide bed.

For a few wild moments, the Abenaki part of him actually contemplated snatching her up, throwing her over his horse, and riding away with her into the wilderness. He would build them a snug little wigwam on the shores of some remote northern lake and fill it with a bed of fragrant balsam. And on that bed he would spend the days and nights loving her like crazy until—

Delia's foot landed on a clump of hawkweed and her ankle twisted beneath her. She staggered sideways, falling, and his arms went out to catch her. His face was so close to hers her breath bathed his cheek, warm and moist and sweet. His chest flattened her breasts and he could feel the vibration of her thundering heart. His rocklike, pulsing sex fit perfectly between the cleft of her legs, and unconsciously he moved his hips, pressing harder.

Her breath caught on a ragged sob.

He raised his head to look down into her face—at the tawny, brimming eyes; the parted, wet lips; the sweet, delicate curve of cheek and jaw . . . He came within a hair's breadth of crushing his mouth down over hers and to hell with the fact that her husband and all of Merrymeeting were watching.

"Let go of me, Ty . . . *Please,*" she whispered in a deep-throated appeal.

He released her just as the fiddles screeched to a halt and she fled from him. Ty looked around him as someone tuned up a hornpipe and the others lined up for the next dance. Everyone seemed oblivious to the drama that had been unfolding before their eyes.

That's because nothing really happened, Ty told himself. But he knew it for a lie.

Everything had happened.

Chapter 16

⌢⌢⌢⌢

A t the sound of the door opening, Delia whipped around,
her hand fluttering to her throat.

"I didn't mean to startle you," Nat said.

"I just didn't expect you . . . so soon." Delia faltered.

Nat avoided her eyes. "It took the girls a while to settle
down, but once they got into b-bed, they fell right to sleep."

"It was a long day for them."

Nat's glance drifted around the room, flitting from the calfskin chest to the pine dresser with its earthenware pitcher and
basin, to the calico curtains fluttering in the open window.
And carefully avoiding the bed in the corner. "Long day for
us too," he said.

"Aye . . ."

The damn bed, Delia thought, filled the room. It was a
fine cord bed of painted black ash, with downy quilts and a
feather mattress. It looked soft and inviting, and she yearned
to stretch out on it in sleep. But first . . .

A hot flush of nervousness washed over Delia. She stepped
closer to the open window where the cool night breeze could
bathe her face. It was so quiet she could hear the silky whisper of the cornstalks and the rustle of the pine boughs. In the
distance she caught the soft hoot of an owl. There was a
tactile quality to the night, a velvety blackness. The heel of
a fading moon gave off little light.

Inside, a betty lamp bathed the room with a soft glowing
luster. Nat pulled the wick out with the pick to make it burn
even brighter. He prowled the room, limping badly, the floppy
sea boots he had to wear to fit over his wooden foot slapping

231

loudly against his shins. Delia wondered if his stump got to hurting by the end of the day. A crutch leaned against the wall by the empty hearth. Perhaps he normally removed the wooden foot when he came in from working the fields.

She swallowed, clearing her throat. "Nat? Why don't you take off your foot, if it's paining you?"

He swung around to stare at her, his mouth drawn into a tight line. "The only one ever to see my stump was my wife."

But *I'm* your wife now! she wanted to shout at him. "I only meant it wouldn't bother me to see you footless."

As soon as the words were out, Delia cursed her flapping tongue. But to her surprise Nat actually laughed. It only lasted a second or two and was more of a chuckle than a laugh. But it dissipated some of the tension in the room.

In the silence that had followed Nat's laughter, his eyes flickered over to the bed. "Frolics make a break from the work, but there's always double the chores to do the next day. We should be getting our rest."

"Aye . . ." Delia squeaked.

He crossed the distance to stand before her.

His big hands encircled her arms. He stared down into her face, his expression grim now. Then he lowered his head and pressed his lips against hers.

There was no commingling of tongues, no open mouths. He barely moved his lips. Yet Delia's throat spasmed as if she would gag. She stood it as long as she could before twisting her head aside and fighting to keep from choking. She couldn't look at Nat, but she heard him heave a sigh. It almost sounded like a sigh of relief, as if he, too, had wanted only for the kiss to be over.

He reached in back of her, pulling the shutters closed and slipping the latch in place. In silence, he turned away from her and began to undress.

Delia supposed that she, too, would have to remove her clothes, but she couldn't move. Nat had discarded his coat and waistcoat when they first came home. Now he pulled his shirttail from the waistband of his breeches, untied his kerchief, and drew the shirt over his head. His chest was smooth and hairless and very white, his muscles flaccid and ropy. A small paunch sagged around his middle.

As he hung his shirt on a wall peg, he felt Delia's eyes on him and looked up. His flushed face darkened even more. "Is something the matter?"

Delia jerked as if he'd shouted at her. She brought her hands up to the front of her short gown, but they were shaking so uncontrollably she couldn't manage the buttons.

He gestured weakly at the door. "Perhaps I'll just step out for a minute."

Delia nodded dumbly and after Nat had left the room, her eyes squeezed shut in relief.

She hurried to undress. There were four pegs on the wall. Two were in use with Nat's things; two were empty. Mary used to hang her clothes on them, Delia thought, her chest tight with repressed tears. What, she wondered, had Nat done with all of Mary's things?

Besides the new short gown and petticoat, Anne had also made Delia a nightrail for her wedding night. The yoke and cuffs were embroidered with eyelet lace that Anne had found in her scrap box. Delia paused only a few seconds to admire the nightrail before pulling it on. She ran a brush rapidly through her hair and then slipped into bed. The sheets were smooth beneath her bare legs, but cool, and she shivered. She debated turning off the lamp on the calfskin chest beside the bed, finally deciding Nat might prefer it left on.

Nat was so long in returning that Delia had almost drifted into sleep. She turned over drowsily at the sound of the door opening, then tensed as he entered. He hesitated in the doorway before coming toward the bed. Their eyes met, then pulled nervously apart. He wet the corner of his mouth with his tongue.

She remembered the feel of his mouth on hers. She hoped he would just do . . . what he had to do without any more kisses. She shut her mind to the memory of another mouth—warmer, firmer lips and probing, thrusting tongue . . .

Nat extinguished the lamp and the room plunged into darkness.

The mattress sagged as he dropped down on it. He sat with his back to her. Delia heard clunking sounds as his big boots came off, then the mattress moved again and there was a rustle of clothing as he pulled down his breeches. She could see the shadow of his shape, bent over, and realized he was removing his wooden foot. She heard the flap of leather slapping on wood and then the creak of the ankle hinge. Did all married couples undress in the dark? she wondered. It seemed strange to her suddenly to realize that she wouldn't be able to see Nat's face while he made love to her. But then, she thought gratefully, he wouldn't be able to see hers.

A draft of cool air washed over Delia as Nat pulled the covers back, getting into bed. She lay stiff and tried to keep from trembling. Yet when his hand reached across the space between them and touched her breast, she jumped.

He moved closer. He wrapped his arm around her waist and pulled her almost roughly against him. Delia's leg rolled, falling inadvertently against his loins. For the briefest second her knee pressed against his small and flaccid sex, before she straightened with a jerk, and he twisted away from her.

Sliding his legs off the bed, he sat up, keeping his back to her. During all this neither had made a sound and Delia suddenly became aware of the noisy rasping of her own breathing.

"I can't do it," Nat said.

She swallowed around the enormous lump in her throat.

"I'm sorry, Delia . . . but I just can't do it. She's only been dead three months, my Mary." He spoke away from her, into the darkness, his voice thick with pain. "We were married for ten years. Ten years we slept together in this bed. Every night but for the births of our girls and the times I went to Wells for muster days. She is—*was*—the only woman I've ever . . . It's nothing against you, Delia, but I just can't . . ."

"Nat, please. I understand." She pushed herself half upright, leaning back against the pillow.

He twisted his head to look at her. It was too dark for Delia to make out the expression on his face. "This afternoon when I saw you coming down the stairs and later watching you dance, you looked so pretty. I thought maybe . . ." His voice trailed off. She felt him shrug. "But even the thought of . . . It makes me feel so guilty. To think of touching another woman. I know she's dead, I *know* it, but I can't help feeling I would be betraying her . . ."

Tentatively she reached out and touched him on the shoulder. "There's nothing that says we have to do it right away."

His breath came out in a loud sigh. "No, no. There's nothing that says . . . that. And, besides, with you being a virgin, you'll need more time anyway. Until we get to know each other better," he added hopefully.

Delia blessed the darkness that he couldn't see her face. It hadn't occurred to her that he would expect her to be a virgin. She almost laughed hysterically—he had gone from believing her a whore to thinking her a virgin! *Oh, Lord above us, Delia, how d' ye get yersel' into these predicaments?*

"Delia?"

She released a fluttery breath. "Aye, that's what we need, Nat. Time to get to know each other better."

Relief made Nat laugh nervously. The mattress shifted as he stood up. Gripping the bedpost for balance, he hopped over to the crutch by the hearth. He secured it beneath his armpit and turned back toward the bed. "Delia . . . ?"

Her throat made a loud clicking noise as she swallowed. "Nat, there's no need for you to—"

"Delia . . . I think for the time being I'll bed down elsewhere. There's a shakedown in the linter. I can spread it out at night and roll it back up during the day. Truth to tell, my Mary always accused me of snoring loud enough to wake the d-dead. You'll get more rest with the b-bed all to yourself."

He lifted his shirt and breeches off the wall peg, tucking them beneath the arm he had braced on the crutch. He paused with his hand on the door latch. "You did look pretty this afternoon, Delia. I felt proud to be standing up with you, to be taking you to wife."

"Th-thank you, Nat."

The door opened, throwing a glowing red light from the keeping room fire onto the bed, then it shut behind him.

Delia slid back down beneath the quilts. Rolling over, she buried her face in the pillow. Her throat clutched on a sob, but she fought it down. She felt so alone. She wanted to be held, touched, loved. But not by Nat, not by just any man.

It was Ty she wanted.

* * *

He didn't love her.

That's what he told himself. Yet if he didn't love her, why was he skulking out here in the dark, staring at the open window of the room where she would soon lay in the arms of her new husband?

He leaned against a stone wall built of the rocks that Nat Parkes had laboriously cleared from his fields. Ty could feel the roughness of the stone through the thin material of his shirt. The night was cool, but he was sweating. There was a tightness to his chest and his muscles were so tense they ached.

He straightened suddenly as she came into view, silhouetted against the yellow light of the window. She was alone, staring out into the night and, though he knew it was impossible, Ty imagined she could see him standing beside the wall beneath the trees. He leaned forward, yearning to call out to her.

Then Nat appeared and took her in his arms.

The sight of Nat plundering her sweet mouth caused Ty to whirl around and slam his fist on top of the wall, again and again, until the skin broke and splatters of dark blood appeared on the stone. The yellow light winked out and Ty heard the shutters clatter closed. His head fell back, his eyelids clenched tightly shut, and the cords of his neck stood out like ropes. His fist throbbed with pain. He wanted to howl, to scream the Abenaki cry of war and death.

He pushed himself away from the wall and trotted back into the forest. He was afraid of what he might do, of what he *wanted* to do, which was to burst into Nat's house and snatch Delia out of her bridal bed, to carry her off with him. To make her his again and again until he was cured of her, until the hunger was satiated, the obsession satisfied.

He made no sound as he ran through the wilderness. But he was dangerously oblivious to his surroundings. The image of Delia in Nat's arms, of their mouths locked together in passion, consumed his mind.

He broke into the clearing where his cabin stood beside a bend in the river. The sound of the rushing water was no louder than his own pounding pulse. He tossed his head back and looked up at the fading sliver of a moon. For a moment the moon blurred and he had to blink.

"Delia!" he shouted, disturbing the dark silence. "Damn you, Delia," he whispered. "Damn you, damn you, damn you. I'm not in love with you. Do you hear me?" He was shouting again. "I am not, goddamn you, in love with you!"

One morning three days later, Nat Parkes and his two daughters sat at the board table in the keeping room finishing up their breakfast. The house was filled with the aroma of burned beans, for Delia had scorched the porridge.

Nat thumbed through the worn, dogeared pages of his almanac. "This hot, dry spell we've been having isn't due to last long," he said. "And August is supposed to be a wet one this year. We'd best start to get the hay in today."

Delia walked around the table with the voider, clearing it of the breakfast dishes. She took away Tildy's porringer to reveal a ring of thick bread crusts. She hurriedly tried to scoop them into the voider, but she wasn't quick enough.

"Tildy, finish your bread," Nat said sternly.

Tildy's lower lip trembled. "But, Papa, it's too hard!"

"Ma's bread was always nice and soft," Meg stated predictably. She sneered at Delia.

Delia had made the bread the evening before, putting it in the oven to bake overnight, banking the fire with ashes to keep it hot. She had been proud of her efforts—until this morning when she had taken the somewhat blackened loaves out of the oven and bitten into a piece of the tough, crusty bread. It was almost inedible.

Delia kept her head bowed, but she could feel Nat's censorious eyes on her. "N-never mind. I can soak it in water and feed it to the pigs."

"But that's wasteful, Delia."

"What would ye have me do with it then?" she snapped at him. She felt close to tears. After only three days she knew she was going to be a miserable failure as a farmer's wife.

At the crack of dawn on the first day Nat had milked the goat for her, showing her how it was done and making it very clear that milking was a special favor a man did only rarely for a woman. The next morning, Delia tackled the chore herself, and the hateful beast tried to eat her hair, then kicked the stool, knocking over the bucket when her back was turned.

She returned to the house with a scant inch of milk in the bottom of the piggin and Nat hadn't bothered to hide his disappointment.

The next day she took the hoe to the garden, only to be told by a gloating Meg that after three hours of work in the broiling sun the weeds she thought she had dug up were instead beets and turnips, and what she had taken to be healthy vegetable shoots were in fact the strangling roots of the skunk cabbage weed.

"Delia's gone and ruined Ma's garden," Meg had tattled to a frowning Nat when he came in from the fields for dinner.

And I've started this day by ruining breakfast, Delia thought with despair. She dreaded what new disasters the rest of the day would bring, for the chores—and thus the opportunities for mistakes—were endless.

Already that morning she had mucked the barn and forked in fresh hay, scattered grain for the hens, gathered eggs, and milked the goat—and all that was before fixing the bean porridge which she had managed to scorch. She sighed now at the sight of the bowls of uneaten food. Then she noticed that all the noggins of hot chocolate were empty. She had made it with fresh goat's milk and sweetened it with molasses, something she dimly remembered her mother doing.

At least, she thought with a tiny spark of pride, I didn't manage to burn *everything*.

"I've got to get at the haying," Nat said, startling Delia by slamming the almanac shut and getting to his feet. She noticed guiltily that his homespun breeches were missing a knee buckle. She had promised she would sew it back on last night, then promptly had forgotten about it. The bit of pride she had felt earlier faded and she sighed loudly. She would never make a good wife.

Nat beckoned to Meg. "Come lend me a hand with the haying, girl. Delia, when you're done with the housework we could use your help as well."

Delia drew in a deep breath, summoning her courage. "Nat? I'd like to go into Merrymeeting sometime this afternoon for an hour or so . . . to take a lesson from Mrs. Bishop."

He paused and turned to look at her. "Has she agreed to

teach you how to spin then? I don't know, Delia. The haying's more important at the moment."

Delia wet her dry lips with her tongue and twisted her hands together behind her back. "Not to spin. She's teaching me my letters."

He slashed his hand through the air. "You've no time for that now. No use for it either."

"But I've only just started to learn. I don't want to quit—"

"I've said my piece on it, Delia, and that's final."

Their eyes clashed. "I'm going, Nat. I'll catch up on my chores this evening, but I'm going."

His eyes narrowed and his hand clenched into a fist. He took a step toward her and she steeled herself for a blow, but just then Tildy let out a loud wail. They both whipped around and looked at the table, where the little girl sat rubbing vigorously at her right eye.

"My eye hurts! My eye hurts!"

Delia knelt beside her, pulling her hand away. "Let me see, little puss." Nat came over and hunkered down as well. There was a small, inflamed red swelling on the rim of Tildy's eyelid.

"It's only a stye," Nat said, his voice still tight with anger. "Take her over to Dr. Ty's this morning. He'll know what to do about it."

Delia's heart lurched. "But I don't . . . Maybe Meg can—"

"Meg's helping me with the haying. She knows how it's done and I don't want to have to waste an hour this morning teaching it to you."

Delia wiped the tears from Tildy's fat cheeks with the pads of her thumbs. "It'll be all right," she crooned. "We'll take a walk over to Dr. Savitch's and he'll fix you right up."

Tildy's mouth dimpled. "Will Dr. Ty give me a cookie? Last time, when I cut my knee, he gave me a cookie."

"Why, I expect he will then."

Nat had stood up. He plucked his broad-brimmed felt hat from a peg near the hearth and headed for the enclosed porch and the front door.

"Nat," Delia said to his retreating back, "I'm going into Merrymeeting this afternoon. For my lesson."

Nat's back stiffened, but he kept going. A moment later she heard the slam of the front door.

Meg lingered a moment, her eyes wide but the expression on her face inscrutable. "You made Papa angry."

"Aye, I did," Delia acknowledged, too disheartened for it to matter anymore that Meg hated her.

"Don't you care?"

"Aye, I care. But those lessons are important to me, Meg."

From outside came the sharp sound of her father's voice calling to her. Meg looked behind her at the door, then back at Delia again. "You remember how you said you could teach me to spin the top? Do you think maybe tomorrow . . ."

Delia suddenly smiled. "Of course I haven't forgotten. We'll do it tomorrow. But after the haying's done so's we don't get to riling your da further by neglecting our chores, huh?"

Meg's pinched face relaxed and she even managed a smile. "Meg!"

"You best go. Your da's calling for you."

Meg scurried out the door and Delia removed her scratchy work smock. Tildy followed her into the inner room, chattering about Dr. Ty and cookies while Delia put on her new linen short gown. There was no looking glass in the house, but the windowpanes showed her reflection well enough for her to straighten her hair and put on a calash to protect her head from the fierce sun. She was aware that two bright spots of color stained her cheeks and her heart raced abnormally fast. She didn't care; she was going to see Ty this morning.

Nat owned four acres of salt marsh along the river where his hay grew. As Delia, with Tildy holding her hand, walked along the trail that followed the river, she spotted Nat and Meg at work. Nat mowed the hay with a scythe. Meg followed in the swaths he left behind him, raking it into rows which would later be tied into stocks. The stocks would then be hauled by a sledge to the rick alongside the barn. Delia waved at them, but they didn't pause in their work to wave back.

The river was sluggish that morning. A fish broke the surface, leaping for a fly and startling a great blue heron into flight. They passed patches of strawberries that looked so mouth-watering that Delia promised herself she would stop on the way back and fill her skirt with the luscious ripe fruit. Tildy laughed with delight and pointed as a squirrel darted ahead of them, twitching its red tail.

After a while the riverbank steepened and the trail veered off into the forest. They entered into a midday twilight where sunlight filtered through the thick trees, giving the world a weird green glow. At first it was eerily quiet and then a pair of chickadees began to chirp, trading songs.

They paused on the edge of a clearing and Delia sucked in her breath with delight. Before her was a tidy log cabin with a wide front porch, and surrounding it was a profusion of colorful blooms—beds of blue flag, wild roses, and huckleberry. The river rushed by, creating its own song as it trickled over rocks. Nearby, not too far from a bank resplendent with swaying pussy willows and a thicket of raspberry canes, was a small, conical-shaped hut covered with animal skins and birchbark. It looked to be an Indian dwelling of some sort and Delia wondered what its purpose could be.

Tildy squealed, squirming out of Delia's arms. "Dr. Ty, Dr. Ty, I got a stye! Can I have a cookie?"

A black cat uncurled from beneath the steps and sauntered out to wrap around Tildy's legs. She let out another squeal of delight and plopped down on her bottom. The cat rolled onto its back, purring loudly.

Delia approached more warily, telling herself not to be a wooden-headed fool. But she couldn't seem to stop her heart from beating heavily, and she couldn't seem to take a deep enough breath. She stopped at the bottom of the steps and looked up. From the heat on her cheeks she knew that she was blushing.

He sat on the porch, tilted back on a chair's hind legs, one booted foot braced against the porch rail, an empty flip mug resting on his thigh. His face was shadowed with several days' growth of beard, and sweat dampened his hair. It also glistened on his bare chest, matting the dark hair into sworls around his nipples, trickling down over the ridges of muscle, sliding into the crease of his stomach, and leaving a spreading dark patch on the waistband of his snug-fitting, low-slung buckskin breeches—

Delia sucked in a sharp breath and her gaze flew to his face. He didn't look at all pleased to see her.

"Morning, Ty. You look . . . hot."

"And you look good an' saucy this mornin'. Married life must suit you." He slurred the words slightly and his mouth was slack, his eyes bloodshot. Delia felt a fierce ache of disappointment to find him drunk like this so early in the morning. She would have expected it of her da, but not of him.

"What are you doing lit this time of day?" she demanded, not bothering to hide her anger.

He grinned nastily at her. "It's a continuation of the night before. And the night before that."

She climbed onto the porch. This close his presence was a tangible thing, like waves of heat radiating from a forge. He looked dangerous—unshaven and half-naked as he was. Dangerous and desirable.

His eyes roamed over her, intense and glittering, almost melting her with their fierce heat. Delia had to fight an urge to turn and run back into the cool safety of the forest.

"What brings you out here this morning, Delia-girl? Is it a social call?"

She started, blushed again. "Oh, no . . . there's something wrong with Tildy's eye."

Ty let his chair fall forward. He got slowly to his feet. Calling Tildy over, he squatted in front of her and tilted her face up with gentle hands.

It occurred to Delia that his drunkenness had mostly been an act, although there was no doubt from the looks of him that he'd been drinking heavily lately. He looked, in fact, as if he'd been imbibing steadily for the past three days . . . since the wedding. For a moment Delia had the wild conviction that she was the cause. The thought left her breathless and giddy.

"I got a stye," Tildy announced.

Ty squeezed Tildy's shoulder. "That's what it is, honey." Delia stepped up to them. "Can you cure it?"

He cocked his head and blessed her with that endearing, slanted smile that could so easily twist her heart into knots. "It's as good as done."

Delia followed as he took Tildy inside. She looked around with avid curiosity. The cabin was made of squared logs so tightly fitted that a knife blade couldn't pass between them. It was cool inside today, out of the bright sun, but in winter it would be snug and warm. Delia drew in a deep breath—the air was redolent with the strong, clean smells of pine pitch and the sweet oil he used on his rifle.

The cabin consisted of a single, large room, but a half loft opened onto it from above, and Delia could make out the corner of a low bed covered with bearskins. In spite of the fact that the cabin was in the middle of a wilderness forest, it was luxuriously, almost extravagantly furnished: with an elaborately carved settle, a pair of silk damask chairs, even a sideboard with pewter and glassware. Delia smiled to herself, remembering how he had warned her that first morning that he was a man of refined tastes.

Ty had almost let the fire go out, but he stoked it, tossing on an armload of wood. He hung a tea kettle on the trummel hook, all the while speaking soothingly to Tildy, explaining how she was going to have to put her face over a bowl of boiling water and blink hard so that the stye would burst, weeping itself away.

"And *then* can I have a cookie?" Tildy asked brightly.

Ty's deep laughter filled the cabin, bringing a smile to Delia's face.

"Can I open the toy chest now, Dr. Ty?" Tildy asked in her piping voice.

"Of course."

Tildy headed unerringly for a copper-banded sea trunk that sat in one corner. It resembled a pirate's treasure chest and was, Delia discovered to her delight, a *child's* treasure chest, for it was filled with toys—dolls, boats, balls, marbles, and a tiny replica of a wooden wagon pulled by two miniature carved oxen. Tildy lovingly took out the wagon and began to load it with wood chips from the kindling box.

Delia stared at the man as he watched the little girl at play, a warm smile on his face. Only a man who loved children would have a box full of toys all prepared for when they came to visit. She wondered why he hadn't married yet so that he could have children of his own.

Delia strolled around the wonderful cabin. It held such an odd mixture of the genteel and the wilderness life. In the middle of the board table sat a delicate crystal saltcellar and a silver sugar box with matching silver sugar scissors. Yet from the ceiling near the hearth there hung a splint tray of drying apples. A tall, wrought-iron candelabra was displayed atop a corner cupboard. Yet dangling from a peg by the door was a crude lantern made of cow horn. His clay pipe, squirrel-skin tobacco pouch, and hunting knife lay together on the sideboard, next to a fashionable set of pewter tankards.

Part of the room had been turned over to his profession, displaying his apothecary jars, the mortar and pestle, strange and gruesome-looking instruments, and the set of lancet blades. Some of the medicines in his dispensary she recognized—sulfur for preventing the ague, powdered cloves for toothache, peppermint for indigestion. Others she recognized but had no idea what diseases they cured—sweet basil, chinchona bark, wormwood oil. And still others were strange and unfamiliar.

A pair of shelves on the wall were filled with books and folios having to do with chirugery and medicine. Delia read some of the titles: *The Method of Physic* and *The Direction for Health, Both Natural and Artificial*. One book bound in colorful red calfskin caught her eye and she took it down to study it further, confident in her newfound ability to read, only to discover that the letters looked scrambled, the words making no sense to her at all.

"It's in Latin," Ty said, startling her so that she whirled around. "In case you were wondering."

Delia's shoulders jerked defensively. "Mrs. Bishop's been teachin'—teach*ing* me my letters."

"So I've been told. Such a skill should come in handy when you're out working in the fields."

She turned away from him, angrily thrusting the book back onto the shelf.

When she turned back around she was faced with his broad chest. He took a deep breath and his muscles rippled. He smelled of male sweat, but it wasn't unpleasant. Still, Delia couldn't resist saying, "You could use a bath." She was pleased to see by the band of color staining his sharp cheek-bones that her jibe had hit home.

Then his nostrils flared, his lips tightened. He took a step closer, backing her against the wall. His hip pressed against hers and he trapped her with his hands by clasping the shelf on either side of her head. He brought his face within inches of hers. She could see the individual rough hairs of his whisker stubble, the smile lines at the corners of his mouth, the deep, deep blue of his eyes.

"What are you doing here, Delia-girl?" He growled the words, low in his throat. "What have you come for?"

Delia's chest was so tight, she wheezed. "Tildy—"

"Uh-uh." He shook his head slowly, bringing his face even closer, so close that if she so much as breathed her lips would brush his. "I don't think so, Delia. I think that what you came for is—"

The kettle whistled.

"It's boiling, Dr. Ty!" Tildy exclaimed. "The water's boiling!"

For a second longer Ty's mouth hovered close to hers. Then he swore beneath his breath and pushed himself away from her.

Ty had Tildy stand on a stool, leaning over his large pewter shaving bowl. He poured the boiling water into the bowl. The little girl blinked rapidly as the steam enveloped her face and within minutes the stye had burst. He mopped her wet face with a soft cloth, studying her eye. "Does it hurt anymore, Tildy?"

"Nope. Can I have my cookie now?"

He produced two molasses cookies from a basket on the sideboard. Delia wondered jealously what woman in Merrymeeting had been baking Ty cookies in her spare time.

There was no longer any reason to stay. She took Tildy's hand and led her toward the door. It occurred to her that she should pay Ty for his doctoring, but she had no money with her.

"You'll have to let Nat know what he owes you," she said.

"I'll do that," he answered curtly.

Outside, it had turned much hotter. The air was humid and still, and they could hear the screech of locusts in the cattails by the river. Delia paused on the porch, wanting to ask Ty something, wondering if she dared.

Tildy, her cheeks bulging with molasses cookies, chased the black cat beneath the steps. Delia's glance flickered briefly toward the river and the strange conical-shaped hut. "What is that?" she said, although it wasn't what she had wanted to ask.

It had been a mistake to look at him. His thumbs were hooked into the waistband of his breeches, his legs were splayed wide. His magnificent naked chest rose and fell with his slow breathing. He exuded pure masculine sexuality and she jerked her eyes quickly away from him.

"It's a wigwam," he finally said. "My own private sweat lodge."

"Oh . . ." She breathed, swallowed, sighed. She had no idea what either a wigwam or a sweat lodge was. She blurted out the question that was really on her mind. "Did you promise Nat that the woman you brought him would be a virgin?"

The question startled him. But only for a moment. "What's the matter," he sneered, "was he disappointed?"

She sucked in a sharp breath. "How dare you—"

"Or were you the one who was disappointed?" He took a step to plant himself right in front of her. Angry heat seemed to pour off him in waves. "Didn't Nat manage to please you in bed?"

Their eyes clashed and Delia's chin came up. "Are you always such a bastard with every woman you know . . . or do I bring out the worst in you?"

He gave a harsh, bitter laugh. "Aw hell, Delia. The truth is I'm j—" He cut himself off.

"What? What is the truth?"

"Nothing. Nat asked me if you'd been a whore back in Boston. I set him straight. That was all I told him."

She barely heard his explanation. She was sure he had been about to admit that he was jealous. Jealous of her and Nat? The thought thrilled, confused, and frightened her all at once.

Tildy scooted out from beneath the steps, dragging the cat by its hind legs. The cat came reluctantly, hissing and digging its claws into the soft ground, and leaving tiny, twin furrows in its wake.

"Come on, little puss," Delia said, laughing. Ty didn't move, so she stepped around him "We've got to be getting home now. Your da needs help with the haying."

At the edge of the clearing they turned and looked back. Tildy flapped her hand in a vigorous wave. "Goodbye, Dr. Ty! Thank you for the cookies!"

Ty lifted his hand in a brief farewell. He looked lonely to Delia, standing by himself on his porch in the hot, glaring sun.

Chapter 17

Delia stared at Meg in disbelief. "Do you mean to tell me I'm to drop a couple of chickens down the chimney?"

Meg nodded, her thin face serious. "Ma always cleaned it that way. When it got to smoking bad. They flap their wings, you see, and that knocks the soot out."

"Chickens down the chimney!" Tildy confirmed. "My eyes hurt!"

The fireplace was definitely smoking. It was now pouring in the keeping room in soft, wispy drifts, causing their eyes to burn and tear. Earlier Nat and the girls had had to finish their breakfast outside and the way Nat had stared at Delia, disapproval all over his face, she knew he blamed her for it. Although why it should be her fault, she couldn't imagine.

Still, he had gone to his work in the fields that morning, leaving her with no doubt that he expected her to rectify the situation and that, after over a month of marriage, she was still a failure as a wife.

Now she eyed Meg suspiciously. "You wouldn't by any chance be trying to play a trick on me?"

Meg's eyes went round with wounded surprise. "Of course not! I'm only telling you what Ma used to do. Just ask Papa."

Delia had no intention of asking Nat. Things were so strained between them, they couldn't speak to each other without it ending in an argument. They had gone from feeling awkward and shy, to active dislike. At night, he still slept on the shakedown in the linter. And he spent an hour every day before sundown up on the hill in back of the barn, speaking to his dead wife's grave.

"All right . . ." Delia said reluctantly. "Tell me how it's done."

At Meg's direction, Delia doused the fire with buckets of sawdust and water, which naturally caused the smoke to billow out in dark, choking clouds, covering the keeping room and everything in it with a layer of gray soot. Delia wanted to sob with despair—she'd be all day cleaning the mess, and she'd miss her lesson with Anne Bishop.

Next she went out to the yard and lured the chickens over with a handful of corn kernels. She snatched at a hen, grasping it by the wings and gingerly holding it away from her body. "Now what do I do?" she asked a giggling Meg, as the chicken flapped frantically in her arms, squawking madly. Tildy danced around them, squealing with laughter.

"You carry her up onto the roof and drop her down the chimney."

Delia looked up, way up, at the chimney stack poking through the cedar-shingled roof. She swallowed hard; she'd always been a little afraid of heights. But she felt Meg's judging, challenging eyes on her and so she said, "Fetch me a grist sack then. I can't climb a ladder and carry this bloo— blasted chicken both at the same time."

After some difficulty, Delia and Meg got two of the biggest hens into the sack. They brought the ladder from the barn and leaned it against the lower side of the house. After first taking off her slippery leather-soled shoes, Delia climbed with shaky legs, muttering to herself about how she should have had the sense to stay in Boston where, when a chimney smoked, you hired a sweep.

The roof had been built with a sharp pitch because of the heavy winter snows and she had to claw her way up it on her hands and knees, dragging the squirming sack with her. She didn't dare let her eyes drift toward the ground. Once at the top she straddled the peak and looked down the chimney stack, but all she could see was blackness.

She hollered to Meg, who still stood alongside the ladder. "Meg, go on inside, will you? So's you can catch the hen when she comes down!"

"*Catch* the hen?" Meg shouted back at her.

"Aye!"

After a moment's hesitation, Meg disappeared inside.

"Delia, don't fall!" Tildy called up to her.

"I won't," Delia said in a reedy voice and offered up a silent prayer, asking God to watch over this poor Boston grog shop girl who had wandered onto a Maine farm by mistake.

Taking a ruffled, clucking hen out of the sack, she peered down the chimney again. "Are you ready?" she called out to Meg, her voice tumbling down, then echoing back at her.

She heard a muffled reply, which she took to be an affirmative. Her thighs gripping the roof, she leaned way over and, fighting a silly impulse to shut her eyes, dropped the chicken down the chimney. There was a frantic squawking and flapping sound and then sudden silence.

"Meg?"

"It's stuck! The hen is stuck!"

Delia pushed wisps of sweaty hair out of her face. *Lord above us, Delia, how do ye manage t' get yersel' into these situations?*

She inched her way across the roof and back down the ladder. She paused a moment to saver the blessed feel of solid ground beneath her feet before she hurried inside, and she and Meg looked up the chimney. Blackness.

"It's not making a sound," Meg whispered. "Do you think it's dead?"

"If it is we'll have chicken stew for supper."

"But how are we going to cook *anything* with a chicken stuck up there?"

That was, Delia admitted, a problem. "I know," she said. "I can try to poke her down with something."

She went onto the porch, searching for the most likely looking instrument from among the tools kept hanging on the wall. She decided on her garden hoe.

She thrust the hoe handle up the chimney, but met only empty space. "I can't reach. You'll have to get on my shoulders, Meg, and poke it up there."

Meg's eyes went wide, but she nodded vigorously.

Meg got on Delia's back, holding the hoe. Hunching over,

Delia shuffled into the hearth. She straightened slowly. "Give it a good poke, Meg."

Meg gave it a good poke. The chicken screeched, flapped. Soot and feathers rained down.

Suddenly the chicken came hurtling at them, bringing clumps of cinders and soot in its wake. Shrieking, Meg reared back. Delia's legs shot out from under her, and she and Meg went flying backward, tripping over a spider pan that skidded across the floor, knocking over a half-dozen ax helves Nat had been seasoning by the hearth, and sending them rolling and clattering like bowling pins across the room. Delia landed on her back with a bone-rattling jar. Meg landed on Delia's chest, knocking the wind out of her.

For a moment Delia could only lie there, wheezing and wondering if she would suffocate before she began breathing again. At last she was able to draw in a gasping mouthful of precious air. Pushing herself up onto her elbows, she stared at Meg, who stared back at her—two pairs of white eyes in charcoal-black faces. "Are you all right?" Delia croaked.

Meg sat up, rubbing her forehead. "I bumped my head." She giggled. Delia bit her lip.

Soon their loud, breathless whoops filled the house. The chicken, which had miraculously managed to survive the fall, raced around them, trailing a broken wing and clucking indignantly.

Suddenly from the yard came the sound of Tildy screaming.

Thoughts of wolves and Indians and other such horrors sent Delia lurching awkwardly to her feet. Grabbing the hoe as the only handy weapon, she raced outside, with Meg following.

At the sight of them, Tildy began hopping up and down and pointing. "Nanny goat's in the garden! Nanny goat's in the garden!"

"Aooow!" Delia shouted, enraged, raising the hoe above her head and running to the rescue of the precious garden that she had been slaving over these past weeks. "I'll get ye for this, ye bloody she-devil!"

Delia fully intended to brain the hateful beast, but she had to get within striking distance of it first. She chased the goat around the garden, growing angrier by the moment as it tram-pled what was left of the vegetables with its sharp hooves . . . and then the sound of a man's laughter penetrated her fuming consciousness.

She stopped abruptly and whipped around. Tyler Savitch stood there laughing. Laughing at her.

She sucked in her breath at the sight of him. He was na-ked—or as near to naked as he could be without scandalizing the countryside. He wore only a pair of high moccasins with fringed tops tied around his legs just below the knee and an Indian-style breechclout that was so brief it covered only the necessities, leaving the vast expanse of his long muscular thighs completely bare. A butchered haunch of some enor-mous, black-haired animal was slung over his shoulders and rivulets of blood trickled down his brown, naked chest.

She stared openmouthed at him, at the magnificent, naked savage sight of him, and her throat went dry, her breasts drew up tight. Then she realized what she was doing and came to herself with an expulsion of pent-up breath and a sharp jerk.

She advanced on him, brandishing the hoe. "What the bloody hell are ye laughing at, ye jackass!"

Ty chortled some more. "I swear, Delia-girl, you have been as hot-tempered lately as a kettle of fat."

How dare he accuse her of being hot-tempered? she fumed, stalking toward him and waving the hoe menacingly in the air. He hadn't been around in weeks, so how could he *know* the state of her temper?

But when she got within smelling distance of him, she recoiled from the reek of the meat he carried. "Pee-uw!" she exclaimed.

Ty's eyes moved insolently over her, starting with her hair, which had tumbled out of her cap, roaming across the angry features of her soot-stained face, dropping down to linger when they encountered the hoe handle pressed tightly be-tween her full, and quivering breasts—and his lips pursed slightly as if, Lord above us, he was thinking of kissing her there!

Finally, his eyes fell down to her bare feet, which caused a tiny twitch of his lips. They traveled back upward, pausing again at her breasts before settling on her face. He grinned. "Been cleaning the chimney?"

"What are you . . . Why are you . . . Damnation!" Her fingers clenched around the hoe handle. She wanted to hit him—but then, that might do serious damage to that beautiful body. "What is that awful, smelly meat?" she asked instead.

"I thought you and Nat might want a piece of the bear that's been raiding your corn."

Delia remembered Nat mentioning a few days ago that a bear and her cub had been at the corn rows all along this end of the river. She looked askance at the huge piece of meat, wrinkling her nose. "What do I do with it?"

"Well," he drawled, his smile widening irresistibly, "you scorch off the hair and hide, spit her on a birch pole, and roast her over a big, hot fire. Then you eat her."

"Eat a bear!" Delia snorted. "Not bloody likely, I will!"

Meg and Tildy had managed to shoo the goat out of the garden and now they came running up. Tildy's eyes grew huge at the sight of the bear haunch. "Did you kill that big bear all by yourself, Dr. Ty?"

"Yup. Wrestled her down with my bare hands."

Tildy's eyes filled her face. "Golly!"

"Go on with ye!" Delia scoffed.

Ty cocked a brow at her. "What? Don't you believe me?"

He couldn't have . . . surely he couldn't have . . . but then he was awfully brave and strong. And raised by the Indians . . .

"You didn't!" she protested.

He threw back his head and laughed with delight. "No, brat, I didn't. I shot her from behind the safety of a nice big rock from a good ten yards away."

She couldn't help laughing with him. Oh, but it was so good just to look at him. She hadn't seen him in so long, since a few days after her wedding, although she had hoped every Sabbath day he might decide to come to the Meeting. And every time she went into Merrymeeting, her heart beat wildly at the possibility that she might run into him—at the Bishops', or the general store, or the grist mill. Yet she never had. *Just let me see him,* she had prayed. *Just let me see him and talk to him, if only for a few minutes.*

Yet when her prayers had gone unanswered, she knew it was for the best. She had no right to be thinking of Tyler Savitch in that way.

"Girls," Ty said, although he kept his eyes fastened on Delia, "why don't you run into the house and see if you can find me an old scrap of flannel to wrap around this meat?"

The girls ran off, eager to be of help and chattering excitedly between themselves.

A sudden silence descended on the clearing. It was so quiet Delia could hear the drone of the bees around the timothy and paintbrush. The sun was a hot silver ball in the sky. A warm, moist breeze carried the smell of newly mown hay.

Ty stared at her with avid intensity, his eyes boring into her. "How have you been, Delia?"

"Fine . . . Oh, fine, fine . . ." She realized she was nodding like a fool and made herself stop it. But it wasn't as easy to control what was happening inside her: the familiar pounding of her heart, the turmoil of emotions that made her throat ache and her eyes burn.

"Has Nat been treating you well?"

"Yes, yes," she lied. Or partly lied. At least Nat didn't beat her, but that was the best of what could be said about what went on between them. "He's out clearing a new field over yonder ridge just now."

Ty nodded, his face impassive. "That's good." He hefted the meat on his shoulders, the tendons of his strong hands flexing. "I'd like to put this into the springhouse, if you don't mind. The bitch is heavy," he added, his lips slanting into a lopsided smile.

Delia blushed—more from the effect of the smile than his profanity.

Behind the house was a natural spring well covered by a cedar-shingled shed. Delia leaned her hoe against the shed's wall and pulled open the door, which protested with a loud squeal of its rawhide hinges. It was cool inside the springhouse, but it offered Delia little relief. She felt hot from the inside out, as if her blood were boiling.

Ty slung the bear haunch over a branched iron hook. The muscles of his back bunched as he lifted the heavy meat above his head. His dark hair was plastered in damp tendrils against his neck. The skin of his chest and thighs had been browned by the summer sun. Shamelessly she wondered if he was brown all over.

"We, that is, Nat and I were wondering why we never see you at the Meeting," she blurted out and was instantly sorry. He would know now that she looked for him there.

He turned and smiled mockingly at her. "I'm not much of a believer."

"You don't believe in God?"

He shrugged. "I believe in the *gitche* manitou, who is not a god but the spiritual force that dwells in all things." His eyes flickered to the carcass hanging from the hook and a strange sadness came over his face. "That's why I sang a song of apology to the bear's spirit, explaining why I had to kill her."

Apologize to the bear's spirit? She looked at the leather bag nestled against his chest that he had said contained a symbol of his guardian spirit. He was an educated physician, yet he believed in heathen things. What a strange man he was. Delia wondered if she would ever understand him. But then, he was two men really and she doubted he understood himself.

Kneeling by the spring, Ty drew a bucket of water and sluiced it over his chest, washing off the blood. The water ran through his chest hair, funneling into a narrow line that disappeared beneath his breechclout. Delia watched his hands as they moved over his own hard, corded muscles. She longed to brush them aside and do it for him. She knew such a thought was wicked, forbidden, a sin. But she couldn't help it.

She handed him the rag that hung from a nail on the wall and was used as a towel. But he didn't dry himself. Instead, he dipped the rag in the bucket and stretched to his feet, coming up right in front of her. Flustered by his nearness, Delia made an inadvertent choking sound low in her throat.

Two fingers curled under her chin and he tilted her head up. With slow and gentle strokes, he wiped the soot and dirt off her face. Her eyes drifted closed and she reveled in the feel of his touch, so innocent and yet so arousing. A place, a secret place deep in her womb, contracted with a fierce, hard craving. She felt suffocated with yearning. She wanted, wanted, wanted . . .

She pulled away from him, stumbling slightly. His hand closed around her shoulder to steady her. "Delia . . . ?"

Oh, God.

"If you ever need me for anything, anything at all, will you come to me?"

The question both surprised and warmed her. Still, it was hard to find the breath to answer him. She had to clear her throat and moisten her lips. "You know I would, Ty."

He expelled a soft breath. His head dipped, came closer. Her eyes became riveted on his lower lip—full, sensual, inviting. For one horrifying moment she felt herself leaning into him, lifting her hand to run her finger along that lip—

The springhouse door banged open and the girls barged through. "Will this do, Dr. Ty?" Meg asked breathlessly, holding up a large piece of worn blue flannel.

"Perfectly," Ty said, his voice strained. Delia's legs were shaking so badly she had to lean against the wall. They carefully avoided each other's eyes.

It took only a minute for Ty to wrap the bear meat in the flannel. Afterward, there was no reason for him to linger and he did not. With the girls skipping ahead, Delia walked with him to where the wagon ruts led into the forest toward the river. They didn't speak, nor did they look at each other. They both knew that another second alone in the springhouse and they would have been kissing.

And that once their lips touched they would not have been able to stop.

Chapter 18

The final strains of "A Mighty Fortress Is Our God" bounced off the stark, bare walls, and the boards of the high, square pews creaked as the congregation took their seats.

Hot August morning sunlight shone through the clear windowpanes and the air within the new meetinghouse was stuffy with an underlying smell of sawdust. To her horror, Delia felt a sneeze coming on and tried to stop it by pinching her nose between her thumb and forefinger. Glancing up, she caught Nat frowning at her from beneath his thick blond brows.

Flushing hotly, she let go of her nose and the sneeze burst out of her, echoing in the heavy silence and earning a round of stifled snickers and a smirk from Meg. Nat's frown deepened into a scowl.

"Delia sneezed," Tildy announced in a loud stage whisper, which brought more muffled laughter.

"Sssh!" Nat snapped harshly, just as the Reverend Caleb Hooker mounted the pulpit.

The pulpit stood high above the pews and had a curved front. Above it was a sounding board to aid in the projection of the minister's voice, although Caleb's mellifluous baritone rarely needed such assistance.

The Sabbath-day service of prayers, hymns, psalm readings, and sermons had been going on for two hours now, but there was still another hour to go. And that was only the morning service. After a community dinner next door in the Sabbath house there would be another two hours of worship in the afternoon, although by then the pews would be considerably emptier.

Delia felt a pinprickly tingling in her buttocks and she squirmed on her seat, earning another frown of disapproval from Nat. Her chest heaved as she swallowed a sigh, for she knew that on the way home this evening she would be subjected to another of his tedious lectures, which always ended with the pronouncement that *his Mary* would never have done such and such a thing.

Caleb cleared his throat, turned over the hourglass, and launched into his sermon. Delia let his voice drone on at the edge of her consciousness. She amused herself by watching the members of Merrymeeting's Congregation of God's Saints fight off drowsiness and try to keep from squirming when *their* bottoms went to sleep.

Constant Hall, the gristmill owner, who also served as the village tithingman, walked up and down the aisle with a fur-tipped rod in his hand, which he used to awaken slumbering worshippers. He was, Delia noticed, being kept busy on this warm and sultry morning. When Sara Kemble's head began to nod and a soft snore puffed from between her fat lips, Delia had to bite the inside of her cheek, hard, to keep from giggling.

The reverend had meandered onto the subject of sin—fornication, to be precise—and the interest of the congregation had picked up predictably, when the door behind them groaned open and everyone turned in unison to gawk. Unconsciously, Delia uttered a soft exclamation of surprise and delight.

Tyler Savitch stood within the doorway, resplendent in a scarlet coat, brocade waistcoat, and moss-green breeches. Lace spilled from his cuffs and fell in folds down his chest. Tall, satiny black boots encased his long, finely molded calves.

Although every eye was on him, he stood still and looked slowly around the church and Delia realized with a sudden lurch of her heart that his gaze stopped only when it found her. For one incredible moment—so short she afterward wondered if she had imagined it—he cast her a warm, intimate glance that sent a rush of blood surging through her body.

Then he flashed the entire staring, openmouthed congregation a delightful smile that was a boyish mixture of cockiness and bashfulness, and slipped into a back pew. A few more seconds of stunned silence was broken by a loud rustling noise as everyone turned to a neighbor and whispered.

"Ahem!" The Reverend Caleb Hooker's deep voice cut through the sibilant chatter. "Dr. Savitch, we are honored that you have decided to grace us with your presence, albeit a bit tardily . . ." Caleb grinned broadly and several people laughed out loud. "But now that you *have* arrived, do I have your permission to continue?"

"Amen, Reverend!" Ty boomed out heartily, to another chorus of laughter and a loud snort of disgust from Sara Kemble.

Caleb reassumed his serious expression and picked up the threads of his sermon. The minutes dragged. Delia didn't know where she found the fortitude to resist turning to look at Ty again. Before long her shoulders ached from the strain of sitting tense and unmoving.

At last the interminable service was over. The tithingman opened the church doors and the worshippers spilled out into the bright, broiling sun. Caleb stood at the entrance, exchanging pleasantries with his flock. Feigning a difficulty with the heel of her shoe, Delia let Nat and the girls go on ahead while she lingered inside, sitting on the edge of the last pew until the church had emptied. Suddenly confronted with the prospect of having to come face to face again with Tyler Savitch, Delia's courage had deserted her. During the two times she had been around him since her wedding she had managed to make an utter, heartsick fool of herself; she was determined not to do it again.

Nothing is going to happen, she tried to reassure herself. The whole town is here, so what could possibly happen?

He could smile at you and your heart will melt. He could laugh and your blood will sing. He could touch you, even accidentally, and you will fall to pieces at his feet . . .

"Delia, are you all right?"

She looked up with a start . . . into the Reverend Caleb Hooker's concerned face.

She smiled brightly to hide the sudden rush of disappointment that the wrong man had appeared to inquire after her well-being. "Oh, I'm fine, Reverend. I'm just collecting myself before going out into that heat."

"It's as hot as the blazes out there today," Caleb agreed. He dropped onto the seat beside her. His answering smile was shy and a bit tentative. "Delia, I wonder if I might discuss something with you . . ."

Delia's throat froze up. She nodded mutely, sure he was going to remind her that she was a *married* woman and her continued infatuation with Merrymeeting's bachelor doctor was a scandalous, wicked thing.

"It's about my sermons."

Delia's breath left her in a loud rush. "Y-your sermons? But I didn't fall asleep this time, honest, I didn't. Maybe I looked a bit distracted and all, by the heat, but . . ." Delia knew she was babbling, but she was so relieved she didn't care.

Caleb's head fell back as he laughed. "Oh, Delia! There, you see. That's just my point. You're such a practical-minded girl. I was wondering . . . I've gotten the feeling my somnolent sermons are somewhat of a disappointment to the good folk of Merrymeeting and I wondered if you could advise me on what to do about it."

Delia chewed on her lip, debating whether to give Caleb the benefit of her opinion. "Well, it's only a thought . . ."

"Go on, Delia, please. Bless me with some of your sage advice."

Delia suddenly became aware that Ty was standing in the doorway, speaking with Colonel Bishop. She heard the colonel ask Ty's advice about a bowel complaint that had been plaguing him and Ty prescribed nanny-plum tea.

She took a deep breath and gave Caleb another bright smile. "Well, if it was me, I mean if I was you, I'd stoke up the place a bit with more mention of hellfire and the awful wages of sin and God's fearsome judgment. And I'd go a little easy on those bookish subjects they taught you at Harvard."

Caleb's lips twitched, but he nodded seriously. "Ah, yes, I see . . ."

"And don't be afraid to name names."

"Name names?"

She nodded vigorously. "Aye. People come to the Meeting as much for a chance to gossip and see their neighbors as they do for one of your sermons, beggin' your pardon, Reverend. So you might want to mention, for instance, that Hannah Randolf's baby is due next month and with seven boys the Randolfs are praying for a girl. And Cap'n Abbott brought in a shipment of French cloth goods yesterday. Also it's been a good two months now since Dr. Savitch gave me that inoc— uh, that prick with the lancet . . ."

"Inoculation," Ty supplied, sauntering up to them.

"Aye. Inoculation." Completely forgetting her earlier resolution, Delia allowed her eyes to roam to his face, unable to hide any longer her wonder at seeing him today, so unexpectedly. Her happiness blazed forth with her smile. "And I haven't dropped dead from it yet. Nor have I caught the smallpox neither—*either.*"

"I'm beginning to get your point," Caleb said. He stood up, clasping Ty's hand, and a grin twisted his lips. "Perhaps I should make an announcement that at long last Merrymeeting's distinguished physician has achieved salvation."

"That might be a bit precipitate," Ty warned with a laugh.

His eyes caressed Delia's face. They sent messages with their looks, subtle messages that spoke of the joy they felt simply being in each other's presence.

But that was impossible—wasn't it? She was used to seeing desire flare in those deep blue eyes. Hunger and lust. But if she didn't know better, she almost would have thought that this time she saw—

Oh, quit being a wooden-headed fool, Delia McQuaid! She'd humiliated herself enough in the past by imagining Tyler Savitch felt something for her when he did not. Her heart couldn't survive being broken again. Besides, she was married now. It was wicked even to be thinking of Ty except as a friend. Still, when his eyes glanced her way a second time she couldn't help becoming lost for just a moment in those burning indigo depths.

That was not only wrong, but also too hard on her heart, and so she broke the contact by turning to the minister. "I do have one other suggestion, Caleb . . ."

"Oh-oh. Take care, Reverend," Ty said, with a teasing smile. "She'll be writing the entire sermon for you next."

"Which might not be a bad idea at that," Caleb responded in all seriousness.

Colonel Bishop appeared in the doorway just then, calling Caleb outside. Delia realized that in spite of all her good intentions, she and Ty had wound up alone together again. But they were safe here inside the meetinghouse, weren't they?

"Don't worry, brat," Ty said, uncannily reading her mind. "I promised myself I would be on my best behavior today." He presented her with his lopsided smile and the crook of his arm. "Shall we join the others and get something to eat? All this good behavior is damn hard work and I'm starving."

Laughing, Delia stood up and laid her palm on his arm. "Shame on you, Dr. Savitch. Cussing in church!"

The material of his coat was warm and smooth under her fingers, the flesh beneath it hard and tense. She realized immediately that it had been a mistake to touch him, even in so innocent a manner. She let go of his arm and took one step away from him.

"Delia . . ."

She waited, her heart thundering, her head light. But waited for what she didn't know.

"Have you eaten any of my bear yet?" he said, his lips quirking into a lazy smile . . . and Delia's heart melted.

Shuddering, she made her eyes go wide. "Are you daft? I want nothing to do with that smelly meat."

Ty laughed and her blood began to sing.

But when he slipped his arm around her waist to lead her down the church aisle and out the door, she didn't fall to pieces at his feet. She only felt like doing so.

To Delia's relief she spotted Anne Bishop and waved, disengaging herself from Ty's embrace, which was making her feel all hot and shivery both at the same time. "Anne! You're just the person I want to see," she exclaimed, falsely gay.

Anne's furrowed face frowned to cover her pleasure. "Have you finished reading Bacon's *Essays* yet?"

Delia's eyes dropped to her shoes. "Well, not completely. I've been sort of busy . . ."

Anne snorted loudly. "Busy! Busy slaving for that man of yours and his two unappreciative younguns."

Delia clasped the older woman's ropy hands. "Oh, Anne, quit fussing at me and listen. I've the most wonderful idea!"

Ty and Anne Bishop rolled their eyes at each other. Catching them at it, Delia pretended to be insulted.

"It really is a good idea, Anne. I've decided you can be Merrymeeting's schoolmaster!"

Anne's bony shoulders jerked in surprise. "But I'm a woman."

"So? I would bet you any man we found wouldn't be a cobbler's patch on you. Besides, we haven't found a man to do it yet and the children keep getting older by the day. What's more, you'd be saving Merrymeeting the ten pounds Boston keeps fining us for not having one."

Anne exchanged looks with Ty, a spark of excitement smoldering in her eyes. "No town has ever had a woman for a schoolmaster."

"True," Ty said, smiling. "But then, I doubt there's a law specifically forbidding it."

Anne sniffed. "Only because it hasn't occurred to anybody yet. Anyway, the folk around here are a stodgy bunch. They don't hold much with breaking tradition."

"True," Ty said.

"But you can talk them around, Ty," Delia put in, giving him a look that said she thought he could do anything.

Ty's smile faded a bit. "Now wait just a —"

"Still, I do have more book learning than any other body in The Maine—man, woman, or Indian," Anne stated.

Ty gave up, laughing. "True again. Unless Delia's managed to catch up with you."

Anne snorted. "I suppose I could mention it to Giles. Oh, the heck I will. He'd only say no if I ask him. That man couldn't see a hole through a ladder with his eyes wide open. No, I'll just *announce* it to him as if it were already done and decided."

Laughter and the delicious smell of roasting corn wafted from the open door of the Sabbath house. Lost in thought, Anne went through it, mumbling to herself about hornbooks and primers and birch paper, and shaking her head.

Delia turned to find Ty's eyes fastened on her, a strange expression on his face. "What are you looking at?" she demanded, blushing.

"You. You astound me sometimes, Delia."

Delia mimicked one of Anne's snorts as she followed the older woman through the door. "Well, don't stare. 'Tisn't polite."

"That was some bear ye killed t'other day, Ty," Sam Randolf said. He was spooling new rungs for a bed. With his mushrooming family he always seemed to need a new bed. "The bitch must have been near big as a mountain."

"Maybe." Ty grinned around the pipe bit between his teeth. "Truth to tell I was so plumb scared I had my eyes squeezed shut the whole damned time."

The other men all laughed and nodded, although they knew Tyler Savitch could never have shot that bear if he'd been quaking with fright and kept his eyes closed. But a good Maine man never bragged about his accomplishments. He let his friends do it for him.

Ty leaned over and plucked an ember from the fire with a pair of smoking tongs. As he put the coal to the bowl of his pipe, his gaze wandered across to the women's side of the room, where Delia sat, watching Elizabeth work her spinning wheel. For the hundredth time that day their eyes met . . . then parted.

Elizabeth Hooker caught a spoke with the knob of her "wooden finger," spinning the big wheel, stepping backward and expertly controlling the draft as the yarn twisted off the spindle. As Delia studied the girl's deft, quick movements, her mouth drew taut and her forehead furrowed in concentration. Even then Ty thought her beautiful.

He thought her more beautiful still when Hannah Randolf said something to her in a teasing voice and she tossed back her head, her full lips parting as she laughed with delight—although the joke must have been on her. It hadn't been easy for her, Ty knew, but slowly Delia was making herself accepted among the women of Merrymeeting and he felt a strong jolt of pride as he thought of her guts and persistence.

Ty had come to the Meeting just to see her; it was no use

trying to pretend otherwise. But he told himself it was because he felt responsible for her. He wanted to be assured that she was happy, that her life with Nat Parkes was a good one. He wanted to see if after a month and a half of marriage, Delia McQuaid had grown to love her new husband. And if Nat loved her. Maybe if they did, then he could forget about her.

He should have known better.

Every time Delia spoke to her husband, Ty felt a sickness eat away at his gut. If she so much as smiled at the man, Ty's insides roiled and his fists clenched. Once, during dinner, she had leaned intimately into Nat, her breast pressing against his shoulder, her hand on his arm, and she had said something that brought a blush to Nat's gaunt cheeks. Ty had almost come bounding out of his seat intent on murder—of *her*, not Nat. He wanted to wrap his hands around her throat and shout at her: "You don't love him, damn you, Delia! It's *me* you love. Me!"

Christ, what had she *said* to Nat to make him blush like that? Was she referring to some intimate game they'd invented to while away the long nights out on their farm?

He still couldn't bear the memory of that night, her wedding night, when he had seen Delia go into Nat's arms. In the long, late, and empty hours since, lying on his own solitary bed, he had burned with hot jealousy and seething desire as images overwhelmed his senses—of Nat plunging his hard sex between Delia's legs, sucking her taut nipples, plundering her mouth with his tongue. Sometimes if Ty was especially lonely and vulnerable, the images would blur and it was himself that he would see with her, not Nat. His sex would stretch and grow hard, and he would make such passionate love to her, this fantasy Delia, that he would lose control, spilling his seed and shattering the dark quiet of his lonely cabin with his hoarse cries of release.

No woman had ever done that to him before, so why this one? Why Delia McQuaid—a common little tavern wench, barely eighteen, with a hot temper and a penchant for trouble? Why was it *her* smile, *her* eyes, *her* laugh that haunted him, when he had never been haunted by another's? Why her? Even married to another man, she still bedeviled his days and ruined his nights. Why the *hell* couldn't she let him alone?

But even as he raged silently against her, her presence in the room pulled him, drawing him to her. But he didn't see the prim farmer's wife in her hood and short gown and petticoat. He saw the girl who had lain naked on his shirt in the Falmouth woods, her glorious hair unbound, her mouth parted wetly, her legs spread wide for him, welcoming him into her virgin's body—

"Do you reckon they're whipped, Doc?"

Ty's head snapped up to find Obadiah Kemble peering at him earnestly with his tiny, pumpkin-seed eyes. "What?"

"I was saying the Abenakis have let the hatchet stay buried for three years now. I was wondering if you figure it's because they've been whipped."

"Shee-it," Sam Randolf drawled, tossing his shaggy red hair. "I know you lived with them Injuns when you were a boy, doc, but even you gotta admit there's no whupping them without killin' them first."

"It's true there's no word in the Abenaki tongue for surrender," Ty said, as he tried to gather his scattered thoughts. There was a tight ache in his gut that for once had nothing to do with the maligning of a people he loved. His thoughts, his heart were still too full of Delia. "But there are several Abenaki words meaning peace," he added, knowing ahead of time that supporting peace would do little good.

And, indeed, all the other men except Caleb Hooker shook their heads, mumbling to themselves. There hadn't been real peace in The Maine since the first English fishing sloop had sighted the Maine shore over one hundred years ago.

Nat Parkes, who had been sitting in sullen silence, whittling teeth for a rake, suddenly looked up to glower at Ty. He voiced aloud the others' thoughts. "There won't be peace until the last Abenaki is dead. It's either them or us."

At first Delia had to strain to hear the men's conversation. But one by one the other women fell silent as they too picked up the talk of the Indian threat.

Sara Kemble tsked loudly, shaking her head so hard her mobcap ribbons fluttered. "Shame on Dr. Savitch, defending those children of Satan. Of course one shouldn't expect dif-

ferent from a boy whose mother allowed herself to be taken
captive by those savages.''

''You make it sound as if she went willingly!'' Delia protested.

''She lived with them, didn't she? She let one of them take
her as his squaw. A decent woman would have killed herself.''

''Suicide is a sin,'' Elizabeth said calmly, and Delia looked
at her in surprise, for she rarely took part in the other wom-
en's discussions, preferring to keep her thoughts to herself.
And in the past, even the mention of Indians would bring
Elizabeth near to swooning with fright.

''My Sam is right,'' Hannah Randolf said, rubbing her
swollen belly nervously. ''It's been so long since there's been
any Indian trouble. I hope we aren't getting complacent. Remember what happened the last time—''

Hannah cut herself off by biting her lip so hard she drew
blood. Everyone turned of one accord and looked at Anne
Bishop. The woman's gaunt face was bloodless and a corner
of her mouth twitched spastically. Alarmed, Delia stretched
out a hand to the older woman. ''Anne?''

Anne stood up so abruptly she knocked over her stool.
Whirling around, she fled the house. Delia started after her,
but Hannah Randolf snatched Delia's arm as she went by. ''I
really think it's best if you let her be.''

''But . . .''

''Her last living boy was captured and tortured to death by
the savages,'' Sara Kemble related, her eyes glowing with
relish. ''Three years ago it happened, right here in Merrymeeting. We were warned of the raid in time, but Willy
Bishop was out tracking an elk and he got caught outside the
stockade. Anne and the colonel—all of us watched the whole
thing from the sentry walk. They tied the Bishop boy naked
to a cross right in front of us, then slashed into him with
knives, over and over. And then they stuck flaming pine
splinters into the gashes they had made in his flesh. It went
on for hours. The screaming was something awful. But he
was out of musket range, so no one could even put him out
of his misery.''

''Oh God.'' Nausea rose in Delia's stomach and she

squeezed her eyes shut. They snapped open again at the sound of a heavy thump.

Elizabeth Hooker had fainted.

Caleb and Delia stood up together as Ty emerged from the bedroom. "H-how is she?" the young reverend asked, his voice hoarse.

"She's sleeping now," Ty said. "She only fainted, Caleb. There's nothing for you to worry about."

Caleb nodded, his throat working with suppressed emotion, then he slipped quietly into the bedroom, shutting the door behind him.

Ty and Delia looked at each other, trying to read the other's thoughts while hiding their own. "What happened?" Ty finally asked.

"Sara Kemble ought to have her tongue bored through with an awl," Delia said, mincing no words. "She told us what happened to Anne's son. Are they really so cruel, Ty—your Abenakis?"

A muscle jumped in his cheek. "They can be."

He was hurting inside. She could see it in the tight set of his mouth, in his dark, brooding eyes. She yearned to cradle his head against her breast and soothe away his pain.

Oh, Delia, you are such a fool. The man stays away from you for days on end because every time you get near him you embarrass him with your stupid mooning ways. Now here you are about to do it again. So she scowled at him to cover all these treacherous feelings.

Ty misunderstood the reason for her frown and a bitter smile twisted his face. "What's the matter, Delia? Are you pitying me because I had to witness such atrocities as a child? Or are you wondering if I participated in the sport myself?"

"Did you?"

"Would it matter?" He shook his head mockingly, a cruel set to his mouth. "Ah, Delia, Delia . . . Can this be the same tavern wench who threw herself at my feet *begging* for my love? Do you fancy yourself too good for me now, brat?"

She gasped, unconsciously bringing her fist to her breast as if to stifle the pain. His words had cut her so deeply, she thought she might be bleeding inside. Slowly, she lifted her chin, although it trembled a bit. "I'm married now, Ty. And I don't *fancy* anything for you at all."

His eyes darkened until they were hard and smooth like polished stones. His fingers clasped her arm, digging into her flesh. "Are you telling me you love Nat?"

"Let go of me. You're hurting me."

His fingers tightened their grip until tears started in her eyes. His jaw was clenched so hard, the muscle throbbed. "Answer my question. Are you in love with Nat?"

"He's my husband."

Ty's head snapped back, nostrils flaring. He flung her arm away as if it suddenly burned him. Spinning on his boot heel, he jerked open the door. Then he stepped aside, bowing sardonically and gesturing the way with his hand. "You should be getting back to the Sabbath house, Mrs. Parkes. Your *husband* must be wondering where you are."

Her head high, Delia swept through the door. Outside, the wind had come up. It whipped her skirts, plastering them against her legs. Nat had brought the wagon to the front of the Sabbath house and was already hitching up the mare. The Reverend Hooker had canceled the afternoon's Meeting and the weather was brewing up a storm anyway. Steely clouds piled up over the mountains in the distance. The pines swept the sky with their boughs and flocks of ducks scudded overhead, trying to outfly the coming rain.

Delia paused on the front stoop and turned to look into Ty's face. Her arm throbbed where he had grabbed her. "Goodbye, Ty." How it hurt to say the words.

It hurt even worse to hear them, especially in that cold, indifferent voice. "Goodbye, Delia."

Squaring her shoulders, she turned away from him. The clouds opened up as she stepped into the road. The hot earth began to steam from the rain.

Chapter 19

The wheel hummed and Elizabeth stepped backward quickly—one, two, three steps, holding high the long yarn as it twisted and quivered. Then suddenly, she glided forward, letting the yard wind onto the spindle. Back again, then forward, back, forward, spinning, spinning . . . The thread mounted on the spindle as the humming vibration of the wheel entered her body and the world around her dimmed, faded . . . disappeared.

Whoever was at the door had to knock twice before she even heard. She stopped the wheel, frowning at this intrusion. Perhaps if she ignored the person he would go away.

The knock came again, more insistent this time.

Elizabeth opened the door the barest crack and peered out, then pulled it wider and actually smiled. "Oh, it's you, Dr. Savitch."

Ty stepped into Elizabeth's immaculate kitchen. His gaze went around the room, taking in the shining brass pots hanging from the summer, the copper kettle and porcelain dishes on the dresser, the spinning wheel with its full spindle. He smiled at her. She noticed he carried his physician's bag.

"Is someone in Merrymeeting ill, doctor?"

"No. I came to town specifically to see you, Mrs. Hooker."

"Me?" She laughed nervously. "Oh, you mean because I fainted yesterday. But I'm all right now, really. Would you care for some tea?"

Ty lowered himself into a leather-covered chair. "Yes,

thank you. I thought you might want to talk to me about *why* you fainted.''

Elizabeth shuddered as she reached for the kettle. "It was the talk . . . about the savages."

"Uh-huh. And how long has it been since you last bled?"

The kettle clattered to the floor, its lid rolling beneath the table. Hot color flooded her cheeks—how dare he ask her such a personal thing!

She felt a pair of strong hands land on her shoulders and she looked up into his concerned face. He smiled at her again, a gentle, knowing smile that strangely banished her embarrassment. "Let me get the tea," he said. "You sit down."

Elizabeth obeyed him. She clenched her hands together on the table in front of her. "I've been ill in the mornings," she admitted in a tiny voice. "And I haven't . . . done what you said for over two months. Do you think I could be expecting?"

He laughed softly. "I think it's highly probable."

"Oh!" A baby! She was going to have a baby! Elizabeth wasn't sure what she thought about it. Caleb, she knew, would be ecstatic at the news. But she . . . she thought she might be frightened.

Ty squatted down beside her, taking her hands. "Would you let me examine you?"

"Would it mean . . . would you have to touch me?"

"Only a little. You can leave your clothes on."

His eyes pinned her. They were very blue, she realized, bluer than the bay outside. His eyes disturbed her. She was afraid he saw things no one else could see.

He cleared the table of her saltcellar and sugar dish and scissors, then she lay down on it at his direction. He reached beneath her skirt and shift. When he touched the bare flesh of her stomach, she jumped.

His smile was calm and kind. "Sorry. I should have thought to warm my hands over the fire first."

She shook her head, biting her lip. Her muscles clenched so tightly they burned. But as his hands moved over her, the tenseness eased. It was as if he soothed aches she hadn't known existed. Blood, flesh, bone seemed to melt and run together into a hum, like the sound her wheel made as she

spun. It seemed she *was* the wheel, spinning, spinning, spinning . . .

She hadn't realized he was no longer touching her until she
opened her eyes. He looked down at her, a grin curling his
mouth. "Our suspicions were correct, Mrs. Hooker. You're
pregnant." He held out his hand, helping her to sit up. "The
water's boiling. Shall we have that tea now? Do you have any
sassafras? It's good for morning sickness."

She nodded mutely. Now that it was over she was horribly
embarrassed. No man except her husband had ever touched
her so intimately. And to think she had actually *enjoyed* the
feel of his hands on her body! For one horrifying moment
she thought she might have fallen in love with the doctor.
But when he turned around from filling the teapot with hot
water and she looked at his handsome features, she knew she
was being ridiculous. She liked the man because he was good
and kind, but looking at him did not make her heart leap as
it did when she gazed into Caleb's dear face.

She almost giggled out loud. No doubt it was all the fault
of her condition. It put fanciful ideas into her head.

The doctor poured from the pot into two of her pretty blue
and white porcelain cups, then cut a piece off the sugar loaf
and dropped it into her tea. She had just lifted the cup to her
lips when the door was flung open and Caleb burst through.
He was so out of breath he had to gulp in air before he could
speak.

"Sara Kemble . . . she said she saw the doctor—Lizzie,
what's happened? Did you faint again?"

Elizabeth startled both Caleb and herself with her exuber-
ant, girlish laughter. "Oh, Caleb, silly. I didn't faint. I feel
wonderful. I'm going to have a baby!"

All the color left Caleb's face. He looked dumbstruck.

"You're going to be a daddy, Reverend," Ty drawled.

Caleb pushed a shaking hand through his pale brown hair.
"Oh, my God . . ." Elizabeth had stood up when he first
barged into the kitchen. Now he rushed to her side, pulling
the chair out and hustling her into it. "Sit down, for heaven's
sake, darling. Should she be standing up like that?" he asked
Ty. "Shouldn't she be in bed? Criminy's sake, Ty, don't just
stand there. *Do* something!"

Ty's eyes, brimming with laughter, met Elizabeth's and they shared a conspiratorial smile. "Come fetch me when the pains start and then I'll do something." Laughing, Ty picked up his physician's bag. "In the meantime, if you all will excu—"

Caleb seized Ty's arm. "You're not leaving?"

Ty rolled his eyes. "I can hardly hang around here for the next six months until she starts laboring."

"But—"

"Caleb, you're being silly," Elizabeth scolded.

"Remember the sassafras tea, Mrs. Hooker," Ty said, easing past the young reverend, making for the door, and giving her a wink. "It's not only good for morning sickness, it also soothes the nerves of expectant fathers."

Caleb came out with him onto the front stoop.

"I can see you were trying to humor Elizabeth," he said. "And I appreciate that, Ty. But you can be straight with me."

"Jesus, Caleb. You're not the first man to father a child. And Elizabeth won't be the first woman to give birth. She's stronger and healthier than she looks. She'll be fine if you take it easy. Both of you." Ty gathered up his pacer's reins, then turned back to impart one last piece of advice. "Oh, by the way, you can enjoy marital relations up until the last month or so."

Caleb's head snapped up and his face darkened. "Why did you tell me that? Did Elizabeth ask about it?"

Ty shrugged. "No, she didn't. The way you've been acting I just thought you'd want to know she won't break, and you won't hurt the baby, if you and she get to feeling amorous from time to time during the next few months."

"Oh . . . uh, Ty?"

Ty waited patiently while Caleb rubbed the back of his neck, ran his tongue over his overlapping teeth, and studied the toes of his shoes. "Ty, in your experience, do most wives . . . get to feeling amorous very often?"

Ty's brows went up. "I haven't exactly had a whole hell of a lot of experience with wives."

"But you've had your share of women?"

Ty didn't bother to deny it.

Caleb laughed shakily. "Well, a divinity student hardly has the opportunity to . . ." He sucked in a deep breath and met Ty's eyes, finishing with a rush. "Elizabeth and I were both virgins when we married and I want to know if you think most women enjoy lovemaking."

"Yes, I think they do."

Caleb looked away. He shuddered once, hard. "It's me then. God, she must hate me."

Ty looped the pacer's reins back around the post. He studied his friend's face, noting the deep bite of a terrible sorrow. "You're imagining things. Elizabeth loves you, Caleb. A blind man could see that."

"Maybe so." Caleb's throat spasmed and he had to blink rapidly several times before he could go on, while Ty politely looked away. "But how can a woman love a man when she hates to be touched by him? I make love to her as little as possible and I do it as fast as I can, to spare her the pain, but it disgusts her, I can tell. *I* disgust her."

Ty's head snapped around. "Pain? She still feels actual pain? Are you sure?"

Caleb nodded, rubbing a hand over his face. "Y-yes. Every time. She's so darn small. I make her cry. I try and get it over with quickly, to spare her, but it still hurts her."

Ty heaved a huge sigh. He couldn't believe he was actually going to do this. He nodded toward the parsonage's front door. "Do you have any brandy back in there?"

"Well, yes, as a matter of—"

"Fetch it then. You and I are going to have ourselves a little talk, Caleb my friend, and I think we're both going to need to be a little drunk to get through it."

Delia worked a smidgen of salt pork onto the end of the hook, then wedged the alder pole into Tildy's dimpled fists. "There you go, puss," she said, rubbing the little girl's blond curls. She dropped the line with its bait into the river. "See if you can catch a fish now."

Tildy wriggled her bottom along the bank, getting closer to the water. Her mouth was screwed up in fierce concentration, for she expected to feel a nibble at any moment. She picked up the cornhusk doll that lay across her lap and handed it back to Delia. "Fix a pole for Gretchen too."

"Don't be silly," Meg Parkes proclaimed from her perch on a nearby rock. "Gretchen's only a doll. She can't fish."

"She can so!"

"Hush now, girls." Delia selected a tiny twig and began to tie a piece of twine around the end of it. "I see no reason why Gretchen can't fish."

Meg stuck out her tongue at her little sister. Tildy reciprocated, showing a mouth stained purple from the blackberries they'd been snacking on while at the river. The smell of the ripe fruit filled the air, cloyingly sweet.

"If you girls are good"—Delia equipped Gretchen with her own tiny pole and sat her on a doll-sized rock near the water's edge—"I'll show you later how to catch a fish with your bare hands."

Meg sniffed dubiously.

Delia laughed. "You'll see. An old Indian I met taught me how to do it."

As the hot noon sun climbed above the treetops, mist began to rise from the high green grass along the riverbank, still wet from yesterday's rain. Nat had taken a cartload of freshly threshed grain to the gristmill and Delia felt guilty, as if she were sneaking out behind his back, like a child playing hooky from school. There were dozens of chores waiting for her back at the farm, but when Meg had suggested going fishing Delia had immediately leaped at the chance to spend more time alone with Nat's girls. Since the day the hen had gotten stuck in the chimney, Delia had sensed a weakening of Meg's hostility toward her and she intended to press her advantage.

The tip of Tildy's pole dipped sharply toward the water. "I got one!" she screeched. "Oh, Delia, Delia, I got a fish!"

Tildy stood up and tottered two steps into the water. Meg hurried to her side, grabbing her around the waist. "Hang on tight, Tildy, and I'll pull it in," she said, grasping the end of the wriggling pole to help.

Tildy jerked away from her sister. "By myself! I can do it by myself!"

As Delia tried to intervene, her skirt brushed against the

cornhusk doll, knocking it off its perch and into the water. Within seconds, it had floated out into the middle of the river where the current grabbed it.

Tildy was the first to notice and she screamed. "Gretchen fell in the river! Gretchen's *drowning!*"

Delia shoved the little girl into her big sister's arms before Tildy could think of going after the doll herself. Then, pulling up her skirts, she waded in.

Away from the bank, the current was much stronger than Delia had realized. The water was also very cold and soon her legs were numb. Luckily, the doll snagged on a rock or Delia would never have been able to catch up with it. But the river seemed suddenly much deeper; it had risen above her waist. She took another step—it rose to her breasts.

The rushing water was a roar in her ears, but even so Delia could hear the echo of Tildy's hysterical screams. The rapids tugged at her skirts as she leaned precariously over, stretching her fingertips toward the doll. She was inches shy.

She took one more step . . . and the water closed over her head.

Given his head to find his own way home, Ty's horse walked slowly between the cart ruts along the river. The hot sun beat down on them mercilessly. A fish hawk circled lazily overhead and the vivid green wild rice and marsh grass waved in the sultry breeze. A pair of squirrels chased each other up a nearby tree, chattering noisily. Ty cursed them. As a result of his and Caleb's "little talk," Merrymeeting's doctor was in a foul mood.

Part of it was due, he knew, to the roiling effect of the brandy bubbling through his veins so early in the day. But a bigger part, a *very* big part, was filling his breeches right now with the most uncomfortable state of arousal he'd ever experienced. It was all the fault of the explicit sexual advice he had just been pouring into the Reverend Hooker's tender and eager ears. He wasn't sure what sort of effect all that randy talk had had on Caleb, but he sure as hell had managed to talk *himself* into one hell of an erection.

"Damn!" Ty rose up in the stirrups, seeking some relief. *What you need, Savitch, you lustful old bastard, is a woman.*

The warm, hard pressure in his crotch was a painful reminder that he hadn't held a woman, a real live woman, in his arms since a certain afternoon in Falmouth woods. The trouble was he didn't want just any woman.

"Delia-girl," he muttered grimly between his clenched teeth, "you'd better hope to God our paths don't cross any time soon." In the condition he was in at the moment, he'd throw her down on the ground and take her, married or not. Willing or not.

Such was Ty's self-absorbtion in his own miserable state that the screams didn't penetrate his consciousness for several seconds. He was just about to kick his horse into a canter, for the noise came from ahead of him, when a movement in the water to his left caught the corner of his eye, and he jerked his head around, hauling on the reins. A body was caught in the current, being swept out toward the bay.

Just then Meg Parkes stumbled around the bend with a screaming Tildy in her arms. She was sobbing something of which Ty heard only one word—but it was enough to freeze his heart.

Delia.

"Stay there!" he flung over his shoulder, pressing his knees hard into the pacer's sides. He urged the horse back along the bank—if he had any hope of pulling Delia from the churning rapids, he was going to have to get downriver from her. Looping the reins around the saddle pommel, he pulled off his coat, casting it aside along with his cocked hat. With his thighs, he maneuvered his horse, sending the panicked animal splashing across the marshy ground and crashing through the brush.

He was ahead of Delia now, but there wasn't much time. Kicking free of the stirrups, he jumped from the horse, landing on his moccasined-feet on the soft ground, knees bending to absorb the shock, and then he was wading fast into the river, pumping his arms hard. When the water reached his chest, he struck out swimming.

He had only one chance to snag her body as it was carried by him and he almost didn't make it. For one terrifying second, his fingers groped nothing but water before becoming entangled in her hair. Even then he almost lost her twice, as they were carried along side by side on the current, before he was able to wrap his arm around her chest and get a good grip. He was sure she was already dead. Her tiny frame was a sodden weight in his arms and her face, from the one glimpse he'd gotten of it, was blanched and lifeless.

He flung her onto the grassy bank and scrambled up after her. He pressed his fingers against the pulse point in her neck . . . and felt nothing.

"No!" he screamed, grabbing her shoulders and shaking her, as if he could shake the life back into her. He clutched her face, pressing his mouth onto her blue, lifeless lips. *"No!"* he screamed again.

It wasn't Edinburgh University that had taught Dr. Tyler Savitch how to try to revive a person who had drowned. He had seen his Indian father Assacumbuit do it once, bringing back to life a child who had fallen into the lake near their village. He did to Delia what Assacumbuit had done to the child, pumping her arms up and down in a rowing motion and squeezing her chest.

He did it over and over, unwilling to accept that he had lost her because the reality was unbearable. He had seen Abenaki shamans try to blow life back into the dead and he did that, too—pressing his mouth over hers and breathing into her, hard.

Suddenly her head lolled to the side. She coughed once and then a second time, and then water poured from her mouth and nose, and she was retching.

He held her head up so she wouldn't strangle, making it easier for her to draw air into her heaving lungs. When the choking finally stopped and her breathing slowed, he gathered her into his lap, pressing her head against his chest while he rocked her back and forth. His eyes squeezed tightly shut and he buried his face in her hair. "Ah God, Delia, Delia. You scared the living hell out of me."

"Ty?" Her fists wrapped around the wet linen of his shirt and she clung to him, rubbing her face against his chest, her breasts heaving. She felt so damn small and insubstantial in his arms. Christ, he'd come so close to losing her.

Suddenly she jerked away from him, trying to push to her feet. "Oh God, the girls, Ty! Where are the girls?"

He held her down. "They're all right."

She still hadn't quite recovered her wind and the slight struggle had her gasping again for air. "B-but, Ty . . ."

"They're upriver a little ways. I told them to stay put. At least Meg had enough sense to run for help rather than try to jump in after you." He ran his hands over her face, reassuring himself that she was all right. "Delia, what happened?"

She twisted her head aside and pushed against him, harder. "G-girls . . . have to go . . . They'll be . . . terrified."

Ty hesitated, torn between his unwillingness to leave Delia and the knowledge that he was going to have to go back for the Parkes girls, when his problem was solved. He spotted Meg running down the road above them, Tildy still in her arms.

"There they are. You stay still."

"But—"

He clutched her shoulders. "Delia, for the love of God, will you for once, just once, do what I ask?"

He reached the girls before they could start down the bank. Meg stood at the top and watched him come with huge, frightened brown eyes. "Is she . . . is she . . . ?"

"She's all right," he said quickly. "What happened?" He squatted down to get a look at Tildy. The little girl had lasped into intermittent, hiccupping sobs, but beyond that she appeared to be all right.

"W-we w-were f-fishing and—" Meg's throat caught on a sob.

"Never mind," Ty said, to head off her growing hysteria. He squeezed her shoulder. "You take Tildy back to the house and put some water on the fire. I'll bring Delia along in a minute. She's all right now, but she needs to get her wind back."

Meg nodded and wiped her nose with the back of her hand. Then she turned and started obediently back down the road.

Delia tried to stand as Ty returned to her. "Don't get up," he ordered, more sharply that he'd intended. "I want you just to sit there in the hot sun a moment and recover your breath."

He sat down alongside her, letting his eyes fill with the sight of her. Her wet hair was plastered tight to her head and her tawny eyes looked huge in her white face. Her lips still

had a bluish tinge and occasional tremors shook her chest.
Her soaked clothes were molded to her curves. He could see
the outline of her full breasts and her nipples, puckered tight
from the cold water, stood out sharply beneath the thin, wet
material. Christ, even half drowned she was adorable.

Their eyes met and slowly a smile spread across her face.
"You saved me from drowning again, Ty. Thank you."

His mouth slanted up in answer. "Who were you trying to
kiss this time, brat?"

She started to laugh, but ended up coughing. She sucked
in a deep breath, then sniffed, rubbing at her nose with the
back of her hand, the way Meg had done a moment before.
"It was Gretchen who fell in the river. I tried to go after
her."

"Gretchen?" Ty's heart skipped a beat and he whipped
around, searching the white-capped water for more floating
bodies, even though by now it would be far too late.

Delia reached out, clinging to his shirt again. "Don't, Ty!
Gretchen's a doll." Suddenly her chest jerked and she started
to cry. "Oh, poor Tildy. I've lost her doll."

"A *doll!* You jumped in the river to rescue a doll?" Unconsciously, his hands closed around her upper arms and he
shook her. "Jesus God, Delia, you can't even swim!"

"I f-forgot."

He crushed her against him, so hard she grunted. "God-
sake, Delia!"

She wriggled out of his arms. "Don't shout at me, Ty."
Wincing, she pressed her palm against her midriff. "My ribs
hurt. I think you bruised them."

Furious anger washed over Ty, so powerful he started to
shake with it. My God, he'd almost lost her over a doll! What
the hell was she thinking to go jumping in the river after a
doll when she couldn't even swim!

"I ought to put bruises on your backside is what I ought
to do," he said through gritted teeth.

She glared at him, while he breathed fire back at her. Then
her mouth puckered and she started to laugh.

"It's not funny!" he bellowed. Did she have any idea what
it would have done to him to lose her?

"Oh, but, Ty, it is." She pressed her hand to her mouth

to stop another laugh. "You look so cute when you're angry."

"Cute!"

"You ought to see yourself. Your eyes get all dark and stormy, and your brows soar up, and your nostrils flare—there, see, just like that, like a bull what's getting ready to charge."

"That's not anger you're seeing, Delia. That's lust."

Now he wanted to laugh at the look on *her* face. "Lust?" she squeaked, scrambling to her feet and backing away from him, her arms pressed across her breasts like a frightened virgin guarding her virtue.

He came up after her, slowly, inexorably.

"Lust," he said, his face set with determination. "I've been lusting after you for so damn long I've forgotten what it's like to feel normal. Do you know what an Abenaki warrior does when he wants a woman, Delia?"

"Oh, Lord above us . . ."

"He takes her."

"But, Ty, I'm . . . Ty, you can't!"

"Can. Will, Delia."

It had started out as a teasing game, a way to pay her back for calling him cute. But at some point it had stopped being a game. He wanted her beneath him, screaming with passion. He wanted her and he was going to have her.

She saw it in his eyes. She whirled to run and he grabbed her. He closed his fingers tightly around her scalp and slammed his open mouth down hard on hers. For a moment she melted against him and met his thrusting tongue with her own, and God, but she tasted so hot and wet and sweet. He thought he'd die from the hunger she unleashed in him.

Then suddenly she bucked against him, her two clenched fists pushing at his chest as she struggled to tear her mouth from his. He kept his hand pressed against the back of her head, but he lifted his lips a scant inch off hers to speak. "Delia, my love, don't fight—"

"Bastard! Let go of m—"

He kissed her again. But there was no surrender this time. She fought him with all her might, flailing, kicking, panting

raggedly against his open mouth. Her chest heaved and she
began to choke.

He let her go. She backed away from him, pressing a shaking hand to her mouth, coughing as she tried to gulp in
breathfuls of air. He reached out to help her, but she flinched
away from him.

"Delia . . ."

At last she turned her face toward his . . . and he had never
seen so much hurt in a woman's eyes. It filled him with such
self-loathing that he shuddered.

"How could you do that to me, Ty?" she asked in a
strained, tormented voice. "You have no right. No right to
treat me that way."

"Ah God, Delia, you've got it wrong. I didn't—"

She stumbled away from him, trying to run, and fell to her
knees. He swung her up into his arms.

Sobbing, she beat against his chest. "What are you doing?
Put me down!"

His arms tightened around her. He welcomed her blows;
he only wished she'd hit him harder. He spoke gruffly to hide
his emotion. "Shut up, Delia. I'm done assaulting your damn
virtue for today."

She went quiet as he carried her up the bank and down the
cart trail toward the farm.

"I'm not that kind of girl, Ty," she finally said in a hurt,
quavering voice that broke his heart.

"Aw, Delia-girl, I know you're not. It's me. I'm the bastard, remember?"

She breathed a tiny sigh and relaxed against him. After a
moment she nestled her cheek against his chest. It felt good,
Ty thought, to hold her like this in his arms.

Simply hold her.

Chapter 20

The barn smelled of grain dust and manure. Delia paused in the doorway and watched Nat as he threshed wheat with a hand flail. The air echoed with a steady thumping sound as he knocked the kernels out of their heads and onto the floor. He had just reached for a hayfork to toss aside the straw when he looked up and noticed her standing there. She carried his musket across her shoulder and wore his hat on her head, cocked at a jaunty angle.

He leaned on the hayfork, his chest pumping as he regained his breath. A tentative smile stretched his wide mouth. "You look like you're fixing to attend the muster days in my stead, Delia. Are the others here already then?" he asked, and she saluted in reply. It actually made him laugh.

He set the pitchfork aside and plucked his coat off a nearby hay bale, shrugging into it. "Are you sure you don't mind my leaving you and the girls alone?"

"We'll be all right, Nat. You mustn't worry." Delia stepped forward to help him on with his fly coat, smoothing it across his shoulders. It reached halfway down his thighs and was of a bright blue wool, the color of a summer sky. His wife had made it for him. His first wife.

Delia couldn't resist adding, "After all, you attended the muster days when your Mary was alive and she didn't mind."

The coat clashed sharply with the dark green of his buckskin breeches, which were part of his militia uniform. Delia had been surprised when Nat had told her he was to attend the muster days in Wells tomorrow with the other able-bodied

283

men of Merrymeeting. "The fine's five shillings if you don't turn up," he had said when she questioned him.

"But surely a man who's missing a foot should be exempted," she protested, forgetting to guard her tongue. Nat had reacted predictably.

His chin jutted forward with pride. "I might not be able to rehearse the military manual with the others, Delia, but I can still contribute my time. Colonel Bishop has me serving as his adjutant. My Mary and I thought it was the least I could do."

Delia started to explain that she hadn't meant her comment as a criticism of his physical abilities, but she held her tongue. She had learned from bitter experience that with Nat her explanations only made matters worse.

Now, Delia wordlessly took the hat off her dark head and put it on her husband's blond one. She'd decorated the brim with a sprig of pine and a ribbon cockade. Handing him his musket, she followed him out the barn door. A group of men waited in the yard, their hearty laughter filling the air. They were like young boys, Delia thought, all set to go on an outing and wound up tight with the excitement of it.

For the men of Merrymeeting the muster meant a five-day excursion. A day by coastal sloop to get to Wells, three days there, and another day back. From what the other women had said, Delia suspected the muster was an excuse for the men to carouse away from their wives' censoring eyes as much as to rehearse the military manual. The mornings were reserved for drilling, true, but the afternoons were filled with horse races, shooting matches, and other manly sporting pursuits. The evenings were spent in drinking bouts during which gallons of flips were consumed. Only Colonel Bishop, who had command responsibilities, and Nat, who didn't drink anything stronger than spruce beer, seemed to take the militia muster seriously.

Nat went inside to tell the girls goodbye and pick up the rest of his equipment—shot pouch, powder horn, tomahawk, and wooden canteen. Delia searched the men in the yard, looking for a particular dark head and sharp-boned, handsome face. Instead a flash of distinctive red hair caught her eye.

She advanced on the burly blacksmith with her fists on her hips. "What are you doing here, Sam Randolf? I thought your Hannah was expecting any day now."

Sam whipped around to face her, his big jowls coloring. "Aw shucks, Mrs. Parkes . . ."

"She's already freshening," Obadiah Kemble put in, his tiny black eyes darting back and forth. "And it's a breech birth, so it's hard tellin' when the brat'll get here. We got ourselves a pool going and right now your Nat looks to be the winner if it comes tomorrow, as the doc's predictin'."

Delia scowled, not bothering to hide her disapproval. "All the more reason for you to remain at your wife's side, Mr. Randolf."

Sam looked at the ground, shuffling his feet. "Aw heck, Mrs. Parkes. Hannah'll be all right. She's birthed me seven lusty boys with barely a whimper. She don't need me. I'd only get in the way. An' Doc is stayin' with her."

"Hunh! I'm surprised *he* isn't going with the lot of you."

"Normally he does," Obadiah put in. "Even though physicians are supposed to be excused from the militia. But him being so wilderness-wise and all, the colonel likes to use him as a scout. Besides, you know the doc. He doesn't want to miss out on all the, er, mustering."

Nat emerged from the house just then, carrying a chattering Tildy in his arms and with Meg at his side. Tildy clutched her new doll tightly in her fist, an Indian girl with a deerskin dress, a tiny shell necklace, and a cap made of wampum— the purple-dyed seashells the Abenaki used for money.

Ty had brought the doll around the day after Gretchen had been lost, but Delia missed him because she had been inside, trying to work Mary's spinning wheel and producing nothing but slubs. Later, when Tildy had proudly shown her the doll, Delia had astounded everyone by bursting into tears and running into the inner room, slamming the door behind her.

When she emerged later that evening, Nat told her Tildy had named the doll Hildegarde. "Where does she come up with these names?" he'd asked her with a nervous laugh, eyeing her askance and no doubt wondering if she were about to start blubbering again.

Delia couldn't explain even to herself why Ty's generosity

had made her behave like a wooden-headed fool. Every time she looked at the doll, she wanted to weep with a mixture of pride in Ty and an aching regret that she would never have the joy of presenting him with a child of their own to cuddle and spoil.

But Delia wore a smile now as Nat and the girls came out of the house. He kissed Tildy before handing her to Delia, squatting to give Meg a hug. "You girls behave and mind Delia."

Meg said nothing, but Delia saw the girl's chin take on a stubborn jut and she repressed a sigh.

Nat shouldered his musket as he and the men started down the trail toward the bay, where the coastal sloop waited to sail down the estuary on the forenoon tide. At the edge of the forest, he turned and waved. Delia and the girls waved back.

"Bye, bye Papa!" Tildy cried, blasting Delia's eardrum.

When Nat's figure had disappeared around the bend, Meg turned to Delia, a slight smirk on her face. "How come you aren't crying? Ma always cried when Papa went to Wells for muster days."

"She did?" Delia asked, surprised. She couldn't imagine the paragon Mary Parkes succumbing to the weakness of tears.

"He didn't kiss you goodbye," Meg said, her eyes on Delia's face to gauge her reaction. "He *always* kissed Ma goodbye."

Delia sighed. "Don't you have chores to do, Meg Parkes?"

Delia decided to chop wood that afternoon.

The morning had begun with a dense fog that left everything wet and smelling of the sea. But by the time Nat left, the fog had been melted by the sun, although a shimmering haze still swathed the horizon. It was September now; the days were growing shorter and the trees were beginning to get a tinge of color on the ridges. The corn was high in the fields; it would be tasseling soon.

Delia had thought this morning that the nights were coming on cool and it would soon be time to take the extra blankets out of the calfskin chest in the inner room. She decided to surprise Nat by laying up a good stack of firewood while he was gone—hickory, because it produced the best and hottest fire.

She worked behind the barn, piling the chopped wood onto a sledge to be hauled into the shed and stacked later. The thunk of the ax biting into the wood bounced off the thick trees of the surrounding forest. When she paused to rest, Delia could detect the pungent smell of moldering pine needles and hear a partridge rustling through the nearby cornrows.

She thought of Ty. Thunk! The ax split the wood with a resounding blow. She imagined it was his head she pounded.

He was at the Randolf house right now, attending to Hannah. Delia was tempted to walk there, to call on Hannah and offer her help, maybe bring a pot of baked beans or a pan of pone with jelly. But she knew if she did such a thing it would really be an excuse to see Ty and she couldn't lie to herself in that way.

Thunk! This time it was her own head she imagined she struck.

It had been three weeks since Ty had fished her from the Kennebec and though she hadn't seen him once during all that time, there wasn't a minute when she hadn't thought about him, reliving that kiss over and over in her mind. She could still feel the heat of his lips on hers, as if he had left a permanent, searing brand. She was furious with him for thinking he could use her in that way—as a happy answer to his manly desires. She was furious with herself for still loving him, for kissing him back and wanting him so shamelessly. Was she no better than he thought her to be—no better than a two-shilling tart, a way for a man to spend a quick hour or two of his time?

Thunk! She worked her frustration out on Nat's head now. Nat, her so-called husband, who still slept on the shakedown in the linter. Who couldn't even give her a peck on the cheek when he was going away for five whole days. There might not be any love between them, but they were man and wife. Maybe if Nat became her husband in fact as well as name, she could get Tyler Savitch out of her blood, out of her mind, out of her heart.

Out—thunk! Out—thunk! Out—thunk!

The ax Delia used had a head made of brittle iron that often cracked in cold weather. It was heavy and hard to swing, wobbling as it approached the mark. Delia didn't notice that the wobbling was becoming worse and worse with each swing she made . . . until the head came flying off the helve.

The ax head flew through the air, slicing into Delia's petticoat and thigh in passing. She stood looking at the headless handle in shock, feeling nothing—and then a burning, searing pain tore a scream from her throat.

She pressed a hand to her thigh. It came away dripping with blood. Flinging the ax helve to the ground, she limped over to lean against the bevel of the chopping stump. The pain was so fierce it darkened her vision and sent the breath wheezing from her lungs. She set her teeth to keep from fainting and lifted her skirt, afraid of what she would see.

What she saw made her reel dizzily and she almost fell off the stump. The cut was jagged and deep, and blood welled out of it, satiny and glutinous, so dark a red it looked almost black. Shuddering, she pressed the heel of her hand to the gash, trying to stop the bleeding.

She heard the linter door slam and Meg's high-pitched voice, calling her name. She opened her mouth to answer, but couldn't summon the strength. The dark edges around her vision were spreading. She blinked and looked into Meg's horrified face. "Get Dr. Ty . . . he's at . . . baby . . . Hannah Randolf . . ."

The darkness covered the world now except for two tiny pinpricks of light. Then even they winked out.

Minutes, or perhaps it was only seconds later, Delia felt wet lips brush her cheek. She forced open her eyes to find a dimpled face pressed close to hers. "Did you cut yourself with the ax, Delia?" Tildy whispered loudly. "Are you going to have to get a wooden foot like Papa?"

Delia smiled, or thought she did. The world had gone black again.

Dr. Tyler Savitch willed his hands to stop shaking as he tied the tourniquet around Delia's slender thigh. He tried not to think that if the ax had sliced so much as an inch deeper, it would have severed the artery and she would have bled to death long before he could have gotten to her in time.

Christ, why did she keep *doing* this to him? He had tried so hard to protect his heart, to distance himself from her so that he couldn't be hurt. But it had all been to no avail—he cared, cared too damn much, in spite of himself. It was if she were deliberating dancing with death to flaunt in his face the fact that if he lost her he wouldn't be able to bear it.

Against his will, his bloodied fingers drifted up, hovering over her precious features. They were twisted in pain and Ty would have sawed off his own leg to spare her this. He suddenly realized she was more valuable to him than his own life. He would sacrifice anything for her. Anything.

Her lids fluttered open. "Ty . . . ?"

He leaned over, pressing his lips to her forehead. "I'm here, my love."

"The ax broke, Ty. It cut my leg."

"You'll be all right. I'm going to sew it up in a minute. But first I'll have to carry you into the house."

He positioned her arms around his neck and lifted her slowly, but still she cried out. He thought she might have fainted again by the time he got her inside and laid her down on the inner room bed, but he saw that her eyes were open, although they were dark with pain.

"I'm sorry I keep gettin' myself into these predicaments, Ty. I'm such trouble t' ye all the time."

"I'm used to trouble from you," he said, brushing her cheek with his knuckles. "You and trouble seem to go together like fleas on a mule."

A weak smile trembled on Delia's lips as her eyes drifted closed. Ty turned around to Meg, who hovered in the doorway, a wide-eyed Tildy clinging to her hand. "Does your father have any rum or brandy in the house?"

Meg's head jerked. "Y-you mean the big bottle of medicine?"

"Yes. That's probably it . . . Bring a mug, too. And put some water on to boil."

Meg came back with a brandy bottle and a noggin. "Take Tildy and wait out in the keeping room. Shut the door." Ty held a nogginful of brandy up to Delia's lips. "I'm going to make you good and drunk, Delia-girl."

Her mouth curled into another smile. "You wouldn't be tryin' t' take advantage of me, would ye, Tyler Savitch?"

Ty's throat closed up. He couldn't answer her; he couldn't even smile.

In spite of her protests, he relentlessly poured the brandy down her throat until she was close to passing out. He cleaned the gash thoroughly before sewing it up with a bone needle and a piece of the sheep gut that he carried in his physician's bag for such a purpose. She whimpered only a little as he did it, although she was still conscious. He spoke to her while he worked, telling her she was the gutsiest wench he'd ever known.

With Meg's help, he found Nat's hoard of pigtails—the small, twisted ropes of tobacco used for smoking and chewing. He opened the twists, picking apart the tobacco leaves. These, combined with some puffball fungus he had in his bag, would act as an astringent. He packed it all around the cut, then wrapped her thigh with a bandage made from an old torn sheet. When he was finished he stood above her, looking down with an unconscious scowl on his face.

Her golden eyes glittered brightly back at him, glazed from a combination of the brandy and the pain. "Don' ye start shoutin' a' me, Ty," she slurred.

"We'll discuss your carelessness later," he said sternly.

" 'Twasna my fault . . . Shouldn't ye be wi' Hannah?"

"She had the baby an hour ago. It's a girl."

"Oh, tha's nice. I wish I could have a baby." She added something that sounded like "your baby," but he couldn't be sure, she had slurred the words so.

He eased down carefully beside her on the bed, positioning her so that she leaned against his chest, her hair spread over him like a black lace fan. He wrapped one arm around her waist, his hand resting on her stomach. He felt her sigh.

She peeled his hand off her stomach and held it out, matching her slender white fingers to his long, dark ones. Suddenly she erupted into a drunken little giggle. "Ye have magic hands, Ty. Since the first, I felt those magic hands an' I fell right in love wi' ye, wooden-headed fool tha' I am."

Uncomfortable with her words, with the frightening feelings they evoked within him, Ty's fingers closed around hers. He brought their clasped hands back to her lap and changed the subject. "Your leg's going to hurt like hell for a few days. You'll have to stay off it. Maybe I'd better send someone to fetch Nat back."

She stiffened in his arms, twisting her head around. "N-no, Ty. Don' do tha'. Don' send for Nat. Pleassse."

Ty felt cold with sudden dread. She could expect Nat to give her what-for over her carelessness, but fear of a scolding didn't provoke that sort of panic in a wife. Unconsciously, his arm tightened around her and he brought her closer against him. "Delia, why are you so afraid of Nat? Does he beat you?"

She slung her head from side to side, bouncing against his chest. "No, no . . . Da used his fists on me alla time. Not Nat. He never so mush as touches me." Her ragged laughter ended on a hiccup. "Nat don' touch me a-tall."

He stared into her face. Her tawny eyes impaled him, piercing his heart.

"Nat don' love me, Ty. He still loves his wife. An' ye don't love me. Nobody loves me."

He could feel her heart trembling beneath his hand. His own chest rose and fell, rose and fell. The movement fluttered the ruby-faceted strands of her hair. Her skin was so pale it was almost transparent. Her lips . . . her lips . . . Ty's head dipped; he had to taste those lips . . .

"Why don' ye love me, Ty?"

His mouth hovered, but didn't fall. He was so afraid, so goddamn afraid. "Ah God, Delia, I—"

. . . *do love you.*

The words, although they caught in his throat, resounded in his heart.

I do love you.

Delia opened the door onto Ty's dark and scowling face. He stood before her, looking incredibly handsome and overpoweringly masculine in his fringed hunting shirt, open almost to the waist, and his tight buckskin breeches and knee-length boots.

"What the hell are you doing up?" he demanded.

As always the color leaped to her face at the first sight of
him; there wasn't a thing she could do about it. To cover her
consternation, she wet her lips with her tongue, drawing his
eyes to her mouth. "Oh, Ty. I couldn't stay in that bed another minute. And, besides, Nat's due home this evening and
I'm way behind with my chores."

His eyes remained fixed on her mouth. Then his jaw
clamped tightly shut, his brows lowered, and his scowl deepened. With no warning, he swung her into his arms and
headed for the bedroom. It always felt so wonderful being
held, being touched by him. For the briefest second she let
her cheek fall against his broad chest. The rough linen of his
hunting shirt was warm and smelled like him.

Damn the man.

"Ty, put me down!" she cried.

"In a minute."

She suspected from the stiff way he held her that he might
have wanted to dump her on the bed like a sack of turnips,
but he laid her down gently. He pressed his hand against her
forehead. "Damn it, Delia, you've got a fever."

"I'm only hot because it's so muggy today." She pushed
herself up on her elbows. "Ty, I've got a million things—"

He pressed her back down. "Nat won't be home this evening. There's a bad storm brewing, a nor'easter by the looks
of it. The sloop won't have set out with weather like this on
the way."

Delia looked out the window. It was true that black, omi-
nous clouds were piling up overhead, their low bellies snagging on the distant hills. The air smelled salty and damp, of
the sea and rain. The wind whipped through the trees in
intermittent gusts, making a low moaning sound that drowned
out the sifting noise coming from the barn where the girls
were winnowing the grain their father had threshed four days
before.

Ty cupped her chin in his hand and turned her head. "I
want your word you'll stay off that leg again today."

"But—"

He put his fingers against her lips. His touch was warm

and soft. Delia stopped herself just in time from pursing her lips and kissing them. "Your word, Delia."

She nodded slowly.

His hand fell, leaving her lips feeling naked. "Now tell me what chores you have to do and I'll do them."

Her eyes rounded in disbelief. "You'd do women's work?"

His mouth slanted crookedly. "For you, I would. Only don't tell anybody or I'll never live it down."

She lay in bed while he did her work, drifting in and out of sleep, lulled by the sound of his voice speaking to the girls. She'd never had this luxury before, having Ty in the same house with her. Once, he brought her a cup of mint tea. He sat beside her on the bed, drinking with her, and they talked. Not about anything earth-shattering, but Delia knew she'd never been happier.

A storm struck with violent fury late that afternoon.

It had grown dark and the wind began to blow harder and steadier. It made a mournful wailing sound as it whistled through the eaves. Suddenly the rain poured down and the wind caught it, flinging it like buckets of water against the house.

Delia got out of bed, limping over to the window to pull the shutters closed. As she did she saw Ty coming back from putting the mares in the barn, running across the yard in his long-legged stride. The rain slashed down in sheets of black water, instantly turning the clearing into mud.

She hurried through the keeping room, hitching her stride to favor her wounded leg. Delicious smells wafted from the direction of the hearth and she cast a passing smile at the girls, who were setting the table with Mary's fine pewterware.

She met Ty at the front door as he was cleaning his boots on the scraper. The rain had plastered his shirt against his body, detailing the contours of his muscles. Water fell in rivulets down his face from the soaked tendrils of his dark hair. His eyes glinted silver-blue in the weird half light.

"You're soaked!" she exclaimed, laughing and repressing the urge to brush the wet hair from his eyes.

The creases beside his mouth deepened with his grin.

"That wind out there is strong enough to lean on," he said, panting.

He slouched against the porch wall to pull his boots off so he wouldn't leave muddy pools on the floor that he had cleaned and sanded for her. She couldn't help noticing how his wet buckskins clung slickly to his slender hips and long, lean thighs, seductively revealing . . . everything.

"Take that shirt off before you catch a chill," she said, pretending to scold to cover the thudding of her heart. "I'll dry it by the fire while we eat supper. You are staying for supper, aren't you?"

He tossed another grin at her. "Damn right. Since I fixed it."

"Hunh. From the way I heard it, you had poor Meg and Tildy doing most of the work."

He peeled off his wet shirt as he padded in his stocking feet into the keeping room. Her eyes fastened onto the sight of his broad, smooth back, tapering to a narrow waist and tight buttocks, and her insides felt warm and melting. "Oh Lord above us . . ." she prayed on a sigh.

Normally supper was the lightest meal of the day, but Ty and the girls had prepared a feast. Roast turkey, succotash, bake-kettle biscuits, and for dessert a blackberry pie. He sat opposite her at the table, with a blanket draped around his shoulders. The firelight bronzed his bare chest and struck golden lights off his rich brown hair.

She watched him as he speared a piece of the turkey with the point of a knife. "I'm sorry we don't have one of those newfangled eating tools like they have up at the Bishops'."

His lips curled up as he chewed and his eyes smiled. "Don't you like my cooking?" he asked when he noticed she wasn't eating.

"Oh, no, it's delicious, Ty."

"I made the biscuits!" Tildy proclaimed.

"You did not," Meg countered. "*I* made them. You only stirred the batter a few times."

Delia put a biscuit smeared with molasses into her mouth. "Mm-mm," she crooned, rolling her eyes. The children laughed. Ty laughed, too, and a warmth uncurled deep within her stomach at the rich, throaty sound.

But she was too excited to eat. She had dreamed of such a moment hundreds of times—sitting across the table from Ty of an evening, sharing a meal and talking of the day's events, with the chatter of children to interrupt them.

"Did you hear that it's official, Ty—Anne Bishop's going to be Merrymeeting's schoolmaster," she said.

"Thanks to you." He gave her such a warm smile that she blushed. "Bringing you here to Merrymeeting was the smartest thing I ever did."

Delia's cheeks pinkened even more with pleasure. "Anne's really the one who's doing it all. She's starting the lessons up after the harvest. In her library."

Ty's eyes danced. "I also heard that Sara Kemble promised to write the authorities in Boston and inform them that our new schoolmaster is really a *mistress.*"

"Oh, no!"

"Oh, yes. Whereupon Obadiah threatened to take a switch to her if he so much as caught her looking at paper and quill." They all laughed at the picture of the diminutive Obadiah going after the huge Mrs. Kemble with a switch.

Ty wouldn't let Delia clear away the dirty dishes, ensconcing her instead on the settle with her leg propped on a cushioned stool. With the girls' help, he soon had the keeping room set to rights and they all joined Delia around the fire.

Tildy crawled into Ty's lap. "Tell us a story about Goosecup."

"Goosecup?" Delia asked, smiling.

"*Glooscap,*" Ty said, correcting the mispronunciation. "He's the giant who came down from the sky in a stone canoe to people the land on the edge of the sunrise with men and animals."

"Go on with you!" Delia scoffed.

"Oh, but it's true," Ty said, looking as if he truly believed it. "Once, in the days before the light of the sun first touched the earth . . ."

Under the guise of listening to the story, Delia openly watched the animated face of this man she loved so much. She let his soothing voice wash over her as he spoke of the giant Glooscap, who with his magic belt of wampum could change himself into any form; of the great battle he fought

to save the Abenaki people from the rule of his evil brother
Malsum, another giant with the head of a wolf; and other
strange spirits: Keskum, the frost giant; and Wokwotoonok,
the north wind giant, who was even now unleashing his fury
on the world outside their snug little clapboard house. She
watched him and she thought: when he marries and has children of his own, this is how he'll be. Oh, how she envied
the woman who would come to know the joy of living with
such a man.

She realized with a start that Ty's voice had slowed and
faded. "And there," he said, low and soft, his eyes locking
with hers, *"kespeadooksit . . . our tale ends."*

Delia jerked her gaze from his, finding a sudden fascination with the flames in the hearth. "It's late and you girls
should be in bed," she said in a voice that croaked. Ty started
to get up, but Delia stopped him. "No. I'll see to them. I've
been sitting about all day long and I feel the need to stretch."

When she came back down after tucking the girls in bed,
she paused in the doorway to look at him. They had not lit
the tallow dip, so the only light in the room was the fire. He
lay sprawled before it, sitting on the bench with his back
braced against the table. He'd discarded the blanket, and his
chest was bared to the flames. He had drawn a tankard of
spruce beer from the brew kettle in the corner and it rested
in his lap. He looked rumpled and lazy and adorable.

A log on the fire fell with a burst of sparks and a licking
of flame. He turned, fixing her with eyes that seared her with
their intensity.

"They went right to sleep," she said. *Damn, why did her
voice keep croaking like a frog's?*

"That's good." Draining the tankard of beer, he set it on
the table. It was so quiet she could hear the ticking of Mary's
lantern clock and the sound of the rain dripping off the eaves.
For the moment the wind had eased.

She came into the room, although she didn't sit down.
"They'll probably wake up in the middle of the night though,
screaming about cannibal giants who devour little girls."

His mouth slanted into a delightful, lopsided smile . . .
and her heart flipped over.

"Glooscap will watch over them." He stretched his legs

out, linking his fingers behind his head, elbows spread wide. The movement rippled the muscles on his chest and exposed the dark shadow of the hair beneath his arms to her fascinated gaze.

The room suddenly seemed too small. They hadn't touched once all evening, not even accidentally. Yet she had never been more aware of him than she was at this very moment. Nor more aware of how much she loved him. And how much she wanted him.

She could barely breathe from the pressure in her chest. "Ty, I thank you for all you've done today. But it's not right . . . your being here now. I think you ought to leave."

His eyes blazed up at her so fierce and hot she had to stiffen her spine to keep from swaying. "What are you afraid of?"

"You," she whispered throatily. "And myself."

His arms fell as he straightened, slowly. He stood, bringing himself up right next to her. He still didn't touch her, but he might as well have. He was stripping her naked with his eyes.

"I love you," he said.

For a moment a fierce joy flooded her, so raw and bright it was like the sudden flare of a pitch torch. Then reality returned. And with it anger.

She slapped him, hard. So hard his head snapped to the side and he emitted a tiny grunt of surprise. When he swung his face back around she hit him again, on the other cheek this time, and harder.

She would have slapped him a third time except she realized he was doing nothing to defend himself. He stood rigid before her, his hair tumbling over his brow, his face flushed an angry red beneath the gray shadow of his beard. Her palm burned and her heart was splintering into little pieces at her feet.

"I love you," he said again.

"Damn you." She had to gulp in drafts of air to keep from sobbing, from screaming . . . from dying. "Damn you, damn you, damn you . . ."

"I love you, Delia," he said a third time. "I know it's too late, but I . . . I just thought you should know."

He plucked his shirt from the peg where it hung by the fire

and headed for the door. He stopped to put his shirt on, along with his boots.

He paused with his hand on the latch. "Delia . . . ?"

"Go!" she screamed at him. "Go! Go! Go! I hate you!"

He went.

But as soon as the door shut, she stumbled after him. Her fingers fumbled with the latch, then stilled. She pressed her cheek against the wood and slid slowly to her knees, moaning and crying his name.

Chapter 21

The nor'easter blew for three days. It brought with it two gifts from the sea.

They heard about the gifts when the militiamen returned on the sloop from Wells. Lobsters, the men said. Lobsters in such numbers had been washed ashore that they could be collected by the wagonload and used as fertilizer for the fields. And something else had come with the tide as well—a cannon off a shipwrecked French privateer.

All of Merrymeeting gathered on the green with their carts and wagons for the trip down to the beach. Just as they were about to set off, Ty rode out of the forest on his pacer, looking—in his fringed buckskins, knee-high moccasins, and fox-fur cap—more savage than the wilderness from which he'd emerged. Delia's eyes went immediately to him, but when he turned in her direction she quickly found something on the other side of the green to engage her fascinated attention.

He loves you! her heart sang, a refrain it had been singing for three days. *He loves you!*

And then, as always, came the dirge that would cause her eyes to burn with tears and her chest to feel tight and weighted with despair. *Too late. Too late. Too late.*

"You ever been to a clambake, Delia?" Nat asked. He sat on the cart seat beside her, relaxed and smiling for a change.

Her husband.

Delia forced a smile and shook her head. "No, I never have, Nat. It sounds like fun."

Too late. Too late. Too late.

"And good eating too." He turned to Meg and Tildy, who

299

sat, legs stretched out, in back of the cart. "Isn't that right, girls?"

Nat had been softening lately. Although they were still solemn, the haunted look had left his gray eyes and on occasion he even managed a few smiles. Delia had expected him to scold her over her carelessness with the ax, but he'd appeared more genuinely concerned than angry. He'd reacted that way as well after she'd nearly drowned herself trying to rescue Tildy's doll.

"There's a goodness in you, Delia," he had said that evening just before bed. "A real goodness. It shows especially with the girls. They're coming to love you. Even Meg," he'd added, producing a half-smile. Then his eyes had searched her face as if seeing her, really seeing her, for the first time.

The ten-mile trail to the beach was nothing but a pair of parallel cart ruts. As they followed the estuary, Delia could see that, indeed, thousands of lobsters had been washed ashore during the storm. They carpeted the ground, their shiny gray shells glinting wetly in the sunlight. Many still lived and the earth seemed to be undulating like waves with their movement.

By the time they arrived at the beach the carts were filled with the lobsters. Snagged between two lichen-covered rocks among debris from the wrecked ship awaited the sea's second gift—a cast-iron, three-pound cannon. The men gathered around it, talking excitedly among themselves, for one shot from such a weapon would scare off a whole tribe of Abenaki on the warpath.

"We could drag her back to the blockhouse with an ox team," Colonel Bishop said, rubbing one ruddy cheek. "She's been partly spiked. Do you think you could get her to fire, Sam?"

The red-headed blacksmith caressed the cannon's barrel almost lovingly. "Aye. But we haven't any shot. Too bad that French bang-boat didn't part with the cannonballs while she was givin' us the cannon."

"She'll discharge a load of musket balls though and that can be just as effective," Ty said. He glanced up in time to catch Delia's gaze on him. She glared, then looked away.

"All we need is a fuse and powder," he finished, frowning at Delia's stiff back.

With the wagons loaded down with the crustacean fertilizer and the cannon dispensed with at least in theory, the folk of Merrymeeting settled down for the main event of the day— the clambake.

It was a beautiful afternoon for a "bake". Usually in the summer months a fog bank lay like a dirty gray blanket just off the shore. But the storm had blown away the fog and the horizon where sea met sky was a sharp blue line. The air was clear enough to ring and the sun bright enough to blind the eyes, and sea birds slashed and wheeled across the cloudless sky.

As they would need several fires for their "bake," the settlers split into groups. Nat led Delia and the girls over to their neighbors, the Sewalls, and soon they were joined by Sam and Hannah Randolf and their brood. Delia was amazed to find Hannah up and about already. The women ooohed and aaahed over the new baby, who was nestled snugly within a pilgrim basket, sucking on a pap bag. Meg and young Daniel Randolf immediately got into an argument over who could eat the most clams.

Delia was sure Ty would soon amble over to their fire and she tried to arrange her face into the mask of polite indifference she intended to present him with that day. She waited, tense with anticipation, her eyes following his every move while pretending not to.

He joined the Bishops instead.

Each group laid stones in a circle and kindling on top. The fires were lit with a tinderbox—a quick strike of steel against flint, a flare of gunpowder, a glowing wick held to bits of birch bark. Armloads of wood were piled on the flames until the fires blazed. The stones had to get good and hot.

At low tide they walked the shingled beach, raking the sand and mud for clams to the accompaniment of the roaring, booming breakers, for the surf was high because of the storm. Delia had uncovered a small green crab and was poking it with a stick when a familiar voice behind her said, "Be careful, Delia-girl. Those are mean little devils. They latch onto a toe or finger, and they don't let go."

She straightened with a snap and started off down the beach away from him. His hand fell on her arm, jerking her around. The abrupt movement pulled the stitches in her thigh and she set her teeth on a cry of pain.

Ty's eyes bored into hers, unrelentingly fierce. "Do you intend to spend the whole day alternating between glowering at me in fury and pretending to ignore me?"

"You flatter yourself, Dr. Savitch. Until this moment I hadn't noticed you were here."

"We have to talk," Ty said between his teeth.

"I can't imagine what we could have to say. Oh, perhaps you wish to discuss your recompense for sewing up my leg. I'll speak with my *husband* about it. We're a little short of hard money at the moment, so would a couple of chickens suffice? Or perhaps a suckling pig?"

Ty ground his jaws. "Damn it, Delia—"

"Excuse me, doctor, but I see my *husband* is trying to get my attention." She brushed past him, hurrying toward Nat, who was busy untangling a bright orange starfish from Tildy's hair and not even looking in her direction.

By the time the clams were gathered, the fires had reduced themselves to embers. The hot stones were swept off with a spruce limb and the buckets of clams were dumped on top the stones. Onto the clams went lobsters and over it all a pile of rockweed to hold in the steam.

When the seafood had been cooked and eaten, and washed down by jugs of cider and spruce beer, the settlers began to gather up their children and gear, preparing for the journey home. Delia looked carefully to be sure Ty wasn't watching her.

He wasn't. He was over by the cannon, deep in conversation with Colonel Bishop and Sam Randolf, no doubt planning how to haul the weapon back to Merrymeeting. Convinced there was no danger of his following her, she told Nat where she was going and struck off down the beach, limping a little on her sore leg. She had been puzzled by something all afternoon and she wanted to get a closer look at it.

"It" was an enormous mound of oyster shells, higher and broader than any building she had ever seen. Guano covered

the mound like a thick dusting of snow. Periwinkles had burrowed into the crevices and in places white barnacles were
glued to the packed shells in bands. She ran her palm over
the tightly packed shells, rough and sharp and smooth in
turn. She couldn't imagine how such a thing had come to be
there. Surely the mound had been created by man, for it was
too unnatural to be a product of nature. But if man made this
oyster-shell mountain, toward what purpose? There was an
ancient, mysterious feel to it; she thought it had been there
for years, perhaps centuries.

She felt his presence before she saw him. She turned slowly
to face him. The most beautiful man she had ever seen, all
the man she could possibly want, the man she loved. The
man who had said, too late, too late, that he loved her.

"Delia—"

"Don't you dare tell me you love me, because I bloody
well don't want to hear it."

"I love you!" He had practically shouted it into her face,
and Delia cast a panicked look back down the beach, fearful
the others had heard. She whirled around, limping toward
another mountain of shells. He followed.

When she got within ten feet of the mound, she stopped.
She had to tilt her head way back to see the top. She flapped
her hand at it. "What the bloody hell are these things?"

"Nobody knows. They were made by people who lived
here thousands of years ago. The Abenaki call them the
oyster-shell people, but no one knows what they did with all
those oysters, whether they ate them or used them for fertilizer or—"

"How long?"

Ty shrugged and a lock of hair fell across his brow. "Nobody knows—"

"How long have you loved me?"

His intense eyes searched her face. "Since that afternoon
on Falmouth Neck. Maybe since I came upon you fishing
with that old Indian. Hell, maybe since I first looked down
on you sprawled so indecently and seductively on my bed."

"You bloody bastard. Why did you wait so long to tell
me? Instead you kept shouting in my face that you *didn't* love

me, and you let me go and *marry* another man. Well, I hope you're bloody miserable now. I hope you're suffering!"

"I am suffering, Delia."

He looked it. His skin had a greenish tinge and his eyes were bloodshot. Dark bruises marked the hollows above his sharp cheekbones. He looked as if he was suffering from the aftereffects of too many flips.

And a broken heart, her own heart cried.

"I'm suffering, Delia," he said again.

"Good!"

She whipped around and headed further down the beach, picking her way through the gleaming piles of brown, rubbery rockweed exposed by the tide. She stumbled over one and he steadied her with a hand under her elbow. She jerked it free.

"What are you doing following me like this? Do you want all of Merrymeeting to know you're lusting after your neighbor's wife?" In fact, they were out of sight of the others now, the oyster-shell mounds blocking their view of the clambake fires.

"I'm not lusting after you," Ty said.

"Bloody hell you're not."

"Stop cursing. You sound worse than a—"

"Grog shop wench?" She stopped and turned to face him.

She pulled off her cap, tossing her head, and the wind snatched at her hair, billowing it about her face in a smoky cloud. She stood before him and she knew—with the sun capturing the red lights in her hair, setting it afire, and the wind whipping roses into her cheeks, and the sea spray moistening her lips—she knew that she was beautiful.

She watched his eyes grow dark with desire, saw his breath quicken and the pulse in his neck begin to throb. And she knew, too, what she would find if she looked down.

Deliberately, she let her eyes fall to his crotch. His sex, thick and rigid, strained against the confines of his tight breeches. Proof of his hunger, of his need, of his desire.

She stared at it for a long moment, then let her gaze travel slowly back up his chest, to his face, where a band of hot color stained his cheekbones. She almost felt sorry for him then. Because, being a man, he couldn't hide what he felt.

He couldn't know that beneath her heavy short gown her breasts were tightening, that beneath her petticoat her knees were quaking, that between her legs . . . between her legs was a hot, wet craving that ached to be satisfied.

She sucked in a deep breath to steady herself—which drew Ty's eyes down to her breasts, and his blush deepened.

"All right, damn it, I am lusting after you," he ground out, with a soft moan. "But, Jesus, Delia, there's more to it than that. I love you. I want to live with you, to marry you."

"I'm married to Nat."

"You don't love Nat!"

"How I feel about my husband is none of your business."

He had turned half away from her, but he spun back around. His arm snaked out and he crushed her against him, bringing his mouth down over hers before she could draw breath to protest.

And then it was too late for protesting. She didn't even offer token resistance—her emotions were too raw, her body too vulnerable. He kissed her and she kissed him back, ravenously, plundering his mouth with her tongue, opening her own mouth to his sweet, hot invasion. When the kiss finally ended, they were both gasping for air, and she had knotted her fingers into his shirt to keep from sinking into the sand at his feet.

He turned his cheek, rubbing it in her hair. "Ah, Delia my love, my life. Come away with me—"

"I *can't*. You know I can't," she cried, her face contorted with misery. She had wanted to make him suffer, to make him ache with love as she had ached. But revenge wasn't sweet; it was bitter, bitter, and she was the one who was aching and suffering. "I can't," she moaned.

He bracketed her face with his hands, tilting it up to meet his eyes. "Then tell me you don't love me."

That's what she would do. She would tell him she didn't love him and then he would leave her alone, to suffer in peace. "I . . . It doesn't matter. I'm married. I—"

His mouth came down to capture hers again, but this time she wrenched her head aside at the last moment. His hand splayed her neck, lifting her chin. His thumb rubbed along the column of her throat, slowly, agonizingly . . .

"Let me go," she pleaded.

"What if I don't? What if I carried you off with me right now? Deep into the wilderness where no one could ever find us."

Her blood was a roar in her ears, sounding louder than the ocean breakers at their backs, so loud she could barely hear her own breathless reply. "Y-you wouldn't . . ."

"Wouldn't I?" His thumb continued to move, up and down. His mouth was close to hers again, only a breath apart. She thought she might faint. "An Abenaki savage would steal you away and to hell with your white man's laws and morality," he went on, as relentless as his stroking thumb. "I'm part savage, remember? Maybe all savage when it comes to you. And what's more, from the way you kissed me I'd say it's what you want, Delia-girl."

She twisted her head away from his grasp, backing up a step. "I'd fight you, Ty, every step of the way. I'd fight you until I escaped." His face tightened, but it was with hurt this time, not anger. Tears flooded her eyes. She seized his hands, clinging to him. "Oh, Ty, why am I fighting you? It's killing me inside to have to fight you . . ."

His fingers tightened around hers. "Then come away with me."

She turned from him, pressing her knuckles hard against her mouth to catch a sob. Her cheeks were drenched with tears. "Please, please don't ask this of me. I can't. I can't."

He pulled her back around. His fingers brushed the wetness from her face. "Ah, love, love . . . don't cry."

"I can't leave them, Ty. I made a promise, to Nat and to his girls. A promise before God. You think that because I'm a woman I have no honor, but I do."

Pain flickered in his eyes. "But I thought you loved me."

She gazed up into his beloved face. "I love you. You've always known how much I love you. But what of Nat? He married me in good faith. He entrusted his children to me. And the girls, Ty, they've come to care for me. How cruel it would be for me to walk out of their lives like that, so soon after they've lost their ma. How could we be happy, knowing they were suffering? I just couldn't live with myself if I betrayed my honor in that way. And if I can't live with myself, how can I hope to live with you?''

He cupped her cheeks, staring deep into her eyes, letting all that he felt show in his own. "Delia, my wonderful, wonderful Delia. Your honor, your dignity, your strength—they're all the reasons why I fell in love with you."

"Then you understand . . ."

His hands fell from her face. "Ah hell, I understand." He flung his head back, gazing up at the sky. Pain twisted his lips and drew taut the cords of his neck. "But, Christ, I love you so damn much. Without you, I—" He swallowed, shuddered. His eyes fell to hers. Never had she seen such pain. "I *need* you, Delia."

She couldn't bear it. She ran away from him, back along the beach. And he let her go.

He turned toward the sea. He squeezed his eyes shut. When he opened them again the ocean was still there, wide, blue. Empty.

"God," he whispered. It was the sound of despair.

"The answer is no and that's final!"

Delia cast a look over her shoulder at the girls cowering together in the keeping room. She followed Nat out the front door, shutting it behind her. He had sat down on the stoop to pull on his golo shoes—the loose canvas boots with short tops and woolen soles that he wore for muddy work. He was going to the logging camps that day.

"Nat, it'll only be for a few hours every morning."

"No." He stood up, awkwardly stomping his heels down into the boots, wincing at the pressure he put on his stump.

"But all the other children in Merrymeeting will be going to the new school," Delia said, trying to keep her voice low and reasonable. "They'll feel left out."

He took off his hat, ran his hand through his straw-colored hair, then jammed the hat back on his head. "They're only girls. What do they need book learning for? And, besides, I can't spare them. There's too much work around here. Maybe if you . . ." He didn't finish, but Delia knew what he'd been about to say. *Maybe if you were better able to pull your own weight.*

Nat picked up his felling ax and started across the clearing. His tall figure, in his bright blue woolen fly coat, stood out in stark contrast against the blazing fall foliage.

She ran to catch up with him. "Remember what the reverend said about it being a Christian parent's moral duty to teach their young to read the Scriptures?"

He turned to glower at her. "You teach them, Delia. Or have you managed to learn anything during all those hours you've spent up at the Bishops', *supposedly* learning your letters." He set off again, blue coattails flapping around his thighs.

Delia's chin took on a stubborn jut. "I'm taking them, Nat!" she hollered after him. "With or without your permission!"

He swung around, his clenched fist raised. "Goddamn you, woman!" It was the oath more than the fist that caused her to take a step back. It was the first curse she'd heard come from Nat's mouth. "My Mary never gave me such aggravation in ten years as I've had during three months with you. I wish to God—" He cut himself off and turned on his heel, starting for the third time down the trail.

Again, she ran to catch up with him. She had to grab his coat sleeve and spin him around. "You wished you'd never married me," she finished for him, her face taut with controlled emotion.

She had given up her love and all hope of any real joy in life because of a promise she had made to this man. She was determined now to see the promise fulfilled. She would *make* their marriage work. "But the fact is we *are* married, Nat," she pushed on. "And the sooner you come to accept that I'm not your Mary, maybe the easier it'll be for both of us."

"Mary is—"

"Dead!" She grasped his arms, shaking him. "She's dead, Nat. But I'm alive and I'm your wife now and I need you . . . We need each other."

He pried her hands loose. "Take the girls to school. Do whatever you want." He emitted a ragged laugh. "You'll do it anyway. Now let me go. I got to get up to the camp."

There was a chill to the October air that morning and in the lumber camps, deeper in the hills, it was even cooler.

The countryside was a rainbow of colors. The lime-green and tawny gold of aspen and birch, the smoky purple of ash, the orange and brilliant red of maples—all were set off to dazzling perfection by a background of deep, rich evergreen.

But Nat Parkes never paid much attention to the beauty of nature. He saw nature as a thing to be bested, a field to clear, a tree to chop down. As he looked at the stand of majestic pines stretching before him, he saw only a lot of hard, blister-popping work.

On that day the men of Merrymeeting were joining up with cutting gangs from two other settlements along the Kennebec to clear a mast road for the coming logging season. During the next couple of weeks, a great swath would be cut through the forest. Then, in the deep winter months, the tall pine masts would be chopped down and hauled on big sleds over this snow-packed road to the riverbank to await the spring drives. Once the river ice melted sometime in late March, the masts would be floated down the Kennebec to Merrymeeting and there shipped to England to be fitted onto the King's ships. Logging was how Maine farmers supported themselves and their families between the October harvest and the first planting season in April.

Under Colonel Bishop's direction, the men were broken up into cutting crews. Normally, men from the same settlement worked together, but that morning Nat found himself attached to the group from Topsham, who were one short because a man had fallen off a hayrick just that morning and broken a leg. For a cutting partner, Nat chose a young man who reminded him of a youthful version of himself. They both had the same tall, rangy build; they even had the same thatch of straw-colored hair, although the boy's face beneath the thatch wasn't nearly as battered and rugged as Nat's.

They started up the trail. "You hurt your leg?" the boy asked, noticing the hitch in Nat's stride.

"Ay-up," Nat responded, not bothering to explain. If he did the boy would only want to see his wooden foot. As Delia had that first day. Delia . . .

The boy, Nat noticed, was wearing only a thin linen hunting shirt and he was shivering. "You should have worn a coat,'' Nat said out the corner of his mouth, panting slightly as they hiked up toward the stand of trees that had been alloted to them.

"Didn't figure on it being this cold up here," the boy answered, smiling in spite of Nat's scowl. "That coat of yours certainly looks good and warm."

"My wife made it. She's good with the wheel and the loom." Nat had developed a trick of forgetting for whole minutes at a time that Mary was dead. He was thinking, anyway, that he wore the coat not so much to keep warm, but because its bright blue color made him stand out in the woods. It was easy to get killed working the logging camps. A tree could split or topple in the wrong direction; a dead branch, called a widow-maker, could slip lethally from above; logs could roll off the sled to crush or maim a man. Oh, there were plenty of ways to die in The Maine. A woman, he thought with a sudden bitter, piercing pain, could get the throat distemper and be gone within a week.

Nat selected a tree by notching it. His muscles bulging like thick strands of rope, he swung the felling ax, taking the first bite. Then he was joined by the boy, who cut at the opposite side, swinging in counterpoint. Because of his wooden foot, Nat had to put most of his weight on his good one, which made his swing awkward. It was effective nonetheless; he was pleased to see his cuts went deeper than the boy's.

The sound of the ax thwacking into the wood echoed in the still air. The ax took pie-sized chunks out of the pine, and the men's swings were fast and steady. When the tree was close to toppling, the boy stood back to let Nat finish it off. The tree shuddered and swayed against the sky, then fell with a sharp crack like thunder, filling the air with debris.

Silence descended and the dust settled. In that moment the sudden quiet was pierced by the sharp, prolonged wail of a wolf. The boy shivered.

"I told you you should have worn a coat," Nat said, although he himself was now sweating after the work of swinging the ax.

The wolf howled again, sounding closer this time, and Nat

frowned. Another way to die, he thought. Get pounced on and eaten by a pack of wolves.

He tightened his grip on the helve of his ax and took a notch out of the next tree.

Elizabeth and Delia walked side by side, following the ruts in the cart trail as it led to the farm. Beside them the dying, empty cornstalks rustled in the breeze. The corn had been harvested the week before and now the ears hung by braided husks along the rafters in Delia's kitchen, long rows of gold and maroon. They'd had a bee for the husking, but although Ty had been invited, he hadn't come.

Delia glanced sideways at her friend. Elizabeth was five months along now and she was blooming with it. She had a habit of every few minutes rubbing her rounded stomach, as if assuring herself the baby was still there. She did so now and it made Delia smile.

"It's good of you, Elizabeth, to come all the way out here to teach me how to work that blasted spinning wheel."

"Oh, I don't mind." Elizabeth's face was bright and relaxed. Oddly, Delia thought, the pregnancy seemed to have done a lot toward reconciling the young reverend's wife to life in the wilderness. "Each wheel has its own peculiarities," Elizabeth explained. "That's why it's best I show you on your own."

"It's Mary's wheel."

"Yours now."

Nat wouldn't agree, Delia thought, although she didn't say so. As they passed the orchard, she noticed that last night's wind had knocked down a lot of apples from the trees. She took Elizabeth's hand. "Let's gather up some apples and roast them while we're spinning. It will make a nice treat for the girls when they come home later after their first day of school."

"You're good with those girls," Elizabeth said, laughing as she allowed Delia to lead her toward the orchard. "I imagine you and Nat are anxious to have one of your own."

Delia looked quickly away so that Elizabeth wouldn't catch the sudden rush of tears that filled her eyes. She would never have a baby as long as Nat slept on the shakedown in the linter. She didn't want Nat's baby anyway; she wanted Ty's.

Delia made a basket of her short gown and they began to fill it with the shiny red fruit. Elizabeth joked that her skirts were too full of baby to find room for apples. Their laughter rang in the clear October air.

A bevy of migrating ducks flew by, so many that for a moment they blotted out the brassy autumn sun and the flap of their wings sounded like a windstorm. It seemed dark and suddenly cold, and in the distance they heard the cry of a wolf.

Elizabeth shivered and the old fear crept back into her eyes. Her hands curved around, protecting her stomach.

"Something's wrong . . ." Delia said. It was a feeling she had; her da would have said someone had just spit on her grave.

Instinctively, she turned toward the house . . .

She screamed.

Nat buried his ax in a nearby stump and hunkered down before the fire, warming his hands on a noggin of hot cider. Raw blisters stung Nat's palms and he winced as he pressed the noggin to his hands; it seemed it always took a couple weeks of swinging the ax to build up a good pad of calluses.

Nat let the talk and laughter of the other loggers flow around him as the crew took their mid-morning break. He didn't know too many of the men from Topsham and he wasn't much interested in what they had to say. He was too busy thinking of what Delia had said, or rather shouted, at him earlier that morning . . . about him having to accept that Mary was dead and that he had a new wife now.

Delia.

He wished he knew how he felt about her. She aggravated him no end sometimes. But he had to admit she'd turned out to be wonderful with the girls, gentle and loving. She was pretty, too. Some days when he'd look at her his breath would catch. Even when they were courting, Mary had never made him picture—

But he slammed his mind shut on that disturbing thought. He thought of sons instead. He could use some boys around the farm. It had always disappointed him that Mary had given him girls. Delia was slim around the hips as well, but there was a lustiness about her that made him guess she'd breed boys.

Thoughts of a lusty Delia in bed beneath him, breeding sons, caused a stirring in Nat's loins. It wasn't the first time this had happened, but the erection always wilted before it fully bloomed because of the guilt, the gut-wrenching guilt, that came with it. He couldn't hurt, couldn't betray, Mary in that way. He knew he'd never manage it anyway—not with picturing Mary looking down from heaven, watching them.

He decided to think about something safe. The slaughtering, for instance. That would have to be done next week. The hogs would have to be butchered to fill the pork barrels for the coming winter. And there were the windrows in the field he'd cleared last July that needed burning before the first snowfall—

Just then he spotted Colonel Bishop coming down the trail from the direction of the Merrymeeting camp, which was three miles to the east of them, on the other side of the hill. The mast agent walked briskly, swinging his elbows, a musket hanging lightly from one big hand. Nat hadn't brought his musket with him today, but now for some strange reason he was possessed with a sudden, fervent wish that he had. He didn't know why, except that maybe it had something to do with hearing the wolf howl again. His eyes were drawn across the fire to the boy, who had stood up as well. The boy felt it too, whatever *it* was, but this time it was Nat who shivered.

Suddenly there was a soft whistling sound. Colonel Bishop flung up his hands, arching his back, before falling face first onto the ground. For two seconds all was stunned quiet . . . and then the forest erupted into a cacophony of bubbling yells, bloodcurdling whoops, and screams of terror.

Naked and painted, brandishing war clubs and tomahawks, the Abenaki warriors seemed to come swarming out of the forest, like wasps from a disturbed hive. For a moment Nat stood frozen, watching as one bent over Colonel Bishop's body to take his scalp and jerking up in surprise when the curled bobwig came off in his hands. Hysterical laughter bubbled in Nat's throat at the sight of the Indian's shocked face, laughter that was choked off when in the next second a Topsham man fell across Nat's feet, his head almost sliced clean off his neck by a tomahawk.

My God, Nat thought, his mind reeling in horror, I'm going to die. He lunged for his ax buried in the stump several feet away.

He didn't make it. An Indian pounced on the ax, jerking it free with a triumphant yell and sinking it in the back of a man who ran past him. The crackle of gunfire joined the whooping war cries and stinking black clouds of smoke drifted over the camp. From behind him, Nat heard his felling partner, the blond-haired boy, screaming in horror and he whirled in time to see a war club swing from the bronzed fist of a tall, naked Abenaki warrior . . . a club swinging hard and fast toward the boy's unprotected face . . .

And Nat ran.

Terror squeezed the air from his lungs and blackened his vision. He had been swift on his feet once, tall though he was, but that was before he'd lost his foot. He staggered across the camp, heading for the cover of a stand of spruce, the stand he had been clearing just a few minutes earlier. He heard a footfall behind him, felt hot rancid breath on the back of his neck. *Die,* his panicked mind raced, *I'm going to die.* He tried to run faster. His wooden foot twisted beneath him just as he felt a searing pain on the back of his head. He swung around, throwing up his arm, and then he was falling, falling back, falling down, down, down into blackness.

Flames crackled, licking at the cedar-shingled roof with fiery fingers, and smoke clouds billowed over the clearing, raining hot soot and ashes. A horse's panicked whinny ended in a scream as its throat was slashed with a scalping knife, and the blood sprayed and gushed in an arc through the air. It was the bay mare, the wedding gift from Ty.

They had tried to run, but they hadn't gotten beyond the edge of the orchard before more savages emerged from the forest, surrounding them. The Indians played a game with them now, enclosing them in a loose circle, taunting them with cackles and whoops, and tossing their knives and tomahawks from hand to hand. The metal blades gleamed wetly, reflecting the dancing flames.

Elizabeth clung to Delia, one arm pressed protectively across her swollen belly, her breaths sawing in her throat. "My baby," Elizabeth kept moaning. "Oh God, please don't let them hurt my baby . . ." Delia slid her arm around Elizabeth's waist, drawing the girl against her. Unknowingly, she still cradled the apples in the lap of her short gown.

The warriors were naked, without even a breechclout to cover their sex. On their chests, in red ochre, were painted identical heads of snarling wolves. Their faces were painted as well, each one differently. One had vermilion stripes across his cheeks, like three slashed and bleeding cuts. Another resembled an owl with his face smeared in yellow, his eyes ringed in white. Flames from the burning house glistened off the grease that liberally coated their bronze skin. They smelled sweetly rancid, like butter left in the sun too long.

Over the crackling flames Delia heard the clanging of the blockhouse alarm bell. Suddenly one of the men took a step toward them. He was tall, with mammoth shoulders, and he wore a necklace of strange beads that fit snugly around his thick neck. His lips pulled back into a snarl-smile, revealing even white teeth. He fired a sentence at them, something quick and fast and menacing.

Delia's throat worked as she tried to talk. "I d-don't understand. I don't s-speak Abenaki."

His hand whipped up, pressing the knife blade against her throat, deep enough to slice the skin. She felt the blood, cool and wet, trickle down her neck, but she forced herself to look up into the Indian's beak-nosed face and willed herself not to show fear. His eyes were as hard and black as obsidian, and merciless.

The arm cradling the apples fell to her side and the fruit rolled onto the ground. The Indian stepped back and with a short, harsh laugh, speared an apple with the tip of his knife. As he bit into it, those even white teeth flashed in the sun.

Another fist lashed out, gripping a hank of Elizabeth's hair. He said something in his guttural tongue that made the others whoop and cackle and laugh some more.

Elizabeth emitted an animal-like whimpering sound and her eyes rolled. Delia dug her nails into the girl's arm. "Don't faint. If you faint they'll scalp you." There were fresh scalps hanging from their arrow quivers and the handles of their tomahawks, so fresh they dripped blood onto the ground. One looked like Nancy Sewall's reddish-brown hair.

A high-pitched yipping sound came from the river. It must have been some sort of signal, for suddenly the taunting game, if it was a game, was over. The women's wrists were quickly bound in front of them with leather thongs, which were attached to short leashes, and they were dragged at a fast trot into the forest.

They ran for a long time, long enough for a stitch to form in Delia's side and her lungs to start burning. She was afraid for Elizabeth, that having to run like this would harm the baby. From time to time she would twist back to be sure Elizabeth, who ran behind her, was all right—only to be jerked forward by the leash with such force that her arms were nearly pulled from their sockets.

They slowed as they climbed into the hills, and Delia realized they were heading toward the lumber camps. Hope welled within her at the thought that they might still be rescued.

It died with a gasp of horror a few moments later as they were dragged into a clearing strewn with bodies of slaughtered men. The air reeked of blood and gunpowder and fear. More Indians, naked and oiled and painted, cavorted around the campfire like red devils straight from hell. Another, smaller raiding party emerged from the woods across the clearing, bearing one prisoner on the end of a leash: Sara Kemble.

She had been run hard as well. Her face was as purple as a beet root and her cheeks puffed as she drew in drafts of air. When she saw Delia and Elizabeth she screamed at them, "They've killed the Sewalls. Killed and scalped them, the murdering savag—"

A fist in the small of Sara's back sent the air from her lungs in a keening wail. Delia started toward her, only to be pulled up short by the man who held her leash. Elizabeth continued to stare straight ahead, not even blinking, as if she were oblivious to her surroundings.

An Indian danced in front of Delia, waving his tomahawk and yipping like a dog. Delia recoiled, then uttered a cry of shock for the man had Colonel Bishop's yellow bobwig perched backward on his grease-coated black head. Eyes wide with horror, she looked more closely at the bodies strewn around the logging camp. She found the colonel by his shiny shaved head. He lay sprawled across the trail, an arrow in his back. Hot tears clogged Delia's throat. Poor Anne.

She started to turn away, unable to bear the sight, when she noticed a slight flickering of the colonel's eyelids. Just in time, she froze her face to keep from showing any reaction, for surely if the savages discovered he was still alive he'd be slaughtered within seconds.

Slowly, the colonel's eyes opened and fastened onto her face. He was trying to send her a silent message. A message of hope, of warning? She couldn't tell. Then his eyes focused on something in back of her and they widened a bit, darkening with horror. At that moment Sara Kemble screamed, only to have the scream cut off by the back of her captor's hand. As if pulled by an invisible power outside her will, Delia turned around.

The big Indian who had cut Delia's neck was bent over a body at the edge of the clearing. Delia gasped with horror for she saw long, rangy legs wearing golo boots that were twisted awkwardly together like a pigtail, and the blood-soaked coattails of a blue fly coat. The Indian blocked her view of the man's head, but then he shifted a bit, revealing a bloodied pulpy mass of smashed and unrecognizable flesh that had once been a man's face. Delia emitted a tiny, whimpering cry. Slowly, the Indian straightened, turning toward her and grinning demonically.

Tossing back his head, he howled, a long, penetrating wail of triumph, and swung his fist into the air. And from the fist dangled a scalp of straw-colored hair.

Chapter 22

〜〜〜◦○◦〜〜〜

"**E**asy, easy," Ty crooned softly, as he worked the barbed arrowhead slowly out of Colonel Bishop's shoulder. "Easy now."

The arrow came free with a sudden, sucking pop. Blood welled up out of the hole it left. Ty pressed a wadded cloth against the wound, his nostrils flaring at the stink of the blood, which seemed part of the air he breathed, like mist.

"Am I going to live?" Giles Bishop gasped in between sobbing breaths as Ty helped him to sit up.

"You'll be dancing with Anne at the Christmas frolic." Ty leaned the colonel against the tree trunk and held a noggin of water to his pinched lips. "I see you lost your hair."

The man wheezed an unsteady laugh and started to reach up to rub his bald head, then grimaced from the pain. He looked slightly befuddled, as if he weren't quite sure what had happened. "What are you doing here, Ty?"

"I was over in Topsham, setting a broken leg. I heard shots and saw the smoke. From the looks of it I'd say all the homesteads along this side of the Kennebec are burning." He tried not to think of Delia. If she were dead, it had already happened and there was nothing he could do about it. Later he would bear the pain of it. If he could.

As Ty crouched on one knee beside the colonel, he looked around the clearing, at the carnage the Abenaki war party had left behind. He thought that after ten years of living with it, he should have been inured to death, but the sight brought a sharp stabbing pain behind his eyes, as if splinters had been jammed under his lids. Splinters under the eyelids—it was a favorite torture of the Abenaki.

He forced himself to study the dead. With guilty relief, he realized this must have been the Topsham crew, for he saw no Merrymeeting men. Then he spotted a familiar bright blue fly coat, although the face of the man who wore it had been smashed beyond recognition by an Abenaki war club.

Colonel Bishop noted the direction of Ty's gaze. "Nat Parkes," he confirmed. "I watched them take his hair." Then his eyes widened as he suddenly remembered. "And they've got—"

A twig snapped beneath a man's foot and Ty's hand gripped his musket. It was already primed and ready to fire, and he sighted it into the woods, toward the snapping twig. He didn't really think it was an Indian, however; the man was making too damn much noise.

"Don't shoot, Ty! It's me." Sam Randolf barged out of the forest, followed by two other Merrymeeting men. "We heard shots and—Keerist!" he exclaimed when he got a good look at the slaughter in the clearing.

Ty felt a hand on his arm and looked down into Colonel Bishop's white, sweating face. "I started to say . . . they got his wife."

"Sam's wife?"

"No, Nat's wife. Delia. The savages have Delia and Mrs. Hooker. And Sara. Sara Kemble."

Ty went cold all over. There was a fierce rushing sound in his ears, as if he'd just stepped beneath a waterfall. "How were they painted?" he heard himself ask from a long way away.

"Wolf . . ." Giles Bishop sighed as he drifted into unconsciousness.

Ty looked northeast, up into the blue spruce-covered hills. *Malsum,* he thought. The wolf, totem of the Norridgewock tribe.

Delia's feet were bruised and bleeding from the unseen roots and stones that lay beneath the short brown needles carpeting the ground. She was so thirsty her mouth felt as if it had been swabbed with a dry cotton rag. Every breath was bitter-sharp, like the bite of an ax into a tree.

They followed a deer trail, and the meshed sunlight that filtered through the thick canopy of trees was fading now. They'd been running steadily since they'd left the lumber camp, a ground-eating, loping gait that the Indians managed easily, but that soon had the women gasping for air and stumbling from exhaustion. When they tripped, their thighs and calves were thrashed mercilessly with the leather thongs.

At least their hands had been unbound and Delia had one arm around Elizabeth, half carrying her. Elizabeth had embraced her fear like a shield, withdrawing deep inside herself to a place beyond pain, beyond awareness. Even the cut of the lash brought no response, not even a moan. Delia was afraid that if she didn't drag the girl along, Elizabeth would simply sit down in the middle of the forest and watch the tomahawk fall without a blink of her pale gray eyes.

Delia knew the savages would murder them if they couldn't keep up, because they'd almost killed Sara Kemble. They had gone barely a mile when the fat woman had tripped over a root and landed with a jar that sent her mobcap tumbling over her eyes. She'd remained there on her hands and knees, her breath whistling like a tea kettle, sobbing and cursing. One of the Indians, a man with a horribly pocked face, had stood calmly over Sara, his war club raised in the air, within a split second of bringing it down on her bowed head.

"No!" Delia had cried, unthinkingly throwing herself against the man's arm, throwing him off balance. It had been a terrible mistake, for he'd whirled on her, his lips peeled back in a snarl, the war club raised again, at her this time. She had seen the promise of her death in his eyes. Eyes that were hard and flat like chips of polished coal.

Suddenly another Indian had stepped abruptly between them. This one was taller and broader than the others and obviously their leader, for one curt word had stopped the fall of the club. Then he'd seized Delia by a fistful of hair, growling a spate of words at her, and though she couldn't understand him, there was no mistaking his meaning: she was not to be so foolish again. He'd thumped her collarbone with his pointed finger, hard enough to make her cry out. *"Lusifee!"*

he'd said, causing the other Indians to laugh, although there wasn't a trace of humor on his face.

Delia, hauled up on her toes, had her face brought up to the man's broad, naked chest. It was smooth, brown, and hairless. His rank sweat made beads on his greased skin. Oddly, he wore a rosary around his neck. She realized he had been the one with the strange necklace who had tauntingly taken a bite out of her apple. The one who had scalped Nat. *Nat . . .*

"Lusifee," he said again, poking her a second time and giving her a rough shake before he shoved her down the trail in front of him.

They'd had only one brief rest after that, when the Indians had paused long enough to unearth a cache of breechclouts and leggings, with which they quickly covered their nakedness before setting off again at a loping jog. It was obvious they feared pursuit and wanted to put as much distance as possible between themselves and the Merrymeeting Settlement.

Night had almost completely fallen by the time the Indians stopped. They chose as a campsite a small moss-covered clearing with a feeder stream running through it. The women immediately fell on their knees before the creek. Delia thought she had never tasted anything so wonderful as that delicious, icy water. But she was only able to wet her mouth with it before being jerked away from the stream by her hair. The captives' wrists were again bound and this time they were each tethered to their own Indian, as if they had been allotted like slaves to a master. Delia was tied to the big one with the crucifix around his neck.

Throughout the interminable day, their captors had been steadily dwindling in numbers, peeling away to disappear into the surrounding forest until only three remained. Now they built a small, almost smokeless fire, and one of the Indians brought out pieces of pemmican and parched corn from a bearskin pouch. Then they did a strange thing—they crossed themselves before they ate, in the Papist manner.

The men sucked and gnawed on the pemmican and nibbled noisily on the parched corn, laughing and taunting the women who watched them hungrily. All except Elizabeth, who stared straight ahead, seeing nothing.

"Please," Sara Kemble finally said in a tiny, hoarse voice. "Aren't you going to feed us?" But the Indians ignored her.

Delia studied the man she was bound to, seeing prominent cheekbones, a broad nose with a low bridge, and heavy-lidded, slanting black eyes. Straight black hair, unbound and unadorned, framed his face. From the way the others had all deferred to him she decided he must be some sort of chief. While the other men laughed and grimaced, his face never changed expression. There was an aura of utter cruelty to this man; he was as hard and sharp as the blade of his tomahawk. Although he had saved her earlier, Delia had no doubt he could kill them all on a whim.

There was something else that made her think she could expect no mercy from this man. From the war club tied to the leather strap across his chest there swung a scalp of yellow hair. Nat's scalp.

The Abenaki caught Delia looking at the scalp and lifted it, running his fingers through the bloodstained strands of hair. His lips curled into a tight, evil smile.

"Ye bloody, murderin' bastard," she snarled at him beneath her breath, secure in the knowledge that he couldn't understand English. He must have picked up the tone, however, for his eyes narrowed and his lips thinned, although he said nothing.

Delia stared at him, letting her hate show on her face; for the moment she was like Elizabeth, beyond caring what he did to her. For the first time since she had witnessed the slaughter in the logging camp, Delia was free of the need to concentrate all her thoughts on summoning the will to put one foot in front of the other. Now her mind fastened fully onto the horror of Nat's death and her grief was a sharp, stabbing pain in her heart, raw and heavily laced with guilt. Their last words had been such bitter ones. And she couldn't bear thinking of Tildy and Meg, who had lost their father so soon after burying their mother.

At least the girls were safe, she comforted herself. They had to be. She had seen no children's scalps dangling from any weapons. She offered up a prayer of thanks that all the children had been within the strong, secure walls of the manor house taking lessons from Anne Bishop when the murderous savages had struck.

When they finished eating, the men passed around a pipe, smoking in silence. Looking at the sharp-boned, dark-skinned face of her captor, Delia was reminded of Ty and a calmness descended over her fevered thoughts. There was no doubt in her mind that Ty had survived the raid and that he was coming after her. It was only a matter of time and she was going to have to work at keeping herself and the others alive until he could find them.

The tobacco made the men drowsy. The night darkened and grew colder. Delia glanced at Elizabeth, hoping she had fallen asleep, but the girl still stared unseeingly at the shadowy trees beyond the flickering firelight.

Suddenly Sara Kemble began to rock back and forth, whining softly to herself. "I shouldn't be here. It's all Obadiah's fault. He sent me to deliver that chair to Mrs. Sewall. I didn't want to go." Sara's captor eyed her askance and his fist tightened around his club. But Sara continued to moan, oblivious. "I never liked Nancy Sewall. I'm glad she was scalped. Glad, do you hear? But I shouldn't be here. It's Obadiah's—"

"Shut up!" Delia hissed at her. "Do you want a tomahawk buried in your skull?"

Sara fastened beady, malicious eyes on Delia's face. "They killed your Nat. Killed and scalped him and it serves him right for marrying you. I told him you were nothing but a grog shop tart. But he didn't listen to me. Oh, no. I'll wager he's sorry now."

Delia set her teeth on a scream of rage and looked away. But the anger immediately gave way to an almost overwhelming desire to throw herself down and sob and beat the ground with her fists. *Oh, Nat . . . Nat . . .*

Sara's outburst had caused her pockmarked captor to burst into a low singsong chant. Suddenly he jerked to his feet and began to dance, enacting a pantomime of that morning's raid. He gestured at the other two, inviting them to join him, but although they nodded and punctuated his chants with high-pitched whoops, they remained stretched out lazily before the fire.

He ended the dance by leaping high, stabbing the air with his war club. Throwing back his head, he cupped his hands around his mouth and gave voice to the sharp, prolonged wail of the wolf.

He killed Sara Kemble the next morning.

They had set out just before dawn, turning in the direction of the Kennebec. At the riverbank the Indians uncovered a large six-man, birchbark canoe that had been hidden in the brush, camouflaged by spruce boughs.

Sara plopped down on a boulder by the water's edge and refused to get into the canoe. "I'm not going, thank you. It could tip over. I could drown." She said it politely, the way one would turn down a second cup of tea.

Snarling in anger, her captor lashed at her with the end of her leash, but it had no effect. "No, no, no," she said, shaking her head like a stubborn child. "I'm not doing it and you can't make me."

Delia watched as rage darkened the Indian's scarred face. She started to climb out of the canoe, thinking she could coax some sense into Sara, when she was jerked back by the end of her tether. She landed with a rattling jar, one of the thwarts jabbing into her hip. The bright blue sky above wavered and dimmed as tears of pain filled her eyes . . .

Elizabeth screamed, a thin, piercing sound that sent a pair of ducks flapping across the water. The scream was followed by a horrible gurgling sound coming from the bank. Delia scrambled to her knees, wrapping her hand around Elizabeth's mouth, cutting off a second scream and pressing tight enough to leave a bruise. "Sssh, Lizzie, it's all right," she whispered softly, turning the girl's head away from the gruesome sight on the shore. "Don't scream. It's all right now."

The pocked-face Indian got into the canoe, carrying Sara's blood-splattered mobcap and her faded, graying brown hair. Elizabeth was crying hysterically beneath Delia's hand.

Delia's captor yanked her back by the hair, tearing her hand from Elizabeth's mouth and releasing an outpouring of sobs, like pulling a plug from a dam. "Don't kill her!" Delia screamed, for the girl's cries sounded frighteningly loud, shattering the peace of the spruce-lined river.

The big Indian's fingers bit into Delia's arm as he pulled her away, shoving her down into the bow of the canoe with his hard, greasy body. He barked a command at her, but Delia struggled against him, lashing out with her feet and fists, sure that if she didn't stop Elizabeth's crying, the girl's captor would kill her with one blow from his tomahawk.

Delia's nails raked through the soft flesh of the Indian's cheek. He hissed at her and sent her reeling from a vicious blow across her face. For a moment the world grayed and dimmed, then she struggled upright again. But Elizabeth had at last stopped the sobs on her own, by pressing her fist into her mouth.

Putting the back of her wrist to her bleeding lip, Delia glared at the man who had struck her. Never, never had she felt such hate. "I spit on ye, ye bloody bastard, ye murderin' savage, ye . . ."

His hand lashed out, encircling her throat and jerking her head up. He brought his face close to hers. The cuts her nails had made on his cheek dripped bright red blood. "Understand this," he said in perfect, unaccented English. "Savage I might be, but I am no bastard. My parents were married at my birth. And my people call me the Dreamer, although you will call me master."

Delia set her teeth on the retort that wanted to fly out of her mouth. The pressure of the hand against her Adam's apple increased, cutting off her air.

He stared at her for a long, long moment, until Delia's vision began to blacken, then he let go of her throat and, picking up a paddle, pushed the canoe out into the current. "Come, *lusifee,*" he said, while Delia struggled to keep from gasping as the air rushed back into her lungs. "Let us see if you can show the same spirit when it comes time to run the gauntlet."

The gauntlet.

Delia hoped the terror she felt didn't show on her face. To prove she was unaffected by his words, she forced a nonchalant smile. "My name is Delia," she croaked.

The smile had no effect on that impassive face. "You have no name now but *awakon,*" he finally said. "Slave."

Delia's smile wavered only a little bit. "Then what does *lusifee* mean?"

But he merely stared at her, his eyes as cold and as black as a frozen pond.

They heard the sounds first—whooping, strident cries, the staccato beat of drums, the baying of dogs. The smell came next—a nauseous odor of putrefying fish. Sight came last—a clearing beside the shores of a great, silver-plated lake palisaded by majestic dark blue spruce.

Within the clearing stood a village of longhouses and wigwams, surrounded by a stockade of tree trunks twelve feet high. Around the village lay fields of cornstalks, their dry leaves crackling in the evening breeze. Heaps of alewives, fertilizer for the cornfields, decayed in piles outside the stockade, stinking up the air with an oily, rotting smell. Flames of pine knots flickered in the gray dusk and smoke coiled upward from lodge tops and dozens of small, open fires. The air resounded with the din of shouts and yodels, yapping dogs and throbbing drums.

The canoe glided onto a gentle shore. At the Dreamer's sharp command Delia climbed awkwardly, with legs that were stiff and cramped, onto a pebbled beach. Ignoring the man's fierce glare, she turned to help Elizabeth. Tiny shivers racked the girl's slender body and her lips were blue with fear. Delia started to comfort her, but the hypocritical words stuck in her throat.

For she had seen the gauntlet.

The gates to the stockade were open. Starting from the entrance and stretching to a low wooden platform in the middle of the village wound two parallel lines of men, women, and children. Armed with digging sticks, clubs, and thorny branches, they chanted a haunting *ai, ai, ai* sound, over and over, to the incessant beat of the drums.

The Dreamer stopped so abruptly that Delia, who was tethered by a thong to his wrist, almost walked on his heels. A Jesuit priest in black cassock and skirt strode out between the gates, swinging a censer that filled the air with wispy trails of incense. He stopped before the Dreamer. To Delia's astonishment, the big warrior knelt on the ground at the priest's feet and bowed his head for the man's blessing.

The priest fixed his fanatic blue gaze on the prisoners. He was an extremely thin man, all fleshless bones and pallid skin. His lips were two sharp diagonal slashes beneath a nose that curved like a fish hawk's beak.

The Dreamer jerked so hard on Delia's leash that she had to grasp his arm with her bound hands to keep from falling to her knees. His flesh was marble-hard and slick with grease, and she clung to him, swaying dizzily, before he flung her off him.

She was almost fainting from fatigue and lack of food. It had been four days since she had eaten, except for a few roots and nuts she had managed to forage for herself and Elizabeth while on the trail. Even above the stink of the alewives, she could smell the savory aroma of roasting meat and she thought she was capable of begging for it on her knees. She had been hungry many times in her life, but never like this.

The Dreamer barked an order at her in Abenaki. She stared back at him, trying not to show her fear. But fear was a metallic taste in her mouth, like blood.

"Strip!" the Dreamer barked again, in English this time.

Delia stared down the long line of Abenaki, ready to lay their clubs and sticks across her bare flesh. The whooping of the men and the strident screeching of the women and children had risen to a crescendo. Some of the women and girls had turtle shell rattles and bear claw bracelets tied to their ankles and knees, and they stomped their feet, shaking the rattles in time to the beat of the drums. A few boys played reed flutes, while others swung long cords of shells in circles over their heads, producing a grating, eerie whine.

For the first time Delia noticed the scalp poles that encircled the platform, marking the end of the gauntlet. Dozens of scalps—dried, stretched on round hoops, painted and decorated—flapped from the poles in the lake-cooled breeze.

In the Boston grog shops, Delia had listened to stories about white captives being forced to strip naked and run the gauntlet. Usually they didn't make the women prisoners run it, she had heard, but sometimes they did. Sometimes . . .

The Dreamer's face appeared suddenly before her, his lips pulled back in a sneer. "Strip, *lusifee*. Now."

A thin, blue-veined hand fell on Delia's arm. "I suggest you obey," the French priest said, his words heavily accented, "or he will cut the clothes from your body. And he will not do it gently."

God protect me, Delia prayed, and with trembling fingers unlaced her bodice. Her short gown and petticoat had been ripped and stained by the arduous four-day journey, but she had never realized what an armor were a woman's clothes, even if they were only rags, until she stood naked before the Dreamer's cold eyes and the mob of screaming, bloodthirsty Abenaki.

"You!" the Dreamer snarled, pointing a stiff finger at Elizabeth. "Strip."

Elizabeth stood unmoving, sunk deep within her well of fear. The Dreamer took a step forward, his knife flashing.

"No!" Delia grasped his arm, cringing at the cold, greasy feel of his flesh. At the sight of the knife, Elizabeth's eyes had rolled back in her head and she had crumbled slowly to the ground. "You can't make her do it," Delia cried. "Can't you see she's with child? It would kill her."

He stared at Delia, a look of incredulity on his face. "She runs. Unless you are willing to take her place."

Delia's legs began to tremble, but she nodded, swallowing hard. "Aye. I'll do it in her stead."

He stared at her for a long moment. Then he said, almost sadly, *"Lusifee.* You will not survive it twice."

Delia looked down the long double row of club-wielding Abenaki, all screaming for her blood. Her chin came up.

"I've survived my share of beatings," she boasted, to shore up her wavering courage. "Aye, an' by experts too. No pack of bloody, ignorant savages'll defeat Delia McQuaid."

The Dreamer grabbed her arm and flung her forward. "Run! Run hard!"

Delia ran. She pumped her arms and legs so fast the first blows merely glanced off her back. But the Abenaki were more loosely packed toward the middle of the gauntlet and they had more play to swing their clubs. The sticks and cudgels seemed to fly at her from everywhere. The pain when they landed drove the air from her already heaving lungs and stole her vision.

She flung her arm up to protect her face and worked her legs harder, her toes digging into the soft earth. The platform loomed up directly in front of her and she knew with a thrill of triumph that she would make it.

Then a child Tildy's age stuck a stick between her legs.

She toppled forward like an axed tree, without even time to fling out her hands to break her fall. Her teeth bit through her tongue, and blood, hot and salty, filled her mouth. Her ears rang like a carillon of bells. The Indians swooped down on her with their weapons, beating her mercilessly.

She struggled to her hands and knees. Blood trickled into her eyes from a cut above her brow. The child who had tripped her swung his stick at her face, but she grabbed it from his hands and whacked it across the nearest pair of shins. The woman jumped back, howling in surprise and pain, dropping her club. Snatching it up, Delia swayed to her feet.

"Aooow!" she howled, as she went after them. She was no longer Delia Parkes, the respectable farmer's wife. She was Delia McQuaid, the grog shop wench, and she turned on her attackers, flailing the club, screaming every disgusting, filthy epithet she'd learned on the waterfront slums of Boston. She was hitting back at everyone, her drunken father, the topers who had pawed her in the Frisky Lyon, Nat who had belittled her and made her feel worthless, Tom Mullins who had stolen her kisses, and Ty. Ty who had stolen her heart, while guarding his own until it was too late, too late . . . She struck back at them all, all the men who had battered and used and pulled and twisted her this way and that, trying to make her into the woman *they* wanted her to be, instead of the woman *she* wanted to be—

Stunned by her snarling rage, the Indians began backing away from her savage, swinging club . . . and then a numbing blow knocked the club from her hand.

She whirled around, panting, flinging her hair from her eyes, tensing her body for the slash of the Dreamer's tomahawk that would end her life.

But it was not the Dreamer she faced.

If anything, this man was even taller and broader. But he was at least thirty years older. Dark gray strands liberally streaked his long, black hair, and lines scored his sharply chiseled face, fanning out around his olive-black eyes and bracketing his hard mouth. He wore a heavily fringed doeskin shirt and long kilt that were gaudily decorated with dyed porcupine quills, bird feathers, and shells. Around his neck hung a French silver gorget and on his head he sported a beautiful beaver hat with a white plume. Delia had thought the Dreamer was chief of his people, but she knew immediately it was this man who ruled.

The look he gave her froze her blood and she was sure he was about to order her death. Instead, he turned to those who had formed the gauntlet and were now packed into a tight angry group. He asked them a question, gesturing at Delia. The Indians immediately erupted into hot speech, pointing at her and shaking their fists.

Suddenly the Dreamer burst from the crowd. He said something in a sharp, harsh voice that cut off all the shouting. Then he threw a defiant look at his chief.

The black-robed priest appeared at Delia's side. "Normally, it is the women who decide a prisoner's fate," he said in a dry, indifferent voice. "And they are saying you should die at the stake." He glanced pointedly at the torture platform. "They say you have the heart of a warrior and so you should die a warrior's death." His thin lips curled into a sardonic smile. "You should be flattered."

Delia wasn't the least bit flattered; she was terrified. She looked at the tall Indian warrior who had called her his slave. She had to swallow twice to dredge up enough saliva to speak. "And the Dreamer," she said loudly. "What does he say?"

"He has claimed you for his second wife." It was the chief who spoke this time, in clear English, his voice ringing in the sudden stillness.

Relief and horror washed over Delia in alternate waves. She wasn't going to die at the stake, but the alternative . . .

"But what if I . . ." She gave the Dreamer a weak, pathetic smile. "That is, I'm very honored, but I . . ."

Delia, ye wooden-headed fool. Shut up afore ye find yerself tied t' a stake an' bein' basted like a Christmas goose.

The Dreamer's dark eyes raked over her in a hard challenge. "I will *take* you for my woman, *lusifee,*" he said.

But another voice, deeper and harsher, cut through his words.

"The woman is mine!"

Chapter 23

❦

Tyler Savitch strode unarmed through the gates of the Abenaki village.

The Dreamer's face registered shock, then a gloating triumph. "Have you come here to die, Yengi?"

"I have come for my woman." He spoke in Abenaki this time, and to one man only. Assacumbuit. His stepfather.

For a moment Ty saw fierce emotion flare up in the grand sachem's eyes. Then they glazed and hardened. There was no feeling on that chiseled face, for an Abenaki warrior never revealed his heart. Ty tried to keep his own face blank, but he doubted he succeeded as well. It had been ten years since he had seen this man. A man who, as a child, Ty had adored. The man he still thought of in his heart as his father.

Assacumbuit's glance flickered over to Delia; Ty's did not. He had yet to look at her, although he knew she had run over to kneel beside Elizabeth's unconscious form.

"She is your wife?" the sachem said.

Ty was tempted to stretch the truth, but he would sooner have ripped out his tongue than lie to this man. "I would make her my wife."

The Dreamer stepped between them, his face flushed with anger. "I have taken her. She is mine now."

Ty turned his head slightly, pinning the Dreamer with his eyes. The hatred the two men felt for each other twanged, tense and tight, like a bowstring stretched between them. "And I will take her back again," Ty said.

"You will have to kill me first."

"Then I will kill you."

"You can try—"

"Enough!" Assacumbuit's voice slashed through the air, effectively silencing both men. "The pair of you have changed little since you were boys. If you wish to be so foolish as to fight over a worthless woman, I will allow it. But"—he held up his hand—"this time it will be no boy's contest. It will be a formal duel, and to the death. Are you both sure the woman is worth it?"

Ty and the Dreamer exchanged mutual looks of scorn and contempt. They would be fighting over much more than a woman, and all the Norridgewocks knew it.

Assacumbuit's sigh was almost sad. "So be it."

At last Ty turned toward Delia. Slowly, she stood up. Love and joy blazed from her face as her eyes devoured him, and he returned the look. Unashamed and unafraid at last of the great love he bore for this one woman, Tyler Savitch let all the emotion he was feeling show in his expression. This weakness elicited a snort of contempt from the Dreamer, but Ty didn't care. He loved her and the whole damn world might as well know it.

She was naked and her poor body was covered with cuts and bruises. But she had fought back. He thought he would never forget the sight of her, swinging that club, bellowing curses, battling for her honor. He had never seen anything more brave. His pride in her brought a tight ache to his chest. Heedless of those who watched, he walked up to her. He stroked a bruise on her cheek, just once and lightly with his finger. Then he unlaced his shirt, pulling it off and bringing it down over her head. His hands lingered on her shoulders, gently cradling her neck.

"Oh, Ty, what was all that about? What's happening? Why the bloody hell couldn't you speak English so I'd know what's going on?" she burst out, unable to contain herself any longer. It was so typical of Delia, it brought a smile to his lips.

"I have to fight the Dreamer to get you back."

Delia gasped and her eyes flew to the huge warrior, who watched them with a sneer on his lips. "Oh, Ty, he'll kill you!"

The remark stung Ty's male vanity to the quick. He

dropped his hands from her neck. "I appreciate your confidence, Delia."

Tears formed in her eyes. "But he's so . . . He's wearing Nat's scalp."

"I saw it." Her obvious respect and fear of his rival's prowess brought a rush of jealousy surging through Ty's blood. "Do you *want* him to win, Delia? Is that it?"

For a moment anger flared in her eyes. "Oh, don't be a bloody f—" She choked on a tiny sob. Reaching up, she cupped his cheek with her soft, warm hand. The feel of it and the husky sound of her voice almost unmanned him. "Oh, Ty, I couldn't bear to lose you. I might as well kill myself."

He couldn't afford to indulge in any more emotion and so he hardened his face. He removed her hand. "Neither one of us is going to die," he said curtly.

He turned and walked away from her. "Oh, damn the man!" he heard her exclaim beneath her breath and he scowled to keep from smiling. *Ah, Delia-girl, you gutsy wench . . . God, but I love you so much.*

Ty was led to a small wigwam to prepare in private for the coming battle. In typical Abenaki fashion, and in spite of what he had said to Delia, he not only prepared himself to fight, but he also prepared himself to die.

He stripped naked and rubbed his skin with bear grease. He painted his face to represent the sky at sunrise, yellow at his chin that blended to white—a symbol of the dawning of the new life he would have with Delia after he had won her. Once, he had believed there was magic in the ritual painting; perhaps a part of him believed it still.

He touched the amulet pouch around his neck, which contained a symbolic fragment of the Thunder Spirit, his personal manitou. Throwing back his head, he sang his death song, a prayer that if he was to die let him meet death as a man, with courage and dignity. It was a chant that he had rehearsed all his young life and then not uttered once for ten years. But he sang it now, with feeling and belief, a guttural wailing that would have frozen the blood of the Merrymeet-

ing folk who called him Dr. Ty and thought of him as a
civilized man.

The last haunting notes of the song died away. Ty lowered
his head in thought and he thought not as an Abenaki who
put all his faith in dreams and spirits and fate, but as an
Englishman, who put his faith in logic.

He thought of his enemy.

Once, he had called the Dreamer his brother. They had
hunted and fought, danced and feasted together. They had
sung together in the sweat lodge. They had called the same
man father.

But between them there had always been a competition that
was almost savage in its intensity. They were close in age,
the Dreamer being only a year or two older, and the Abenaki
boy had always been bigger and stronger than Ty. But on that
long, arduous march to Quebec with the image of his father's
murdered body fresh in his mind, Ty had learned the power
of endurance. He was smaller than the Dreamer, but he was
tougher.

When the Dreamer proved better at archery and spear-
throwing, Ty spent hours practicing until he had mastered the
skills. In swimming and foot races, in wrestling matches, Ty
always won because, while he might come up short in physical strength, mentally he just wouldn't quit.

The only thing he could never beat the Dreamer at were
the visions. Like the other Abenaki boys, Ty had made his
spirit trek of fasting and deprivation and had received his vision of the Thunder Spirit, Bedagi, from whom he took his
name. But that had been his only experience with the spirit
world. Yet the Dreamer had been given visions constantly,
even while still a small boy. To the Abenaki, visions were
wonderful and powerful things, and the Dreamer garnered
much awe and respect because he was so continuously
blessed. But Ty was Yengi, and no matter how many races
or archery matches he won, his flesh would always be white.
Ty had often thought that if only he, too, could be visited by
the visions, then he would be more accepted by the clan. He
would be Abenaki. But the visions never came. More than
anything, Ty had bitterly envied the Dreamer his dreams.

Yet the bad blood between Bedagi and the Dreamer went

beyond their childhood rivalry. Assacumbuit had been married to the Dreamer's mother when he brought the Yengi slaves home with him from Quebec. But Assacumbuit in turn became a slave to the tiny, silver-haired woman, a slave of passion. He set his first wife aside, divorcing her and taking Ty's mother as his only wife. The Dreamer never recovered from the shame of this rejection. Nor the fear that he, along with his mother, had been set aside in Assacumbuit's heart, that the Yengi boy had become the grand sachem's most beloved son. The woman had died, but her son lived, and as long as he lived the shame and the fear were kept alive in the Dreamer's heart.

So Ty knew that the Dreamer would be fighting for reasons far more personal than the right to possess a woman. It meant he would be merciless and driven. But it also meant his pride would be vulnerable. Perhaps he could be taunted into anger, and anger, Assacumbuit had once taught Ty in a valuable and painful lesson, could make a man reckless, could lead him into committing a mistake. A fatal mistake.

Just then the deerskin flap to the wigwam was plucked aside and a boy entered, bearing the shield and weapon that Ty would use in the coming battle.

The weapon was a *casse-tête*, an Indian war club. Its head was carved from a hickory knot and studded with jagged flints and animal teeth. A tuft of hawk's breast feathers dangled from the handle. Ty had once killed an Iroquois warrior with such a weapon and he had never forgotten the feel and the sound of the man's head splitting open like a ripe melon. No matter how many lives he saved as a doctor, he knew he could never erase that particular memory from his mind.

The boy put the club in Ty's hand and Ty steeled himself not to show his sudden revulsion. The shield the boy carried was wrapped in skins, for it possessed magic properties and so had to be kept covered when not in use. Nor must it ever be touched by a woman's hands. It was made of rawhide, emblazoned with magic fetishes, and painted and decorated with feathers.

As the boy reverently unwrapped the shield, Ty's eyes widened in surprise and pleasure, for he recognized it immediately. The shield belonged to his father, Assacumbuit, and it was magic, indeed, for it could do far more than simply deflect the Dreamer's blows. When Ty's stepbrother saw their father's shield in his rival's hand, he would know which son Assacumbuit favored. All the old feelings of shame and fear and envy would rise again, like floodwaters, within the Dreamer's breast. He would be vulnerable then and Ty would defeat him.

Pine torches hissed and flared in a circle around the torture platform. The thick middle post, where prisoners were bound and subjected to the agonies of fire and the knife, had been removed. But the scalps of past raids still swayed in the smoky air from the four poles that supported the platform where the two men would fight each other to the death.

Delia was brought to stand before it, beside the grand sachem. The iron-haired warrior bestowed an unfathomable look on her before turning his attention forward again.

One of the Indian women had cruelly slapped Elizabeth awake. Then she and Delia had been led through the village by a pair of stone-faced old women. Delia was surprised at the size of the village. They walked down actual streets, past conical-shaped wigwams and longhouses built of timber, with thatched roofs and elm-bark shingles.

They were taken inside one of these longhouses where they both were fed a bland, mushy pumpkin stew. Then Elizabeth, who seemed more enclosed than ever within her wall of fear, was carried to a bed of furs, where she immediately fell into a deep sleep. Delia, meanwhile, was bathed and clothed in a simple one-piece dress and leggings of soft deerskin. Her hair was brushed and plaited with thongs.

Now, standing beside the Abenaki chief, she strained her eyes for a sight of Ty. She was so tense that every inch of her felt raw and exposed, as if she had been flayed. She couldn't imagine how the Tyler Savitch she knew, the healer with those gentle, magic hands, could defeat the brutal Abenaki warrior.

"If Ty dies I'll kill your great Dreamer myself," Delia declared fiercely to the man beside her. "An' with my bare hands. Aye, see if I bloody don't!"

The sachem raised surprised brows at her. A corner of his mouth twitched. "I can see why my son calls you *lusifee.*"

"Your son? The Dreamer is your son?"

"They are both my sons."

Delia's eyes widened. *"You're* Ty's Indian father?"

The man said nothing.

"If you're Ty's father," Delia persisted, "then how can you allow him to do this?" She gestured at the platform. "Can you bear to watch him die?"

The sachem gave a tiny shrug that was more French than Indian. "He does it for you."

She grabbed the man's arm, heedless when he stiffened. She was so desperate and so afraid for Ty, she had to struggle to keep from bursting into tears and her chest jerked with the effort. "I will go to the Dreamer willingly, as his second wife," she pleaded, her nails unconsciously digging into the man's stony flesh. "If you'll spare Ty's life, I will give myself to your son. Your Abenaki son. You have my word."

The man drew breath in a soft snort. "You are a woman. You have no will in the matter." After a moment, he fixed her again with his unreadable eyes. "Why do you assume that it is Bedagi who will lose? Perhaps you don't know him as well as you think."

The drums, which had been throbbing softly, suddenly grew into a thundering roll and a great cheer erupted from the watching crowd. Delia's head jerked around as two men leaped from opposite sides onto the platform and she gasped with shock.

If she hadn't known it was he, Delia would never have recognized Ty as the naked, greased, and painted warrior, who looked as cruel and as savage as the man who faced him. But seeing them now together as they circled each other, Delia was also horrified at how much bigger the Dreamer was than Ty, who was hardly a small man. The Abenaki was a veritable giant.

The two opponents circled each other in a semi-crouch, each with a lethal-looking club in one fist and a puny shield in the other. They swung a couple of tentative blows, feeling each other out, and the crack of the clubs striking the rawhide shields drowned out the cries of the watching crowd. Then

Ty shook his shield and said something to the Dreamer in a low, cutting voice that brought the Abenaki's head whipping around to his father. For a brief moment, Delia saw hurt, bright and hot, flare in the young man's eyes, and in that moment Ty struck.

The Dreamer recovered but barely in time, taking the numbing blow high on his shield and stumbling backward. Again Ty spoke in that lilting, taunting voice. Snarling with rage and swinging his club, the Dreamer waded into the attack.

Once, one of the Dreamer's blows landed beneath Ty's shield, striking his thigh with a sickening thud and eliciting crowing whoops from the crowd. It left a horrible and bloody gash in his flesh. But Ty merely sneered another taunt, which produced a bellow of rage from the Dreamer and another vicious swing of his club. Ty met it with a cross-blow and the cudgels slammed together like two dueling broadswords. And then he laughed.

"What is he saying? Why does he keep doing that?" Delia asked the sachem, who of course didn't answer. She wanted to kill Ty herself. Why was he deliberately taunting the Dreamer when it was only making the man angrier, and deadlier?

Soon, the fight began to take its toll on the men's stamina as more and more blows connected with tender flesh. Their breathing grew labored; their oiled muscles strained, glistening in the torchlight.

Then the Dreamer got lucky. One of the jagged flints on his club snagged a sinew on Ty's rawhide shield, tearing it from his hands and sending it sailing like a plate over the heads of the whooping crowd.

The Dreamer's mouth stretched into a smile of triumph, which slowly dissolved when Ty didn't back off as expected. Instead, with a bloodcurdling war cry, Ty launched into an attack. The Dreamer, his cudgel already whistling forward with what he had thought would be the killing blow, saw it fall uselessly where Ty had been. The Dreamer blindly raised his shield, but Ty knocked it aside, not with his club but with a lashing kick of his foot. He followed the kick in one continuous movement with a blow of his balled-up fist to the Indian's solar plexus.

The Dreamer's mouth pouched like a fish's as he gasped for air. His grip on the shield relaxed a fraction and Ty easily knocked it from his hand. Enraged, the Dreamer lunged at Ty with his club raised, but Ty nimbly stepped aside and, swinging his foot up, brought his heel down hard on the back of the Dreamer's knee.

The Dreamer's legs buckled and he started to stumble forward, but it was Ty who stopped him from falling. Gripping a fistful of his greasy black hair, Ty hauled him backward, slamming a knee into the Abenaki's arched back.

He pressed the length of the knotty club against the Dreamer's exposed throat, slowly exerting force until the man's face turned dark purple and his eyes began to bulge. A breathless hush had fallen on the crowd. Everyone knew that with a simple flexing of his powerful arm muscles, Ty could break the other man's neck.

Ty's breath came in retching gasps, rivulets of sweat shimmered on his oiled skin. His eyes clashed with Assacumbuit's. "The woman is mine."

For an interminable moment the sachem's face was impassive. Then he jerked his head in a quick nod. "The woman is yours," he stated. "As is the Dreamer's life."

"I'll take the woman." Ty relaxed the pressure of the club and released his grip. "This life isn't worthy of my trouble."

The Dreamer slipped slowly to the wooden floor, his head hanging as he gagged and choked. A shocked murmur coursed through the crowd at this insult—to throw a man's life back in his face as if he were an enemy so puny he was not even worth the killing.

Assacumbuit said nothing. He simply turned and walked away.

Ty flung down the cudgel and swung off the platform. Delia waited, white-faced with relief, for him to come to her. As he approached, she saw the sharp stamp of exhaustion on his face. Raw cuts and purpling bruises scored his body. She hadn't been able to follow the exchange between Ty and his father. All she knew and cared about was that Ty had survived, and she wanted to wrap her arms around him and hold him close.

He paused in front of her. But when she looked into his eyes she saw nothing but emptiness.

"Ty . . . ?"

He started to raise his hand as if he would touch her face, then let it fall. He walked past her, following Assacumbuit into the night.

Ty let the tent flap drop and paused, waiting for his eyes to adjust to the dim, firelit interior of the lodge. It was empty except for Assacumbuit, who sat with regal grace on reed mats before the hearth, leaning against a backrest. Draped around his shoulders he wore one of the trappings of his rank—the magical eagle-feather robe.

Ty walked stiffly toward him, for in spite of just having spent an hour in the sweat lodge and taken a swim in the lake, every place where the Dreamer's club had landed was aching and sore. "You sent for me, my father," he said, when he stood before the grand sachem.

Assacumbuit raised his head, fixing Ty with his unfathomable black eyes. "I am not your father."

Ty was careful not to let the hurt show in his face. But along with the hurt he felt anger and he summoned that forth instead. "You sent me back to the Yengi and as a dutiful son I obeyed. But before then I called you Father for ten years. The past can't be changed."

The sachem gave his characteristic French-like shrug. A few years before, Assacumbuit had journeyed to France to be a guest at King Louis's court. He had been knighted by the great Sun King and presented with a sword. Along with the sword he had picked up a few French habits, including the shrug.

"The past is finished," he said.

Swearing softly, Ty flung his head back and stared at the smoke hole in the ceiling.

"Sit and smoke with me," Assacumbuit ordered. "And stop sulking like a woman because you cannot make things back into the way they never were in the first place."

A dark flush stained Ty's cheekbones. Then he laughed.

The old fox had never in ten years raised a hand to Ty, but he could use words like a whip, and many was the time Ty had felt their sting.

As Ty settled himself, Assacumbuit prepared the pipe for smoking. It was the calumet, the sacred pipe. Its bowl was carved from the valuable red pipestone that came all the way from the land of the Ojibway, the Great Lakes. It had a reed stem carved with an intricate design and decorated with feathers.

Assacumbuit smoked first. He sent a puff skyward, an offering to the *gitche* manitou. He passed the pipe to Ty, who repeated the ritual and passed it back. More puffs were dedicated to Earth, Sun, and Water, and then to the four points of the compass. Only after the ritual was completed would they speak.

The concoction they smoked was called *kinnikinnik,* a mixture of tobacco and other plants known for their vision-enhancing properties. The smoke it produced was making Ty feel euphorically light-headed. Too much more of it, he thought as he took the pipestem yet again, and I'll be floating up there on the ceiling.

They smoked for a long while in silence while Ty waited, for the grand sachem must be the first to speak.

"You fought well tonight," Assacumbuit finally said.

Ty flushed at his father's praise, for it was rarely given. "I was well taught."

Assacumbuit snorted softly. "That chop to the back of the knee—I didn't teach you that."

"The Yengi universities are dangerous places," Ty said, and the old warrior actually smiled.

He passed the pipe to Ty. "You made a mistake, however."

Ty drew deeply on the calumet, inhaling the smoke. It was working wonders on his bruises. He was numb all over now and the world was beginning to blur nicely around the edges. "Oh? What mistake was that?"

Assacumbuit nodded at a skin-wrapped bundle in a far corner of the lodge. His eyes glinted with amusement. "That wasn't my shield I sent to you. It was another's. A warrior, in fact, who was a terrible coward and died early in battle."

Ty laughed softly. He felt almost giddy from the effects of the smoke, and relief. He found that he was glad Assacumbuit hadn't favored him over his own blood son. He also felt a quiver of fear at the realization that he had taunted the Dreamer over the magic of a shield that had no magic at all. Ironically, because he had been unable to kill Assacumbuit's only blood son, he had instead heaped such shame upon the man that the Dreamer's fate would now be worse than death.

Assacumbuit drew deeply on the pipe, his lids fluttering closed. "My son has a weakness and you wisely exploited it. But you have a similar weakness. You both must learn to draw your power and your pride from within yourselves."

Ty tried to pull his head back from where it floated on the ceiling. "Why have you taken up the hatchet against my people?" he finally said. His voice sounded fuzzy to his own ears, as if he spoke through a blanket.

"Then you admit at last that the Yengi are your people," was the sachem's answer, which was no answer at all.

"I live among them now. Thanks to you."

"You lived among the Abenaki once."

Ty clenched his jaw and tried again to gather his scattered thoughts. With Assacumbuit, a conversation, even in the best of circumstances, was often like fencing with a ghost. He tried a different tack. "What is the French black robe doing here?"

"The Yengi are as countless as the sands. We have scarcely a place left to spread our blankets."

"And so? What does that have to do with the black robe, who I might point out is Yengi as well?"

"Your brother and those who follow him have taken the French god as their own."

"Ah," Ty said, for in spite of Assacumbuit's circuitous way of speaking and the cloud in his brain made by the *kinnikinnik,* he was beginning to piece together the reason behind the raid on Merrymeeting. An Abenaki sachem was elected to the position by the women of the tribe, through whom the hereditary lines passed. He was chosen for his abilities; it was not a birthright. Nor was his rule absolute. The decision to go to war was determined by council, but any warrior seized with the desire was permitted to organize his own raid at any time.

The attack on Merrymeeting had been the Dreamer's idea, an idea no doubt fostered and encouraged by his French priest. The Dreamer was campaigning to be the next sachem in a manner not too different from that of a colonial who might run for election to the office of magistrate. But it was a dangerous game the Dreamer played and it could lead to another all-out war between the Abenaki and the English settlers.

"You wish to marry the Yengi woman?" Assacumbuit asked, in an uncharacteristically unsubtle attempt to get Ty's mind off the subject of the raid.

At the thought of Delia, Ty smiled. "Yes. I want to marry her." *I want to bury my heat in her at night. I want to see her face first thing upon waking. I want to spend all my days and nights loving her.*

And then he thought of how he had come to have her—through Nat's death and the Dreamer's shame. And he felt guilt, for he knew he didn't deserve her, not at that cost, and relief that fate had given her back to him anyway.

His father was nodding wisely, as if he had read Ty's thoughts. "She does make the eyes glad to look at her."

"And the heart as well," Ty said. He was finding it easier and easier to admit his love for Delia.

"I, too, loved the Yengi woman who was your mother."

Ty was surprised at this bald statement, and more touched than he would have ever thought possible. It gave him the courage to ask, "Why did you make me go back? They didn't even know I was alive until you told them."

He didn't think Assacumbuit would answer. The man sat so still, his glazed eyes staring blankly from a face that revealed nothing. Then he stirred and looked up, and the black eyes he fastened on Ty were lucid, and uncomfortably penetrating.

"I made you go back because I knew your heart would always be Yengi."

Ty's smile was tinged with bitterness. "My Yengi grandfather accused my heart of being Abenaki. Which is it? I wonder. Do I have two hearts then, or none at all? What am

I?'' he said, unconsciously echoing the cry of despair and confusion he had made to his grandfather five months before.

Assacumbuit merely shrugged. "You play a game with your own head. You know what you are."

"I'm a physician. And since I will be Delia's husband," Ty said, not even aware he had spoken aloud. He felt surprise at the sense of peace that simple statement gave him.

"You are a Yengi shaman? Truly?" Assacumbuit exclaimed with such astonishment that Ty laughed. The old warrior digested this in silence, then he shrugged, setting aside the pipe. *"Wurregan.* Go now. Your bride awaits you."

Dismissed, Ty stood up. But he hesitated. "You've been across the great ocean and so you've seen," he said. "The Yengi are, indeed, as numerous as grains of sand on the beach. Tell your son. The Abenaki must try to live in peace with the Yengi, for you can't hope to defeat them."

"Them?"

"Us," Ty acknowledged reluctantly. "You can't defeat us."

The grand sachem shook his head slowly, sadly. "My son, my son, we have no choice but to try. I would die before I let my heart grow soft."

Delia waited.

She had been left alone inside a wigwam. Remembering that Ty had a smaller version outside his own cabin, she had spent the first few minutes of her solitude exploring the Indian dwelling with curiosity. It was snugly built of a framework of light saplings bent together and layered with long strips of birchbark and hides sewn together. In the center of the single circular room was a primitive hearth—a stone-lined firepit with a small opening in the roof above it to let out the smoke. Mats of woven rushes covered the earth floor, but there was no furniture except for a bed made of balsam boughs and padded with moose hides and bear furs.

A group of Abenaki women her own age had brought her here. She had been stripped and clothed again in a long gown made of soft caribou hide that was elaborately trimmed with porcupine quills and embroidered with colored moose hair and English beads. Around her waist the women draped a girdle of wampum, with tassels made of shells and beads that rattled when she moved. Delia felt more like a queen being pampered by her ladies-in-waiting than an Abenaki captive.

With a show of great respect, the youngest, a girl of about fourteen, lifted a heavy cape made of a single panther hide and let it fall heavily over Delia's shoulders. Then her hair was brushed until it shimmered and spread in waves over the cape. A small headdress of swan's feathers, as white and fluffy as clouds, was placed like a crown on her head.

The Indian women giggled and cast shy glances up at her. Delia had a hard time believing that only two hours ago these kind, friendly people had voted to have her tortured and burned at the stake. No wonder, she thought, Ty so often seemed to be two different men.

After dressing her, one woman told Delia through a mixture of sign language and a smattering of English that she was to help prepare a meal. Then food was brought in: an enormous pink-fleshed salmon, which was put to bake on the hot stones; ears of corn to be roasted in their husks; a stew of beans and squash and squirrel meat bubbling in a bark dish; and finally a haunch of a moose, already cooked and basting in its juices.

The succulent smells reminded Delia of her hunger-pinched stomach, but when she politely asked if she might try a piece of the fish, she was told in between blushing giggles that she must serve her man first and watch him eat his fill before she took a bite of it herself.

Delia huffed with indignation at this injustice. Except for that tiny amount of pumpkin mush, which had had about as much flavor as a bowl of sawdust, she hadn't eaten in four days, and here she was supposed to sit and watch while Ty stuffed his handsome face! Why, she would probably start drooling like a starving dog, provoking him—him with his re-*fined* ways—into calling her a pig, just as he had done once before. Which was why, after the giggling women left, Delia snitched enough of the food to take the edge off her hunger.

There was nothing, however, to take the edge off her impatience.

After being dragged by a leash like a prize cow through a hundred miles of wilderness, being forced to run naked down a gauntlet of screaming savages, then being fought over like a bone tossed between two snarling curs, Delia was like a pot of water on a low fire—slow to boil but nonetheless getting hotter and hotter. Oh, she had a few choice words she intended to say to Dr. Tyler Savitch. Although if Delia knew her man, when he finally got around to coming to her tonight the last thing on his mind would be conversation. But she was determined this time not to surrender to those charming, seducing ways.

With Nat dead—and she squelched the pangs of guilt that came with the thought of Nat's death—she and Ty could now marry. But how could she be sure of him, sure that he would ask her? Not too long ago he had abhorred the very idea of marriage to the likes of her. And she had worked so hard these last months to erase the stigma of her past. She was respectable now, almost a real lady. She wasn't about to undo it all for a night of passion. Just because he had won that awful, ridiculous fight, that didn't mean he had the right to take her like a prize of war.

She paced the wigwam, punching her palm with her fist to drive home her points—she was damn bloody tired of being referred to as a possession that could be *taken*, or *won*, or *owned*. This time she was going to make Tyler Savitch court her properly. Respectfully. Just because he'd finally dredged up the nerve to admit he loved her, that didn't mean she was going to fall right into his arms. Or into his bed.

My woman, he had called her. "Ha! He'll soon find out he has to *earn* the right to call me that!" she muttered hotly to herself. "He'll soon learn that—"

"Who are you bawling out this time, brat?"

Delia's heart slammed up into her throat and she whirled around. Light from the pine knots outside the open tent flap threw his shadow in front of him, obscuring his face. But she had heard the teasing laughter in his voice. And the love.

They stood facing each other, saying nothing. Then he let the animal skin fall, shutting out the night sounds and torchlight.

"Oh, Ty!" Delia cried, flinging herself into his arms and covering his face with soft, fluttery kisses.

He captured her head between his two hands so that he

could kiss her properly. But nothing had prepared either of them for the exploding impact of the first touch of his lips on hers. It was fire to gunpowder, water to parched throats. It was the summer sun blazing up suddenly, hard and fast and hot, in the eastern sky.

It was love and passion and eternal life.

They tried to devour each other with their mouths. She twisted her fingers in his hair, pulling his head down so she could kiss him harder, as if she could fuse her lips to his with the heat of her passion. She probably would have let herself faint for lack of air rather than stop kissing him, but at last he tore his mouth from hers, burying his face against her neck.

His breath blew against her skin in hot, harsh gasps. Their hearts beat together, louder than the Abenaki drums. His hands moved up and down her body, as if he were trying to touch her everywhere at once.

"Sweet, holy Jesus . . ." He swayed unsteadily and she clung to him. He started to pull her head around for another kiss, but she slid from his arms. She was suddenly frightened by her own wanton reaction to that kiss, to him.

Her lips felt swollen and bruised, and she wet them with her tongue, tasting him. "It seems I'm supposed to feed you." Her voice was a hoarse whisper.

"Then feed me," he said huskily, and there was no mistaking his meaning. He took a step—

"Food," she said quickly, backing away from him, sliding around to put the firepit between them.

Ty's laugh was ragged. "Ah, Delia-girl. For such a passionate wench, you are the damnedest, hardest woman to woo." But he dropped gracefully to the ground beside the fire, sitting cross-legged in the Indian fashion.

There were bark plates and bowls, and she filled them with the food, giving them to him one at a time, as she had been instructed by the Indian girl. There were no newfangled forks here; he ate with his fingers, licking them clean between courses. And he kept his eyes on her the whole time he ate. She could feel their heat. It made her skin sizzle, and a place deep inside her, low in her belly, began to burn.

She feasted in turn on the powerful, masculine sight of

him. He, too, was dressed in intricately beaded buckskins—shirt, breechclout, and leggings. The belt of wampum he wore around his waist was identical to hers. With his dark hair, sharp-boned face, and blue eyes obscured by the shadows, he looked pure savage. She remembered him up on the platform, naked and painted, howling his war cry and swinging the club. *I don't know this man,* she thought. *I don't know him at all.* And she was afraid.

Then he smiled at her—that crooked curl of his mouth that never failed to pull at her heart. She looked quickly away so he wouldn't see what he was doing to her.

Suddenly it felt very warm in the wigwam. Delia brushed damp tendrils of hair from her face and fumbled with the shell clasps that fastened the panther cape. It was beautiful, but it was heavy and much too hot, especially with Ty watching her with those burning eyes. She took the cape off and laid it aside, running her palm across the sleek black fur.

"*Lusifee,*" Ty said.

She looked up at him in surprise. "He called me that."

"Who did?"

"The Dreamer."

Ty's smile turned hard. "Well, well. Now isn't that interesting? And what did you call him?"

Delia made a face. "He told me I must call him master . . . What does it mean—*lusifee?*"

He glared at her for a moment longer, then shrugged. "It's an Abenaki term of great respect. I've never heard it applied to a woman before." His eyes glinted now with teasing amusement. "Although if there was ever a woman it suited, that woman is you. It means wildcat."

Delia was pleased with herself, but she also thought it very funny. Her lilting laughter filled the wigwam. "Oh, Ty! And to think I was beginning to suspect it was the Abenaki equivalent for wooden-headed fool." And Ty's warm laughter joined with hers.

A small iron kettle filled with water and hemlock tips began to boil. She filled a hominy ladle with the brew, then dropped in a piece of maple sugar. But when she started to hand the ladle to him across the fire, he shook his head. "Bring it to me."

"But—"

"Come here, damn it."

She brought the drink around to him. He took the ladle from her hands and set it on the ground. Then his hand shot out, grabbing her wrist, and the next thing she knew she was sitting on his lap with a powerful arm wrapped around her waist.

She squirmed—then felt the hard, thick ridge of his arousal pressing against her bottom and went instantly still. "You tricked me!" she protested breathlessly.

"Uh-huh," he admitted shamelessly. He drew her mouth down to his for a slow, delicious, tongue-sucking kiss.

He stopped before she was ready, but only to lay his open mouth against her neck. "Ah God, Delia-girl . . . I can't wait anymore. I want you now."

She oozed against him, flowed into, over him like hot molasses. She was all weak and warm and wet between her thighs. "No . . . we must stop," she said. Or thought she said. She couldn't hear because of the blood rushing in her ears.

He stroked the length of her . . . waist, hip, thigh. Then back again . . . thigh, hip, waist. His lips drifted up her neck, seeking a slow, tortuous path back to her mouth. His hand found her breast and he massaged it roughly through the supple skin dress, his fingers pulling on the nipple until it was hard and quivering and aching.

She struggled against him. Or tried to. Every part of her felt too heavy to move, yet at the same time she had no more substance than the smoke curling up from the fire. "Stop, Ty . . . please . . ."

He flicked her ear with his tongue. She groaned and arched her neck. His lips roamed down the long, white column. He spoke to her, into her, his voice resonating through her blood. "I love you, Delia, Delia . . . And you love me. We're together at last, just the two of us. Free. Let me love you, Delia. I fought for you, Delia. You're my woman now, my—"

"No!"

She flung herself off him, backing away, crossing her arms in front of her in the age-old, purely female gesture of self-protection. "No, not again. I won't let you seduce me again, Tyler Savitch. If you want me, you're going to have to marry me first."

He uncoiled, stretching slowly to his feet. He advanced on her, his eyes glittering hotly. "I think I could seduce you, Delia."

"No—oh!"

He crushed her against him so hard that her denial came on a expulsion of breath. "Yes," he growled, gripping her hips, grinding his blatant, bulging erection into the cleft between her legs.

Her nails dug into his shoulders and her head flung back as a loud moan tore from her throat. Stars, she saw stars through the smoke hole. They were spinning, whirling, and she . . . she was surrendering. "No," she murmured.

He ground his hips again, moved his lips across her neck. "I think I could seduce you easily."

She tried one last time. "No . . ."

His hand splayed her scalp and he pushed her mouth within reach of his lips. "Yes," he insisted, his lips brushing hers in a feathery, erotic caress. "But I won't have to, Delia, my love, Delia, my wife . . . because we are already married."

Chapter 24

$\sim\!\!\circ\!\!\oslash\!\!\circ\!\!\sim$

Her lips parted, trembled, and her eyes opened wide. "Married? No, we never . . ." But Ty was done with talking and he was done with waiting. He smothered her hot, wet mouth with his.

Never had he tasted anything so fine, so sweet as Delia's mouth. She owned him, this woman, body and soul, and he wanted something back from her—even if it was only the short, sharp, exploding pleasure of spilling his seed deep inside her.

Her mouth opened, surrendered, melted beneath his. She sucked at his tongue and he gave it to her. She clung to him and he supported her. She rubbed her stomach against him and he pumped his hips, letting her feel what she hungered for. Then he tried to swing her up into his arms and carry her to the bed without letting go of her mouth, and they wound up stumbling and tripping across the floor, rolling onto the piles of soft furs, still locked together.

He thrust his tongue deeper into her mouth as he tugged up her skirt. He brushed the sensitive skin of her inner thigh and her hips arched off the bed as if his fingers were tongues of fire. She moaned and he sighed, for her flesh was soft there, so incredibly soft that he was afraid it would melt beneath his hand, like strands of silk held to a candle's flame. His hand moved upward, covering her pulsating sex. She groaned against his mouth as his fingers slid between the tender folds, stretching her open. God, but she was dripping wet and hot. So hot.

He expored her with his fingers, smearing her juices over

the downy, curling hairs, whisking his wet thumb back and forth across the hard nub of pleasure until he had her writhing against his hand.

She tore her lips from his. "Oh, Ty, that is so . . . oh, please . . ."

He raised his head to look at her. Her eyes were wide open and dark with desire, her mouth swollen and slack, wet from his kisses. Her gaze fastened onto his face, as her searching hands moved between the folds of his breechclout, finding his erection. Her palm closed around his thick length, squeezing him almost roughly. Her hand was hot and Ty hissed in an agony of desire.

He clenched his jaw, setting the back of his teeth so hard he thought they'd break, and buried his face in the hollow of her shoulder. He felt enormous, so hard he hurt.

"Oh, Delia, oh sweet Jesus . . . It's been too long. I'm sorry . . ."

The wampum belt came off easily, but he had trouble with the waistcord of his breechclout, unraveling the knot in the second before he was about to take a knife to it. He flung the offending garment against the far wall and, spreading her legs wide with his knees, he broached her entrance with the smooth, round tip of his iron-hard erection. He braced himself on his outstretched arms so that he could watch her face as he drove into her. He wanted to bury himself so deeply inside of her that she'd feel him on the back of her throat.

He thrust—and her eyes winced shut, for she was tight, virginally tight. It shocked him for a moment and his buttocks lifted, until he'd almost pulled all the way out of her. Then he eased back into her, more slowly this time, stretching her, filling her. She arched her back and clenched his hips with her thighs, gripping him like a satin fist, sucking him even deeper into the slick, throbbing core of her.

He tried to stroke her rhythmically, but he was incapable of control. Soon he was plunging wildly in and out of her, slamming his hips, and she met his thrusts with such ferocity she almost bucked him right off her. Her violent passion surprised, delighted, and spurred him on. He could hear his own breath as a high-pitched whistling sound as he forced it out through his clenched jaws. She raked her nails across his

back and sunk her teeth into his shoulder. His neck arched
and his mouth opened on a silent scream of pleasure.

"Ty, Ty, Ty," she panted.

"Christ!"

They climaxed together with a shattering release that started
in his toes and shot out the top of his head with the explosive
force of a thousand booming cannons going off at once.

He stayed in her for a long time. Until he'd grown almost
completely soft. Until his heart stopped slamming against his
chest and his lungs started working again. Until he was sure
his body wasn't scattered in little pieces around the wigwam.

He lay mostly on her, his chest flattening her breasts, his
head buried in the crook of her neck, where her hair tickled
his nose. She smelled of the pine forest outside and of the
musky furs they shared and of the erotic scent that was pure
and unmistakably Delia.

He had an irresistible urge to look into her face. Rolling
onto his side and pushing himself up on one elbow, he looked.
And he had to laugh because her expression was the image
of the way he felt—stunned.

Her skin was flushed and damp. Her mouth looked pillaged
and ravished. Gold, starred with green, were her eyes, the
color of the lake at sunset; he drowned in them. The firelight
played with her hair, emblazoning it with ruby lights. It fell
over the furs and across her shoulders like spilled wine. He
scooped it into his hands and held it to his mouth as if he
would drink of it.

As he stared deeply into her eyes, he saw them suffuse
with a soft, dreamy look of love. Languidly her hand came
up and she ran her finger along his lower lip. "Ty . . ."

Emotion thickened his throat. To his astonishment tears
blurred his eyes. He loved her so damn much it *hurt*.

He lowered his head to trace the curl of her mouth with
his tongue. He delved between her lips, flicking her teeth.
Her moist breath blew into him on a soft sigh. Then she
moved her tongue over her own lips, where his tongue had
been just a moment before. He groaned and covered her
mouth with his.

They kissed and kissed. Hot, hard kisses that soon left

them panting and tearing at each other's clothing, desperate now for the feel of warm and naked flesh rubbing and sliding together. He couldn't believe they were kissing like this, with such fierce hunger, so soon after that shattering explosion of just moments ago.

Yet there was no doubt he wanted her again. Already.

Reluctantly he gave up her mouth, but only to move down her neck, where he nuzzled and teased with nose, lips, and tongue. She moved her hands beneath his shirt and over the hard, supple muscles of his back and buttocks, all the while making soft cries of yearning in his ear.

He unlaced the front of her dress, exposing her breasts. Her nipples were puckered and pointed, the surrounding areolas as dark as blueberry stain. He cupped one breast, gently squeezing its fullness and bringing it within reach of his lips. He made a lazy circle of the nipple, then dusted the tip of it with his tongue. But that was too subtle for the mood he was in tonight and he soon had the whole of it in his mouth, rolling it between his teeth, sucking and suckling like a greedy babe.

He pushed her breasts together and rubbed his face in the deep cleft, then thrust between them with his tongue, as he had done to her mouth. "Oh God, wife, you taste so damn fine. I envy our babies—"

She heaved against him with such force that he grunted. "Tyler Savitch, you are a bastard!"

"What—ow!" He grabbed her wrists before she could hit him again, holding them together with one hand and pulling them above her head. He covered her bucking body with his, stilling her. "What have I done now?" he demanded. Then grinned and wriggled his hips. "I mean besides the obvious."

"How *could* you lie to me like that? How could you call me wife and say we're married? Oooh! I've let you seduce me again. I hate you!" Tears pooled in her eyes and she twisted her head aside, trying to bury her face in the furs. "I hate myself," she added softly, miserably.

He took her jaw between his fingers. "Aw, Delia, my doubting bride." He licked the tears where they started to spill from her eyes. "Do you think I would lie to you about something so important?"

He watched the emotions chase each other across her face: disbelief, anger, and at the end an uneasy hope. He had hurt her so often in the past. *But never again, Delia. I promise I'll never hurt you again.*

She swallowed, cleared her throat. "But that's . . . *when* were we married?"

"Tonight," he said, smiling, savoring the rare thrill of knowing he was about to give her joy on this night, as well as pleasure. "Abenaki weddings are somewhat casual affairs. The intendeds dress up in special clothes . . ."

She rubbed her palms across the front of his quilled and beaded shirt. "These clothes?"

"Uh huh." He ran his tongue along her pouting lower lip. "Then the man sends food to her wigwam or lodge. To show that he can provide for her."

She glanced at the remains of the feast by the fire. "That came from you?"

"Uh-huh." He nibbled on her lip, sucking it into his mouth. "And then the woman prepares and serves the food to her man, showing how she will care for him." He kissed her mouth fully, gently. "And then they make love, on a bed of balsam and fur."

She dipped her nail in the crease beside his mouth, then traced his lips. They parted open. He circled her finger with his tongue. "Someone should have warned me," she said.

He tilted his head back to study her face, a little unsure now. She had declared her love so often, he'd taken for granted that she would welcome their marriage. God, if he had somehow managed to lose that love . . .

"If you'd been warned, would you have gone through with it?" he asked, then held his breath.

She laughed low in her throat. "What do you think, Tyler Savitch? I've been wanting you to marry me since I first laid eyes on you," she acknowledged, unafraid as always to reveal her love for him. She traced his features with the soft, sensitive pads of her fingers. "It's just . . ."

Smiling, he kissed her palm. "Just what?"

"I was going to make you court me first. Like a proper lady."

He had lowered his face to her breast and now he slid his hand between her thighs, fingers stroking, parting. "Is this the proper way to court a lady?" he asked, his mouth around a nipple.

She gasped and squirmed as his fingers delved deeper. "Most improper . . . I should think."

He slid out of her arms and off the furs, standing up. There was such a look of surprise and disappointment on her face that he had to laugh. "I'm not going anywhere, greedy brat," he said. "I only want to get out of these damn wedding clothes."

He was out of them in seconds. Tall and strong and naked, he looked down where she lay in wanton abandonment on the pile of furs. Her skirt was bunched around her waist. Her legs were long and slender and painted golden by the fire. The dark triangle between her thighs concealed mysteries he would never tire of trying to solve. Her dress was unlaced and pulled off her shoulders, revealing a pair of perfect, ruby-tipped breasts. His gaze moved up the creamy column of her throat, past parted lips, to lock onto her eyes.

But it was Delia who spoke. "You're beautiful."

He tossed back his head and laughed. "I'm the one who's supposed to say that."

Leaning over, he took hold of her wrists and lifted her up beside him. He reached around her waist, untying the belt of wampum and letting it fall with a soft whisper to the ground. He gathered up the folds of her caribou-skin dress and pulled it over her head. Unconsciously she made it easy for him, raising her arms above her head the way a young child would do.

Her hands came down between them to stroke his chest, fingers tangling in the pelt of soft hair. Her palms moved lower, to his belly, and the muscles spasmed as he sucked in air on a tight sigh. A sigh that turned into a deep groan as her hands found and gently fondled his swelling manhood.

"What are you doing, Tyler Savitch?" she purred in that erotic husky voice of hers, as if she didn't know.

"I'm preparing to consummate my marriage."

She giggled and pressed her naked body against his, rubbing and arching like a cat. "I thought we already did that."

"That was the overture." He took her hand and wrapped it tightly around his thick, surging erection. *"This* is going to be the real consummation."

He cupped her breasts in his palms, lifting them, brushing his thumbs back and forth over their puckered tips. He drew her up so that he could suck one into his mouth. She groaned a little for he sucked hard. She leaned back, her eyes squeezed tightly shut. Clinging together, they fell down among the furs.

He covered her with his body, taking her slender wrists and pinning them on either side of her head, as if he would ravish her. She felt so incredibly tiny beneath him. He was afraid he would crush her. Yet as the same time he was overwhelmed with a purely masculine desire to possess, to take, to make her *his*.

He rubbed his swelling arousal against the wedge of tight, dark curls between her legs and brought his mouth down so close to hers that their noses touched. "Better get real comfortable, Delia-girl," he growled softly, "because this particular consummation is going to take a long, long time."

He began with her mouth. He explored it with his tongue, marveling at its heat, its silky texture. He sucked and nibbled on her lips, telling her between kisses that not even the first maple sap of spring tasted as sweet as her lips. She laughed into his mouth.

With his tongue he traced the firm line of her jaw and the underside of her chin that jutted up so provokingly when she was angry or scared. The thought of that little chin, leading the way so bravely into the world, made him want to enfold her in his arms and protect her from all sorts of unnamed dangers and sorrows. "I love you, Delia," he said, his open mouth pressed flush to her throat. His own throat was so tight, he was surprised the words got out. "You don't need to worry 'bout anything now, 'cause I love you."

He felt her swallow. She tangled her fingers in his hair to hold his head in place. "Ty," was all she said. It was enough.

Her fingers tightened, pulling his head down. She arched her back, pressing her breasts into his face. "Suck me," she said, and the words sent an erotic, burning thrill lashing through him like flame.

He accepted her invitation and feasted on her breasts. He lavished them with compliments and kisses, flattened, massaged, suckled, and worshipped them. He placed his hand low on her belly . . . then followed it with his lips. He planted a loud, sloppy kiss on her stomach, just above her pubic hair, and nuzzled her with his face until he had her laughing. Then he slid his hands beneath her bottom, lifting her to his hungry mouth, and felt the taut muscles clench with shock and ecstasy as his tongue delved between her soft, wet folds of flesh.

"Ty!" she gasped. "What are you doing?"

"Loving you."

"But it's . . . Oh, Lord above us . . ." But her thighs opened wide and she grasped the sides of his head, pulling his face deeper into her in case he had any intention of stopping. Ty smiled as he moved his tongue and lips along her hot, sweet cleft. Delia McQuaid might be hard to woo, but once won she was the most uninhibited lover he had ever known.

He scraped her tiny nub of pleasure with his teeth, then sucked it between his lips. She seemed to swell beneath his mouth. Her head flailed back and forth. Her fingers dug into the fur at her sides and the air was rent with her guttural moans and cries. He felt powerfully male that he could do this to her, wonderfully blessed that she would let him. And when she came, it was against his hot and moist open mouth.

"I love you," he cried against her as the last of her tremors faded away. "Love you . . . love you . . ." He rose over her and came down on top of her, slamming his mouth over hers as he drove into her. She raised her hips higher, meeting his piercing thrust and grasping him so tightly that he shouted.

He withdrew until only the rounded tip of him remained inside her, then delved into her, again and again stroking her clenching tightness. He held back, held back, held back . . . until he thought it would kill him. Then he set his teeth and thrust some more. The blood thundered in his ears; their breathing sounded like a nor'easter gale. Their bodies, slick with the heat of their passion, sucked and popped as they came together and drew apart.

Her legs fell so wide apart, her knees were touching the bed. He heard a pathetic whimpering noise and realized it came from himself. He didn't feel so powerful now. She was grinding him between her thighs, wringing him dry, sucking him empty, reducing him to a poor, quivering male animal who was nothing, nothing, nothing without her.

He had never known such ecstasy.

The fire disintegrated into a mound of coals. The night air was full of the coming winter and Ty pulled the furs close around them.

Sighing sleepily, Delia snuggled into the circle of his arms, burrowing against his broad chest. "I love you, Tyler Savitch," she said, so softly he wasn't sure if it was she, or only his own memory, that he heard.

His arms tightened around her and he pressed his lips to her ear. He spoke to her in Abenaki, crooning the words of a love song. Then he repeated them in English, so she would know . . .

"Sleep, sleep, my beloved. Do not fear the dark . . . for tonight my heart beats with your heart. Tonight we are one."

She slept, but he did not. He leaned on his braced elbow, resting his head on his fist, and looked at her. Simply looked at her. He couldn't believe she was actually his and he didn't want to sleep for fear that when he awoke it would all have been a dream. Besides, he liked looking at her . . .

Hours later, Delia opened her eyes to find him gazing down at her with a bemused expression on his face. She smiled. "What are you staring at, Tyler Savitch?"

His lips brushed her temple. "My wife."

"Oh, her." She laughed and nestled deeply into his warm embrace, shifting so that her back was to his chest, his arms around her waist.

His hands moved up and gently cupped her breasts. "Delia? How awake are you?"

She moved her bottom in a seductive bump and grind. "Do you want to do it again?" she asked with such eagerness that he laughed with delight.

"Yes." He fitted their bodies close together so that she could feel his growing arousal. "Incredible as it is to me, I do. But there's something else I want to do first."

She looked back over her shoulder at him. "Eat?" she said, with even more eagerness.

He laughed again, rubbing noses with her. "Well, we can do that too. Afterward."

She complained, but good-naturedly, when he threw back the furs, exposing their naked bodies to the crisp air. He helped her dress, although they had to search the entire wigwam twice for one of her moccasins. Then he pulled on his shirt, tied on his leggings, and stepped into his moccasins. Snatching one of the furs off the bed, he led her into the night.

The air seemed to crackle with the frost, pinching their skin, and their breath made clouds of vapor around their faces. It was so clear the stars looked close enough to touch. A pair of wolves cried to each other, their howls echoing across the lake.

Ty turned Delia so that she faced north and she gasped with wonder. Bright spears and luminous bands of light shot up from the horizon and fanned across the black sky in rainbow splendor. "Oh, Ty!" she exclaimed. "It's beautiful. But what is it? I mean, how is it happening?"

"The Night Spirit has put on his robe of colored fire," Ty said, then laughed with a helpless shrug. "Actually I don't know what causes it. It's always most dramatic, though, at this time of year."

He stood behind her, wrapping the fur around them both, pulling her close against his chest. They watched the dazzling display in silence for several minutes before Ty spoke again.

"I was so afraid, Delia."

Somehow she knew he wasn't speaking of his fight with the Dreamer. "Of what?" she asked softly.

"Of loving you, in case I lost you. The way I lost my father and mother, and later Assacumbuit and the life I knew here at Norridgewock." There was a tenseness to the way he held her that came from deep within him. "From the very first, I was so damn afraid of falling in love with you, I was

like a kid being dragged out to the woodshed for a hiding—
I fought it kicking and screaming every step of the way.''

She turned so that they were chest to chest and hip to hip
within the fur. She rested her hands on his supple buckskin
shirt and tilted her face up to his. Through her palms she
could feel the low tremor of his beating heart. "Then what
happened to make you stop being so afraid?"

A grin curled his mouth. "Nothing. I'm still scared blue
at the thought that I might lose you—"

"You won't ever lose—"

He stopped her words with his mouth. "Sssh. Don't say
it. You can't know the future. But as terrifying as the thought
of losing you is, nothing could be as bad as never having you
at all. These last months, seeing you married to Nat, knowing you shared his bed and that I might never have the joy of
making love to you again . . ." He shuddered. "I've never
suffered such hell.''

Delia started to confess that her marriage to Nat had never
been consummated, but then she realized such an admission
might have been an embarrassment to Nat. He was dead, but
she owed it to him to protect his pride. So instead she said,
"You have me now, Ty. For as long as we live."

"Aye, I have you now, Delia. You are my wife, my lover."
He rubbed his face in her hair and pulled her tighter against
him, melding their bodies. "And even if I am never to have
you again after this night, this moment, you will remain wife
of my soul. Keeper of my heart."

His words were a balm to her own battered heart. For the
first time she believed, truly believed that he loved her. She
sighed against his throat. "It doesn't seem real . . . that we're
married."

"It's real. But if it'll make you feel better, I'll marry you
again in the Yengi way when we get back to Merrymeeting.
Whereupon I will proceed to plant a dozen of my babies in
your belly. One at a time, of course—"

"A dozen!" She leaned back against his clasped hands to
glare at him. "Tyler Savitch, you'll have me pregnant the
rest of my life!"

He hugged her. "Um, yes . . . that's the idea—"

Suddenly a loud scream erupted from one of the long-

houses at their backs. There was the sound of running feet
and shouting, which set the dog to barking, turning the village into a cacophony of noise.

Ty's head had flung up and he'd gone stiff in her arms.

"Ty? What's happening?"

Throwing aside the fur, he grasped her hand and started at
a run for the longhouse, where the screams were still coming
in short, staccato bursts.

"It's Elizabeth Hooker!" he cried out to her over his
shoulder.

But Delia could tell that even Ty wasn't prepared for what
they found in the lodge. Elizabeth lay on a pile of blood-
soaked furs, her white skin stretched as thin as parchment
paper over the stark bones of her face. Every few seconds
she clutched her stomach and emitted a throat-searing scream.

"God in heaven," Ty breathed, kneeling beside the an-
guished girl. For a moment he hovered there, doing nothing,
and when Delia turned to look at him she saw stark terror on
his face.

Elizabeth screamed again and Delia had to clench her fists
to keep from screaming along with her. "Oh God, Ty, is she
dying?"

"No," he said, suddenly all brisk business as he bent over
to examine her. "No, she isn't dying and she's not losing this
baby either."

Suddenly the door banged open and the devil appeared on
a cloud of sulfurous smoke. Delia's heart almost stopped from
pure terror.

Then Ty said something in Abenaki and she realized the
apparition was some sort of medicine man with a black-
painted face, swinging a perforated bowl that oozed oily,
foul-smelling smoke. He knelt beside Ty, shaking a rattle in
Elizabeth's face and mumbling an incantation.

Elizabeth's blue-veined lids fluttered open, focusing on the
medicine man, and she screamed.

Delia clutched the girl's trembling hand. "Ty, make him
go away. He's frightening her."

"No, I need him. He knows more about healing than I
could learn in a lifetime." He bracketed Delia's shoulders
with his strong hands. "My love, I'm sorry but you're the

one who's in the way." He gave her a gentle smile. "If you want to be useful, you can keep us supplied with hot water."

Throughout the rest of the night and the long day that followed, Ty and the Abenaki shaman worked to save Elizabeth's life, while Delia abided their wishes by staying out of the way except when they asked her to fetch more water or rags. For the first time Delia understood something of the courage it took Ty to be a doctor. He seemed to suffer empathetically with Elizabeth's pain and she knew he would take the loss of any patient, no matter how old or sick, bitterly hard.

The sun was just beginning to set again when Ty suddenly appeared before her. He wrapped his arms around her and clung to her, shuddering with exhaustion and the release of long-suppressed emotion.

He sighed into her hair. "She's going to make it, my love."

Tears of relief stung Delia's eyes. "And the baby?"

He laughed shakily. "That little unborn tyke is a fighter. I can't believe the way he's clinging to life. But, Delia—" He stepped back so that he could look down into her face. He smoothed the hair from her brow. "If the baby is to have any chance at all, he's going to have to stay in the womb for at least three more months, and it isn't going to be easy keeping him there."

She clasped the hand that cupped her face. "We can't go home, can we?"

"Not until spring."

Chapter 25

The hunter studied the cloven-shaped tracks left by his quarry. They were fresh, for the flattened snow crystals sparkled in the fading winter sunlight. He smiled to himself—the hunt would be over soon and he was anxious to be home.

He picked up his pace, gliding effortlessly across the deep, soft snow on wide, flat oval shoes of bent wood frames and rawhide webbing. He saw where the tracks detoured around a pair of birches that grew six feet apart and knew then that the moose he followed was a bull, and a big one. The animal's antlers had been too wide for it to pass between the trees.

When he came to the shore of a frozen lake, the hunter stopped, concealing himself within a thick stand of snow-clad spruces. The ice stretched before him, flat and empty, eerily green in the white winter light. From a distance the man resembled the animal he hunted, for he wore a thick coat of mooseskin and a set of antlers on his head. Holding a birchbark instrument to his lips, he reproduced the deep lowing sound of the bull moose. Then he settled mind and body to wait with the patience and endurance he had learned as a boy.

Now that he was no longer moving, the hunter could feel the belly-shrinking cold. The air was raw and piercing, and in spite of the deerhair stuffing in his moccasins, his feet soon grew numb. Long streamers of clouds flowed in layers across the sky; it would snow again soon. He could smell the snow and feel it in the tight pinching of his nose.

A tree that couldn't take the weight of the ice snapped

suddenly with a crack that echoed like a rifle shot. It startled a snowshoe rabbit, which bounded across the frozen lake, jumping high on his huge hind feet. But the hunter didn't move. He'd been listening for some time now to the moose slogging through the wet drifts, coming his way.

When the moose emerged into the open, he raised his enormous head and sniffed the air. The hunter lifted his short, powerful bow, knocking a cane arrow into the sinew string. The moose turned his head. Man and animal, hunter and hunted, locked eyes.

Tyler Savitch pulled back the bowstring and let the arrow fly.

The arrow, flighted with eagle feathers, flew true. It sliced into the animal's thick neck, and blood from the jugular vein spewed into the air like the blow of a whale. The great animal swayed, sinking onto his foreknees in the deep snow, dying in silence. The hunter threw back his head and sang, thanking the spirits for their gift, and the music seemed to bounce off the sky.

Ty butchered and quartered the animal where it fell, leaving a portion of the entrails and some meat as a gift for the other predatory birds and beasts with which he shared these hunting grounds. He had to carry the meat in pieces the two miles down the trail to where he had stashed his toboggan. He used parfleches—rawhide containers—carrying the heavy packs on his back by a tumpline of coarse bark webbing.

The going was much easier once he got the meat onto the toboggan. Like snowshoes, the toboggan was an Abenaki invention—a sledge made of a board about a foot wide, its front end turned up, which could be dragged by men or dogs across the snow. The toboggan made a swishing sound as it slid through the drifts and the icy pellets squeaked beneath Ty's snowshoes. But in spite of the heavy load he pulled, Ty's pace was swift. He had been away from his wife all day and he missed her.

Coils of smoke rose blue against the sky, smelling of burning spruce. Ty topped a rise and paused to look down on the village spread in the valley below. The thatched roofs of the longhouses were dirty gray against the pure white background. The wigwams, snow-laden cones, resembled white wasp nests.

The dogs' baying announced Ty's arrival and women emerged from the wigwams and lodges to relieve him of his burden. The meat would be taken to the smokehouse where it would be cured. Part would go into the village's communal stores, but the bulk would go to the clan of families Ty hunted for. The muffle he kept for himself. The fleshy part of the upper lip and nose of the moose was a delicacy reserved for the man who had slayed the great beast.

As he made his way to his own wigwam, Ty passed the bare poles of other lodges that had been stripped of their hide and fur walls. In winter, when food was scarce, many families chose to leave the permanent village and follow the game animals into the snow-laden forest. Because of the pinching cold, everyone, even the dogs, was indoors.

"Delia-girl!" Ty sang out happily, as he unstrapped his snowshoes, whacking them against a pole to knock the packed snow from the webbing. He pulled aside the flap and, ducking low, entered his lodge. "Where are you, woman? I'm cold and tired and starving for a kiss . . ."

The last of his words faded and the smile dissolved from his face as he realized the wigwam was empty. No doubt she was next door at Assacumbuit's longhouse, visiting with Elizabeth and the baby. Still, he couldn't help feeling disappointed that she wasn't there to greet him, especially since he'd fantasized all afternoon about the taste of her mouth and the feel of her breasts filling his hands. He wanted her.

He laughed at himself. Hell, when *didn't* he want her? The only thing that tore him from her side was the need to hunt for food. If they could have lived on love alone, he wouldn't have left the wigwam at all.

The air inside was warm from the fire and redolent of bayberry candles and steam from a French kettle that sat on the coals, bubbling with a mush of corn, acorn, and cattail.

As he dropped down on the mats beside the hearth to take off his wet moccasins, Ty scooped up a ladleful of the mush and tipped it to his mouth. His stomach was suddenly reminding him that he'd eaten nothing all day except a small piece of *quitcheraw*—a cake of parched corn sweetened by maple sugar—and he'd probably trekked a good twenty miles all told, most of it dragging the laden toboggan behind him.

He smiled when he saw that Delia had left a birchbark pail of melted snow by the fire so that he would have warm water to wash with on his return. After living alone all of his adult life, this seemed the greatest luxury to Ty, having a wife to anticipate his every need. He was especially blessed with Delia; she seemed to know what he wanted even before he did. He had tried to tell her all this pampering wasn't necessary—he would be the happiest man on earth simply for the joy and excitement she brought him in bed. Her answer, he recalled now with a fond smile, had been to quit being a wooden-headed fool. He felt himself grinning inanely at the mere thought of her. God, but he loved her. Delia, his wife . . .

A shudder of utter horror passed through him at the memory of that day on Falmouth Neck when she had told him she would make him the best wife ever, and he had rejected her and the love she offered. For the hundredth time he thanked his guardian spirit Bedagi, the *gitche* manitou, and the Christian God as well for giving him a second chance to take this rare and beautiful woman to wife.

His stomach full and his feet warmed, Ty now scowled impatiently at the door, feeling suddenly most neglected. He was feeling ill from a lack of kisses. He mentally counted backward—it had been eight hours since they'd last made love. If they weren't careful, a certain valuable part of his anatomy could atrophy from lack of use.

Ty was up and pacing the wigwam. Damn it, this was serious. Where was she? Surely one of the other women had told her he was back by now. Grumbling another curse, Ty shoved his feet into his now-dry moccasins. He shrugged back into his moosehide coat, picked up a parfleche of the fresh meat, and headed out the door. Obviously he was going to have to go and get her and bring her back to his bed, where she belonged.

On entering the longhouse, Ty was met with an astonishing sight. Assacumbuit, that great, proud warrior, was shuffling in a little dance around the fire, bouncing Elizabeth Hooker's bundled baby in his arms. He was singing, too—a made-up song about a *waligit wasis,* a handsome baby with hair the color of cornsilk, who would grow up to be a tall, strong hunter and warrior, a great sachem of his people. The baby made little oohing sounds of delight, while Assacumbuit's daughter-in-law, Silver Birch, kept her head bent to hide her amusement.

Ty set the parfleche down by the door and entered the lodge quietly, unwilling to disturb this remarkable scene.

Although there were no windows in the longhouse, bars of dust-moted sunlight came through the smoke holes. The lodge was rectangular in shape, fifty feet long and divided into separate living cubicles, but with a paved central fireplace. The smoke from many fires had blackened the rafters. Even for the Abenaki, whose dwellings were more permanent than most of the other eastern tribes, this lodge was fairly old. Both Ty and the Dreamer had lived in it as boys.

Assacumbuit's dance ended with a flourishing jig. He whirled around on his toes . . . and froze at the sight of his grinning stepson. For the first time in Ty's memory the mighty warrior appeared embarrassed. He actually blushed!

"The brat looked like he needed to burp," Assacumbuit said gruffly.

"Ah, I see," Ty replied, his grin widening. "And were you trying to jiggle it out of him?"

The grand sachem snorted with pretended disgust. "Here, woman, take him." He held out the wriggling bundle to Silver Birch, who put the baby back in his cradleboard, hanging it from a center pole.

"So," Assacumbuit said, "there's been a rumor singing through the village that the Yengi shot with one arrow a moose with antlers big enough to fill a wigwam."

"Um," Ty acknowledged modestly. "There's a parfleche by the door."

Silver Birch exclaimed with delight as she unwrapped the meat. "Look, Father-in-law, he has brought us the muffle!" She turned grateful eyes on Ty. "But you must take it back with you. It is the hunter's reward."

"Nevertheless we accept the generous gift," Assacumbuit put in quickly and Ty hid a smile. The old warrior was known to trade a pair of beaver hides for the delicacy, which when made into a stew had a flavor of the sweetest spring chicken.

Crooning nonsense words, Ty dangled a string of painted bone dice in front of the baby, who stared back at him with unblinking gray eyes.

Every time he looked at this child, Tyler Savitch the physician was struck anew by the miracle of life. Five months ago, when he had seen Elizabeth Hooker tossing and screaming in a pile of blood-soaked furs, he had been struck with horror, assailed by the memory of his dying mother. If Delia hadn't been watching him with those big golden eyes, so full of love and faith, he might have given in to his fear. But he couldn't bear the thought of failing Delia, and so he had fought for Elizabeth and her baby as if he could defeat death through willpower alone.

The baby's hold on life had been tenuous throughout the following three months, until his early birth in January. It had been impossible for Elizabeth to leave her bed, let alone make the arduous journey back to Merrymeeting. Now they would have to wait until the warmer weather, when mother and baby would both be strong enough to travel.

Ty had spent two weeks tracking down the old timber beast, Increase Spoon, to have him take a message back to Merrymeeting for Caleb and the others, letting them know that both women were alive but that they wouldn't be home until spring. He and Delia both fretted over Nat's orphaned daughters, but they knew Anne Bishop would care for the girls until they returned. Ty didn't think Nat had any relatives, except for a distant cousin in England, and so he and Delia planned to adopt the girls as soon as they got back to Merrymeeting.

Ty suddenly became aware that all his cooing and rattling was a source of considerable amusement to his father. Laughing, he tossed the dice string in the air, catching it one-handed, then dropped down beside Assacumbuit by the hearth. An elk intestine, stuffed with meat, hung from a forked stick over the fire, filling the lodge with the sizzle of splashing fat and the aroma of bubbling grease.

Silver Birch, the Dreamer's pregnant wife, watched Ty from beneath shyly lowered lids, her hands neglecting her work. She had been tanning a deerhide by rubbing it with a mixture of brains, elm bark, and pureed liver. Her mother, blind and stooped with age, sat beside her, bent over a stump mortar, grinding corn. Molsemis, Assacumbuit's five-year-old grandson, played with a miniature bow and arrow, shooting at a target painted on the far wall. There was no sign of Delia or Elizabeth.

"Where are my women?" Ty asked casually, although inwardly he was a little alarmed. He had been sure he would find Delia within Assacumbuit's lodge, gossiping with Elizabeth and fussing over the baby.

Assacumbuit shook a gambling bowl up and down lazily, rattling the dice, no doubt hoping to entice Ty into a game, something which Ty fully intended to avoid since he always lost.

"Ice fishing," the old man said.

Ty's brows quirked up. "Elizabeth as well?"

"*Ai*. Your *lusifee* thought the fresh air would be good for her." The baby in the cradleboard above their heads let out a loud gurgle. The sachem glanced up, his black eyes as warm as glowing coals. "He's a fine boy. You ought to take the *awakon* Elizabeth as your second wife." Ty had bought Elizabeth from her captor for five beaver hides, so Assacumbuit considered the girl Ty's slave.

Ty laughed at the old man's blatant attempt to acquire another grandson. "Haven't we been through all this several times? Elizabeth already has a perfectly good husband. And Delia would wrap my innards around the torture pole if I so much as *thought* about taking a second wife."

Assacumbuit chuckled. "The *lusifee* would truly have you singing your death song."

A soft giggle came from Silver Birch. But when Ty looked at her, all he could see was the top of her bent head. The middle part in her shiny black hair was stained vermilion and she wore a finely quilled dress with a string of red and blue glass beads. She had dressed in this elaborate way every day for the past five months. She dressed for the return of her husband, the Dreamer, who was never coming home.

Shamed and scorned by the tribe for losing the fight to a mere Yengi—even if the Yengi was Assacumbuit's stepson— the Dreamer had walked out of the village that night. He had not returned, nor had he been seen by anyone since. The Norridgewocks, all except Silver Birch, suspected he had gone to the sacred mountain, Katahdin, where he had sang and danced and fasted until he entered the spirit world of his dreams.

The wind came up, rattling the bark shingles on the lodge. Ty stirred restlessly. He wanted his wife.

"Keep your stick in your breechclout a while longer," Assacumbuit said, reading Ty's mind and causing him to blush. "A man should not allow himself to become a slave to his appetites. Especially his appetite for a particular woman."

Too late, Ty thought with an inward laugh.

He started to stand up. "I think I'll just—"

Assacumbuit's hand fell on his arm. "Rest easy, my son. They've been gone only an hour and I sent the brother of Silver Birch to watch over them."

Reluctantly Ty settled back down.

The grand sachem grinned and shook the dice bowl. "Now, how about a little game while we wait, *ai?*"

Stuffing her hands deeper into her bearskin muff, Elizabeth Hooker peered through clouds of her own breathing into the hole they had cut in the marsh ice. "I don't see anything," she said.

"You can't see them. They're buried deep in the mud," Delia informed her, proudly showing off her newfound knowledge.

She poked around the unfrozen mud in the bottom of the hole with a flint-tipped spear. The young warrior, Pulwaugh, watched critically, chewing vigorously on a wad of spruce gum but doing nothing to help, for it was woman's work.

"Ty showed me how to do this," Delia said, mostly for the benefit of the young Abenaki, who, she suspected, spoke more English than he let on. "The great Yengi warrior Bedagi isn't too proud to teach his woman how to hunt for eels."

Suddenly she gave a sharp jab. Exclaiming with delight, she straightened, bringing up a pair of eels with yellow bellies that squirmed on the barbed tines. "Two of them!"

"Ugh!" Elizabeth shuddered, backing away. "They're horrible!"

"But delicious. Haven't you eaten smothered eels before?"

Elizabeth shuddered again. "Yes, but I didn't know they looked so . . . so disgusting when they were alive."

Laughing at Elizabeth's foolishness, Delia strung the eels onto a pointed stick that was already heavy with the smelt they had fished from a hole in the lake with a sinew line and corn for bait. Suddenly the sound of demonical laughter disturbed the winter silence, a long, ghostly *hoo-oo-oo*.

Shading her eyes from the winter glare, Delia looked up to see a white loon circling overhead. "Glooscap's messenger," she said, with a dreamy smile. "He's predicting a storm."

She never saw a loon now without thinking of a certain afternoon on the lake. In November, after the first dusting of snow, the weather had suddenly turned warm again, like summer. The Norridgewocks had taken advantage of the good weather to prepare for the coming winter—preserving food, making and repairing weapons, utensils and clothing, hunting for game. Ty decided to take Delia into the forest to show her how to set rabbit snares.

He *had* taught her some things about setting the snares. He showed her how to make the nooses of twisted bark fiber. He told her she must do them in fours, as four was a sacred number because of the four winds and the four compass points. He had taught her a song to sing when she found the traps empty, to drive away the bad-luck spirits.

But it was too beautiful a day for such serious concerns and before long they found themselves floating on the lake in a canoe, Delia slouching lazily with her back against Ty's warm chest, secure within the circle of his arms.

At first their talk was only interrupted by occasional kisses, but soon the talking grew less and less and their kisses got longer and harder, until the canoe began to rock dangerously.

Delia struggled halfheartedly in Ty's embrace. "Ty, stop," she protested. Her heart was palpitating rapidly, although it wasn't because of the near capsizing. "Remember what happened the last time you tried to kiss me in a canoe."

Ty's lips made a flank attack on her mouth by sneaking up her neck. "The way I remember it," he murmured against her throat, "you kissed me."

Delia's laugh was a deep, contented purr. "Was I really such a brazen hussy?"

"Be a brazen hussy now," Ty offered, and followed the invitation by slipping his hand inside the loose neckline of her buckskin dress to fondle her breasts.

Suddenly, crazed laughter rent the air above their heads as an enormous, muscular bird crashed onto the lake beside them, dousing them with an icy spray, rocking the canoe, and almost giving them an unwanted bath in the snow-fed lake.

Startled, Delia sat up abruptly, clutching her opened dress tightly to her chest. She looked into the lake where the bird had dived, but all she saw were the ripples. "What the bloody hell was that?" she demanded so indignantly that Ty burst into crazy laughter of his own.

Just then a sharp beak poked out of the water, followed by an iridescent, greenish-purple head. Then the whole bird popped up, still wearing his gaudy summer plumage of black and white checkered coat and striped collar. His tiny beady eyes fixed on Delia and he yodeled.

Delia heard an answering yodel and her head whipped around, for the sound had come from Ty.

The bird raced in a circle around their canoe, so fast he was almost paddling upright on the water on his big webbed feet. He let out a long, drawn out *hoo-oo-oo*. Ty *hooed* back. He laughed, *aha-aha-ha-ha*. Ty *ha-haed* back. He yodeled, *ha-ha-loooo*. Ty *ha-looed* back.

As Delia stared at her husband's smiling, beautiful face, her heart filled up with so much love she thought it would burst. For of all the many facets to this man—Dr. Ty, the healer; Tyler Savitch, the refined gentleman; Bedagi, the Abenaki warrior—Delia decided she loved this Ty the best.

Ty, the little boy, who could play with a loon.

A touch on her arm brought Delia back to the present. She looked into Elizabeth's rosy-cheeked face. "It's starting to snow again," the girl said. "Don't you think we should be getting back?"

Delia was about to agree—for big flakes were now falling from the sky—when the roses were blanched from Elizabeth's face and she let out a squeal of alarm, pointing back in the direction of the woods.

Pulwaugh turned first and he, too, let out a sharp-pitched cry. The hand that fell to the tomahawk at his waist trembled badly. "It's a ghost!" he exclaimed.

"Nonsense," Delia scoffed. She had never known a people worse than the Abenaki for believing in spirits and ghosts. " 'Tis only a man."

The man, although tall and broad-shouldered, was wraith-thin. His clothes were mere rags that flapped in the wind and his long black hair whipped around his face like a torn flag. As they watched, he raised his hand in the manner of the French priest bestowing a blessing.

"Why, it's the Dreamer," Delia said. She thought sadly of Silver Birch, waiting every day in the longhouse for her man's return. "Perhaps we should go talk to him. He looks cold and hungry."

Pulwaugh shook his head angrily and snapped a series of orders at them, all the while gathering their gear and herding them toward the village. Delia obeyed without an argument. The truth was she was afraid of the Dreamer. She certainly wasn't going to approach the man alone.

As they followed their own snowshoe tracks toward home, Delia looked back toward the lake. The Dreamer still stood there, watching them. He looked like a giant black crow, silhouetted against all that white brilliance, and Delia suppressed a superstitious shudder . . .

For crows were supposed to be the harbingers of death.

The wind knifed through his tattered buckskins and icy flakes swirled around his head. But the Dreamer was impervious to the cold. His eyes followed the three figures as they shuffled away on their snowshoes and disappeared into the curtain of falling snow. Wrapped up in furs as they were, he couldn't see their faces, but then he didn't really care. Dizzy and light-headed with hunger and a fever, he was lost in his own world of dreams.

He thought he might be a spirit now, although he wasn't sure. He lived among the spirits on Katahdin, the greatest mountain. No Abenaki had dared such a thing before, or at least dared such a thing and lived to boast of it.

The Abenaki dwelled and traveled within the woods and

on the waters beneath, but the Katahdin was sacred. It was the home of Pamola, the Storm Spirit, a beast with the wings and claws of an eagle, the arms and torso of a man, and the head and antlers of a moose. Pamola, in his rages, unleashed his winds and lightnings and snowstorms on the hapless humans below. To venture up where Pamola had his lodge was to invite a sure and terrible death.

Yet the Dreamer had climbed to the very top of Katahdin and there he had been visited with visions unlike any he had ever beheld before. They were strange visions, fragmented and ephemeral, and he didn't understand them yet. Understanding of the dreams would come later and then he would act upon them. For every Abenaki knew that disaster followed if a dream was not fulfilled. A man must take the path shown to him in his dreams or risk the vengeance of the gods. They were gifts from the gods, to show a man the way, and such gifts should never be ignored.

The Dreamer thought of the power of the visions and threw back his head and laughed. His laughter sounded crazed, like the loon's, and it echoed over the frozen lake. He laughed again and, taking a glass bottle from between the ragged folds of his mooseskin coat, he pulled the cork out with his teeth and poured the fiery brown liquid down his throat.

It burned, causing him to gasp and his eyes to tear. But the effect was almost immediate. The visions came, wavering before his eyes, and he squinted hard as if he could bring them into focus.

Assacumbuit had once warned him the visions that came from the Yengi's spirit water were not true visions. And the black robe said the Yengi god, who was the one true god, frowned upon the drink. But the Dreamer had forsaken the black robe's god. He had ripped the god's totem beads off his neck in disgust and ground them to dust on a rock beneath his heel. There had been no *keskamzit*, no magic, in those beads.

But there was *keskamzit* in the spirit water and he drank more of it, welcoming the dreams. This time the vision that appeared before him was sharper than the others. He could see Yengi, hundreds of the pale-skinned men, flowing over the earth in great rushing rivers. And at their head was *lusifee*, the panther. Suddenly, a great wolf emerged from the forest, slaying the panther with one mighty slash of his sharp fangs. The panther died and the rivers of Yengi flowed back into the ocean where they were carried away by the tide.

The vision faded, leaving the Dreamer stunned . . . and euphoric. Flinging back his head, he uttered a full-throated war cry. At last, at last, the gods had shown him his destiny.

The wind gusted and Delia ducked her head, trying to protect her face from the stinging, icy pellets. Her legs burned and trembled with exhaustion. The awkward toe-in way of walking on the snowshoes used muscles she hadn't known existed. She followed Pulwaugh blindly, trusting he knew the way, for she had long since become disoriented in the universal whiteness.

Elizabeth stumbled and the young man stopped, lifting the girl into his arms. Delia heaved a sigh of relief as the shadowy outline of the village palisade loomed before them. The sigh turned to a cry of joy as a man appeared out of the swirling snow.

"Ty!" Delia exclaimed. She covered the last few feet at a shuffling run, throwing herself into his arms. She felt so safe within his hard embrace. The sad, yet frightening image of the Dreamer had followed her home.

Ty hugged her against his chest. "I was afraid you'd gotten lost in this storm," he said, shouting to be heard above the wind.

Pulwaugh carried Elizabeth toward the grand sachem's longhouse and Delia started to follow, but Ty led her firmly toward their own wigwam.

"But, Ty, I was going to take the eels to your father," Delia protested once they were inside and he was taking off her fur hood, rubbing her wind-chapped cheeks with his hands.

"Do it later. Besides, he's been spoiled enough today with people bringing him delicacies." His hands stilled. He tilted her face up to his and his breath trailed across her lips. "Spoil me for a change. Give me a delicacy."

She loved spoiling him. She moved her mouth the fraction of an inch it took to put her lips into contact with his. His lips were warm, tender; their kiss was hard, draining. Her head fell back and her eyes squeezed shut as his lips moved down her pulsing throat . . . and then the Dreamer's black, ragged image appeared before her eyes. She shivered.

"Are you chilled?" He ran his hands up over her shoulders and down her back, his gaze lovingly caressing her face. "Let's go to bed. I'll soon have you good and warm. Hot, in fact—"

She pulled back slightly from his embrace. "Ty, we saw the Dreamer. Out by the lake."

A crease appeared between his brows. "Are you sure?"

"No . . . not sure." She closed her eyes, trying to conjure again the strange, crowlike image. "That wooden-headed fool Pulwaugh thought it was a ghost."

"If it was the Dreamer, it probably was a ghost."

"No, it was a man, a real man. And it was the Dreamer. I could feel it." She opened her eyes. "What are you scowling at *me* for?"

His face relaxed into a rueful smile. "Aw, hell, Delia. I'm just jealous, I guess. I wish you were a little less impressed with the man."

"I'm not impressed with him. He frightens me."

"Forget about him. Think about me." He cupped her bottom, tilting her hips toward his. "Do you know how long it's been—"

"Ten hours."

"God, it feels like ten centuries." He took her hand and put it between his legs. His manhood stretched and swelled, pushing against her palm. She could feel the heat of it through the pliant leather of his breechclout. "There, see," he said, his voice strained. "I'm dying for you, Delia."

She assumed the haughty face she had worn for her customers at the Frisky Lyon, while below, her hand was daringly squeezing his turgid sex. "Then why, sir, are ye standin' here a-talkin' me t' death?"

Groaning with need and anticipation, he lifted her, carrying her to his bed where he fell upon her greedily, his lips locking on hers in another deep, shattering kiss.

Long, breathless minutes later, he ended the kiss by growling against her mouth. "I hated coming home and finding you gone, Delia-girl. Don't ever leave me like that again."

Delia smiled to herself, for she knew that nothing short of death would make her leave Ty.

Chapter 26

⌒◯◯⌒

Ty dashed a ladleful of water on the red-hot stones. Moist, suffocating steam rolled up, filling the tiny wigwam.

"It's too hot, Ty," Delia protested, panting a little. She lolled naked against a backrest, feeling wonderfully relaxed and wanton.

Ty opened the entrance flap a crack. He picked up a brush made from the tail of a porcupine. "Come here," he said.

She came to him eagerly, positioning herself between his legs. It had become an afternoon ritual with them, performed almost every day. The steambath, the hair brushing, the talk . . . and the love. The Norridgewocks had merely thought it a Yengi idiosyncrasy when Bedagi had built his own private sweat lodge so that he could share the pleasure with his woman.

Ty drew the brush through his wife's long, black hair. It slithered and coiled wetly around his hands and over his thighs. Delia purred. She felt tingly all over from the steam generated by the water on the hot stones, and the steam generated by his touch, by the presence of his warm and wet and naked body pressed in intimate places against hers.

"Do you think your cabin was burned during the raid?" she asked lazily. "I can't bear to think you've lost all your fine things."

"They were only things." He set the brush aside and pulled her back to lean against his chest.

"But your mother's moccasins, Ty. And all your books and—"

He stopped her by kissing her mouth. "They don't matter.

379

I have you now and you're all I care about.'' He rested his chin on her shoulder. "I would've had to build another cabin anyway. The old one was too small to accommodate my dozen babies.''

She turned her face aside so he couldn't see her smile. "Aye. And the three wives it'll take t' give ye those dozen babies,'' she said tartly, although she liked the idea of having a houseful of children. Hers and Ty's . . . and Nat's. She wanted Tildy and Meg as much as she wanted children of her own. "I keep thinking of the girls, especially Meg. Poor Meg. She took her ma's death so hard. Now her da . . .''

Gently, he squeezed her shoulders. "They still have you.''

"But I'm not there.'' She twisted her head around. "When can we—''

He placed his finger over her lips. "Soon, love of my life. At the first sign of spring.''

He moved away from her to pour a bit more water over the stones. Steam wafted between them. He stretched out on his side and her eyes moved over the length of him—naked, hard, and beautiful. She wanted him to make love to her.

No, she wanted to make love to him.

Leaning back on her elbows, she thrust her chest out. Her breasts, firm and full, pointed saucily toward the low domed roof, their nipples dark and puckered. Her eyes took on a smoky cast, and her knees fell brazenly apart, one of them just brushing his thigh. Beads of water glistened in her dark triangle of tight curls, like dew caught in a web.

His chest trembled with silent laughter. "Are you perchance tying to seduce me, you wanton wench?''

"Hunh. Wishful dreamin', Tyler Savitch.''

He pounced on her and they rolled together over the reed-matted floor. She wound up on top, straddling his thighs. Her eyes widened at the sight of his splendid arousal.

"Do you see something you might like, sweetheart?'' he drawled.

"Oooh,'' was all she could manage, as a coil of heat, blazing red as the fiery stones at her back, unfurled deep between her legs.

She ran her palm up and down his rampant length, admiring it, manipulating it, worshipping it. Enjoying the beautiful thought of what she could do to it. She pressed her lips to the round swollen tip of it.

Ty sucked in a sharp, hissing breath.

Her mouth closed around it, and she sucked on him.

His thigh muscles tightened until they quivered, his fingers became ensnarled in her hair, his hips lifted . . .

She drew as much of him as she could into her mouth . . .

His mouth fell open. "Oh, sweet heavenly Je . . . ah . . ."

She sucked in her cheeks, drawing her lips along the length of him. She traced the pulsing veins with her tongue. She scored him lightly with her teeth, until he could bear it no longer.

"Oh God," he cried. "Enough . . ."

He pulled her up by the hair. She pressed her knees on each side of his slender hips and, rising up, impaled herself on him, deep and hard, and she gasped aloud as he seemed to pierce to the very core of her and his huge thickness packed her full. She ran her fingers over his chest, tracing the hard slabs of muscle, leaving little trails and swirls through the moisture on his dampened chest hair and steam-slick skin. Leaning forward, she cupped her heavy breasts with her own hands and lifted them, presenting her swollen nipples to his lips as if offering two ripe juicy strawberries for his degustation.

And he licked, nibbled, tasted.

He rose up, she sank down. Slowly at first, and then with greater and desperate urgency. Their bodies melted, flowed together as she rode him, sliding up and down on his thick length, faster and harder. Their breathing was choppy, harsh, muffled by the hot, steamy air. She was burning, burning, burning from the inside out.

He thrust up, hard, and she slammed down, driving a harsh cry out his throat as he pumped and pumped and pumped into her, and she melted over him, and they were one.

Small aftershocks still tremored through her body as she opened her eyes onto his face.

He blinked the sweat from his eyes, swallowed. Breathed. "Delia that was . . ." But he couldn't finish. He seemed shattered, and she felt shaky inside. In pieces. As if a giant hand had picked her up and rattled her like a gourd.

His glistening chest expanded as he sucked in another, deeper breath. "I think I'm going to live," he said.

Her wet hair slapped against his arms as he drew her head down and took a slow and loving kiss from her mouth. Then he laughed and bucked his hips, lifting her off him. "Let's take a snow bath."

Delia shrieked, trying to fend him off. "No, Ty!"

Heedless of her kicking feet and flailing hands, he carried her out the wigwam. Sky, sun, snow—all were white, the blinding, brilliant, bleached white of the purest ice. Minute crystals floated in air so cold it burned.

A big snow drift, fluffy and loose like a pile of goose down, loomed before them. Delia shut her eyes. "Oh, Lord above us . . ."

The snow was so dry it squeaked, and so cold it snatched the scream from her throat. Her muscles, fluid and loose from the steam and the heat, tautened with the snap of a bowstring. The cold was like the slash of a blade, so sharp she couldn't feel it.

And then she did—and it was like the water dashing onto the red-hot stones. She sizzled, she bubbled. She burst into hard and vibrant life.

His face floated above hers. Tiny diamond chips of snow dusted his flaring brows. Bright splashes of color heightened his cheekbones. His eyes were so blue they outdazzled the glare of the sun on the ice, and they burned with love, so that lying naked in a bed of snow, she felt not cold but warmed by the heat of his look.

His mouth slanted into a crooked smile. "God Almighty. I'm freezing my balls off!"

Laughing, clinging together, they fought their way out of the snow drift. They were halfway to their feet when Delia fell to her knees again. "Oh, Ty. Look . . ."

A spot of bare earth showed through the snow and from it emerged a tiny blue flower in the shape of a star. She brushed the flower once lightly with the tip of her finger. Looking into his shining face, her own face mirrored back his love and happiness and promise. They said it together.

"Spring."

* * *

Spring was noisy.

The snow plopped and thudded as it fell from drooping branches. Mist formed over the lake and river ice as it creaked and groaned, and cracks slithered and twisted across the once glassy surface. The steady drip of icicles thawing off the trees and roofs pattered like rain. Everywhere was the sound of water—flowing, running, gurgling. After so many months of snow-shrouded silence, the noise of spring battered the ears.

One day the wind changed direction, becoming warm and damp against the skin. The sap began to rise in the maples; young ferns and flowers poked through melting snow. The first tiny leaves of the birch and beech unfurled. Nature sang, a single loud repetitive note.

Spring.

The folk of Merrymeeting had waited out the long winter, each according to his nature—with resignation or impatience or hope.

The dead were mourned and buried but life went on, marked by the passing months. In November, they gave thanks for the harvest, with pumpkin bread and popped corn and roasted chestnuts. Hollowtide marked the slaughtering time with cracklings and sausage. For Christmas there were greens and minced pies, and in March they rang in the New Year with mead and hardened cider-brandy. On Good Friday they baked hot-cross buns.

Those farmers along the Kennebec who had been burned out in the raid set up housekeeping within the stockade. Along the inside wall of the palisade were low sheds whose roofs served as firing platforms. The families bedded down in these sheds at night. They cooked and lived communally in the blockhouse by day. Most of the men still logged the great pine masts that winter, but they went out in gangs, heavily armed. They built a small but stout garrison house at the central logging camp, and some of the men, those without womenfolk, remained up in the hills after the first big snowfall.

Colonel Bishop sent out scouts to cover the Sagadahoc Territory in fan-shaped wedges around the settlement. Those families who lived within Merrymeeting proper, and those who still dared to remain on their isolated homesteads, al-

ways had one ear cocked, listening for the alarm bell warning
of another raid. But feelings of security increased when each
scout returned to report the same emptiness in the woods.

It was the second week in March and just about the time
they were scraping the bottom of the pork barrel, when the
ice broke up in the Kennebec with such a shattering and a
roaring that it rattled the ground like an earthquake. There
was a jauntiness to the steps of the men coming down from
the logging camps that day and the women were heard to sing
as they went about fixing supper. But in blew a blizzard that
night, dumping another foot of snow, and it was cold enough
the next morning to make a body's toes jingle. It was The
Maine's peculiar sense of humor, the old hands said. Spring
was still a good ways off yet, but the promise was there.

It had been that sort of winter—full of both promise and
disappointment.

Sam Randolf, the blacksmith, had cursed and spat and
pulled out tufts of his red hair, but by February he thought
the cannon would fire if they were ever to put a slow match
to priming powder. They pointed the cannon upriver and
dared the Abenaki to come back and fight like men, now that
they were ready for them. "We'll bang the bastards stoutly
this time," Sam Randolf said. They hadn't tested the cannon,
though. They didn't have the extra shot.

In spite of the Indian scare, the settlers prepared for the
season's plowing and planting, for farms that lay idle soon
became full of hawkweeds and hawks. When Colonel Bishop
lamented to his wife about the danger of working the isolated
fields, his wife's tart reply was, "You can either die hungry
or you can die scared." Having no answer to that, the colonel
occupied himself with busily scratching his head. Wigless,
he was growing his hair back out and it itched to beat hell.

Obadiah Kemble spent the winter drunk enough to pickle
a hog and brought home a squaw from Cape Elizabeth to
warm his bed. He told anyone who would listen that he'd
never had so much fun in his life. The women said it was
scandalous. The consensus of the men was that Obadiah
Kemble, like a man just out of prison, was doing a little well-
deserved celebrating.

Daniel Randolf caught Meg Parkes alone on the veranda

of the Bishop manor house one schoolday morning and kissed
her on the mouth. She punched him so hard with her fist that
she knocked him on his rump and bloodied his nose. Young
Daniel swore off girls for life.

Every night after saying her prayers, little Tildy Parkes
asked Anne Bishop when her new ma was coming home.
Anne always answered, "In the spring." And every morning
on first waking up, Tildy would say, "Is it spring yet?" So
they built a snowman outside the gate of the stockade. His
eyes were made from the buttons off one of the colonel's old
coats, he had a corncob for a nose and a piggin for a hat,
and Obadiah Kemble carved him a wooden rifle to scare off
the Abenaki. "When he begins to melt," Anne said, "you'll
know it's spring."

Colonel Bishop and the Reverend Caleb Hooker got into
an argument early in November—the day the old timber beast
Increase Spoon brought the message from Dr. Ty. They repeated the argument at least once a week throughout the next
five months. Caleb wanted to set off into the wilderness after
his wife. The colonel accused him of being a cussed fool.

"You don't know where she is or how to get there or how
to find your way back once you did get there!" the colonel
would bellow into Caleb's drawn face. "Dr. Ty has found
her and she's alive. He's lived with those savages and he can
deal with them. You'd only wind up with your hair decorating
some scalp pole, which would do her one hell of a lot of
good now, wouldn't it? And her with a babe on the way . . ."

By March, Calab was looking so miserable the colonel found
himself promising to have a steeple built onto the meetinghouse
first thing in the spring, just in the hopes of seeing one of the
reverend's crooked-tooth smiles. He didn't get one.

Then on the first day of April, the sun came up so warm
the snowman lost one of his arms and his button-eyed face,
in the words of Tildy Parkes, "got all squishy."

Anne Bishop, with the Parkes girls for company, took baskets
out to pick spring greens from the edge of the forest along the
east side of the clearing around the stockade. After living on
hog and hominy all winter, the settlers always eagerly consumed
the first tender shoots of dandelions and fiddlehead ferns.

Tildy, who was still too young to distinguish between what

was edible and what was not, was given her own basket to fill. She squatted in front of a promising weed patch, her hanging sleeves trailing in a bank of soggy snow. "Mrs. Bishop, if these are spring greens, does that mean it's spring?"

Anne Bishop swallowed a sigh, for she knew what was coming.

"Why do you think they call them *spring* greens, you ninny?" Meg snapped. She sat her basket down with a thump and scowled at the world.

Tildy's face brightened. "Then when is my new—"

"Soon," Anne said, rubbing the little girl's head. "Delia will be here soon. You've got to give her time to get here."

Meg shocked them both by suddenly kicking her basket, sending it sailing into the trees. "She's lying!" She whirled on Anne, her face red with fury. Then it crumbled and she burst into tears. "You're lying . . . lying . . ."

Anne fell to her knees, gathering the girl into her arms. "Meg? Why are you crying?"

Loud sobs tore from Meg's throat. "You think I d-don't know she's d-dead. The Indians scalped and k-killed her just like . . . just like they did the others. You're only *saying* she's coming back, but she never will. You're lying . . ."

Anne's large hands clasped Meg's bony shoulders. She held the girl at arm's length so that she could look her in the eye. "Meg, listen to me. I stood right there in my front parlor and heard Increase Spoon say Dr. Ty had found your ma and that she's alive. Mrs. Hooker—you remember how she was going to have a baby? Well, Mrs. Hooker had some trouble on account of the baby, so they couldn't make the journey back right away. But the baby's been born by now and likely they're right this minute on their way." She gave Meg a little shake. "Soon now, honey. Your ma will be home soon."

Meg choked on a swallowed sob and her pointed chin came up. "Delia isn't my ma." Then the chin quivered and trembled, and fresh tears pooled in her eyes. "B-but I w-want her to come home. I w-want her b-back with us. I w-want it just like it was b-before . . ."

Anne hugged the girl tightly to her flat chest. "Oh, honey, she will, she will come back. I promise."

"Mrs. Bishop, why is that man running?"

Anne's head whipped around toward Tildy's pointing finger. At the same time the man spotted them and veered in their direction. As he got closer Anne saw he was one of the scouts her husband had sent out the morning before.

"I saw them!" he cried. "I saw them not more'n five miles upriver. They should be here 'long about nightfall."

At the man's words Anne's heart slammed into her throat and her mouth went instantly dry with fear. *Abenakis!* she thought, and clutched Meg's arms so tightly the girl uttered a tiny cry. Then she noticed the big grin plastered all over the man's face.

"Hank Littlefield, you like to have scared me out of what fews years I have left. What the hell are you blatting about?"

He looked at her as if she were a fool not to know right off. "Why, Dr. Ty. Him and the women. And the baby! Mrs. Hooker had herself a baby boy. Hair the color of cornsilk and a cry that'll curl the skin on your back." He whooped a laugh. "I'm surprised you folk didn't hear it all the way down here."

Anne stood up, taking a girl by each hand. She looked down into their upturned faces. "Tildy, Meg. Your ma has come home."

They arrived just as the sun was sinking into the bay. All of Merrymeeting gathered to meet them. The town had put on an illumination to celebrate the event. A big bonfire burned in the middle of the green and a candle glowed in every window.

Caleb Hooker stood at the forefront of the crowd. He was so tense his whole body quivered. Then Tyler Savitch emerged from the forest. The doctor pulled a small travois behind him, but it was empty and two Indian women walked at his side. Caleb took one faltering step forward. Then he saw the cradleboard in one of the women's arms and the flash of blond hair, and he broke into a run.

He stopped himself just in time from crushing wife and baby into his arms. His eyes devoured his wife's face, noting the bloom of health, the clear, shining gray eyes. "Elizabeth . . . Oh, dear God. Elizabeth . . ."

Smiling shyly, Elizabeth lifted the cradleboard and peeled back the fur blanket. "Reverend Hooker, meet your son. Ezekiel."

Caleb's hand hovered over the baby's face, then he gently stroked one fat cheek with the tip of a finger. Ezekiel burst into a loud wail, and Caleb, horrified at what he'd done, snatched back his hand.

Elizabeth laughed. "I think he's hungry."

Ty's arm had encircled Delia's waist as he led her toward the people waiting for them on the green. Delia frantically searched the group for Meg and Tildy and when she spotted them, a huge grin blazed across her face. At a little nudge from Ty, she broke into a run.

Tildy skipped up to meet her, her fat knees kicking up her pinter. She flung herself against Delia's legs. "It's spring, Delia! It's spring!"

"Why, so 'tis, little puss!" Laughing, Delia swung the little girl up in her arms, settling her down on one outthrust hip. She landed a loud, smacking kiss on Tildy's plump cheek. Then turning, she met Ty's eyes as he joined her and they shared a warm smile full of love and promise.

"Hello, Delia."

Delia spun back around. Meg walked toward her, stiff-legged, her arms folded tightly across her thin chest. She jerked to a stop and her wide brown eyes fastened onto Delia's face.

Delia's smile was dazzling. "Meg Parkes, I swear you've shot up like a bean stalk. Why, I wouldn't be surprised if one day you aren't as tall as your . . . as tall as Dr. Ty here."

Meg took two more tentative steps and, after a moment's hesitation, slipped her small hand into Delia's. Again Delia looked at Ty and tears of happiness filmed her eyes.

"I thought the Indians had killed you," Meg said in a tiny, strained voice.

Delia squeezed her hand. "Oh, Meg, I've such stories to tell you and Tildy. Dr. Ty fought a huge giant of an Abenaki warrior to get me back," she said, causing Ty to scowl and roll his eyes.

"Golly!" Tildy exclaimed, climbing from Delia's arms to assault Ty's legs. "Did you really fight a giant, Dr. Ty? Was it Goosecup?"

He tangled his fingers in her curly blond hair. "He wasn't a giant, Tildy. Only a man."

A loud snort signaled Anne Bishop's arrival. "Don't bother turning modest at this late date in your life, Tyler Savitch." She smacked him lightly on the arm with her open palm. "You sure did take your own sweet time coming home," she said in her most vinegary voice. She had yet even to look at Delia.

"Anne?"

Anne's shoulders jerked. Her head fell back and her lips pressed hard together. "Delia McQuaid. I bet you haven't done a lick of reading all winter." Then her face twisted and a sob burst from her throat and she flung herself into Delia's arms.

Everyone crowded around them then, all talking at once. Delia had Tildy back in her arms and Meg had her fist twisted into the fringe of Delia's buckskin dress, as if she were afraid to let go for fear Delia would be carried off again. They all watched Ty while he tried to answer the questions the men fired at him about the Abenaki and whether he thought they'd be on the warpath again this spring.

After a moment Delia became aware of Anne Bishop's tart voice speaking in her ear. ". . . He's been living up at the logging camp all winter. But Giles sent a fellow up there soon as you all were spotted. I expect he's halfway down the mountain by now and coming at a dead run."

"Anne, what are you talking—" Delia began. But the question died in her throat as she saw Ty's eyes lock on something in the distance behind her and a startling change come over his face. It seemed to drain of blood all at once, like water gushing out of a cask after the bung's been pulled. It left his cheekbones standing out in stark relief and his eyes staring wide and dark. He was immobile with shock . . . and something else.

Fear.

At that instant Anne Bishop's hand fell on Delia's arm. "Why, what did I tell you? Here he comes right now."

"But that's—No . . ." Delia said, denying it even as she turned around, suddenly knowing what she would see.

He walked toward her with his long-legged, hitched stride. He had let his hair grow longer and it swung about his shoulders, flashing golden in the flickering flames of the bonfire. The creases in his cheeks deepened with his wide smile. The biggest smile she had ever seen from him.

"Delia!" he cried.

"Nat?"

Chapter 27

"**D**elia!"

Nat Parkes bore down on her with such exuberance, Delia was afraid he would fling his arms around her. She backed up a step, clutching Tildy tightly to her breast, as if she could use the little girl as a shield. "Nat . . . we thought you were dead."

He halted right in front of her, his eyes intently searching her face. He laughed a bit too loudly. "You do look like you've just seen a ghost."

"The 'Benakis hit Papa on the head!" Tildy exclaimed, tugging Delia's hair to get her attention.

Delia stilled the little girl's hands. She stared at Nat and tried to say something, but her face felt so stiff she was afraid it might break.

After what seemed forever she was finally able to force her mouth open. "But, Nat, I saw . . ." She shuddered even now at the memory. "You were dead. The Dreamer scalped you."

Laughing again, Nat ran a hand through his hair, as if reassuring himself it was still there. "Everyone did at first. But it was the boy from Topsham you saw. He was cold that day and I lent him my coat," he rushed on at her look of disbelief mixed with confusion. "When the Abenakis attacked, I . . ." He flushed vividly. "I ran. I made it as far as the timber line when one of them got me from behind. He smacked me on the side of the head with a war club and I fell backward, into a ravine. I guess it was too much trouble for the savage to come after me for my scalp. Or maybe he got distracted by somebody else. Anyway, I lay there unconscious for a good six hours.'' His glance flickered over to Ty. ''The doc had already started after you by the time I was found. Later, we sent word back with Increase Spoon. I guess you didn't get it?''

Ty said nothing. He didn't move. Delia was afraid to look at him, but then she couldn't stop herself. Slowly, she turned her head.

His face still wore that expression of utter horror, as if he'd been given a glimpse of his own death. Then his eyes clashed with hers and his grew hard with challenge. She wondered what he wanted her to do. Did he expect her to declare their relationship to Nat right here and now, before Nat's children and all of Merrymeeting?

She shook her head slightly, sending him a pleading look, then felt her heart clench with pain as she saw his mouth twist into a bitter, scornful smile.

He spun around and strode off, back toward the wilderness forest from which they had emerged. *Ty!* Delia cried out to him silently as she watched his stiff figure diminish into the tree-shrouded darkness. *Please don't leave me to face this alone. I need you. You're my hus—*

She clapped her hand over her mouth, cutting off the thought the way she would a scream. Her head snapped around and she looked into a pair of pale-lashed, solemn gray eyes. The beaming smile had faded and a more familiar frown was back in place.

''Delia?'' Nat said.

Nat. Her husband.

Delia pushed the spruce beer jug filled with hot water to the foot of the pallet, then tucked the blanket snugly under Tildy's round, dimpled chin. ''You rest your feet on that, little puss. There's frost in the air tonight.'' She brushed the curls off the little girl's forehead and kissed the soft, pink skin.

''But Mr. Snowman lost his arm today, Delia.''

Delia's mouth turned down in a sad, exaggerated frown. ''Oh, poor Mr. Snowman. I'm so sorry. Shall I order the sun not to come out tomorrow so he won't melt off any more of Mr. Snowman's appendages?''

"Don't be silly," Tildy said with a snort, sounding like a miniature version of her caustic big sister. "It's spring now. Mrs. Bishop said when spring came Mr. Snowman would melt and my new ma would come home." Her face suddenly crinkled with worry. "You're home now, Delia, aren't you?"

Delia kissed the smooth forehead again, her throat constricting tightly. "I'm home, sweetheart."

"You won't go away again, will you? Promise?"

Helplessly, Delia's head fell back. Her eyes squeezed shut. "Oh, Tildy, I'm not sure I—"

"But you *have* to, Delia!" Tildy cried, a sob gurgling in her throat. "Please promise. Promise you won't go away again. I didn't like it when you were gone. Papa went up to the camps and he wouldn't come back. And Meg cried a lot, didn't you Meg?"

"Just shut up, Tildy!" Meg snarled, her thin cheeks flushing brightly.

"Don't fight, girls." Delia cupped Tildy's face. Her cheeks were wet and sticky with tears. "Now, you two go to sleep. I'll be here in the morning. I promise you that."

She kissed Tildy again and the little girl pulled her Indian doll from beneath the covers. "Give Hildegarde a good-night kiss too."

Delia obediently kissed the doll's dark face. The she stood up to smooth down the covers, tucking them beneath the hay pallet. The hay rustled as Tildy squirmed, burrowing deeper. The room filled with the smell of summer.

Since December, with Nat up at the logging camp, the Parkes girls had been living with Anne Bishop at the manor house. But tonight Nat had insisted he wanted his reunited family to spend the night alone together in the shed that had been allotted to him within the stockade.

The shed was only one room, but Nat had rigged a curtain down the middle by stringing a blanket on a rawhide rope. Now, Delia dawdled over seeing the girls to bed. She didn't want to go around to the other side of the curtain and face Nat. She didn't want him to start asking her about the winter months spent with the Abenaki, because she wouldn't be able to talk about those times, so full were they of Ty and their love. Their marriage . . .

Oh God, Ty, Ty . . . our marriage.

She knew she had to think about what she was going to do, but she couldn't bear it. The situation was impossible. Nathaniel Parkes was alive and she was married to *him*, not Ty. Ty, the man who owned her heart. Ty, the man she loved above all others, above her own life, above . . .

Anything?

Swallowing a sigh of deep despair, Delia straightened. But as she turned to leave, Meg's voice called out to her from the other side of the room. "Delia? Could you . . . I want to tell you something."

Delia eased down on the very edge of Meg's pallet, careful not to touch the girl, for Meg had so often rebuffed Delia's attempts to show affection that she had long ago learned to maintain a careful distance.

Now she realized instinctively that Meg was ready, more than ready, desperate for a mother's love. And so she leaned over and planted a soft kiss on the girl's thin cheek. "Good night, Meg."

To Delia's astonishment Meg kissed her back. A quick kiss, so light she barely felt it, but a kiss nonetheless.

As Delia pulled away, she saw that Meg was studying her face with enigmatic brown eyes. "Delia? I prayed to God after the Indians took you."

"Thank you, Meg," Delia answered. "I'm sure that's what kept me safe and helped Dr. Ty find me."

Meg swallowed loudly. "I promised God that if you came back, I'd never be mean to you again."

Delia couldn't help laughing. "That was a rather rash promise, wouldn't you say?"

Meg giggled. "I suppose so . . ." Then her laughter dwindled and she plucked nervously at the covers. "I also promised God I would call you Ma if you came back."

Delia covered the girl's hands with her own. "Meg . . . I told you that first day we met I had no intention of trying to take your ma's place. Your ma loved you very, very much, and you loved her, and you must keep that love alive in your heart. I only hope that someday you can come to love me, too. But in a different way, of course. As a special friend."

Delia waited, but Meg remained silent. After a moment,

Delia stood up. But as she turned, Meg's voice came to her, soft and a little fearful. "Good night : . . Ma."

"Sleep well, Meg. I love you."

Delia was startled when she turned around to see Nat standing just inside the curtain, one hand holding it back. After a moment's hesitation, while they stared at each other, she came toward him and he stepped aside, letting the curtain fall into place behind them.

"They missed you," he said.

Delia couldn't reply.

The only furniture in this side of the room was a truncated plank board table and two stools. She saw that Nat had brought a pot of tea and two black jack mugs from the communal kitchen in the blockhouse. She poured the tea into the boiled leather cups and then sat down on one of the stools, gripping the mug in her two hands. Steam wafted up in a soft, moist cloud around her face. She rubbed her palms over the mug's smooth leather side. Her hands were cold. She was cold all over.

Steeling herself, she looked up. The room was lit by a single candle shielded with a hurricane globe that hung from a bracket by the door. It cast harsh shadows across Nat's face, emphasizing the scores on his forehead and the creases around his wide mouth. He stood with rounded shoulders, one hip cocked to take the weight off his stump, his thumbs hooked into the waistband of his breeches. He stared down at the puncheon floor.

Slowly, he looked up and met her eyes. His were serious and perhaps a bit afraid. "I've missed you, too, Delia," he said, so softly she barely heard him. Her disbelief must have shown on her face for he plunged on. "I know I didn't appear to appreciate you much while you were here—"

"I could do nothing right, Nat." The words came out more bitter than she had meant them to, certainly more bitter than she felt.

"No, that's not true," Nat protested, his voice breaking. "You did plenty of things right. Only I was too wrapped up in my own misery to see them."

He came up to her, standing on the other side of the narrow table. She could feel his gaze on her, but she could no longer look at him. She didn't know how to deal with Nat's confession. Battered by conflicting emotions, she was overwhelmed, and so she sat stiff-backed and tight-mouthed, unable even to breathe.

"What is it, Delia?" he asked, a guilty flush darkening his face. "Are you angry with me for not coming after you?"

Delia's hands tightened around the mug. A loud sigh heaved up out of her chest, along with her pent-up breath. "No, of course not. Ty—Dr. Savitch stood a much better chance of finding us. And of bringing us back."

Nat sighed as well, with relief, although his flush remained. "That's what I thought. Although I try to pretend I'm as good as a whole man, the truth is I can't manage walking too far on my wooden foot. And I'm a farmer, not a timber beast. I know squat-all about tracking. I only would have wound up getting myself killed, and Meg and Tildy—I'm all they've got. No, that isn't strictly true now, is it? They've got you."

"But you're their father—"

"And you're their mother." He swung out the stool and dropped into it, leaning his elbows on the table and fixing her with earnest gray eyes. "They love you, Delia. We've seen that tonight. And you love them."

"I do love them, Nat," Delia said hurriedly, relieved to be on this safer ground. "They're wonderful children."

Smiling shyly, he drew a mug in front of him and rubbed his finger around the rim. His eyes flashed up at her, then down again to the table, engrossed in watching his own finger move around and around. "You don't love me though, do you?"

Delia had folded her arms across her chest, her hands clasping her elbows. "Nat, I—"

"Never mind." He pushed the mug so abruptly away from him that tea slopped over the side. "You don't have to explain. I haven't exactly given you cause to love me. Or even like me—"

"I like you, Nat. You're a wonderful man and a wonderful father, a good provider, and—"

"A lousy husband," he cut in, his voice harsh with self-accusation. "At least to you. The Lord knows, we've had our differences before this happened, but it's been a long winter and I've had a lot of time to think up there at the logging camp. I know I've been unfair to you, expecting you to be like Mary when you're . . . when you're yourself. I've thought often about that day we married, about the vows we made to take each other for better and worse. To forsake all others. Yet I've been clinging to Mary as if—''

''Oh no, Nat! You must never forsake Mary—''

''Not forsake the memories of what Mary and I had, I don't mean that. But up till now I've still thought of myself as married to Mary, and that was wrong. Mary was my wife, but she's dead. You're my wife now, my only wife, and that's what I mean by forsaking all others. I'm a man of strong faith, Delia, and I made vows before God. I'd like to start this marriage over and start fulfilling those vows.''

Why now? Delia wanted to rail at him. *Why do you tell me these things now?*

She felt sick—with guilt and pity and dread. She gripped her hands together and forced her chin up. ''Nat, there's something . . . Ty—that is, Dr. Savitch and I—''

A hard knock caused Delia to start so violently that she almost knocked over the pot of tea. The stool scraped loudly across the floor as Nat stood up. With two hitching strides he was pulling open the door.

''Oh hello, Dr. Ty.''

Delia's hand flew to her throat, where her heart now lodged, beating painfully. Nat blocked her view of him; she wasn't sure she could bear to see him anyway. Yet she strained to hear his voice.

His words were flat and toneless. ''Nat. I'd like to speak to my—to Delia.''

Nat stepped back, pulling the door open wider. ''Of course. Come in.''

Ty didn't move. ''In private. I'd like to speak to her in private.''

Delia slowly stood, turning around. Ty was a hulking, faceless shadow standing beyond the doorway. Delia spoke to Nat, keeping her eyes safely on Nat's face. ''I'll only be a few minutes.''

Nat's brow knitted, but with curiosity, not suspicion. ''Sure . . .'' He gestured weakly at the table. ''I'll just have another cup of tea.''

Ty strode away from the doorway and disappeared into the surrounding darkness without looking back, expecting Delia to follow.

She did.

* * *

Elizabeth opened her short gown and put the baby's face to her breast. Ezekiel's mouth opened wide and he latched onto the pink nipple, sucking greedily.

The Reverend Caleb Hooker sat knee to knee on a stool opposite his wife, watching. He was both fascinated and slightly embarrassed. Elizabeth's breast was small but as round as a fall apple, creamy golden in the light cast from the hearth. It occurred to him that he had never before stared so openly at his wife's bared breast. She had always dressed and undressed with her back to him. When they made love, she kept her nightrail on and they did it quickly, in the dark.

A blush crept up Caleb's neck as he remembered the conversation about lovemaking that he'd had with Tyler Savitch all those months before. The doctor had described men suckling at their women's breasts; Caleb had been appalled at the very idea. But now, watching his son feed, he felt a stirring of envy, and desire.

Caleb's blush deepened when he realized Elizabeth had transferred her attention from the top of their son's head to himself. There was an indulgent half-smile on her mouth and a tender cast to her eyes. It was a look he'd never seen before and it confused him.

"You haven't told me what you think of your son," Elizabeth said.

The firelight made the baby's blond head look like a christening cap of spun gold. His lips, which clung so tightly to his mother's nipple, were a deep, rosy pink, the color of persimmon pulp. His fat, ruddy cheeks flexed with his hard sucking. Caleb wondered what it felt like to Elizabeth, to have her nipple tugged on so vigorously. Was it, as Ty had said, pleasurable to a woman?

"He's a beautiful baby," Caleb finally said in awe, his chest constricting tightly. "I feel so strange, though. I can't quite come to grips with the fact that he's mine. My son. To tell you the truth, I'm a little scared."

"I was, too, at first," Elizabeth admitted matter-of-factly, not sounding the least afraid now. It was a startling thought and Caleb had trouble reconciling this calm, self-contained woman with the Elizabeth who had been taken captive and given birth among the savages. During the past months he had been tormented by thoughts of what was being done to her. Now the Elizabeth who had returned seemed a stranger to him.

Caleb leaned forward, studying his clasped hands where they rested on his knees. He swallowed, moistened his lips. "Lizzie? Did they . . . were you treated all right?"

Elizabeth stared into the distance and a frozen expression settled over her face. "In the beginning, it was . . ." She shuddered, disturbing Ezekiel who let out an indignant cry. She switched him to her other breast. "But I don't remember that part very well. Except at night, sometimes, I have nightmares."

Caleb's throat closed around a sob; tears filmed his eyes. "Elizabeth . . ." He blinked hard, trying to hold the tears back. "Will you ever find it in your heart to forgive me?"

Balancing the baby in her lap, she leaned over to stroke his clenched hands. "Caleb, it wasn't your fault."

"But I brought you out here. A thing like this never would have happened to you in Boston." He wrapped his fingers tightly around her hand, clinging to it. He looked up to search her face. "I'm telling Colonel Bishop tomorrow he'll have to find someone else. I'm taking you home, my love."

"I am home. Your ministry is here, Caleb. This is where you belong." Another soft smile lifted her lips. " 'Whither thou goest, I will go.' "

"But the Indian menace isn't over. There could be more raids—"

She pulled her hand away from his, pressing her fingers against his mouth. "I don't think I'm afraid anymore, Caleb. Not so foolishly afraid. Perhaps it's because what I feared would happen to me, happened. And I survived."

He sunk his teeth into his bottom lip, his eyes squeezing shut. "When I think of you in the hands of those savages . . ."

Ezekiel's head dropped from the nipple. Elizabeth got up and tucked him into the cradle Caleb had had Obadiah Kemble make during the winter. It had scalloped sides and flowers carved on the headboard and footboard. The cradle had been a talisman of hope to the reverend, proof of his faith that God would see his wife safely home to him, with their child.

"The Abenaki aren't savages," Elizabeth said. "Oh, they can be cruel to those they call enemy. But then, so can we." From where she stood in the shadows he couldn't make out her face, but he heard an edge of anger in her voice. "Aren't the whipping posts and the gallows cruel? And we were the ones who started the scalping ritual. We English and French and our foolish, wasteful wars against each other over a land that rightfully isn't even ours. Ask any man in Merrymeeting and he will tell you the Abenaki must be wiped out so that we can farm and log the Sagadahoc in peace. Yet they hunted and fished on this land we now call ours long before we did, and in a harmony we will never achieve."

"You would defend them after what they did to you? They are *heathen,* Elizabeth. They don't believe in God, the Father."

"The Great Spirit is our father and the earth is our mother . . ." She came up to stand beside him, staring into the flames. Her hand fell softly to his shoulder. "An Abenaki woman told me that. Her name is Silver Birch and she is the kindest, most generous person I have ever met. She became my special friend even though I was considered—" She laughed, a tiny chirrup that startled Caleb because it was so unexpected. "It was amusing really. They all thought I was Dr. Ty's *awakon.*"

The sound of the guttural Indian word coming from Elizabeth's delicate mouth horrified Caleb. "What?" he croaked.

"His slave. They thought I was Ty's slave."

"Slave!"

She laughed again. "He bought me from my captor for five beaver hides. Silver Birch kept giving me advice on what I could do to entice Ty into taking me as his second wife."

Caleb was so astounded at her glib talk about slavery and being bought that it took a moment for the full sense of her words to penetrate his mind.

When they did his mouth fell open. *"Second* wife."

Elizabeth started guiltily and turned away from him.

"Elizabeth, are you implying—"

She whipped back around, interrupting him and there was a sharp edge to her voice. "You have to understand, Caleb. They thought Nat had been killed. That scalp of blond hair hung from the scalp pole by the torture platform all winter. We saw it every day."

Scalp pole . . . Torture platform . . . Caleb's head reeled. He licked his lips and tried to assume his stern minister's face. "Are you saying Ty and Delia lived openly together in that Indian village as man and wife?"

"Ty saved my life. And our baby's."

"That doesn't mitigate the sin."

"Sin? I thought with sin there had to be intent. They believed Mr. Parkes to be dead. And they were married in a Abenaki ceremony." She knelt at his feet, clutching his thighs. "Oh, Caleb, they are so in love. Never have I seen two people so blessed by love. Together they have found such joy in life. Such joy in each other . . ."

She turned her face aside, but Caleb couldn't miss the color rise high on her face. "Watching them together," she whispered, "you could see . . . you could see the *passion* they shared. Sometimes . . . sometimes I wondered what it would be like, to experience such passion."

Caleb swallowed hard. Since he had found out about her pregnancy, he hadn't dared touch his wife. But he had thought often about all the things Ty Savitch had told him in between hefty swigs of brandy that hot August morning. He had believed Elizabeth would be horrified and disgusted by the acts Ty had so graphically described. But now he wondered . . .

What if, he thought, what if I took her into the bedroom now and undressed her slowly as Ty suggested? What if I kissed and touched her in those places . . . *all* those places . . . ?

But it was Elizabeth who fastened dusky gray eyes onto his face, Elizabeth whose lips parted wetly into a beckoning smile. And in the end it was Elizabeth who spoke.

"Would you make love to me, Caleb?"

Delia pulled herself up the last rungs of the ladder and onto the sentry walk. Ty was there before her, leaning against the round, pointed logs of the palisade, his arms folded in front of his chest, his long, buckskin-clad legs crossed at the ankles. His pose was one of negligent nonchalance, but tension and anger crackled in the air around him like summer lightning.

At five-foot intervals, pine torches burned, thrust into brackets set into the walls. They illuminated Ty's face, showing the dark cast of a day-old beard and the hard, implacable set to his mouth.

Delia wanted to fling herself against his chest. She needed

to be held and comforted by those hard arms. His anger at her hurt and disappointed her, and angered her in turn.

"We shouldn't be meeting like this," she said stiffly. "Nat might suspect—"

"Suspect, hell!" He straightened with a snap, slamming his palms against the peeled logs at his back. "Why doesn't he know by now? When are you going to tell him?"

"I'll tell him when the time is right. I can't just blurt it out at him."

His fingers spanned her upthrust jaw. There wasn't the least thing tender about his touch or in the fiery anger that blazed from his eyes. Yet her whole body hummed with physical awareness of this man.

"You're actually thinking about staying with him," he said, equal measures of bitterness and fury in his voice.

Her eyes clenched shut and she pulled away from him, turning her back. "Oh God, Ty . . . I'm married to him."

He clasped her shoulders, swinging her roughly around to face him again. "You're married to *me!*"

Delia was sure she could actually feel her heart ripping in two. It was like a scream in her mind. She tried to speak and thought she might choke. Surely a person couldn't suffer this much pain and not be dying. "Our marriage, Ty . . . it wasn't real."

He shook her, hard. He pushed his face up against hers and raged at her. "Goddamn you, Delia! It was real to me!"

Then the pine torch beside them hissed and flared, catching the gleam of wetness in his eyes, and she knew his anger was only a facade. He was hurting as much as she.

She looked back at him through her own tears. She touched his cheek, but he jerked his head sharply aside. "Oh, Ty . . ."

Below them the gate to the stockade screeched open and a scout rode through, his horse's hooves clattering on the hard-packed ground. They listened to the gates grind closed, squealing in their straps, and to the thud of the crossbar falling heavily into its brackets. The full moon shining through the spiked palisade cast alternating bars of shadow and light on the ground and on the looming blockhouse. To Delia it made her feel shut in, imprisoned, symbolizing what was happening to her life. She felt suffocated with despair.

Ty's harsh grip on her shoulders relaxed. His hands moved

up and down her arms. His voice was soft, imploring. "Delia, you have to talk to Nat. Explain to him what happened, that he's got to let you go."

She backed away from him, wrapping her arms tightly around her waist as if she had to physically hold herself together. She shook her head, her throat working spastically.

Ty came after her, bringing himself so close she could feel the heat from his body and his breath disturbed strands of her hair. "Tell him, Delia. Tonight. Or I will."

She pushed against him. "Don't you dare! I'll not have Nat hurt for no reason—"

"*Him* hurt! For no *reason!* Jesus, Delia, that is rich. What the hell do you think this is doing to me? Do you seriously think I'm going to stand aside and allow another man to swive my wife?"

She winced at the crudity of his words. To add to all the other emotions that were tearing her apart, there came a sick, chilling dread. Nat had said he wanted to start over. Did that mean he would now want to exercise his husbandly rights on her?

"He won't do . . . do that," she said, more in an effort to convince herself.

Ty snorted a bitter laugh. "He'll do it. He's been without a woman for five months. He'll do it." He clasped her arms, hauling her up against him. "You can't let Nat go on thinking of you as his wife."

She balled up her fists, slamming them against his chest. "I *am* Nat's wife!" She clutched his shirt, clinging to him, and the tears fell at last, in streams down her cheeks, choking her, drowning her. "Ty, Ty, please try to understand. We spoke our vows before God, Nat and I. I made a bargain with him that day we married. He took me out of the gutter, out of a stinking grog shop, and he made me his wife. He gave me a home and respectability, when all I had was a da who drank up my earnings and would sooner beat me as look at me—"

"I was the one who saved you from all that."

Her head snapped up and her eyes changed suddenly from tears to fury. "Oh? The way I remember it, Tyler Savitch, what you did was help yourself to my virtue one afternoon in the Falmouth woods and then hand me over to Nat the next day with the condition that if he didn't like me he could always ship me back—like a cracked teacup or a stocking with a hole in it!"

"Are you going to punish me now for seducing you and then rejecting you? Is that what this is?" He emitted a harsh, choking laugh. "I suppose I deserve it but, Jesus, Delia . . ."

She pressed her face into his neck, her chest heaving with suppressed sobs. "No, no, no . . ." Leaning back, she clung to his shirt, her legs no longer able to support her. "I only mean that Nat doesn't deserve to be deserted now. Although for you, to be with you, I might even be able to do that. But the *children,* Ty. Between their ma dying and me disappearing for five months, Meg and Tildy are terrified of being left alone again. I set out to make them love me, to depend on me, and they do now, even Meg. Think what it would do to them if I just up and vanished out of their lives. Those things I told you on the beach that day still hold true. I don't know if I can walk away from Nat and his children and the promises I made. Not and continue to live with myself."

His hands moved up her back, his fingers becoming entangled in her hair. "But what about me? What about the promises you made to me? You're my *wife.*"

"But I married Nat first and—"

"No! You're mine!" He sucked in a deep, ragged breath. "All right. Forget about the fact that you managed to get yourself married to the both of us—"

"That wasn't my f—"

"Let's discuss love," he went on inexorably, rising anger roughening his voice again as he thumped her in the chest with a stiff finger to punctuate his points. "I love you. You love me. We love each other. Now you tell me. Where do Nat and his girls fit into that little equation?"

She slapped his hand aside. "That hurts."

"Ah, God!" He spun around, flinging his head back. He stared at the sky, his chest heaving. Then his head fell forward and he threw himself back to lean against the palisade. He shoved his fingers through his hair, then let his hands fall helplessly to his sides. "I'm sorry, Delia, but you're scaring me to death. I can't lose you."

Her hands gripped together and she swayed on her feet. "Oh, Ty . . . What are we going to do?"

His voice came to her, barely a whisper. "Come away with me, Delia. Come away with me. Right now. Tonight."

She squeezed her eyes shut, although she couldn't stop the tears. Silence hung long and heavy between them. She could hear his ragged breathing, beneath her own choking sobs.

She opened her eyes to tell him she couldn't do it; she couldn't go away with him no matter how much her heart and soul and body yearned to—but the sight of his face robbed her chest of breath and sent her heart shattering into pieces at her feet.

He hadn't been able to hold back the tears any longer. They filled his eyes and rolled silently down his cheeks. "God . . ." he sobbed. He turned his head aside, ashamed. But the words tore out of him, rough and raw. "Don't choose them over me, Delia. I'm *begging* you. Come away with me . . . Be my wife, Delia. Be my . . . wife . . ."

She would have torn out her heart and presented it to him with her own hands. She would have died for him. She opened her mouth to tell him she would do it, she would leave Nat and the girls and she would go away with him. What did her honor matter when she loved him so?

But then she remembered the frightened sound of Tildy's voice, begging her to make a promise never to leave again. And Meg, making bargains with God and kissing her on the cheek. Calling her Ma . . .

And she couldn't do it.

"Ty, I need more time to think."

He pushed off the wall and brushed past her, striding away so fast he was almost to the ladder before she realized what he was doing.

"Ty!" She ran after him, just managing to grip the sleeve of his shirt. "Ty, don't . . . Where are you going?"

He kept his face turned away from hers. "Leaving you alone to think. To decide whether you love me or not."

"You *know* I love you!"

"Do I?" He swung around, impaling her with his eyes. They glittered at her, hard with bitterness, wet with pain. "Do I?" he demanded again, jerking his arm from her grasp.

And then he was gone.

Chapter 28

❀❀ "Whoa, there . . ." Nat Parkes pulled back on the yoke of the borrowed ox team and the stoneboat slid to a graceful stop. Delia stepped off the flat, runnerless sled, her eyes on the blackened ruins of a chimney that thrust up like a pointing finger amid scorched beams and charred wood.

"I raked through it all last fall," Nat said, noting the direction of her gaze. "I was able to salvage a few pots, but that was about it."

"Hildegarde was saved!" Tildy exclaimed, clutching the Indian doll tightly to her chest as she scooted off the end of the sled. "Hildegarde didn't burn to death."

"That's only 'cause you took her to school with you the day the Abenakis raided," Meg said petulantly. "I wish I had thought to bring my top."

"Your da'll carve you a new top," Delia said, forcing a smile. "Won't you, Nat?"

Nat grunted. Delia looked at his wan, lined face and, to the despair and wrenching sense of loss that was squeezing her own heart on this beautiful spring morning, there was added a piercing melancholy. She thought sadly of Mary's things—the lantern clock, the sampler, the spinning wheel. They were all Nat had had left of Mary and their ten years together and now they, too, were gone forever.

She laid her hand on his arm. "I'm so sorry, Nat."

He shrugged, pulling away from her. "It can be rebuilt now that spring is here. Matter of fact, Colonel Bishop is organizing a raising bee for us next week." He walked back to the stoneboat and began unloading a heavy iron cauldron. "Meantime there's work to be done. I'll get you girls started on the sugaring—Meg, if you'll bring along those sap pails and spiles—then I'll begin on the fields. Seems like the earth spewed out enough stones to choke a whale this winter."

Winter frosts always heaved stones and boulders to the surface of the fields and before any planting could be done, the big ones, in the words of The Maine farmers, "had to be twitched out." The flat-bottomed stoneboats slid easily over a ground made soft and soggy by rapidly melting snow, and were especially useful for hauling away the rocks cast up by winter.

The time for stone-clearing coincided with sugaring time. The sap flowed just right for tapping in the big maples when the nights were still cold enough to freeze sharply and the days warm enough to thaw freely. Nat, with patience and even an occasional smile, showed Delia how the sugaring was done. He chose a big maple, over twelve inches in diameter, and bored a hole with an auger into the sunny side of the trunk, three feet from the ground. Then a spile, or spout, was tapped into the hole and a pail was hung over the end of the spile.

"I'll build you all a big fire in the clearing for the cauldron," Nat said. "When the pails get full, you and the girls can haul them back on the hand sledge and empty them into the kettle." He grinned at her. "There ought to be maple syrup enough to swim in."

Delia tried to return his smile, but she just couldn't manage it.

Nat nodded. "Well then . . ." He waved vaguely over his shoulder. "I'll be over yonder. Should you need me."

Delia nodded back at him. They stood there staring and nodding at each other until Delia, feeling foolish, turned away.

There was a strained awkwardness between them this morning, perhaps because they had never finished their conversation of the night before. When she had returned from that devastating meeting with Ty, Delia couldn't bear looking at Nat, let alone discussing their future as husband and wife. She had pleaded exhaustion and retired to a small hay pallet in one corner of the shed, but she knew Nat had noted her reddened eyes and tear-swollen face and he must have wondered at their cause. But it wasn't in Nat to pry and so he had said nothing. In the end neither had she.

It seemed Delia's very bones ached with sadness that morning and her stomach echoed with a hollow emptiness that was like a hunger which could never be satisfied. It was as if someone she loved dearly had died. What had died was the idyllic love she and Ty had shared. No matter whether she decided to stay with Nat and his girls as her conscience insisted, or to disappear with Ty back into the wilderness as her heart pulled her—whatever she did, the result would be misery.

She couldn't imagine living out the rest of her days without Ty. Once, she had thought it would be enough to wake every morning with the chance of seeing his face that day. But that was before she had awakened of a morning to see his beloved face beside hers on the pillow. His eyes, heavy lidded with sleep, had glowed with love, and she had pressed her lips to his beard-roughened cheek. She had stretched and felt the pleasant ache between her thighs, legacy of the night before, a tender reminder of his rapturous lovemaking. A dream had come true for her, an impossible dream. Ty loved her and had made her his wife. How could she ever give up that dream?

And yet . . . yet . . .

Yet there was Tildy, awaiting the first drop of sap from the end of the spile, a look of fierce concentration mixed with excited anticipation animating her face. Just then it appeared and she squealed with delight. "It's flowing, Delia! The sap is flowing! *Now* can we have some maple candy?"

"Patience, little puss," Delia said, laughing helplessly, yet feeling close to tears as well. "The candy will be a time in coming yet." Her eyes met Meg's and they shared a smile.

Two spots of color, as bright as polished apples, dotted the young girl's cheeks, and her brown eyes glistened like two dark chestnuts. The pinched look was gone from her mouth which curved into a smile. Delia had never seen Meg Parkes look so happy, so at peace.

These children, Delia thought. How can I bear to hurt these children?

She looked upriver toward Ty's clearing. She felt certain he was there right now, raking through the ruins of his cabin. Ruins, she thought. Everything was in ruins. Their homes, their lives. Their love.

Tears formed in her eyes and her heart cried out to him. *Oh, Ty, Ty, my love, my life . . . what are we going to do?*

Delia was wrong.

Ty was ten miles away from the burned rubble of his cabin. He moved through the forest with the silent toe-in walk of the Indian. What he had left in the world he carried with him—his rifle, shot pouch and powder horn, a tomahawk and hunting knife. In a small haversack over his shoulder he carried some food and a change of buckskins. All of his healing herbs and most of his instruments had been lost in the fire that burned his cabin, but those that he'd salvaged he brought with him.

In his heart he carried memories.

If I am never to have you again after this night, this moment, you will remain wife of my soul. Keeper of my heart.

He had meant those words when he had said them, that night of their marriage as they stood outside his wigwam and watched the northern lights. But he never thought he'd be called upon to prove it so soon. Or that it would be so hard.

In the beginning he had almost lost her for fear of loving her. Then he had conquered his fear and let himself love her, only to wind up losing her in the end. But at least this way the loss was of his own choosing. Even in the midst of all his own anger and pain, he had seen in her tormented face last night how her heart was being torn between her love for him and her tender regard for Nat's motherless children. He realized then he had in his power the ability to give her a gift worthy of his great love for her. He would spare her the pain and anguish of having to make an impossible choice by making it for her.

He would leave her.

At the moment he was heading northeast, following the Kennebec because the snow was thinner here, where the sun penetrated more easily through the thick bower of trees. A false euphoria drove him along, the relief from having made and then carried out a dreaded decision. Pain was there, but it was deep within him, like a bruise on the bone. It throbbed below the surface of his consciousness. He hoped that by the time it became full-fledged agony he would be so far away that the temptation to return would be easier to resist. Lord knows, he thought, with a hollow, inner laugh, he was not a man made for self-sacrifice.

He was tempted now, but he wouldn't go back to Norridge-wock. The memories of Delia and their love would be too hurtful there, the way back to her too easily traveled. He would follow the river for a while longer and then strike out west. Assacumbuit had once told him that the land the Yengi called America stretched west all the way to the edge of the world, to another ocean where the sun slept at night. He thought he would just keep on walking until he found the end of the world. There he could be alone with his thoughts of her, his dreams. His memories.

He stopped where the Kennebec forked, although he wasn't the least bit tired. Several times, when Ty was a boy, Assacumbuit had made him run for a day and night without water or rest. Once, when he was twelve, he had been sent naked into the forest with nothing, not even a knife, and he had emerged a week later, clothed and so well fed he had brought his father back meat as a gift. But then, when he was six, he had marched from Kittery to Quebec with a pack as big as he was strapped to his back. His body had been toughened on that march, and so had his mind. He had lost loved ones before and survived, again and again.

And I'll survive this, he told himself. I'll have to. A man, he had been taught over and over by life, endured what he had to and went on.

He sat on a rock at the river's edge, his rifle cradled in his lap. The sun was a warm caress against his face. A strong breeze rippled the water and played the tree boughs like harps. It carried with it a smell of grease and poorly cured hides.

Someone was coming.

It was two people actually and whoever they were, they

made little noise. But Abenaki warriors would have made no noise it all. They had to be timber beasts then. The question was whether they were English and probably friendly, or French and possibly not so friendly.

With slow nonchalance Ty primed and loaded his rifle. He laid it across his lap, his finger curled loosely around the trigger, and waited.

They emerged around a bend in the river five minutes later—Increase Spoon and his girl-squaw. She was practically bent double, enveloped by the pile of hides on her back. Increase didn't carry a thing except for his rifle. He grinned when he saw Ty, showing black gaps in his teeth.

"Ye be huntin' purdy far from home, aren't ye, Doc?" he called out when he got within hailing distance.

Ty waited until the old trapper had pulled abreast of him. "Looks like you had yourselves a good winter there, Increase," he said, nodding at the pile of beaver furs. The young girl stared stoically ahead, but Ty could see that the weight of the pack was causing the tumpline to cut deeply into her forehead. At least she was no longer suffering from the effects of scurvy.

"We be on our way to Mrs. Susannah's trading post up t' Falmouth way. Did ye hear she was getting hersel' hitched up?"

"No, I hadn't. Who's she marrying?" Ty asked, not really caring.

Increase shrugged."Some feller fum Wells. A cooper, he be." He combed his beard with his fingers as he studied Ty hard, a look of confusion knotting his dirt-pitted face. "Ye know I was t' deliver a message t' ye. Now what—ayup, I remember what 't was now. Nat Parkes never did get hissel' kilt and scalped by the Injuns. 'Twas some other feller."

Ty sighed. "I got that message. Thanks anyhow, Increase."

Increase noticed Ty's eyes on his squaw. "Yon Nesoowa's been right as rain since ye had a look at her that day at Falmouth Neck, Doc. I kept her pie-eyed on spruce beer all winter, didn't I, gel?" He smiled fondly at the young Indian girl and she looked shyly at Ty, shifting the heavy pile of furs further up onto the broad part of her back.

"Couldn't you at least share the burden with your woman?" Ty asked.

"Huh?"

"Help her to carry that load of peltry."

"What for?"

Ty sighed again.

Increase wet his lips. "Ye wouldn't by chance got any corn squeezing's along wi' ye?"

"No, sorry." Ty removed the pipe he had stuck through the band around his fox-skin cap and fished in the haversack at his feet for his squirrel skin tobacco pouch. He packed the bowl with the aromatic leaves. "I can offer you a smoke though."

"Kinnikinnik?"

Ty shook his head. "Plain tobacco."

Increase looked disappointed, but he took the proffered pipe. Like the Indians, the trapper carried fire with him, hanging from his hunting strap in the form of a smoldering punk enclosed within two large clamshells and wrapped in a deerskin bag. He used the tinder now to light the pipe.

"Ye know, I'm beginnin' t' feel like a postrider," he said around the bit in his mouth. "What wi' all them messages I been carryin' backwards and forwards. You and the Corn'l Bishop an' now some feller over t' Penobscot has got me runnin' every whichaway."

"What message are you carrying now?" Ty asked, mainly to keep the conversation going.

"Boston done sent a bang-boat up the Penobscot Bay couple weeks back. She leveled the mission at Castine with her cannon an' managed t' kill the old black robe, Sebastien Râle, in the process. Now them Abenakis over thataway are scalpin' mad. They've taken up the hatchet, all official-like, after a big powwow of all the tribes, and they're buildin' themselves scalin' ladders so's even the forts won't be safe."

Ty snarled with disgust at colonial policy. If anything was sure to rile up the Abenaki against the settlers, it was murdering their favorite French priest. "Do you know where they're aiming to strike first?"

"Well, ye know better'n most folk how them Abenakis've never been predictable. But if I was t' guess, I'd say Merrymeeting, only 'cause there's been some crazy Injun mouthin' off lately at the powwows 'bout a vision he had or somethin' and— Hey, what the hell?''

Increase Spoon stared with astonishment at the empty rock where a second ago Dr. Tyler Savitch had appeared to be relaxing, lazily taking in a little sun. Increase looked around him—up the river where a smelt jumped, down the deer trail that led into the forest, both empty except for a squirrel who stared back at him, whiskers twitching. Finally, he looked down at the smoking pipe in his hand to be sure he hadn't dreamed the whole thing.

"Now what in blazes d' ye think set him afire?'' he asked of no one in particular.

Shrugging, he resumed his way downriver. His squaw, Nesoowa, walked silently behind him.

One half of his face he painted white, the other black so that he resembled a victim burning at the stake. It was fitting, for in the visions he saw his own death by fire. He welcomed his death with a singing heart. He would immolate himself so that his people might survive; it was a fitting way for a warrior to die.

The spirits visited him all the time now. He no longer needed the Yengi spirit water to summon them. They showed him the same dream, over and over, so that he would not forget or betray his destiny.

He understood the dream clearly, as clearly as if it were written in the pictographs of his people's language. The rivers of Yengi who covered the earth were led by *lusifee,* the wildcat. But in the dream *lusifee* was slain by *malsum,* the wolf, and the Yengi tide receded, back into the ocean from which it had come. In the dream, the wolf killed the panther and the Dawn People regained their lost hunting grounds.

The Dreamer's eyes fluttered closed. He saw the face of *lusifee*—her tangled black hair, her pointed chin, those catlike glowing, golden eyes.

Still with his eyes closed, he took the red ochre and drew on his chest the image of the snarling wolf, totem of his tribe. Throwing back his head he gave the wolf's howling cry. "I am the Dreamer!'' he sang. "I am the Dreamer, leader of the wolf people. It is we who will kill the mighty *lusifee*. It is we who will drive back the Yengi tide!''

The Dreamer was aware on the periphery of his entranced consciousness that most of the Abenaki tribes had once again taken up the hatchet against the Yengi. But the fate of the Dawn People would never be decided in that way. The spirits had spoken. It would be the Dreamer, and the Dreamer alone, who would bring *lusifee* back to the Norridgewocks where she would be burned as was her fate before Bedagi had interfered. She would be destroyed and the Yengi would leave the land of the Dawn People, forever.

Why *lusifee*, the totem spirit of the Yengi, would choose to inhabit the body of a worthless woman, the Dreamer knew he would never fully understand. But then, the Yengi were an aberrant race; his father had once told him of some Yengi tribes which were ruled by female sachems. If they could choose women as their chiefs, then he supposed it was possible for a guardian spirit to inhabit the body of one of their females. That she was no ordinary woman, he had seen with his own eyes, for she had the courage, the ferocity of a warrior.

She was *lusifee* and she must be destroyed.

So the Dreamer prepared himself both for battle and for death. He smeared the bear grease over his body, he painted his chest and face, he sang his dream song to the heavens. He prepared himself to return to the place where he had captured *lusifee* the first time.

The visions had promised she would be there and the visions never lied.

The air was sweet with the odor of boiling sap. When Nat Parkes paused in his work of twitching rocks onto the stone-boat, he thought he could almost hear the sap dripping into the pails.

From time to time he had stopped and gone over to give Delia and the girls a hand hauling the filled buckets on the ledge over to the boiling kettle. He kept the fire fed with wood, too. He did these chores for Delia, to make the sugaring easier for her. He had things he needed to make up for with Delia. A lot of things.

He didn't clear away all the stones from the field; some he left in scattered heaps. He had read in his almanac that stones made good manure, as they supposedly leached into the soil and the ground around them was said to sprout three times the crops of ordinary dirt. Earlier Delia had asked him about the heaps of stones and when he explained—a bit sheepishly, for the theory sounded like an old wive's tale even if it had come out of the almanac—she had actually smiled. He realized it pleased him to make her smile.

He looked for her now and saw that she was among the maples, tapping in more spiles. The girls were tending to the fire. With everyone's attention focused elsewhere, Nat slipped away from the stoneboat and followed a familiar path up the hill behind where the barn used to be, before the savages had burned it.

The marker remained untouched, although weathered by a winter exposed to the elements. Last year at this time she had been dead but three weeks. The stone had been freshly carved, the letters white scars in the smooth, gray granite, the dirt covering the grave mulchy brown and raw. Now the letters were black and the granite was pitted and scarred with tiny cracks. The ground had sunk at bit around the stone and sprouts of weeds were coming up through the patchy snow.

Removing his hat, he knelt beside the marker, tracing the letters of her name with his fingers.

Mary . . .

You know the course of my thoughts these last weeks, while I've waited for Delia to come home. For I could feel you there, listening to me. It's not that I love you any less . . .

He shut his eyes for a moment, then sat back on his haunches. He dangled his hat between his outstretched knees, his wrists resting on his thighs. *Mary, I'm going to have the house rebuilt next week and Obadiah Kemble is making us a new bed. And, Mary, I intend . . . I intend for Delia and me to share that bed as man and wife. If this hurts you, then I'm truly sorry, for you know in ten years I never once set out to deliberately hurt you. And I certainly never thought of taking another woman to bed, or even looked at one in that way. But I've considered it and I've decided maybe where you are now you don't much care about such things as the pleasure*

*of the flesh anymore. I hope that's true because . . . because
there's more to marriage than two people sharing the same
house, Mary, and I'm wedded to Delia now.*

He swallowed, rubbing his mouth with the back of his
hand. Slowly he stood up. *But it won't change how I feel
about you. And I hope . . . I hope it won't change how you
feel about me.*

A terrible doubt blossomed in Nat's mind, a doubt whether
the Mary he knew and loved felt anything at all anymore.
But the thought was too terrible to contemplate and he ham-
mered it down ruthlessly. If he believed for just one moment
that nothing of Mary existed beyond the bones in this grave
he—

A piercing scream split the air and Nat flung his head up
in terror. For a moment he was sure the sound had come
from the grave at his feet.

Then the scream came again and a cry of *"Delia!"* in
Meg's voice, and he spun around, stumbling and tripping in
his haste to get back down the hill.

Delia struggled in the arms of an Abenaki savage. As he
tried to drag her back with him, deeper into the forest, her
feet left furrows in the soggy snow. It was the girls who
screamed. Delia fought her abductor in awful silence, claw-
ing at the arm that had a stranglehold around her neck.

For one shameful, paralyzing moment Nat's feet slowed as
fear squeezed his chest. Like a fool he had left his musket
back on the stoneboat, too far away from him to retrieve it
and shoot the savage before he disappeared into the woods
with Delia. Nat looked frantically around him, wondering if
more Indians lurked within the forest, ready to spring out at
him.

Yet he was running again, toward the naked, painted man
who wrestled with Delia . . . with no thought now but to
save her.

Lusifee fought with the spirit of the wildcat that inhabited
her soul and the Dreamer was shocked by the weakness of
his response. His arms felt weighted to the earth with stones.
His legs trembled with the effort it took to drag the Yengi
woman with him. His breath labored in his chest, like mourn-

ful, dying gusts of wind, and he shook his head to rid it of the blurry film that covered his eyes.

The Dreamer saw the tall, yellow-haired man lumbering awkwardly across the fields and he felt at the thong around his waist for his scalping knife. *Lusifee* almost broke free of him then and he saved his grip on her only by tangling his fingers in her hair. He threw back his head to utter his war cry, but he thought he might have laughed instead.

The man with the yellow hair came on. He had no part in the vision; he was a gnat, easily squashed. The Dreamer drew back his hand and flung the knife at the man's chest, but his arm felt strangely weak and his aim was wobbly and low. He would have missed altogether, but the man's left foot seemed to collapse beneath him in that instant, so that he lurched sideways, flailing his arms to regain his balance and throwing himself directly into the path of the knife.

The knife buried itself in the man's stomach.

Still, the man came on, several more stumbling steps before he slipped and collapsed on the trailing edge of a bank of melting snow. "Nat!" *Lusifee* screamed, tearing free from the Dreamer's grasp. She flung herself toward the fallen man. "Nat!"

It wasn't a noise that made the Dreamer's head snap up then, but a premonition as strong as any vision. He saw a spirit in the guise of a man emerge from the trees to the right of him. He saw the spirit's long arm come up to point at his chest. He saw a flash of flame . . .

He never heard the shot that killed him. But if he had he would have likened it to the sound of thunder.

Ty took the precious few seconds necessary to reprime his rifle and ensure the Dreamer was dead before he pulled Delia off Nat. He gave her a little shove toward the sap kettle where Meg and Tildy were huddled together, sobbing hysterically.

"Get the girls and get to the blockhouse now, Delia! Tell Colonel Bishop an Abenaki war party is headed for Merrymeeting."

Delia looked down at hands that were covered with blood

She turned hollowed, shocked eyes onto Ty's face. "Ty . . . Nat is . . ."

He shook her slightly. "Delia! You've got to warn Merrymeeting and get those girls safely inside the stockade." He shook her again, harder. "Do you understand?"

She nodded, her teeth sinking into her lower lip.

"Good." Seizing her jaw, he landed a hard, swift kiss on her mouth, then whirled her around, sending her forward. "Now run, Delia-girl. Run like God Almighty!"

She ran. He watched her until she reached the girls, picking Tildy up into her arms and taking Meg by the hand, until all three of them had started down the cart tracks toward the village.

He knelt beside Nat. Gray eyes, dark with pain, fastened onto his. "Doc? My stomach hurts."

"You've got a knife in your belly, Nat," Ty said. He wished he had some mandrake root to ease the man's pain. "I'm going to have to pull it out of you."

Nat jerked a nod on a sobbing breath. "Delia . . . ?"

"She's all right. So are your girls . . . Bear down, Nat. This is going to hurt like hell."

The knife was buried deep and it came out hard, and Ty was afraid he'd killed the man. But Nat's breaths still came, in stertorous gasps, in between his screams. Ty staunched the welling blood with his wadded-up shirt, listening all the while for the sound of the fort's warning bell, which would mean that Delia and the girls had arrived safely, although he knew that even at a fast run it would take them at least a half hour to get there.

Ty thought he would have to build a travois to carry Nat to Merrymeeting until he noticed the stoneboat in a nearby field. He led the ox team over to Nat and as gently as he could lifted the man onto the sled. The movement had started Nat screaming again, but once on the stoneboat the screams faded, and Ty hoped for Nat's sake that he had fainted.

Nat sighed and his head lolled. "Mary . . ."

"Hang on, Nat. You're going to make it if you just hang on."

Nat's hand flopped as he tried to lift it and his glazed eyes cleared a moment, fastening onto Ty's face. "Tell Delia . . .

sorry. Was going to make it up to her . . . Never got the chance . . .''

Ty squeezed the man's shoulder. "You tell her yourself. When we get to Merrymeeting."

Nat's eyes closed and he drifted on a tide of agony. The pain was a living thing in his gut. He could picture it, eating at him the way tongues of flame ate at a pitch-covered log. It sizzled, crackled, burned. It was too much to bear and he hoped he would die soon.

Mary . . .

He felt so close to her now. For the first time since she had died he thought he could actually hear her voice. And the image of her, which had been fading of late, was suddenly in sharp focus before his eyes, as if she leaned right over him, her face mere inches from his. He was sure he felt her lips brush his forehead. *I'm coming,* he told her. *Soon, soon . . .*

For a brief moment the agony faded and lucidity returned and in that moment he felt guilty for wanting to die. He would be leaving his children, a wife. But the guilt was small compared to the fierce yearning to have the unbearable pain stop . . . and the joy, the incredible joy and anticipation at the knowledge that soon, soon he would see his Mary. They would be together again. This time forever.

Bells. In the far distance he heard bells. How odd, he thought, that there would be bells in heaven. The blue sky overhead began to blaze with white light and the ringing grew louder. The white light was cold, very cold. But he didn' mind because the cold was numbing the fiery pain in his belly. Soon, he thought, soon, soon . . .

"Mary . . ."

Ty heard Nat's roughened whisper and glanced down words of reassurance on his lips. Words that died when he saw the open, lifeless eyes.

The stockade's warning bell carried far on the clear sprin; air. Settlers from the other nearby farms streamed out int the road on foot, horseback, and carts. They carried wit them the things that they would need for a long siege. Th oxen were not known for being fleet of foot, but the roa was muddy and deeply carved with ruts and the sled move easily over it. Soon the Merrymeeting green came into viev then the mast house, the Bishops' manor house, the meeting-house and parsonage, and finally the stockade.

The palisade gates were open for the streams of refugees, but men prowled the sentry walks, rifles pointing into the surrounding wilderness forest. Inside the walls the stockade resembled an anthill that had been knocked over, with people scurrying in all directions, seemingly to no purpose.

The blockhouse door banged open as Ty drove through the gates and Delia stumbled out. She paused on the threshold, her gaze flying first to Nat's lifeless body on the sled and then to Ty's face. He could hear screams coming from inside the blockhouse—Meg crying, "Let me go!" over and over.

He met Delia halfway. He longed to take her into his arms, but he was afraid she would misinterpret his motivation. In-stead, he tried to give her comfort with his eyes. "He died on the way here, Delia. I tried, but there never really was a chance."

She reached up and stroked his cheek. "Thank you, Ty," she said softly. And then she went to Nat.

She sat on the sled beside him and picked up his hand, bringing it to her lips, and she cried. Ty turned his back on them, but not out of jealousy. Out of understanding.

The sun went down and it grew cold. In the windows of the sheds beneath the walls, lacy white ferns of ice grew in the corners of the windowpanes. The moon came up, round and white, like a hard-packed ball of snow. It bathed the surrounding forest in a bright, silvery light.

A scout had returned just before sunset. He had seen the Abenaki war party—over two hundred strong. They were stopping to raid a few isolated farms and trappers' cabins along the way, but there was no doubt Merrymeeting was their main objective.

Tyler Savitch, Colonel Bishop, and Sam Randolf were grouped around the cannon. The weapon's long, black nose pointed menacingly east, the direction from which the Pe-obscot Abenaki were expected to come.

His face looking ruddy as a scrubbed beet in the torchlight, Colonel Bishop glared at the cannon as he heaved a dubious sigh. "Are you sure this thing'll fire, Sam?"

"Hell, no." Sam kicked so hard at one of the spoked iron wheels, he almost knocked his hat off. "For all I know, the damn thing could be no more use than a lace-trimmed nightie. But, aye, I think she'll fire."

The colonel stared over the pointed palisade walls, into the dark, empty night. He pulled his thick lips with his fingers. "We've only shot enough for two rounds. Depending on their numbers, we might not be able to kill enough of them by firing only twice."

"We don't need to kill all that many of them," Ty said. He wrapped his hands around a couple of the logs, and the tendons in his wrists stood out, belying the relaxed tone of his voice. "The threat of the cannon should be enough." He tried to explain the Abenaki method of fighting a war. "They don't believe in dying gloriously on the battlefield. To them the object is to kill as many of the enemy as they can while surviving themselves to fight another day. They don't see running off as a reflection of their courage, so if killing us looks to be too costly, they'll simply fade back into the wilderness and strike somewhere else."

Colonel Bishop's hand fell heavily on Ty's shoulder. "I hope to God you're right, doc. When do you think they'll hit us?"

"Tonight sometime. Most likely just before dawn."

Ty moved down the sentry walk, away from the cannon. He carried his rifle in the crook of his arm, primed and ready to fire. He would use it when the time came because he didn't want to die and he didn't want Delia to die. But he also knew that every time he pulled the trigger, every time he saw an Abenaki fall, he would feel terror that it was Assacumbuit, his father, whom he killed.

He felt more torn than ever before in his life, more torn than during those first frightening, lonely months after Assacumbuit had brought him to Wells and turned him over to his grandfather. Was he Tyler Savitch, the Yengi physician? Or was he Bedagi, son of an Abenaki sachem? Now, as then, the choice seemed to have been made for him. He was Yengi by blood and so that was the life he must live, the life he must fight and now kill for.

He leaned sideways against the rough wooden wall an

looked up at the sky. It glittered with stars and the broad band of milky light wove across it, like a fat, luminescent eel swimming just beneath the surface of a black lake. The Abenaki believed the Milky Way was the star trail to the spirit land. If the men of Merrymeeting had their way, there would be many an Abenaki warrior on that trail come morning.

"Ty . . . ?"

He straightened and turned slowly around. She came to him, his love. The skin around her eyes was drawn and pale. Her mouth trembled. Silently he opened up his arms and she came to him.

She leaned against him, her cheek to his chest, and heaved a deep, sad sigh.

"How are the girls taking it?" Ty asked.

Her arm wrapped around his waist, she burrowed deeper. "I don't think little Tildy really understands. But Meg . . . she cried herself to sleep. Why did he have to die, Ty?"

"We didn't wish his death," he said, answering her unspoken thought. He supposed some guilt would always be there, for the both of them, because Nat's dying had given them back their love. No, they would have always had their love. Nat's dying had given them back their future, and their joy.

He tensed his arm, hugging her to him in silent understanding. After a while, a long, long while, she raised her head.

She traced his lower lip with her finger. "I love you, Tyler Savitch."

He kissed her. Not with passion and not with hunger, although that was there, as always, deep within his heart.

He kissed her with love.

They poured out of the woods in the wavering gray light of false dawn, their bloodcurdling war cries cracking and splitting the frigid air.

Sam Randolf held the slow match to the powder in the top of the breech. Colonel Bishop stood beside him, his hand raised in the air. "Wait, wait," he said softly. "Let them get closer. Make it count, Sam, make it count . . ." He chopped his hand down. "Now!"

The cannon exploded, discharging a load of musket balls, nails, and other bits of scrap iron into the swarming mass of Indians and scaling ladders. The shot boomed like thunder across the sky, bouncing over the water, and stinking black smoke choked the air. The war cries turned to screams.

Coughing from the smoke and cursing as his flesh came into contact with the hot metal, Sam Randolf swung the barrel around to load the second shot.

But Colonel Bishop's hand fell on his arm, stopping him. "Never mind. Look, the doc was right. They're running!"

Sam whooped. "We licked the pus clean outta them with just one shot!" he cried. Then he reloaded the cannon anyway and everyone waited in tense silence, in case the Abenaki were of a mind to come back.

Ty didn't wait. He climbed down from the sentry walk and emerged through the palisade gates, into the clearing, where a dozen bodies sprawled like scattered bowling pins.

He went to see it any still lived. And if he knew them.

Epilogue

Tyler Savitch stuck a carrot into the middle of the snowman's face, then stepped back, the better to survey the overall effect. Unfortunately, the carrot was withered and gray and bent in the middle. It gave the snowman a slightly sinister cast.

Tildy giggled, tugging at the fringe of Ty's buckskin coat. "He looks silly. That snowman looks silly with that nose."

Ty glanced down at his adopted daughter. A smile of pure joy played around his mouth—a smile it seemed he had been wearing without respite for the last eleven months. "I'm afraid I must agree, little one," he said, imbuing his voice with the proper degree of gravity. "Perhaps we ought to go inside and think what to do about it over a noggin of hot chocolate."

Tildy ran back toward the house, shouting in her excitement and frightening a rabbit that had hopped, twitching cautiously, into the clearing. Although a late March blizzard had dumped deep drifts over the land, the little girl moved easily on the path that Ty had shoveled just that morning.

Ty was proud of the house. It was a full two stories tall, newly built last spring. They'd had a raising bee the week right after their wedding. Ty had teased Delia, saying he was building the house big enough for *all* their children—Meg and Tildy and the dozen babies he planned to give her.

Ty had just started after Tildy when the door flew open and Meg came hurtling out. Her hair blew in wild brown tangles around her face and she clutched at her flour-dappled apron with two tight fists.

"Dr. Ty! It's coming! The baby's coming!"

For a moment Ty stood frozen, utterly incapable of moving. His heart slammed up into his throat and he couldn't breathe. He'd long ago lost count of the number of babies he had delivered, yet suddenly he was as frightened as an apprentice physician on his first case.

"Dr. Ty!" Meg cried again.

Ty almost slipped on the packed snow in his haste to get inside the house. He sent Meg and Tildy upstairs to play, then threw open the door to the keeping room, sending white clouds swirling into the air from the pie dough that lay amid a dusting of flour on the table. He tripped over a broom left lying in the middle of the floor and almost fell into a washtub full of soaking copper pots. For the past two days it seemed Delia had been caught up in a frenzy of wifely activity and it was driving Ty crazy because he was terrified she would strain herself or hurt the baby.

But at the moment she sat fairly quiet on a stool before the fire, cursing like a tavern wench at the knots in the embroidery of a sampler she was trying to fashion . . . looking radiantly beautiful and immensely pregnant.

She glanced up and laughed at the expression on her husband's face. "Now don't you go getting all nervous on me, Tyler Savitch. I'm scared enough as 'tis without my doctor having a fit of the vapors."

He had hurried over to kneel beside her, rubbing his hands over the monstrous mound of her stomach. "When did you feel the first pain? Was it just now?"

She caressed his bent head. "Oh no," she said calmly. "Sometime after breakfast, I think."

"Christ, that was hours ago! Why didn't you say something?"

"I thought I was only having a touch of indigestion from that lumpy porridge you fixed us this morning."

There was a note of hysteria in Ty's laughter. He heard it and tried to calm himself by tensing his jaw so hard he appeared to be scowling. Straightening, he kissed her roughly on the mouth. "I've never had a fit of the vapors in my life," he stated, and hoped she didn't notice how his hands trembled. "Only women get those."

"Hunh. You men think—" Suddenly a spasm of pain twisted her face and her whole body contorted.

"Jesus," Ty groaned. For a moment he almost thought his stomach had cramped in sympathy.

"That was a big one," Delia said, panting, a moment later.

He smoothed the hair off her damp forehead. "That's good, Delia-girl. Don't fight them." He gave her a shaky grin. "I'm doing enough of that for the both of us."

He helped her into the room he had prepared downstairs, undressing her and seeing her settled onto the birthing chair. He examined her and saw that it would not be long.

The contractions were coming at regular intervals and only a few seconds apart. Delia gasped and tensed with each one. Ty wished he could have the baby for her; he hated the pain women had to suffer to bring children into the world.

"Why don't you go ahead and holler," he said, sitting beside her and picking up her clenched hand to plant a kiss on her white knuckles.

Stubborn and gutsy to the end, Delia shook her head, biting her lip hard as another contraction racked her. He was filled with such love for her. And such fear. *I won't lose her*, he swore to himself to quiet the erratic beating of his heart. *She's strong and healthy. Women have babies every day. I won't lose her.*

"I love you," he said. "Oh, Delia, Delia, I love you, girl."

Pretending a professional detachment he didn't really feel, he talked her through it, telling her when to push and when to relax. A long two hours later, Ty's firstborn child emerged from his wife's womb and into his steady hands. The baby was slick with blood and crying lustily, and he held this tiny scrap of humanity, *his* baby, and stared at it with wonder and awe. Tears of an incredible, piercing joy flooded his eyes. For the first time in his life Ty thought he truly understood the meaning of the word "blessed."

Ty lifted his head and looked into his wife's eyes, eyes glazed with pain and shining with triumph. He held the baby up so that she could see. "We have a son, my love. A beautiful, perfect son."

Delia was too exhausted to do more than smile, but that smile said it all.

Ty had Delia in bed and the baby all clean and swaddled, and he was just about to put him in his wife's arms when the door creaked open and two little heads poked around the jamb. "We heard a baby crying," Meg whispered.

Ty grinned proudly, showing off his son. "Why don't you girls come in and say hello to your new little brother."

Tildy stared at the baby, her brow creased in disappointment. "But he's so teeny. How're we going to play with him? And he's funny-looking, too. All wrinkled and purple like a prune."

Meg thumped her sister in the side with her elbow. "Shush up, Tildy Parkes! That wasn't nice!" But Ty could tell from the look on Meg's face that she shared her sister's opinion and he had to bite the inside of his cheek to keep from laughing.

Delia beckoned the girls to the bed, where she kissed them in turn. "He'll be big enough to play with in no time," she said, her voice weak, but her face glowing with happiness.

"But he doesn't even have any hair," Tildy protested, still unconvinced, and Delia and Ty shared a smile.

"His hair, like the rest of him, will grow," Ty said. He herded them toward the door. "Now why don't you girls do me a favor and go fix us some supper and give your ma a chance to get some rest. Having a baby is hard work."

The girls reluctantly left the room and Ty stretched out on the bed beside Delia, their sleeping son cradled between them. Now that it was over Ty thought he just might sleep a month himself.

Delia rubbed her finger across the tiny features, laughing softly. "I do hate to admit it, Ty, but he does in a way resemble a prune."

"He's beautiful," Ty insisted.

She turned her head and met her husband's eyes and her face grew serious. "I know you wanted a girl. Are you disappointed?"

"Of course not. Besides, if we have a dozen of them, one is bound to end up being a girl."

She tried to scowl at him, but her lips betrayed her by quivering. Ty kissed them.

"I would like to call him Willy, after Anne's son," she said. "And we'll ask her and the colonel to stand as godparents."

Ty smiled his agreement. "And next year we'll take him up to Norridgewock and introduce him to his grandfather."

"Oh yes, Ty! Assacumbuit will adore him. Remember how he kept wanting you to take Elizabeth as a second wife just so he could acquire another grandson?"

Ty thought of his father. Assacumbuit would be pleased to have another grandson. And proud. There had been intermittent fighting all summer and fall between the Abenaki and the settlers. But Ty had found his peace in Delia and he knew now he would always belong to both worlds.

Delia was so quiet he thought she slept. He leaned up on one elbow to study her beloved face. She was so beautiful, his Delia, so strong, and he loved her so. "Damn," he muttered as more embarrassing tears filled his eyes.

A smile curled Delia's lips and her lids fluttered open. "Thank you, Ty," she mumbled behind a big yawn.

His arm tightened around her. "What for? You did all the work."

"For giving me a baby. Your baby. And for loving me."

"Aw, Delia, Delia." He said her name with wonder and with joy. And he kissed her with passion and love and tender promise.

She spoke softly as she drifted into sleep and he lowered his head to catch her words . . .

"I do love you, Tyler Savitch."

Author's Note

Cotton Mather's experiments with smallpox inoculation, and the attack on the mission at Castine and the subsequent death of the French Jesuit Sebastien Râle, have been anticipated by several months for the purposes of this story.

In 1724, the Abenaki stronghold at Norridgewock was overrun by the British, and many of the Abenaki warriors and their families withdrew to Quebec. However, there are still communities of Abenaki living on reservation lands in Maine. In 1980, the Penobscot and Passamaquoddie tribes of the Abenaki nation were granted a settlement of $81 million from the state and federal governments because their lands had been unfairly taken from them by the early settlers.